the *devil* to *pay*

Also by Gaylord Dold

*Schedule Two*
*Bay of Sorrows*

THE MITCH ROBERTS SERIES

*The World Beat*
*Rude Boys*
*A Penny for the Old Guy*
*Disheveled City*
*Muscle and Blood*
*Bonepile*
*Cold Cash*
*Snake Eyes*
*Hot Summer, Cold Murder*

# the *devil* to *pay*

## gaylord dold

THOMAS DUNNE BOOKS

st. martin's press ✿ new york

THOMAS DUNNE BOOKS.
An imprint of St. Martin's Press.

Design by Nancy Resnick

Library of Congress Cataloging-in-Publication Data

Dold, Gaylord.
    The devil to pay / Gaylord Dold.
        p.      cm.
    ISBN 0–312–19257–6
    I. Title.
    PS3554.O436D48    1999
    813'.54—dc21                                    98–42392

First Edition: February 1999

10   9   8   7   6   5   4   3   2   1

None of us can help the things life has done to us. They're done before you realize it, and once they're done they make you do other things until at last everything comes between you and what you'd like to be, and you've lost your true self forever.

—Eugene O'Neill, *Long Day's Journey into Night*

The most wonderful thing about life seems to be that we hardly tap our potential for self-destruction. We may desire it, it may be what we dream of, but we are dissuaded by a beam of light, a change in the wind.

—John Cheever, *Journals,* 1958

I

# the geronimo motion

*a* bourbon heartburn woke Jack Darwin at one in the morning. He lay in near dark listening to foghorns moan across the bay, gripped by the anxiety of forgetfulness. He tried to remember how many whiskey sours he'd drunk at Marge's on Mason Street, counting forward through each drink as if he had willed himself an injection of truth serum. When he reached the fourth drink, he tried willing himself to forget Marge's on Mason Street, its yellow-amber ambience on that dank November evening, its tinkle and clank of glassware and dishes, its harsh guffaw of lawyers laughing at each other's jokes, their braying like the sound of a hundred ill-begotten mules. Then, for a moment, just as he rose and put two feet on the carpet, he felt like begging God for an explanation of these Sunday night expeditions to the Financial District, some clear delineation of the loneliness that froze itself inside a person, the false conviviality of it all, which was in actuality an excuse to drink not four, but six or eight, or ten or eleven whiskey sours, a number, after all, too large to remember accurately, though enough to render a tremendous fiery ache behind the ribs, just near the heart.

Placing two feet on the floor, Darwin drank half a glass of milk, which he had left on the nightstand in advance, thought of his dead father, and for a longer time contemplated the corridors of his present life, which he found empty, dust-ridden, and quite contemptible.

At half past two he woke again, this time from a terrible dream involving car crashes, howling sirens, dripping blood on wet pavement, a regular werewolf of a dream. The light in the room, or lack of it, had shifted like cargo in the hold of a wooden galleon, its subtle weight and glaze sifting in from lamps in the Marina, an omnipresent sulfur blur on the face of the electric clock near his bed, its click-click dooming each second to eternity while outside the sky held cloud shapes suspended on dim pillars.

Now the wind rose. He heard it clap through eucalypti on the slopes below his house. He walked to the French doors and opened the drapes, studied the city and its famously clichéd bay, Alcatraz and its hulking disused prison outlined by the circular stare of lighthouses in upper Richmond, and beyond that the scattered light from a hundred thousand sources on the hills as far north as Albany.

Suddenly, drops of rain struck the window in front of his face. The city blurred and eucalyptus leaves clattered down as gusts of wind beat in from the ocean. Darwin turned on the bedside lamp, throwing the room into pure white light. On the stand beside him lay a copy of the Geronimo motion, next to that an empty milk glass, ringed by white stains. Across the room, his dressing table was littered with ties, cuff links, combs and brushes, two bottles of expensive cologne, and a single copy of the *Federal Reporter,* second series, open to tiny print. In Darwin's closet were an even dozen suits, a few winter sports coats, many pairs of slacks and twenty or more dress shirts, some far too frayed to wear in public, much less in court, and his beautifully polished shoes, one of Darwin's fetishes willed to him by his father, who had never ventured anywhere except in freshly polished shoes.

Darwin thought about his parents and caught himself gazing at their photographic portraits on his wall. His father stood beside a big bay gelding, the horse kept for him in a stable down in Burlingame—his father, for God's sake, dressed in khaki puttees and yellow riding shirt with epaulets, the face browned by sunny weather, set off in color by the lush white mustache he wore. In the background, high blue sky and puffy white cloud, the coastal range low and green and indistinct. In contrast, Darwin's mother, her photograph in a separate frame, was captured perched in a gazebo at home, the gazebo in summerish glare, enveloping her like a halo, though her sad, somewhat enigmatic smile was set against the intentions of the photographer so that, with her right hand raised as if bidding someone to please stop the process, and her dark piercing eyes fixed in a pleading gaze, she looked like a young girl who has left her girlhood behind and wished it weren't so.

Darwin put on a robe and opened the French doors, letting the rain come inside. He sat down at the dressing table with the Geronimo motion and opened it to page 1, for a time wondering if his wife, Karla, was awake in their room down the hall, realizing with anger that she was undoubtedly asleep, her dreams untroubled by conscience. While he thought about Karla, rain whipped across the room, wind ruffled the gauzy drapes, and he hated his wife with the vastness of violent death.

It took Darwin fifteen minutes to read the Geronimo motion. He spent fifteen more minutes outlining his oral argument, then read the federal case and its headnotes once again, memorizing portions he'd outlined in yellow marker. He was troubled by thoughts of his father again, imagining the old man's reaction to all this concentrated study, his father being a man who'd spent his entire life consorting with executives and shareholders of Standard Oil and Union Pacific. *Criminal law* he might have snorted contemptuously, the husky undertow of sarcasm in his voice. Darwin's thought blurred, confused by the absent specter of his own father, its clash with the knowledge that in slightly under seven hours Darwin would be in state court, a disheveled client at his arm, arguing the Geronimo motion for something like thirty or forty dollars an hour, money he desperately needed.

At four o'clock in the morning Darwin switched off the lamp on his dressing table, the one on his nightstand, and crawled limply and sourly back into bed. The bourbon heartburn had relaxed its grip, and he thanked a nonexistent deity that his father, who had bequeathed Jack his own name, a huge house in Pacific Heights, and a membership in the Burlingame Country Club, had never laid eyes on Karla, would never see what a retread his own son had become, what with clients like Manolo Diaz-Geronimo, a Mexican kid about nineteen years old who had neither money nor friends, and who was looking at three years in San Quentin.

At seven, the alarm woke Darwin, who found himself straddled across the bed still wearing robe and slippers, windows open to a dazzlingly blue sky. His head ached and the memory of Marge's on Mason Street flooded back in Technicolor reality. He showered quickly and dressed in a gray suit, white shirt, and soft red tie. When he was finished dressing, he examined himself in the mirror for the traces of seediness he knew were lurking here, in the harness of bulge forming around his neck, splits of hair in his ears, black circles under the eyes. Just then he thought that growing older would not be so terrible if one had a shred of dignity or peace of mind. And just as the thought passed he told himself what crap it was, because growing old could be soothed only by wealth, its reality papered over by cash, which was probably why lawyers he knew stared at each other like starved wolves, animals lost in a snowy forest at the onset of a hard winter. He wondered if he himself had that same look, the nervous deportment and false conviviality that went along with the look, the weary waxwork of ludicrous pretension that led to Sunday nights at Marge's on Mason Street, where the forest was wood-paneled and reverberated with the clink and tinkle of touched glasses, where the winter was snowy with whiskey sours.

Downstairs the sun-filled kitchen buoyed Darwin's spirits. He always loved the white and gray of the kitchen tiles, the shiny promise of the glass doors that led to a patio and deck that overlooked the bay, window boxes outside filled with geraniums, and the always faintly dusky smell of eucalyptus gum that hovered in the air. As a child Darwin would tumble downstairs every morning to the smell of oatmeal or fried eggs and bacon, and the equally perfumed embrace of his mother's arms, the memory of it lingering in the room like the fragrance of crushed roses. After opening the patio doors, Darwin made toast and coffee, boiled eggs. He walked his coffee out to the deck and looked at the bay, sailboats far away scudding on the cold blue water, whitecaps tipping spray and windblown spume. He put his coffee down on the redwood table and opened the Geronimo motion again.

"Your Honor," Darwin whispered to himself. "This boy Geronimo had no criminal intent when he walked into that bar on Mission Street. I can assure the court of that."

Darwin sipped his coffee and mulled the notion of criminal intent. What the hell was he talking about? "If anybody was ever entrapped, if anybody was simply going along for the ride, this boy is that person."

Darwin shook his head in disbelief. In a fit of despair he walked to the end of his mother's garden and observed her roses. In November they were not in bloom, but he recalled their June loveliness. Down on Bay Street traffic was morning-thick, an urgent artery toward downtown. He tried to control his anxiety by breathing deeply. How long had it been since he had been in court, argued a case? Two years, three? The traffic on Golden Gate Bridge was thick and crawling, a steady stream of vehicles back to the contours of Marin County. There was not a cloud in the sky, which had been washed clean by the night storm.

All right, Darwin thought to himself, entrapment and what else?

Here, the gates of his mind seemed to slam shut, Darwin almost phys- ically disturbed by the hammer of metal against metal that signified brain lock. Here was this boy, Manolo Diaz-Geronimo, who had walked into a bar on Mission Street, sat down, ordered a glass of beer, and fifteen minutes later a stranger had offered to sell him an ounce of cocaine at an incredibly low price. Boom—Geronimo faces three years without parole. Darwin sipped his coffee and reread his brief. He had argued that lack of probable cause was based on the unreliability of the seller, but what the hell did that mean? Nothing probably, and all Darwin had was a years-old federal case out of the Northern Dis- trict of California, something about the unreliability of a protected witness. Maybe that and the baby face of his client. You really have to be kidding me.

Darwin got his boiled egg and toast. He sat down with a fresh cup of coffee. He ate his egg and tried to outline his oral argument. When he finished he rinsed the dishes and closed and locked the patio door, then went upstairs and stood outside his wife's bedroom door. He pushed gently, but as expected, the door was locked. Darwin knocked four times, hard.

"Have a good day darling," Darwin heard from inside. The sar- casm was thick.

"Open the door, Karla," Darwin told his wife.

"I'm not dressed, dear," she replied.

"Just open the goddamn door," he said.

With hands at his side, Darwin waited.

"Don't you have to go to work or something?" Darwin sensed his wife poised on the other side of the door. There was a long mutual silence. "Jack, you know we don't have anything to say to one another." Strangely, and without warning, the door opened and Darwin shud- dered in surprise. His beautiful wife wore green satin, her long black hair tied behind her head with a green ribbon. Darwin's heart ached with anger and desire.

"It's going to be a long day for me," Darwin began. "I have to be in court at ten."

"All right, darling," Karla said tonelessly. She placed one slim hand on the doorjamb and leaned.

"We have to fix things or end them," Darwin said.

"Jack, you know I'm happy the way things are."

Karla cast a glance over Darwin's shoulder, perhaps looking at something, perhaps not. It was a way she had of destroying Darwin's existence while creating definite emotions in him at the same time. It was a sexual thing, deeply scarring. "And besides," Karla continued, "you can't afford a divorce right now, can you?" Karla smiled piteously. "Can you really, darling?"

"Why don't you just go away?" Darwin said. It shamed him to say it, but he meant it nonetheless.

"Now Jack, you know I love this house. I've grown very attached to it, the garden and the views. This house means a lot to me, Jack."

"You slut," Darwin said. He had not raised his voice. It was a point of honor with him never to raise his voice. This protocol was something his father had insisted on all those years, like polishing one's shoes, like owning a good bay gelding down in Burlingame.

"That's a trait you cultivated in me, Jack, didn't you?"

"Just go away. Why don't you?"

"Jack, we've had this conversation every morning for a year. It isn't getting us anywhere. And it is so boring."

"Do me a favor, Karla," Jack told her. "Try not to spend so much money. You could do that for me at least."

"Oh, Jack, you're silly. That's another trait you loved in me. You knew when you married me you created certain expectations. You know you did. You traded on them, didn't you?"

Darwin swallowed hard. This doctrine had become an article of faith with his wife. Like all doctrines, it contained a kernel of truth. Of course it did. Darwin's house, Darwin's gold Mercedes, the family breeding—Darwin had made use of it all in his pursuit of Karla.

"You sound like a lawyer," Darwin said finally.

"It's too bad you don't, isn't it?" Karla said.

She laughed her twinkle-laugh, the one where she opened her mouth and breathed hard like Marilyn Monroe.

"I'm going to say this plainly," Darwin said. He stepped forward a single pace and placed his foot in the doorway. The look on his wife's face darkened. Darwin hoped it was fear he had put there, but he doubted it. "I've begun to take criminal appointments. I've got to earn some cash. You know as well as I do that I can't go on bleeding money like this. The trustees who handle my funds won't continue to advance principal against my current debts. I have got to try to make ends meet somehow. I'm taking a teaching job down at the law school after the first of the year. Classes start in January. After Christmas I'm going to get you out of this house and change my life. You've sucked my blood for four years. You won't be sucking it much longer."

Karla tugged the door closed an inch or so. Standing two feet away from his wife, Darwin wanted her physically as much as he ever had. That part refused to die somehow. He wondered at its persistence, the strong hold it had over him.

"That was a terrific speech, Jack," Karla said. "But I've heard it a dozen times, remember?"

Darwin removed his foot and Karla pushed the door closed. Darwin's heart raced wildly now. "I mean it, Karla," Darwin said to the door. "I mean it, I really do."

"Go to work, Jack," Karla said.

Downstairs, Darwin picked up his briefcase from the kitchen table and went out to the flagstone walk. He retrieved the morning *Chronicle* and got inside his old Volvo, which was parked in the driveway. He switched on the ignition and the car filled with classical music. He sat with his eyes closed listening to the music, unable to make himself drive away. He opened his eyes and studied the rows of stucco mansions, each a quiet rectangle of rectitude, red tile roofs, manicured hedges, rows of eucalyptus and sycamore. A few expensive cars were parked here and there, late-model BMWs and Audis. The music engulfed him, and he imagined he could smell his wife, her odor like lemon and earth. He remembered the night a few weeks after they'd met at the cemetery where his parents were buried. After a dinner date they'd gone up to the house in Pacific Heights during a rainstorm. They'd shared a few glasses of wine, and then had gone upstairs to Darwin's bedroom and made love on the floor in front of the open French doors. Rain, borne hard on a Pacific gale, swept over them. As they made love, Darwin didn't notice the rain or the cold wind at all, or the sound of foghorns on the bay. He had been transported in ways he thought not possible.

Now, sitting in the old Volvo with classical music around him, Darwin realized why he'd opened the French doors last night, why he'd let rain pour onto the carpet, why he'd sat in despair as the storm raged. He was reliving something wasted, something already dead, something shameful, but something he thought he needed, but that he really didn't. This effort to relive his desire for Karla had exhausted him. It wasn't Karla who drained his blood every Sunday night. It was Darwin himself.

He finally backed out of the driveway. On the way downtown he practiced his Geronimo speech. It had a nice ring—Geronimo! For a moment he felt hopeful, almost enthusiastic. Perhaps he could reestablish his law practice, get a grip on his life. Then in traffic on Lombard a void returned. *Criminal law* his father would have growled. It would have been a polite growl, for Darwin's father never sneered, never lifted a brow. And Darwin's father never raised his voice.

He thought of their narrow walk-up on Potrero Hill as a dry-docked schooner, an elegant sailing vessel, himself the retired captain, a man with many years at sea—Amos Vorhees, the sage and mariner of Army Street. And on mornings like these, sunshine pouring through the many-windowed bedroom upstairs, Vorhees in fact felt clever, as if he'd kissed the Blarney stone, and mounds of good luck had gushed forth. Turning slightly on his side, he ran one hand inside his wife's nightie to feel the smooth bulge of her belly, his hand playing over her nipples lightly, sliding down her lower abdomen where he thought he felt the baby move, a subtle moment of life, the stirring of seed. His wife arched her back, rising from the depths of a dream. Vorhees studied the Marine Corps photos on his walls, the worn flowered wallpaper, the rows of windows through which he discerned high blue sky, an after-rainfall morning.

His wife purred and touched his hand.

"You'll be late for work," she said.

"You're a very practical woman," Vorhees laughed. "But it will never happen."

Vorhees pulled the nightgown up and looked at her belly. It was smooth and black, unnatural really when you thought about it.

"You will," she said. "You'll be late."

"You don't answer reveille every day for twenty years, then miss work because you want to stay in bed with your wife."

"I might could change your mind," his wife said.

"You might could," Vorhees told her.

They were quiet, listening to church bells. The sound of the bells slipped through the air, making an almost palpable shimmer on the window glass.

"Can you feel her there?" his wife asked. "She's moving."

"Feeling for a way out," Vorhees said.

"Two more months," his wife said. "Now, I'm sure it's time for you to go to work." His wife pushed away his hand. "She'll be out soon enough. Then we'll see how an old man like you enjoys doing diapers."

"I can hack it," Vorhees said. "*Semper fi.* I'm one of those few good men you hear about."

"Outstanding," his wife said.

Vorhees got out of bed, showered, and dressed. His wife stayed in bed, enjoying the warm sun. She sat upright, watching her husband dress, resting her back against four pillows.

"What you got going?" she asked.

Vorhees struggled with the knot in his tie.

"Alisha," he said, "you wouldn't believe it if I told you."

"Try me, Sergeant," she said.

"I'm meeting this shavetail lawyer named Winston Docking. We busted a doper named Manolo Diaz-Geronimo. We did a reversal on him a couple of months ago and some jackass lawyer named Darwin filed a motion. My guess is that Winston Docking is the last lawyer on the district attorney's list right now, so he's got the case. I'm supposed to testify what a dangerous guy this Geronimo is, or supposed to be. It's what we marines call shit duty. Forgive me."

"And how does an old marine such as yourself look credible doing shit duty?"

Vorhees posed for the mirror. Short hair going gray, oil-well eyes, the half-remembered frightened look of a semiprofessional boxer. "Hey," Vorhees said to the mirror, "I look fine, just fine."

"Looking pretty ain't the same as looking credible."

"You think this Darwin could Johnnie Cochran me?"

"Nobody could Johnnie Cochran you, honey."

"Well, I never used the *n* word for ten years, that's for sure."

"You use it plenty, mister," his wife laughed.

"Nigger this, nigger that," Vorhees said. "That's all I seem to hear."

"Okay, nigger, get to work," his wife said.

Vorhees sat on the edge of the bed and kissed his wife. He was amazed at how large she'd become with her pregnancy, and it often worried him. Her discomfort was obvious, and sometimes when he thought about the child inside her it frightened him. Perhaps bringing a baby into a world like this was selfish, almost self-serving. Certainly, Vorhees had seen much of life, starting on the streets of the Western Addition, two tours of Vietnam in the military police, then the narcotics unit at SFPD. And in all those years he'd witnessed plenty of human frailty, breakdown and accident that sent people and their parts flying off in all directions. Sometimes it was all he could do to see people as human, not as insects with brutal instincts. He was old enough to realize that the best intentions could be blown away in the slightest gust of ill wind, and that most men and women were separated from their own centers by the most fragile of margins. What could Vorhees do? He volunteered for Big Brothers, he helped with basketball camps for kids, and at times he cut the dopers and street hustlers some slack. But in truth, the center was just as close by as the edge. He'd known men at Da Nang who'd loved the color and violence of death, and would sit on bunkers and smoke spliffs and goof on the Rolling Stones while the muffled sound of mortars and rockets swelled in the near background. Even Vorhees found himself getting off on the violence at times, and he'd have to check the emotion. And even though he was black, he understood the cops who got off on beating Rodney King. He hated the race part, but it was deeper than race. It was a kind of addiction that made these men do the things they did, some species of deep and resonant spiritual memory nurtured by economics all these years, by genetic structure, history, science, television, the whole rotten business of modern life. Our better instincts, where were they?

Alisha kissed his ear. "You okay, honey?" she asked.

"I've got a surprise," Vorhees said. "After the first of the year I'm being transferred to homicide. I passed all the tests. I get a new grade too. The money isn't much more, but it's a better job. I just heard yesterday."

Alisha hugged him. "That's wonderful," she said. "Why didn't you tell me last night?"

"I wanted to think about it. Let it sink in. I wanted to tell you when the sun was shining."

"I'm happy for you."

"At least I'll get away from the bars on Mission Street."

"You'll be my big black Ironside."

"That honky?" Vorhees laughed. "He didn't know shit."

Vorhees got up and looked in the mirror, adjusted his tie. He was getting thick at fifty, but he tried to keep himself in shape with basketball and a little jogging. It was impossible to say how many years of life he'd lost to the narcotics squad. Five, eight? "I'll call this afternoon," he told Alisha.

Vorhees took Van Ness to the Civic Center and parked his car in the public underground garage. He hadn't seen a day this beautiful in the city for weeks, and all the bums and homeless were outside enjoying the weather. They sat in front of plywood shacks, cadging for dimes and quarters, drinking the first muscatel of the day. The current mayor had suspended the city's constant battle against the street people, the feeling being that it was just as useless as battling pigeons. Vorhees had lived all his life in California, and even he was thinking that maybe it was time to bail out. Did he want his daughter to grow up in the city, stepping over drunks as she walked the sidewalks?

Vorhees passed weapons check on the first floor and took the elevator to three. The young assistant named Docking had an office at the end of a row of cubicles down a long hallway of frosted glass. Vorhees found the nameplate and peeked around an edge of frosted glass. He saw Docking, who looked very innocent, sleek black hair moussed and gelled to style, tortoiseshell frame glasses, an impeccable gray suit.

"Vorhees," he said.

Docking nodded and the two men shook hands. Vorhees towered over the lawyer, a head taller at least.

"I've been studying the Geronimo file," Docking said. He offered Vorhees a metal chair and Vorhees sat. In this part of the third floor maybe forty lawyers had their offices. There was a steady muffled sound of words being processed.

"I've looked over your report," Docking said. "It looks pretty straightforward to me."

"Thanks," Vorhees said. He did not volunteer information to lawyers, even friendly ones.

"I've read the defense lawyer's brief, have you?"

"No, I haven't."

"Well, he's trying to get the case dismissed before trial. Do you have any reason to think that this might happen?"

"You're the lawyer," Vorhees said. "You'd have to tell me."

"It's a clean bust, isn't it?" Docking asked. Docking looked up from his papers, thinking he might have said the wrong thing.

Vorhees smiled. "It's as clean as they come." Vorhees tried to see if there was any coffee, but there wasn't. "I sat in a bar on Mission Street and watched this guy Geronimo buy an ounce from our agent."

"Well, that's good," Docking said, relieved. "As you can imagine, I'm not the most experienced lawyer on the staff. Uh, well, actually, this is my first morning. But I can tell you that Darwin's motion doesn't make any sense to me. He talks a lot about the witness not being reliable. What's that all about?"

"You're asking me?" Vorhees said.

"You know Jack Darwin?"

"Never seen him," Vorhees said. "And I have been around the state courts now for a long time. Look, if it's important to you, we had probable cause. Geronimo agreed to buy the coke. It's that simple. Is there any chance we could lose this bust today?"

"I'd like to say no," Docking replied.

"Will my witness have to take the stand?"

"Who knows? Is he ready?"

"We told him to dress nice and play it straight. He isn't much interested in taking the stand, though. We sort of implied that it probably wouldn't happen. He has friends on the street who might hassle him."

"Well, let's hope he dresses nice then," Docking said.

"Who's the judge?" Vorhees asked.

"Hoffman, in Division Twelve."

"He's as straight as they come," Vorhees said.

"Oh, that's good."

"By that I mean he shits on everybody who comes near him."

Docking took off his glasses. Without them, he looked about sixteen years old.

"That's great," Docking said quietly.

Vorhees read the lawyer's brief and reviewed the police reports. Vorhees wanted to tell Docking to forget all about the judge. He was just a guy who put his pants on one leg at a time, all that old crap. And then it came to Vorhees that Docking looked a little like Tom Hanks, a face like putty, weak chin, narrow-set eyes.

"You'll do just fine," Vorhees said to Docking.

"Can you give me the facts in a nutshell?" Docking asked. Docking glanced at his watch, the time edging toward nine-forty-five.

"We've been doing reversals," Vorhees said.

"Reversals?"

"Oh boy," Vorhees said. "Well, a reversal is where the good guys make a sale of dope to the bad guys. The good guys hold out some cocaine and a bad guy buys it, then the good guys bust the bad guys. As a narcotics officer I'd say it would be preferable to bust sellers, not buyers, but the district attorney and the chief of police decided that this month would be a good month to do reversals." Vorhees shrugged.

"The election coming up," Docking said.

"Something like that," Vorhees replied. "Our seller is a guy named Vincent Alvarado. He's what you'd call a piece of work. But he can string several English sentences together and make himself barely understood. In this game, he's what you'd call a good witness."

"A foot soldier in the war against drugs," Docking said. "You recruited him?"

"Well, he's on the department hook. He's been on the hook for quite a while, snitching and so forth. He's a useful little SOB when he wants to be."

"You mean he's a criminal?"

"Of course he's a criminal," Vorhees said. "Small-time." Docking was new to this game, and Vorhees detected a trace of disapproval in his expression. In a few years Docking would be higher up on the food chain, sitting behind a walnut desk smoking a big cigar, laughing about how they had so-and-so on the hook. Maybe Docking would become a major-league sadist, enjoying his work, watching people squirm.

"You didn't bust Alvarado on a reversal too, did you?" Docking asked.

It was a good question, and Vorhees was surprised at the kid's moxie. Maybe he was okay after all.

"Not really," Vorhees answered. "Vincent has been around a long time. He's a Mission Street regular and right now he's out on parole for a state bust on simple possession. He's only in the joint because it's his second strike. Don't think too harshly of Vincent. He kind of likes the work."

"I'm only thinking about how great our chief witness is, a street snitch out on parole. Some guy waiting for the other shoe to drop. It's my first case and the other lawyer doesn't have a clue, and Judge Hoffman shits on everybody within sight."

"Hey, you're a lawyer," Vorhees said. "You didn't apply for art school and get sent the wrong acceptance package did you?"

Docking broke into a nice smile. Vorhees had to like the kid's attitude.

"When you busted Geronimo, did he say anything?"

"Geronimo doesn't speak much English. I don't speak Spanish. Geronimo probably speaks a little English, but he's too smart to let it all out. It doesn't matter what he said because I was in the bar. I saw it go down."

"What was the deal?"

"Alvarado asked him if he wanted some coke. They're speaking pidgin English and Geronimo says he'll have to go back to the apartment for the money. I tagged along, and when they got there Geronimo pulled out a stash of cash for the down payment. At least Vincent says he did."

"Alvarado wasn't fronting the coke?"

"No way. We have the cash in evidence."

"Well, I hope so. I don't really understand what this fellow Darwin is arguing in his brief, but he may be saying that there couldn't be a sale because Geronimo didn't have any money. There's a lot of hot air in his brief, but that's the gist, I guess." The phone rang and Docking answered it, then had a short conversation that Vorhees tried to ignore. Docking hung up and turned to Vorhees. "Well, the inevitable has happened. Hoffman just went into a huddle with the state police on a major phone-tap warrant. He just put us on hold until at least ten-thirty. You know what that means."

That's just great, Vorhees thought to himself. We could be on hold all morning, into the afternoon. People didn't realize how much time cops spent pacing courthouse corridors, counting fly specks on the wall.

"I'm going downstairs and call my wife," Vorhees said. "Maybe I'll take a walk around Civic Center just to get some fresh air."

"I'll meet you in Hoffman's courtroom in forty-five minutes."

"See ya," Vorhees told the lawyer.

He spent close to an hour in the bright sunshine, strolling amid the trimmed sycamores. He was cadged for quarters so often that he finally visited a bookstore on Turk, killing the time. If anything bothered him it was his own happiness that day. How could he feel this good in such a world?

Looking good was Karla's gift. It came to her naturally, the way motherhood comes naturally to some women. And if she prized one feature, it would be her hair, long and black with auburn highlights she cultivated. Her best look, she believed, was to tie her hair in segmented bundles, tossing the bundles over one shoulder, Roman-epic style. She would wear low-cut blouses and let the hair ride her neck. She perfected moves and made men pant with them, caressing men with her undercurrent of pretend wantonness, smiling just over her shoulder, watching men watch her move. At times she wore her hair loose and down her back like Cher, a style too simple for words. Another part of her talent was her eyes, steely green betraying nothing, not an ounce of emotion or nuance, with a slight violet iris. People told her she had eyes like a young Elizabeth Taylor, eyes that stopped traffic, eyes that caused hailstorms, eyes you couldn't take your eyes off of, eyes to die for they said. And Karla enjoyed turning heads, forcing men to stare after her, catching them in the act, making a point of startling them in embarrassed poses, smiling at the discoveries she made. Whenever she was near a department store she always paused before its plate glass window, gathering in her reflection and sending it back toward the men behind her who were checking her out, imagining their fantasies, practicing a game of double make-believe that had all the whorled intentionality of consciousness itself, which is the same thing as saying that Karla caused confusion, plenty of it. Knowing what she wanted had always been the hallmark of her personality.

And she had wanted Jack Darwin, straight off. In those days, and for years before, she had been working at Resthaven Cemetery, selling "packages" to the grief-stricken or elderly, helping people in their time of need, as the brochures said. She would target clients, especially older men, and go after them in a way that was "supereffective sales," and she was good at what she did, so good that she often won the company sales competition, rendering her dangerous to the men with whom she worked, men with families, men with mouths to feed, men with hard-ons for Karla all the time. She won trips for her work, free tours of Alaska and Cancún, an all-expense-paid journey to New Orleans for Mardi Gras, though the trip had disappointed her when she found the town dirty and full of blacks and drunks, kids who puked in the street and spoke with a drawl.

Jack Darwin was at Resthaven to bury his parents. Karla was just back from a trip to Minneapolis, where she had attended a regional conference. She was dissatisfied with her job. Her new boss, a corporate veteran, had been making snide comments behind her back, not much out of earshot. Sometimes she didn't mind his resentment, thinking that it gave her an advantage over him, but when he began to deprive her of "leads," she rebelled and began to look for other work. And just then, at a crisis in her professional life, Jack Darwin walked into her office looking like little boy lost, grief-stricken and ripe.

Karla knew old money when she saw it. And when you looked at Jack Darwin, you were looking at old money, or at least that's the way Karla understood the matter. He had a nice face, almost naive, a way of trailing his voice away in midsentence that gave him a vulnerability that was appealing. He carried himself well, even though he had been shocked by the simultaneous deaths of his parents in a plane crash. That day, Karla sat Jack down on a plush sofa and surrounded him with her concern, guiding him through the tricky business of death, the funeral, the interment. It took Karla only about five minutes to establish herself with Jack, gliding easily into her normal rapport. He was distracted and tired, needed succor, and if there was one thing Karla could do it was fake sympathy. But then, as she sat talking to Darwin, she felt herself slipping into a real emotion, something that was practically impossible to envision. But there sat Jack Darwin with his blue puppy dog eyes, such an easy mark, too easy.

Karla had swallowed hard, looking outside to the parking lot, seeing Darwin's gold Mercedes. That sight cured her of her sympathy. She loved the gold Mercedes at first glance. And when she looked back at Jack Darwin she saw a tall, nice-looking guy with old money behind him and a storm of expensive cologne hovering around his conservative blue suit. She smiled at him and condoled him with eager pity.

Karla remembered perfectly what she wore the day she met Jack Darwin. It was a gray wool business skirt, a pale blue long-sleeve blouse with ruffled front. She got their meeting going by using her eyes to transfix the client, rinsing him down with her stares, shaking her hair, one of her best moves. While they talked, she touched his hand lightly once or twice, let him look deeply into her eyes, hoping he'd notice the violet iris. An hour later they were walking amid the cypress-lined avenues, down white gravel paths between tombstones. It had been early September, the weather mild, a slight breeze. Just by being herself, Karla put Jack Darwin at a disadvantage, and soon he was talking about his own life, sharing with her his feelings, a thing he would probably never do with another stranger. But Karla knew that death had that kind of effect on people. It made them morbid, made them want to talk, to spill their guts. That kind of talk substituted for tears. It was a form of psychotherapy.

A week later Karla was in her office. When the phone rang it was Jack Darwin on the line. She bit her lip in satisfaction, for though she hadn't given up on him, she wondered why it had taken him so long. After all, she could almost sense him getting hard that day they'd walked on white gravel between lines of gray tombstones. On the phone, in his little-boy voice, he asked her to lunch.

They were married at Christmastime in a small chapel near Lake Tahoe, a ceremony attended only by a local Episcopal priest, one witness, and an elderly woman who played the wedding march on an organ. Jack called it an elopement, and seemed as pleased as a child with a new bicycle, walking his beautiful new bride down the aisle of the chapel while an elderly priest beamed at them. After a two-week honeymoon, Karla quit her job and settled into life at the Pacific Heights house, just the two of them alone in six thousand square feet of carpeted luxury, enough silence to daunt even a confirmed hermit, room after room that smelled faintly of dust and rose water, rooms that seemed inhabited still by the ghosts of Jack's parents. Karla could feel their presence and it haunted her, being surrounded, nearly suffocated, by two unseen personages.

Karla told herself she'd be a good wife. She'd run the household, prepare meals, adorn each room with fresh flowers, play hostess to Jack's many friends from before his marriage. Indeed, she tried, but soon found herself lonely, wandering the house for hours as though she'd lost her way in a dark forest, finding herself watching the hands of the clock moving imperceptibly, agonizingly slowly. She missed her job, grew bored with Jack's devotion to books, his moody silences, his ability to disappear inside himself for hours at a time. Romance had burned to war, each battle a great huffing struggle for power. After four years, it had come to nothing, a fearsome silence punctuated by threats.

After Darwin left for work, Karla showered and put on a pair of dark black wool pants, a blue cashmere sweater with a red rose pattern in front. She drank what was left of the coffee Darwin had brewed and drove downtown to the TransAmerica Building on California Street, took the elevator to the eleventh floor, bay side. Her appointment with the lawyer Herbert Rowe was for ten-thirty, and she wanted to be precisely on time. The office, as she'd hoped, was elegant—mahogany-trimmed, with Boston ferns hanging in pots, quiet piped-in music that wasn't Muzak, and modern art on the walls. The receptionist took her name, then sent her down a long carpeted hallway to a corner office.

When she saw him, Karla knew that Rowe was exquisitely correct. He was a large man with large manicured hands, a florid face, a black suit and red power tie, graying hair, a diamond pinkie ring. Karla loved lawyers who wore pinkie rings. She wanted her lawyers pure, devoid of ideology. She wanted them to look like the thugs they were, empty muscle you could hire to do anything.

"How do you do, Mrs. Darwin," Rowe said calmly.

Really, Karla thought, he's almost too, too. His desk expressed cool efficiency, like a gallows. The computer behind him whispered blue tones into the room, the walls were dense with plaques, diplomas, certificates, and political photos. On Rowe's desk was the photograph of a stout woman surrounded by grinning teenagers. Rowe saw to it that Karla had fresh coffee, then sat down and placed his hands flat on the desk.

"May I ask how you got my name?" he asked her.

"A friend recommended you," Karla said. She shook out her hair, which she was wearing in her segmented style, thrown over the left shoulder. She had brought a black umbrella with her, a brown briefcase for her papers. "The friend is not a client. He's a fellow lawyer, I believe."

"Fine then," Rowe said. "How can I help you?"

"My husband is John Blasingame Darwin," Karla said. "The Second, I believe."

"Yes," Rowe said. "I knew the First." He smiled and clicked a fingernail on the desk. Rowe picked up an expensive fountain pen and wrote something on yellow legal paper. He nodded at Karla, silently asking permission. "John Darwin the First was a lawyer at Kline-James, I think."

Karla looked over Rowe's shoulder, giving him the faraway look, then caught his eye. "My husband is considering divorcing me. I'd be a fool not to think so. He might actually do it someday."

"Nothing has been filed yet?"

"No, not yet. He told me that he was going to file after the first of the year. He's said it before, but this time he may actually get around to doing it. You never know."

"Why would he want a divorce, Mrs. Darwin?"

"First, let me tell you I don't want this divorce. I'm not necessarily happy with the way things are, but I'd like to work on this marriage. We're not perfect, of course. What I'm trying to say is that I want to be a good wife. We hardly talk anymore. It is true that we haven't gotten along for quite some time."

"I see," Rowe said. "How long have you been married?"

"Four years. We had a good year or two. But our relationship just hasn't been working. Now, we hardly talk. I suppose Jack is a good person in his own way, but he's quiet, his friends don't care for me much, and it turns out we have little in common. I've tried to please him, I really have, but I miss working, I miss going out. Jack's idea of an evening is to sit in a chair, drink vodka, read a book."

"And how long haven't you been getting along?"

"For the last year. Perhaps slightly longer."

"Married in California?"

"Yes." Karla told Rowe the date, and told him they had no children. "I've often thought of having them," she said.

"And what did you do before you were married?"

"I was in sales at Resthaven in Belvedere. You know the place?"

"I've heard of it. Have you been married before?"

"No, this is my first. It's the first for Jack as well."

"You call your husband Jack?"

"Everybody does. It separates him from his father, doesn't it?"

"You quit your job to marry?"

"Oh yes. I was doing very well there. I was one of the top people, and I'd worked my way into a very good position. I won sales awards and trips. Jack came along and took me away from all that, as they say. He was dashing, very handsome. I fell for him. It was all so sudden, but he was kind, a real gentleman. He just took me by storm."

"And now, Mrs. Darwin? How do you feel about your husband now?"

"Jack? I love him, of course."

"Well, then, tell me in your own words what you think your problems are."

"Poor Jack has money troubles. That's part of it. He drinks a good deal and his law practice suffers and he tends to blame me when I spend money, even a little. Of course, he never thinks of the money he spends drinking. These days he tends to stay out drinking. Then when he comes home from some bar or other he wants to—well—have sex. It isn't very pleasant to confront that sort of thing every night, night after night. Now he tells me I won't do my duty, if you know what I mean. And it isn't that I mind sex, of course. It's just that I mind sex with a drunken man who stinks of cigar smoke and wants me at midnight." Karla let this story hover between them, awesome with significance. "Do you understand?" she asked Rowe.

"Perfectly," Rowe said. He spent a minute making notes on the yellow pad. He looked up and said, "Before we go any further, I want you to understand something very clearly. I'm going to need information from you, lots of it. Some of it you will consider very confidential. So do I. Wild horses couldn't drag it out of me." Here he flashed a professional smile. "I'll bill you at the end of our session here, after I've advised you of your rights and options. Then you can choose me to represent you or you can choose any other lawyer in town. It's entirely up to you. I hope we can develop a rapport and a level of trust here. If you choose to have me represent you, drop me a note telling me. If you choose otherwise, tear up the bill and accept my best wishes."

"That's very nice. I understand."

"So, first of all, let me tell you that nothing can stop your husband from filing a lawsuit against you. The courthouse is open to everybody. And in California, as in most other states, you could hardly stop this divorce from becoming final if your husband wants it that way. It is almost totally no fault."

"But if Jack sues me next year? What can I do?"

"Let's start at the beginning," Rowe said. "You're not working now?"

"No."

"Nobody lives in the house with you?"

"We live there alone in Pacific Heights."

"Let me ask you, has your husband has ever hurt you physically? Are you in fear that way?"

"Not exactly," Karla said. She paused, looked over the lawyer's shoulder again. "But I am afraid of him. Just this morning he threatened me."

"All right," Rowe said. "How about financially? Can you paint me a picture of his estate?"

"Well, Jack's father made a lot of money." Karla painted Rowe a picture of the house, the landscaped grounds overlooking the Marina, a gold Mercedes, art in the rooms. "The house is free and clear too, his dad left it that way. But I think Jack has trouble with the taxes. In fact, several years may be due and owing. You see, when Jack's father died four years ago he left most of the money in trust, about five million dollars I think. It becomes Jack's when he turns forty-five, which isn't for another ten years. I don't know why his father did that, perhaps he wanted Jack to mature, I don't know. I have a feeling he'll spend his trust money before he inherits it."

"How is that, Mrs. Darwin?"

"If you ask me, I think the trustees advance him money. I can't be sure, but I don't know where he gets his money if it isn't from them."

"But you're not sure?"

"No, not sure."

"Who are the trustees?"

"Men Jack's father knew at the law office."

"And tell me about your husband's practice."

"He's begun to take criminal appointments," Karla said. "I think he did that because the trustees have cut him off. I've heard Jack complain about it when he's been drinking. You have to understand I didn't know any of this when I married Jack. He was a perfect gentleman, gallant, very old-world. Now I find him a drunk and a complainer."

"And sometimes violent too?"

"You could say that."

"And what about Resthaven? Ever thought about going back?"

Karla caught Rowe with her eyes. "Mr. Rowe, let me ask you something."

"Please do."

"How long did it take to build your practice?"

"A long time," Rowe said.

"It isn't any different in sales. I was only halfway to success when I married Jack. I gave away five years of struggle to marry him. Maybe in ten years I could have made it really big. And that was four years ago."

"So, what you've lost is twenty years."

"I see we understand one another," Karla said. "Please don't misunderstand me, Mr. Rowe. When I met Jack, his parents had just been killed in a plane crash at Tahoe. He was sweet. I liked him. I grew to love him. But I won't live with a violent, useless drunk. I won't be taken advantage of either."

"Nor should you," Rowe said. "A woman of your accomplishments has every reason to expect success and happiness." Rowe put down his fountain pen. "Is there another woman?"

"Oh, heavens, I don't think so," Karla said. "Jack has only a little initiative. I don't think his initiative extends to clandestine affairs. He likes to drink and talk to his legal pals. He has a horse down in Burlingame he rides sometimes. Something on the side would tax poor Jack out of his mind."

Rowe swiveled in his chair and spent a moment looking out over the bay, where an oil tanker churned under the bridge. He turned back and said, "Let me tell you what I think. I think you wouldn't be averse to giving Jack his divorce."

"Not under the right circumstances," Karla said.

"Of course," Rowe said. "We understand each other perfectly. But let me tell you this. In California, every member of a marriage partnership owns either separate property or community property. In your husband's case, the house he owned before your marriage is separate property."

Karla leaned forward in her chair. The braided hair fell loose over her shoulder. "I know this for a fact, Mr. Rowe. The Darwin estate didn't close until six months after we were married."

Rowe raised an eyebrow. "You mean your husband didn't own the house until after the marriage? That's a very clever piece of information, Mrs. Darwin. Very clever indeed."

"It's just a fact."

"As to the trust fund, I'd have to review its provisions carefully before giving an opinion. But my gut tells me it's an expectancy and might be community property. This is an area of the law that is still developing. There is always the question of alimony payments."

"What kind of money are we talking about here?"

"What would you say the house is worth?"

"Two million dollars. Maybe more."

"It has back taxes?"

"Forty or fifty thousand."

Rowe put down his pen again. "We're moving pretty fast here, so let's slow down. I want you to understand that if a court held that the house and trust fund were separate property then you'd never get any kind of judgment against either piece of property."

"That would leave me out flat?"

"Well, consider that it is possible that the house is community property. Don't forget that probability, will you? And don't forget that if a court obligates your husband toward some form of support payments, then those payments can become judgments if not paid, and then can become liens against the house and the trust."

"That just means I'd have to fight for my money."

"It could be difficult, of course. Let me ask you, does your husband have a will."

"A will? Not that I know of. Why do you ask?"

"I'm just checking the possibilities. But before we go away half-cocked, let me tell you that regardless of the property situation, your husband would be foolish to try to walk away from this marriage expecting not to get, how shall I say, nicked. We'd take him to the cleaners, Mrs. Darwin."

"I see," Karla said.

"Has he ever pushed you? Punched you, forced you to have sex?"

"A little. It's a fine line."

"I know it's hard to speak about. But for a woman like yourself, a woman of accomplishment, a substantial career, a woman who finds her husband a drunk, and an abusive drunk at that, a ne'er-do-well, a failure who can't manage his family and professional situation—well, I see a woman like that, especially an articulate and attractive woman, having no trouble obtaining a substantial settlement if divorced. It happens all the time, especially in California. Executing against the property is a problem, but the house can be sold for cash."

"And the trust fund?"

"I'll research the matter if you wish."

"I like the way you talk," Karla said.

"I thought you might," Rowe told her. "Still, every lawsuit is an adventure. A risk, so to speak. Anything can happen in court and there are no guarantees."

"How much?" Karla said.

Rowe smiled. "Half of everything," he said. "Of course, you might have to wait a few years to execute against the trust."

Karla picked up the photo of a woman and teenagers. "Your family?" she asked. Without waiting for a reply, she said, "You're a lucky man." Karla was unconscious of the irony in her tone. Indeed, perhaps Rowe was undressing her in his fantasies right now, running his hands through her long black hair.

Rowe walked her to the door. "I'd be delighted to represent you, Mrs. Darwin. And perhaps you shouldn't wait for the first shot to be fired. It's an option, you know."

"I'll think it over," Karla said. She walked down the long carpeted hallway, aware that Rowe was standing in the doorway watching.

Karla ate lunch alone at Carlisle's near Union Square. She shopped at I. Magnin and spent $140 on two silk scarves and a jeweled coin purse. She considered the money an advance against Jack's trust fund, money she was owed for looking so good. After all, Jack had wanted a trophy wife, and everybody knows that trophies are expensive. Outside I. Magnin she paused in front of the plate glass window, giving men a good view of her ass. They tried not to look, but couldn't help themselves. It was so sad Karla had to smile.

•   •   •

Amos Vorhees sat at the prosecution table in Division Twelve, Superior Court of the State of California, Honorable Ernest T. Hoffman presiding. It was ten-thirty and he was alone in the marble silence.

Vorhees sat nervously, anticipating the hearing, occasionally glancing at the clock above the judge's bench. To Vorhees' immediate left were fifteen red leather jurors' seats behind a walnut enclosure, behind them portraits of judges on the wall, and high above the portraits a row of leaded-glass windows letting in hazy gray light. Spending time in empty courtrooms was nothing new to Vorhees. In detective parlance it was downtime, wasted hours you could have been in the real world chasing down bad guys, doing paperwork.

Shortly before eleven, Docking brushed through the padded doors and sat down next to Vorhees. He banged his briefcase heavily on the prosecution table. Its echo seemed to startle the young lawyer, who flushed and looked around to see who had heard.

"The judge is still tied up," he said angrily.

"How long, any idea?" Vorhees asked.

"Soon, very soon, they say," Docking said ironically.

Docking opened the briefcase and spread out his work papers, notebooks, police report, brief, two Parker pens, a spare legal pad, and some Xerox copies of case law. He danced his thumbs along the glass-covered top of the table. Vorhees closed his eyes, listening to the faint rush of traffic on Van Ness. Five minutes later the padded doors swung open, and a deputy led in Vincent Alvarado.

"Oh my God," Docking sighed.

Vorhees blinked and looked at Alvarado. There he was, Alvarado, a cocky kind of guy with an attitude, flashing Vorhees the thumbs-up, a toothy funked-out smile. He was a bird-boned kid with attractive features, high cheekbones, a dusting of acne, black wavy hair, and superb white teeth. He was wearing baggy purple pants tied at the waist with what Vorhees thought might be a drapery sash, a flame red shirt with Victorian frill at the cuffs. Over his arm Alvarado was carrying a cheap imitation patent leather topcoat that had cracked in the cold weather. On his head he wore an Oakland Raiders ballcap backward, gang style. Vorhees turned to Docking, who hadn't taken his eyes off the witness, Docking biting his lip involuntarily. Vorhees knew the deputy, who could barely suppress a laugh.

"Vincent loves clothes," Vorhees told Docking.

"I'm impressed," Docking muttered. "Couldn't he be tutored a little?"

"I can't hold this guy's hand," Vorhees said.

"Well, you know what I mean," Docking muttered again. "You didn't see O. J. in his county jail orange did you?"

"Vincent isn't in prison orange is he? Besides, he's hip to his job. He'll be okay."

The deputy led Alvarado to a public seat just behind Vorhees. Alvarado nodded to Vorhees again, courting favor of some sort. Vorhees looked away, up to the frosty glass for a sign of the outside world. He could see a gull wheeling riotously, Vorhees envious of the bird's freedom. There was not a cloud in the sky, a rare day in late November. Vorhees found himself thinking about his wife, the child growing inside her. He wondered if she was upstairs or down, what she was doing. He felt Docking tap his elbow.

The lawyer named Darwin had come into the courtroom. Behind him the defendant Geronimo was being led by two deputies, the man gaunt and tall, his black hair tied behind his neck by a red bandanna. Next to Geronimo, Darwin seemed an open book, sandy hair, pale blue eyes, hawk nose. Vorhees wondered why he'd never seen this lawyer around the courthouse. What was he, mid-thirties? Knowing most of the criminal lawyers as he did, Vorhees wondered how Darwin had failed to show up on the screen before now. Vorhees watched Darwin empty his briefcase onto the defense table, then pat his client on the shoulder and engage him in a brief conversation. Geronimo failed to respond. An interpreter came into the courtroom and sat down at the defense table.

Vorhees leaned back. "You're looking good, Vincent," he said. "Very professional."

"You like my ensemble, man?" Vincent said.

"Listen to me, Vincent," Vorhees said quietly. "You tell it straight, no bullshit. If there is any bullshit, I'll break your fucking arm."

"No need, my man," Vincent said. "I know exactly where you're coming from, my man."

"You went into the bar, you offered the coke for sale. Geronimo bought an ounce and you went to his place for the cash. You didn't pressure him, you didn't make any sweetheart deals. You got the street price, am I clear?"

"Sure, man," Vincent said. "I know the text."

"Good, I'm glad you know the text, Vincent. Listen to the lawyer's questions, think for a minute, then answer. Keep it simple and don't volunteer anything."

Vincent went into a pout. "Why you got to be this way, man?" he said. "I thought we was friends."

Vorhees turned back to Docking.

"Nice prep job," Docking said. "Where'd Vincent get the coke he carried?"

"From me," Vorhees answered. "Is it relevant where Vincent got the drugs?" Vorhees asked finally.

"Probably not," Docking said, reading a case. "I just wanted to know."

Vorhees had to feel sorry for Docking, a kid of twenty-five and already in the trenches. The way Vorhees looked at things, being out on the street wasn't half as bad as doing your fighting here in this marble-and-walnut jungle. While Vorhees was thinking, Jack Darwin got up and walked slowly over to the prosecution table. Docking got to his feet and the two men shook hands, exchanged some small talk.

"I'm asking for evidence," Darwin told Docking.

"On what grounds?" Docking said. "Hell, I don't even know what your issues are."

Vorhees tuned out the lawyers. He had managed to read the Darwin brief, but it seemed too technical to be understood. After all, Vorhees knew what he needed to know, the rules for probable cause, grounds for a search, how to make a solid confession stand up, when he could run a bluff, how to kill a man under the departmental guidelines. What else did he need to know? In the background Docking was saying, "You talk a lot about criminal intent."

"Well after all," Darwin said, "there wasn't really a crime committed here, was there?"

Before Docking could reply, a door opened behind the bench and a clerk and bailiff filed to their places. Moments later, Hoffman appeared, a tiny bluff man with a bald head, graying muttonchops, beady eyes. The bailiff made his call to order and there was a long silence while the judge organized his paperwork.

"Your motion, Mr. Darwin. State of California against Manolo

Diaz-Geronimo." The voice of the judge echoed in the marble room. "I knew your father, didn't I?" Hoffman said.

"Probably so, Your Honor," Darwin said.

More silence. Vorhees looked back at Alvarado, who was still sulking.

"The charge here is possession of cocaine with intent to sell. By the way, I apologize for the delay. I think you've been told the reason, so let's get going here. It's already eleven-thirty."

Vorhees studied Geronimo, who didn't move a muscle or look at the judge. He seemed barely to breathe.

"Proceed, Mr. Darwin," Hoffman said.

"Uh, thank you, Your Honor," Darwin said, standing. "Uh, I think there are two main points in my brief. The first is about general principles. Under the criminal law, there must be some demonstrated criminal intent on the part of the defendant, or there can be no crime. That is to say, there has to be some known harm to society. If there is no harm, there is no crime."

"Wouldn't this be for the legislature to determine?" Hoffman interrupted.

"Uh, no, I don't think so."

Hoffman looked away, irritated. "I've read your brief, Mr. Darwin," he said. "Have you read the rules of criminal procedure that govern proceedings like this?"

"Pretty much, sir," Darwin said.

"Well, you couldn't prove it by me," Hoffman said.

Docking glanced at Vorhees, relieved that the shit was flowing elsewhere.

"Sir," Darwin said, "I'm only saying that on the facts as alleged, my client committed no crime."

"All right, Mr. Darwin," Hoffman said. "I've read your brief. Twice in fact. I read it twice because I couldn't understand it the first time. You cite one case out of the Northern District of Federal Court here. That case went up on appeal on habeas corpus and it involved the reliability of the testimony of a protected witness in relation to a search. The original motion was one to suppress the fruit of an allegedly illegal search. Am I getting through to you, Mr. Darwin?"

Darwin broke a faint sweat.

"The witness is unreliable, sir," Darwin said, stalling. Darwin pointed to Alvarado. "Just look at him."

Hoffman suppressed a smile. "A point well taken. But we're not talking about his apparel here. Are you aware that the case you cited holds that a protected witness should have been called in the suppression hearing and failure to do so constituted reversible error because a conviction based on his hearsay testimony was unconstitutional?"

Darwin looked at the courtroom clock. Vorhees thought maybe he was hoping for divine guidance. "Shouldn't we hear from the witness in this case as well?" Darwin said.

"I guess we might if I thought you'd really filed a motion to suppress, Mr. Darwin. Your motion is entitled a motion to dismiss. That was my point about the rules of procedure." Hoffman took off his glasses and dropped them on his bench. "What do you have to say, Mr. Docking?"

Standing, and with a slight unconscious bow, Docking said, "Frankly, Your Honor, I don't understand the legal grounds upon which Mr. Darwin seeks a dismissal. Isn't that what he's seeking? His brief reads like a bad lesson in the law of entrapment that stumbled into probable cause. If this is a brief about entrapment, then those issues are reserved for trial."

"Quite correct," Hoffman said. Hoffman squinted in Darwin's direction. "Mr. Darwin, you've tricked up your motion with entrapment language. You're aware that's an issue for the trier of fact? Perhaps you meant this to be a motion to suppress the evidence."

Docking sat down and whispered to Vorhees. "Shit, he's soft-balling this guy because he knew his father."

"Welcome to the big leagues," Vorhees said.

Hoffman was quiet for a long time, tapping his glasses on the bench. "Mr. Darwin, I'm going to give you a chance to fix up this motion of yours. As I read it, you've asked the court to dismiss the case entirely. I can't do that unless there is a formal defect in the information previously filed, or unless there's some prosecutorial misconduct. I guess I could dismiss the case if there was a serious constitutional defect in the arrest. As I read the facts, there isn't anything remotely like that in this case. Do you agree?"

"Uh, in essence, sir," Darwin stammered.

"Welcome to the old boys' club," Vorhees whispered.

"Too bad I'm not an old boy," Docking whispered back.

"Gentlemen," Hoffman announced. "It's getting very near lunch. I'm going to give Mr. Darwin here a couple of hours to reformulate his motion. If I don't, and simply dismiss the motion, we'll all be back here next week anyway when he does. We might as well do it today, don't you agree, Mr. Docking?" Hoffman paused, but continued immediately without waiting for Docking to reply. "When we come back at two, I want Mr. Darwin to argue cogently for a motion to suppress. I'll see you back here, *n'est-ce pas?*" Hoffman rose and walked around the end of the bench, standing five feet from Darwin. "Someday we'll have a chat about your father," Hoffman said. "I knew him when he was quite young."

"Thank you, sir, I'd like that," Darwin said.

"Hell, in fact come on back now," Hoffman said.

Docking turned to Vorhees. "You got to be shitting me," he said.

Darwin followed the judge into chambers, a tomblike interior office tricked up with red velvet drapery, green carpet, half a dozen plush leather chairs. Hoffman sat down behind his desk and lit a menthol cigarette.

"I'm sorry about your dad," he said. "It must have been rough losing them both like that. Your father didn't get to court very often, but I saw him at all the events."

"Yes sir, thank you."

Hoffman took a deep drag on his cigarette.

"What the hell are you doing here, Jack?" Hoffman said.

"I don't understand," Darwin said honestly.

"In my court. What are you doing here?"

"Practicing law," Darwin said.

"Barely, I'd say," Hoffman replied. "You ought to be up at Kline-James, making house calls on rich widows. You ought to be playing golf with shareholders, drinking with the boys at the Fairmont."

"It doesn't appeal to me, Judge," Darwin told him. Darwin sat buried in one of the plush chairs.

"Doesn't appeal to you? With your background? What the hell did you go to law school for anyway?"

"I went to law school because my dad wanted me to. Sometimes that's the way it is in life. I wanted to please him and so I set about pleasing him."

"And criminal law? That appeals to you?"

"Well, this is my first case. I'll let you know."

Darwin felt uncomfortable now, almost angry.

Hoffman nodded slightly, crushed his cigarette, and immediately lit another. "Listen, Jack," he said, "I don't know what's going on here, but that motion you filed could get you called on the Bar Association carpet. You may have something in there, but it isn't clear. You failed to follow the rules of procedure and your case law is bad. If your client had any sense he'd get a new lawyer."

Darwin looked at the door, two oak panels with brass fixtures. "I got him a week ago," Darwin said. "The preliminary hearing is next week and I needed to get the motion on file."

"Look, Jack," Hoffman said, leaning forward. "Get out of here and spend an hour and a half doing some research. At the very least I want you to look reasonable before I overrule you. Besides, the work you've done here today is grounds for appeal by your client. Hell, the scruffiest legal aid lawyer at San Quentin could spot this motion for the turkey it is and spring Geronimo back here in a month. I can't have something like that happening in my system."

"I don't know what I can do in an hour and a half."

"Figure out some grounds for suppression. Hell, I don't care if you headnote some recent case. Just fix it so that it comports with the rules of procedure and give me a California case at least. Then I can overrule you and we can move on."

"I'll do my best," Darwin said.

"Just fix the motion and cover my ass, will you? Not to mention your own ass, okay?"

Darwin got up and shook hands with the judge. He hurried out of the chambers and took the elevator to the ground floor. The vast hall was filled with people going to lunch, lawyers leaving court, secretaries, computer operators, deputies on break. Darwin stopped for a minute at a marble balustrade and realized that his hands were shaking. He stood there for five minutes before his shame subsided, the weak sickness he felt draining through his legs. Outside, he stood on the steps of City Hall and looked at the gray federal building next door, the old public library, the opera house and museum. The day was blue and the sky was filled by wheeling seagulls. Darwin clutched his briefcase and thought about going to the small federal law library across the street. He knew it was quiet and there was a librarian who could help him retrieve books.

He crossed the street and stood on the corner of an intersection. A bum cadged him for quarters. Darwin walked a long block past the law school and stood outside a bar called Frieda's. The bar was crowded with lawyers at lunch. He could smell fried rice and spring rolls, and he could sense the great riptide of whiskey dragging him under.

Nothing powered David Avila like a federal courtroom. He knew many lawyers who felt small inside them, lawyers who would shrink to nothingness when they hit what he liked to call the marble and velvet. He knew some lawyers who didn't sleep for weeks just thinking about their appearance in front of judges and juries, the live wire of anxiety inside them night and day. But Avila fed off the lush hypocrisy of such places, the bigger the better. He loved the marble floors, the dark mahogany paneling, rows of portraits of stern-faced men, black-robed eminences. Invariably he felt a rush of lust when he heard his name called in open court, his name resounding like a totem, a magical incantation. It must be the same feeling an executioner had when he chopped off a head.

And it made him sick how some lawyers bowed and scraped to judges, as if a political hack in a robe had the authority of God himself. Avila knew better, and the knowledge he carried made him the equal of any judge.

That Monday morning Avila was on the courthouse steps observing the bums and panhandlers, the homeless wanderers beside their pitiful plywood fires, the piles of uncollected garbage, scabrous dogs on leashes. He hated it all, and he despised these people, and he wished he could personally tear down their shanties and shacks, their huts and blanket tents. He fantasized about punching bums in the face, kicking them in the ass just for the fun of it.

He considered going to the nearby YMCA to lift weights during lunch hour, maybe taking a steam afterward. He looked at his appointment book and noted the three o'clock with a labor leader in danger of doing fifteen years for racketeering. He thought for a moment, and decided he couldn't do his meeting with wet hair. Instead, tonight he would go to the dojo and do karate, getting his exercise and aggression in the evening after work. He could pick up his weight lifting later in the week, when things calmed down. It wouldn't hurt him to skip a day of lifting here and there, even though he hated the thought of it. And besides, it had been a good morning, arranging bail for two drug mules in Contra Costa County, both of whom were probably heading to the airport and out of the country right now. Avila had their ten thousand each, and if they were ever arrested again, anywhere anytime, it would be worth more than that to Avila the second time around.

Avila crossed the street and walked down a block past the law school. He knew a place called Frieda's that served a decent tempura and rice, some nice tofu, pickled garlic and soy. Most of the time Avila avoided the place because it was a lawyer hangout, but today he needed to stay downtown to be near his office and the three o'clock meet. As he walked, he tried to calculate how much he could get up front from his labor leader, perhaps forty thousand against two hundred an hour and expenses. He could smile at the guy and ask—How do you put a price on fifteen years of your life?

Halfway down the block, Avila paused to watch some law students having lunch. He walked up two granite steps and observed some women who had gathered outside under the locust trees to eat sandwiches. They were wearing halter tops and cutoff jeans, some in shorts and T-shirts, others in skirts or dresses. Avila picked one out, a healthy blonde, and studied her for a long time, getting her in his sights. He liked her cool insouciance, how casual she looked eating her sandwich. He continued to watch until she picked up her books and disappeared inside the glass doors to the lobby of the school.

Down the block he found Frieda's full. But in the corner he saw a man hunched over a glass of bourbon, taking up a table for three. Avila knew the guy, sure he did.

He walked over and stood at the table, his manner saying *Hey there's no tables, mind if I share?*

"Hi there," Avila said. He smiled down at the man, widely. "You aren't John Darwin, are you?"

"That's me," Darwin said. "Do I know you?"

Avila sat down without being asked. "Do you mind?" he said. "The place is packed."

"Sure, help yourself."

"I'm David Avila," he said. "I've seen you around. Maybe your picture in the bar journal. I don't know." These sweet lies were how Avila made his living. He reveled in them and they made him feel alive. He thought he could convince Darwin they shared a history if he had to. Darwin registered something and seemed to brighten. It was an expression Avila understood. Darwin didn't want to drink alone.

"Yah," Darwin drawled. "I've seen you too. You do criminal law, right?"

"Nothing but," Avila said. "It's a helluva way to make a living. But as they say, somebody's got to do it."

Darwin sipped his drink. Bourbon rocks, Avila decided.

"You won't believe this," Darwin said. "But I've got my first criminal motion in front of Hoffman this afternoon at two."

"Hoffman," Avila said sympathetically. "He's a specimen. What's the case?"

"Oh, some poor guy on Mission Street was sitting in a bar. Fellow on the next stool offers to sell him an ounce of cocaine. They go to the guy's apartment, he gets out some money, and in come the cops. Now he's looking at three years without parole."

"They offered an incredible price?"

"Sort of," Darwin said.

"And what's your motion?" Avila asked.

Darwin had that first-drink flush. Avila recognized it rising in him, a faint rosy tint at the gills. Avila knew he was already drinking an imaginary second bourbon inside his head.

"Well, I called it a motion to dismiss," Darwin said.

A waitress came and Avila ordered shrimp tempura, rice, tofu, and designer water.

Darwin was saying, "When I started to speak, Hoffman shut me up and gave me a lecture on the rules of procedure. Then he gave me two hours to fix up a motion."

"You won't find anything in the bottom of that glass," Avila said. Darwin looked surprised. His face reddened further. "And you won't get anywhere with a motion to dismiss. You have to have a technical glitch to get a case dismissed."

"That's what I'm told," Darwin said coldly.

"I'm sorry to be blunt," Avila said.

"It doesn't matter," Darwin replied.

"Look," Avila said. "Don't take offense. Going back to court with a load on isn't a good idea. Besides, I think I can help you out on this case."

Darwin's eyes searched for a waitress and a tray of drinks. He was at the point of no return—either he would drink or he would go to court prepared. Finally Darwin found the waitress and raised his glass, ordering a second bourbon.

"I'd appreciate the help," Darwin said. "Hoffman already told me to change it to a motion to suppress."

"Well, he's right," Avila said. "Hoffman, I've known him for a long time. I could tell you stories."

Avila paused to eat some of his shrimp when it came. He used chopsticks, drank some designer water.

"You're dealing with reversals," Avila said finally. "A reversal is when the cops send people out into the street to sell drugs and bust the buyers. Usually when they bust a buyer, they try to put him to work selling drugs, at which point they bust other buyers. It's a pyramid scheme designed to pick up a lagging bust statistic. The state of California sends sixty or seventy street punks to jail for three years each and you and I pick up the twenty-million-dollar tab."

"It isn't illegal is it?" Darwin asked.

"No, it isn't illegal. It's about the election. Your friendly DA likes the headlines and gets to crow about the war on drugs for a few months. Then it all dies down. Just like Vietnam, it is all about a body count. And it doesn't matter if it's grandmothers and grandfathers. They're bodies too."

Avila noticed Darwin glance at his watch just as the waitress set down a second bourbon rocks. Before Darwin could touch the drink, Avila took out a legal pad from his briefcase and put the pad over the drink. Darwin stared at the pad, the whiskey invisible beneath it. For a moment, Avila thought he'd made a mistake, had gone too far.

"I really think I could help you out," Avila said. "But if you'd rather drink than practice law today, then help won't do you any good. I'm sorry."

"You're right, of course," Darwin said. He smiled quickly at Avila, slightly embarrassed, but willing. Darwin called the waitress and asked her to take away the drink, to bring him a tomato juice. He ordered a roast beef sandwich and a pickle.

"Look, here's what you do," Avila said. "When you get up in court this afternoon, orally amend your motion under Rule twelve to be a motion to suppress. Then demand to examine the complaining witness. What's his name?"

"Vincent Alvarado. He's wearing baggy purple pants and a crimson fluffy shirt."

"Super, terrific," Avila laughed. "Hoffman hates little street shits like that. Hates them worse than your guy, what's his name?"

"Geronimo," Darwin replied. "But look, I don't know what I'd do with Alvarado on the stand."

"Rip him a new asshole," Avila said.

"Well, I do know the evidence code. I've never seen that strategy in it."

"Okay, look," Avila said. He had been making some notes on his legal pad, an outline for Darwin to follow. "You're going to examine Alvarado on his past use of drugs."

"I don't think I can do that. If I remember my evidence code, past conduct isn't relevant. Especially as he's not charged with any crime."

"Go over to the law library," Avila said. "Check out a case called *McLeod v. California*. You'll find it in the advance sheets. Read the case, take it to heart. You won't find it *exactly* on point. It has to do with a search warrant based on the testimony of a convicted felon whose word could be doubted. It has to do with the relationship between credibility and probable cause. Get it?" Avila leaned over and whispered to Darwin. "Credibility is going to get Alvarado on the stand, get it?"

"And you think Hoffman will go for it?"

"I know Hoffman," Avila said. "He'll know your case is bull. But he'll want Alvarado on the stand. Yell and scream about how this case is a reversal and reversals are clogging up the court system. Hoffman will know what you're talking about. Drag Alvarado through his arrest and conviction record. He's probably out on parole right now. Ham it up. Rant and rave. Your whole point is that the cops and the DA are using criminals to bust people sitting quietly in bars. You're going to lose, but at least leave a stain in the road."

"*McLeod* you say?" Darwin asked.

Avila wrote down the name of the case on the legal pad. Darwin ate half of his roast beef sandwich and drank the tomato juice. Avila let Darwin eat, studying the decor of the restaurant, a wall covered with naval photographs, dried coconuts, musical instruments, and rattan matting. Somebody had played the jukebox, an old tune from the forties. Avila finished his tempura and shared some small talk with Darwin, watching every move the man made. Avila was enjoying himself, relishing each second.

"Let me tell you something else," Avila said. "A lot of times these guys offer great deals just to get the ball rolling. Some guy offers to sell a gram of coke for ten bucks and the buyer's eyes light up. Too good to be true. Even if that argument speaks to entrapment, you should bring it up. Lock Alvarado in on a dollar figure, so he can't backtrack on you at trial. They're going to object to all that, but just cite *McLeod* and say you're not attacking anything but credibility for the bust."

"You know," Darwin said, "I was thinking that maybe the deal was too good to be true. I tried to make a kind of contract argument in my brief. I wasn't very clear."

"Now you're thinking," Avila said. Avila took out his money clip and let Darwin see the hundreds and fifties. He found a twenty and tossed it on the table. "Lunch is on me," Avila said. "Good luck. Give me a call sometime, let me know how you made out."

"I appreciate your help, I really do."

"Sorry about the drinking thing," Avila said.

"No, it's okay. You're one hundred percent right."

Avila smiled and walked to the bar, then turned and waved goodbye. Darwin waved back, happy as a lark.

Outside, Avila stood on the sidewalk and looked at his watch. The day had clouded up a bit, but it was still a warm afternoon in fall. He walked the half block to the law school sunporch, mounted the steps, and sat on a granite flower bed. He picked out a female student and watched her—a wan blonde with a ponytail, frail bones, a dusting of freckles on her nose. She sat in pale sunshine leafing through a case book, finishing what was left of a sandwich, sipping iced tea from a paper cup. As he watched the woman, Avila could feel the muscles in his stomach tighten. Something living was heaving around inside his body, something palpable and real. When the woman finished her sandwich, she tossed its paper wrapper into a garbage bin. Avila rose and circled the rectangular sunporch, just a guy out for an afternoon stroll. When he neared the woman, he put on a pair of sunglasses, standing just to her side. He sat down on a granite bench and pretended to enjoy the sun. He studied the lines of the woman's neck, her shoulder blades, the curve of her jaw. Just for a moment, he was back in East L.A., where an orange sun growled down through smog every day, where there were dust motes in the air and the constant groan of heavy traffic. Then the girl turned to face Avila for a moment, something passing between them on its way from somewhere to nowhere. Avila thought the woman might speak, but she didn't. Avila looked at her hips, studied her lips, her eyes. Then he watched her go inside, integrate with other students.

Avila walked a block to the old Federal Building. He took an elevator to the third floor and went into the men's bathroom. He ran water over his face, dried it with a paper towel. For a long time he examined his own features, liking what he saw. There was nothing left of East L.A. now, nothing left of the sour sheets that smelled up his room, the aroma of cheap wine, the ripped shades over all the windows. What did freedom mean unless it meant having no past?

Avila went down the hall and peeked inside the law library. He could see Jack Darwin at a table, head down over a volume of California cases.

Avila took the stairs to the ground floor and hurriedly left the building. He went back to the law school, but his woman had disappeared for good. He went inside the school to its cafeteria, but it was too late for lunch now, and all the students had gone back to class. Something had massed inside his head, causing him pain. Now, more than ever, he needed to lift weights and take a steam. He felt drained and he longed for something to cut the dread.

Fate is invisible, isn't it? Avila decided it was his fate to meet Jack Darwin. But really, fate was just the catalyst for something bigger, something luminous in everybody's future.

Together on the third floor of City Hall, waiting for anything to happen. Vorhees and Docking were quiet while a deputy finished his cigarette, Alvarado off in a dark corner pouting because the deputy was making him wear his ballcap bill forward. "Some gangsta," the deputy had told Alvarado on the elevator, flipping around the hat. Alvarado touched his hat with a painful look of annoyance on his face. Vorhees had already talked Alvarado into wearing his plastic leather coat, just to hide the red ruffled shirt. Maybe because Vorhees was black, Alvarado had zipped on the coat with a protest. In truth, punks like Alvarado didn't bother Vorhees all that much; he found them slightly amusing, guys caught in between roles, not really bangers, not saints either. But even though these kinds of punks didn't bother Vorhees, he still wanted away from narcotics detail, and was counting the days. For one thing, the people you put in jail on narcotics rarely stayed long. You put them in jail, and weeks later you'd see them cruising on Mission or Army Street, as if nothing had happened. Vorhees had to think if you put somebody away for murder, they'd stay.

Vorhees noticed Jack Darwin get off the elevator, a slight flush on his face, but looking fairly happy. Vorhees hoped Darwin appreciated his luck with Hoffman.

"Good afternoon gentlemen," Darwin said. Docking nodded his hello.

Darwin went inside the courtroom and took his place behind the defense table. Geronimo had been brought in already, and Darwin was telling him something through the interpreter. Vorhees went inside and tried to listen, but all he could hear was muffled Spanish. Alvardo came up behind and tried to start a conversation, but Vorhees made him sit down and be quiet. Ten minutes later the clerk, bailiff, and judge took their places.

"Your turn, Mr. Darwin," Hoffman said loudly.

"I want to apologize to the court," Darwin said. He was standing now, holding a legal pad. "My motion should have been styled a motion to suppress the evidence, slightly over one ounce of cocaine, and all the cash seized by the police. The cocaine was brought to the Tango Club on Mission by a police agent, a provocateur. This police agent is in the courtroom today." Darwin gestured to Alvarado, who beamed proudly. "On the grounds announced in *McLeod v. California,* I'd ask that Vincent Alvarado be made to take the stand and explain his actions, his reliability, and his credibility."

"You forgot bias, Mr. Darwin," Hoffman said.

Docking was on his feet. "Wait a minute," he said angrily. "There are no grounds in the evidence code to call this witness. There are certainly no grounds to challenge his credibility as he hasn't testified anywhere yet. He hasn't signed any affidavits. He's an eyewitness, that's all."

Vorhees smiled with satisfaction. On his feet, the kid Docking seemed to move well. Vorhees watched the judge put on his reading glasses, sitting about six feet above them like a god on Olympus.

"Mr. Docking is right," Hoffman said. "I'll ask that you articulate your motion. Give me something to bite on, will you? A reason to call Alvarado to the stand? I presume you've spent the last two hours mulling it over, Mr. Darwin?"

"Uh, yes sir," Darwin said.

Vorhees wondered if Darwin had spent the whole two hours in study, or if he'd stopped by some bar for a quick drink.

"I'd ask the court to notice my case," Darwin began. "In *McLeod v. California*, the supreme court looked at the following facts." Darwin crossed the room and handed copies of the case to Hoffman and Docking. "A sale of marijuana was made by a police agent who'd just gotten out of prison and was being handled by police in Los Angeles."

Docking rose again. "Your Honor, this case isn't in the defendant's brief. It shouldn't be considered."

"Let's hear it, Mr. Docking," Hoffman said. "You're technically right. Let's see how innovative he's become. And as I explained before, we might have to let him come back next week with the same case. Besides, Mr. Docking, all you have to do here is show probable cause for the arrest, all right?"

Docking nodded and sat down heavily. Docking and the judge spent ten minutes reading the case.

"Gentlemen," Hoffman announced after finishing his reading. "This *McLeod* case allows a defense lawyer to examine a protected witness about a transaction prior to the preliminary hearing if probable cause is based solely on the testimony of the protected witness. It kind of says to the state that California can't have its cake and eat it too."

"I beg to differ," Docking said.

"It's a free country," Hoffman told him.

"The *McLeod* case is one in which a search warrant was issued on the basis of the affidavit of a protected witness. You don't have that here. The witness is hands-on to an arrest."

"I'm attacking the arrest," Darwin said quickly.

"Now, that's a second thought if I ever heard one," Docking said sarcastically.

"Better late than never," Hoffman said.

"Your Honor, may I?" Darwin asked.

"Please," Hoffman said.

"This police agent is practicing reversals. He's the kind of guy who makes your docket the mess that it is."

"Oh, come on," Docking said loudly.

"Mr. Docking," Hoffman said, "if I let the examination proceed what harm can there be? Your witness is going to tell me the truth and he'll just repeat himself at preliminary, if we get that far. Am I right?"

"The harm," Docking said, "is that the examination constitutes discovery by the defense. They're not entitled to examine my witness today."

"Look, Mr. Docking," Hoffman said. "I appreciate your position, I really do. But if I fail to examine the witness today, Mr. Darwin will refile his motion and we'll be right back here."

"Then I have no choice," Docking said.

"Call the witness," Hoffman told the clerk.

When his name was called, Alvarado shuffled gang-style to the stand and slumped into the leather chair.

Darwin picked up the police report and stood behind the lectern, just in front of Alvarado. He unfolded the *McLeod* case and his brief and put them on the lectern, just to have some papers to look at. In truth, they were completely useless to him now. Darwin thought back to lunch, trying to remember the advice Avila had given him. Where had he heard of Avila? Darwin took Alvarado quickly through his vitals, name, age, address, occupation. Fry cook, Alvarado told Darwin, that's what he did. Alvarado was twenty-six, but he looked about fifteen.

"And last September tenth you were sitting next to my client in a bar on Mission Street?"

"I sat down next to him, yeah."

"Why Geronimo?"

"There was a seat."

"You never knew him before that day?"

"Nah, I didn't know the guy."

"Just picked him out."

"That's right, man."

"Did the police tell you to pick him out?"

"Nah, they didn't care."

"And when you walked into that bar, you possessed an ounce of cocaine?"

"Object!" shouted Docking.

"The grounds?" Hoffman said.

"It isn't relevant."

"Overruled, Mr. Docking," Hoffman growled.

"Man, you know where I had that coke. In my pocket."

"And where did you get the cocaine?"

"Oh, objection," Docking said.

"Overruled, Mr. Docking, I told you."

Docking sat down glumly.

"Man, you know where I got that shit," Alvarado said. From where Vorhees sat, the kid looked rattled.

"You tell the court," Darwin said.

Alvarado tried to catch Vorhees' eye.

"Well, Five-O give me the shit," Alvarado said.

"You got the drugs from the police?"

"I said I did, didn't I?"

"So, when you went into the Tango you were hoping to help the police make an arrest by selling cocaine to a stranger. Is that about it?"

"That's the game, yeah."

"Somebody, anybody?"

"What do you mean?"

"It didn't matter who you picked out, did it?"

"Not really."

"Have you ever been arrested?" Darwin asked. Docking was on his feet instantly, protesting loudly.

"Prior bad acts aren't relevant," Docking shouted.

"Small-time shit and that," Alvarado said.

"Don't answer!" Docking shouted.

"Small-time shit like what?" Darwin said.

Alvarado glanced up to Hoffman. "Man, do I have to tell about all the shit I done?"

"No, you don't," Hoffman said. "I get the picture though, Mr. Docking." Hoffman took off his glasses and wiped his face with a paper towel.

"You use drugs, don't you?" Darwin asked Alvarado. "You use the stuff you went into the bar to sell?"

Docking rose wearily. "Prior bad acts again, Your Honor."

"We've been through this," Hoffman said.

"It goes to perceptions," Darwin said. "I want to know if he knew what he was doing that day."

"I'd be interested too," Hoffman said.

"Do you need the question read back?" Darwin asked.

Alvarado looked at Vorhees. "I don't use nothing," he said sullenly.

"Were you arrested for using drugs?" Darwin asked.

"I wasn't guilty," Alvarado said.

"You're on parole now, aren't you?"

"Yeah, I'm on parole."

"In fact, you're being used by the police on a regular basis to make arrests."

"Used, hah, I ain't being used."

"They've threatened to send you back unless you sell dope for them, haven't they?"

Docking rose angrily, shouting, "Objection, just a minute!"

"Hey now, boys and girls," Hoffman said. "I want to see all the parties in my chambers. You too, Mr. Policeman."

Vorhees let Docking take the lead, all of them following Hoffman around the bench and through an oak door. Inside chambers, Vorhees and Docking sat together on a red leather sofa. Darwin stood beside a set of drapes. Hoffman lit a menthol cigarette and smoked half of it down in silence. Vorhees knew it was going to be him on the hot seat.

Hoffman looked at Vorhees. "We're doing reversals again, huh? And do you people have any information that leads you to believe that Mr. Geronimo out there is a dealer? Does he have a record? Is he a big-time guy? Or is he just some target in a bar, drinking a cold one?"

"He's an illegal," Vorhees said.

"That's it?" Hoffman asked.

"He has no record, if that's what you mean."

"You know that's what I mean, Officer," Hoffman said.

"Just a minute," Docking interrupted. "If this is about entrapment, then that's still for trial. Let Mr. Darwin use it if he wishes, but not here."

"I'm well aware of the law of entrapment, Counsel," Hoffman said. "But look, my courts are being clogged by these reversals. Illegal drugs are swamping the streets and the police are helping make sales. Please, please."

"It's a clean bust," Vorhees told the judge.

"Of course it's a clean bust," Hoffman said. "I don't doubt that."

"If you want to know about the policy, you'll have to ask the chief of police and the DA." Vorhees shrugged and sank back into red leather.

"So, he's clean but he's illegal," Hoffman said. He picked up a phone and punched through a call. "Nola," Hoffman said, "we've got a serious problem down here in the courtroom. Can you give us five minutes please? I know your time is valuable. So is mine."

Hoffman listened for a moment, then hung up the phone. "Look, gentlemen," he said, "I don't blame the officer here for this policy. We're involved in election politics and things will calm down next month. But for now, I think we need to exercise some fairness."

Docking looked at Vorhees, who raised an eyebrow. Darwin sat quietly, not wanting to interrupt the flow. In a few minutes the chamber door opened, and the district attorney walked inside. She was a handsome, weather-lined woman in a gray business suit, a plain white blouse, and a silk bow tie under her chin. Nola Gettes looked around the room, then settled on Docking, trying to place him from all the other 140 lawyers she supervised.

"Thank for coming down, Nola," Hoffman said.

"What's going on?" Gettes asked.

"The state has a case against a man named Geronimo. He's sitting out in the courtroom now. He's charged with possession of an ounce of cocaine with intent to sell. As you know, that's three years without parole. We've just been chatting about this defendant, how he has no criminal record and was minding his own business in a bar on Mission Street when a police agent, who's out on parole by the way, walked in and offered to sell him the cocaine. I haven't heard much about this, but I suspect it was a really good deal, pricewise."

"It happens," Gettes said, still standing.

"The police agent is out on parole for, dare I say it, doing drugs himself."

"I resent the implication," Gettes said harshly. "Sting operations are common law-enforcement techniques. I thought you knew that, Judge."

Vorhees wished he could smile. It was wonderful to hear someone giving a judge the business. And right in front of everybody.

"Come on, Nola," Hoffman said. "I don't like my courtrooms jammed with innocent men who were drinking a beer. We've got enough real problems without making any up."

"Geronimo is a potential dealer. The streets will probably be safer with him inside."

"I don't think we can speculate," Hoffman said.

"And I'm no Gypsy fortune-teller," Gettes said. "I just enforce the criminal laws against possession of cocaine."

Hoffman worked his jaw back and forth. "That's fine, Nola, but I interpret the laws of this state. And I've been looking at a recent California Supreme Court case brought to me by Mr. Darwin here. I think that case authorizes me to investigate the substance of the drug transaction to find out if it was a fantasy or not." Gettes was about to speak when Hoffman put up his hand. "And I'm not talking about entrapment either, Nola. I think this court can investigate the motives of the seller and can examine the consideration for the sale." Hoffman crushed out his cigarette and lit another. "In short, Nola, I would like this case out of my sight."

"I wish you wouldn't strong-arm me," Gettes said.

"Call it what you will," Hoffman told her. "At trial, I'll give an instruction to the jury that you guys will just love."

Gettes motioned for Docking and Vorhees to follow her outside. They went through an outer office and into the main corridor of the third floor. The halls were full now, lawyers and police officers and family members milling willy-nilly. While Vorhees watched, Gettes leaned against a marble pillar. Her blond hair was bleached and wispy. You could see blue veins working in her neck.

"Do we have a problem with the *McLeod* case?" Gettes asked Docking.

"It isn't even on point," Docking said.

"So, it's just Hoffman," Gettes said. "Does anybody know this Darwin guy?"

Docking shrugged. Vorhees told her he'd never seen the man in his life. "His old man was a star," Vorhees said. "Hoffman said they were friends."

"All right," Gettes said. "Can we offer them simple attempted possession?"

"A misdemeanor?" Docking said in amazement.

"A small fine and Geronimo walks," Gettes said in her hard tone. "I don't want to get all balled up with Hoffman over this little bust, okay?"

Vorhees and Docking followed the woman back into chambers. Darwin had remained by the drapes.

"How about simple attempted possession?" she asked Darwin.

"I'll have to ask my client," Darwin said.

"It's a deal," Hoffman interrupted. "Prepare a journal entry and file it, will you, guys?"

Darwin started for the door to the courtroom. "I'm sure this will be fine with Geronimo," he said.

"I'm sure," Gettes told him.

"Just get the journal entry to me," Hoffman said. "I'll see to it that Geronimo gets out this afternoon. Tell him he'll have to pay a small fine."

"The INS will be waiting for him," Gettes said.

Hoffman tapped at his empty pack of cigarettes. "That's all, boys and girls," he said.

Gettes came over to Docking and Vorhees.

"Let's not forget this guy Darwin, okay?" she asked.

"Okay," Docking said.

"Just remember," the woman whispered. "What goes around, comes around."

Darwin did not tell his client the INS would be waiting outside the jailhouse door, that a van would pick him up and take him down to the border and dump him in Calexico, maybe Tijuana. He simply told the interpreter about the deal and then gathered his papers together for the walk down the three marble flights of stairs to the ground floor of City Hall. All the way down he felt as though a great weight had been taken off his shoulders, as if he'd just been manumitted from breaking rocks on a hot swampy southern day.

Outside the weather was gloriously blue, the sky shot with fall gold. With the sun tipping through the sky, making soft shadows, he thought of Karla and their first trip to Sonoma, where they'd stayed at a spa and taken mud baths together, frolicked in warm springs, made love at night. He remembered the smell of her, lavender. He remembered the color of the grape leaves in early morning, mauve and orange. Then Avila replaced Karla in his head. He tried to recall meeting the man Avila before. Walking across Civic Center a thought came to him. He remembered reading newspaper stories of a huge drug bust on I-80 in the Sierras, sometime in the late 1980s. The CHP had pulled over a rented van with two tons of Mexican weed in the back, one of the biggest marijuana busts in California history. It had been David Avila representing the Costa Ricans in the front seat. It was history-making stuff at the time, though now it would probably be no more than page 10, strictly local. After that, Avila had gotten into bigger and bigger drug cases, some white-collar stuff, a labor case here and there.

Whatever made David Avila tick seemed to work for Darwin too. He knew that without Avila's advice, Hoffman would have sent him home like a baby.

The taste of the bourbon was almost gone.

That was another thing he'd have to thank Avila for. Maybe meeting this guy would signal a change of luck for Darwin. God knew it was something that was overdue.

She slept until ten, about average these days. She did not dream, and when she woke she was utterly refreshed. Lying in bed for a long time, she admired her decorating talent, the room she'd remodeled over Jack's protests, expensive faux pearl wallpaper with tiny bits of stone embedded in the weave, paper that had the luster of shell. The thick carpet was gray, which she thought matched her eyes. And after all the work was done she had gone to Mendocino for a few days and stayed at a spa where she'd first gone with Jack, only this time going alone, leaving Jack behind to calm down before the invoices and bills really started pouring in. That was months ago now, and the issue of the bedroom remodel had been buried under an avalanche of other problems, so many problems Jack probably didn't remember the color of the walls anyway.

She was so used to their daily battles that they hardly even annoyed her anymore. They were a couple with no agenda, and so any event might trigger an explosion, or a long silence, either of which was okay with Karla because by her own reckoning she could outbattle Jack any day of the week. Of course, they shared an occasional desultory dinner beside the flickering TV, Jack making halting conversation in an attempt to break the emotional deadlock. And then there were the nights Jack would stay out late and come home drunk, stomping around like a kid trying to get attention. Sometimes Karla took pity on him and let him come inside her bedroom and make drunken love to her. Or she'd let him take her in the tub, as if she'd been surprised, just to give him a taste. Those were the nights he'd grunt and struggle over her body, afterward taking a quick shower, easing his way into bourbon-racked sleep, while Karla bathed him out of her body. Now, though, Jack had let her alone for more than a month, which was unusual, his longest dry stretch in four years.

Karla washed her hair and dried it, standing in the open air of her balcony. She could see nearly all of the bay from there, tiny boats on the water, the Golden Gate. Jack had talked about going to Tahoe for Christmas before going to work, and she had let the subject drop, pretending to be asleep as he shouted through the door at her. In truth, she hated the log cabin that Jack's father had built in the forest, its remoteness, the cold and the snow, the forced intimacy with Jack and its inevitable failure. For four years Jack had asked her to go at Christmas, and she'd gone twice, giving in to Jack's need to relive something from his past, even going so far as to help him decorate a tree once, making evening hot chocolate, sitting in front of the stone fireplace while Jack pretended to tie flies, watching the flames. Karla marveled at Jack's desire to relive his childhood, thinking of it as something wondrously naive. She hadn't seen her own mother or father for ten years, and she didn't want to see them, their stuffy apartment down in Escondido, her father's misplaced contempt for everything and everybody, their mutterings, money problems, and moral smallness. By the time she left high school, she hated the thought of them. She still did.

With her hair dry, Karla dressed in designer jeans and a knitted cashmere sweater. She drove the gold Mercedes to a flower shop on the Marina and ordered a dozen red roses delivered to her home later that evening. She caught Doyle at the Presidio and crossed the Golden Gate, taking the Belvedere exit past Mill Valley. She drove with the windows open, enjoying this latest in a string of gorgeously blue days, cool air that smelled of salt. Heading toward Belvedere she crossed a neck of the bay and parked in Sammy's Dockside lot. It was about twenty minutes after noon and the lot was jammed. The restaurant was suspended over the water, a pier running above the shallows.

She hurried inside the restaurant and saw David Avila at a corner table, sipping Evian. For a moment, she thought back to their accidental meeting at Marge's on Mason, just a few short months ago. She and Jack had gone to dinner on a Sunday night, one of their last attempts at reconciliation, and when Jack had begun a cribbage game after their meal, Karla saw David Avila sitting at the end of the bar, darkly hand-some, a man who could take away your breath. She had caught his eye. He introduced himself. They made up an excuse to meet later in the week.

"Don't tell me I'm late," Karla said breathlessly, teasing Avila with her tone. She had worn her hair long and straight. With David, there was no need for tricks.

"I saw you drive up," Avila said. "I ordered you a white wine spritzer."

Karla took off her Italian-made sunglasses, two hundred dollars at a jeweler's off Union Square, charged to Jack Darwin. In the past two weeks she'd done three tanning sessions, and her skin was the color of molasses. She liked to call her current look "informal expensive."

A waiter delivered the spritzer and Avila ordered shrimp cocktail.

"I've missed you," Karla told Avila, touching his hand under the table. Avila did things to her, things she thought no man could ever do. It was uncanny the things he could do to her, how he could make her lose power and crash. Karla had always prided herself on having control of every situation. Avila seemed to be a mirror image of herself, only harder and sharper. He made her take chances just like this. They would meet in out-of-the-way places, sometimes in towns like San Jose or Santa Clara. There were times when Karla wanted David to come home with her and fuck her on Jack's bed. "I really have missed you," she said again.

The waiter delivered shrimp cocktail, six huge shrimps around a beveled edge of chopped ice and parsley. Karla drank some of her spritzer and felt giddy.

"I'm glad you miss me," Avila said.

"Jack wants me to go to Tahoe this Christmas."

"Are you going?" Avila asked.

Karla wanted to touch him, his crisp white shirt, the beautifully tailored three-piece blue suit, a pale yellow tie, everything just right, like quartz crystals. Avila had a way of going to the heart of things. He brought a sense of danger and exactitude to whatever he touched. Maybe that was something Karla really liked about him. Down deep, he frightened her somehow.

"Of course I'm not going," Karla said. "I hope we can be together while he's gone."

Avila stabbed a shrimp and ate it. He gazed out at the water and the boats.

"Did you see the lawyer I told you about?" Avila asked.

"I spent an hour with him," Karla said.

"How did it go?"

"I told him Jack was threatening divorce. In fact, he did that very thing again."

"What's the bottom line?"

"He thinks I can get about half the estate."

"Less his fee," Avila said, distracted.

The bay was bright with reflected sun. Karla was in the corner and the sun warmed her.

"Yes, less his fee."

"That means about three million," Avila said.

"That's a lot of money, David," Karla mused.

"That's not much money. What's Darwin worth, six or seven million maybe?"

"You know his money is tied up in the house and the trust. He's just about broke otherwise. And he can't lay his hands on the trust money for ten years."

"You explained all this to Rowe?"

"Yes, everything. He thinks it might be hard to execute against the trust. But the house can be sold." Karla sipped her wine. She felt Avila slipping away. "He said it would be different if Jack ever hit me. But I think Jack is too big a coward to do something like that."

"Suppose Jack dies," Avila said.

"But Jack isn't going to die," Karla said. "If he did, I'd get everything."

"It sounds like you'll get nothing. Not for ten years anyway."

"Perhaps," Karla said. She ran a finger along Avila's cuff. She longed to touch him, search him with her tongue. "Why don't we get married? I could divorce Jack. Surely I'd get something. Then we could be together."

Avila pushed away the shrimp cocktail.

"You want to let your husband's seven million go just like that?" Avila asked.

The waiter came and Karla ordered a small Caesar salad. Avila had nothing, just more Evian.

"I ran into Jack last week," Avila said finally. "It was just a co-incidence. I went to have lunch at Frieda's down by the law school near Civic Center. Your husband was sitting all alone in a corner nursing his first bourbon rocks of the day." Avila looked outside again, lost in thought. "I went over and sat down with him."

"Oh God, you didn't really?" Karla said.

"Why not?" Avila said casually. "There wasn't anyplace else to sit. Besides, we had a nice talk, lawyer to lawyer. He had a criminal motion in state court and I gave him some advice. I talked him out of the second bourbon rocks and sent him off to the law library with a case."

"I remember the night," Karla said. "He'd had a few when he got back and bragged about winning his first case."

"Jack called my office," Avila said. "A few days ago. He said he wanted to thank me. He asked me a few questions about getting criminal clients. He wanted me to think he was a man on a mission."

Karla saw her hold on the afternoon slipping away.

"He could be serious about divorcing me, you know," she said.

"Then I say we head him off."

"Head him off? I don't know what you mean."

"I'm surprised he hasn't filed already. His house may be separate property and the trust is tied up. He could put you out with very little. Suppose we put *him* out? How would that be?"

"David, this talk scares me."

"I'm only thinking out loud," Avila said.

Karla felt something moving inside her, a vestige of fear and the primal emotions David stirred in her, emotions against her will. She slipped off the deck shoes she was wearing and put her right foot on Avila's lap, running her foot in circles around his penis. Avila sipped designer water and watched the sun shine on Sausalito. When she had him completely hard, she began to run her foot up and down, base to tip, tip to base, very slowly. The waiter brought the check, but Karla continued her game with Avila.

"Are you in court, baby?" Karla asked, still working.

"Not until three," Avila said heavily.

"Let's go up to Belvedere again. I want you to remember me all day and all night."

Karla paid for lunch with her Gold Card, then left the restaurant and drove down a hill for about a mile. She cut left across a narrow lane and through a grove of eucalyptus and juniper. Gradually, the grand houses on either side of the lane dropped away and she found a gravel service road that skirted the cemetery. She parked her Mercedes beside a stone wall and waited. There were no houses near, only rows of stone monuments, groves of eucalyptus, the silence of the dead. When she was sure she was alone, she rolled up the tinted windows of the Mercedes and slipped off her jeans. She kept a blanket in the backseat, and she unfolded it and laid it carefully over the leather. She waited until she saw Avila's green Jaguar pull up behind her, and then she crawled over the seat back and lay down in the backseat. Avila got out of his car and slipped into the back with her.

Karla kissed him on the mouth. She opened his zipper and took out his penis and sucked him. He turned her roughly and straddled her from behind, one arm around her neck, nearly choking her as he came inside, working deep. It hurt her and she moaned quietly, both because of the pain and because she liked what he was doing, keeping her head down on the seat while he worked himself harder and deeper inside her from behind, his right arm around her neck, still pressing against her. When he had finished, he rolled away and sat back. Karla stayed where she was, on her knees, half ruined. Her back was slick with sweat and she was out of breath. In the corner of the car, Avila was combing his hair. The pain thrilled her. The coldness of his muscle warmed her.

"I'm going to play with Jack," Avila said.

Karla was flushed now, almost faint. Her legs hurt from being tucked beneath her, and the backs of her thighs were nearly cramped.

"Let's not talk about Jack," she said.

"You *might* get half," Avila said. "If we're going to be together, we might as well have it all."

"Jack isn't stupid," Karla said.

"No, he isn't stupid. But he's weak. He trusts people. He looks on the bright side. That's how he ended up married to you, isn't it?"

Karla tried to embrace Avila.

"Why don't we give Jack his divorce?" she said.

"I never settle a case," Avila said.

"Please, David," Karla said stupidly.

"Let me handle this," Avila said. "I've got to get back to the city."

Karla watched him leave the Mercedes and drive away in his green Jaguar. She put on her jeans and got out of the car and stood beside the stone wall, looking out into Resthaven, where she'd been a salesperson. That life was gone, and another had taken its place. It was the order of things. Now it seemed that something else was going to replace what she had now as well. It was hard for her to think, standing and peering over the stone wall at acres of gray tombstones. When she got home she could look forward to roses and a hot bath. That was about as far as she could see into the future.

Coming home tired, Darwin parked in the driveway and sat silently for a time, regretting his own arrival. He raised the courage to go inside, put his briefcase in the hall closet, and exchanged his suit coat for a moth-eaten gray sweater of his father's that Karla called his "old man getup." In the kitchen he stood looking out the glassed patio doors and across to the Golden Gate, where a stream of traffic headed north on 101 toward Marin County and San Rafael. The gray twilight was dense with mist borne in from the Pacific over the Farallones. It seemed gloomy and morbid to Darwin, the water in the bay the color of slate.

Karla surprised Darwin when she came in through the patio doors. She was sipping a gin and tonic.

"You're not at Marge's?" she said. She did not look at Darwin, but instead stared out at the gathering dark.

"I want to work at home tonight," Darwin told her. His flat distant voice seemed disembodied. "Do you have dinner plans?"

"I'm going down to the Marina. I'm meeting my friend Gina for pasta. Don't wait up for me."

"Great," Darwin said. "Is there anything to eat here?"

Karla said nothing. She clicked the ice in her drink.

"What about Christmas at Tahoe?" Darwin asked.

"Not this year, Jack."

"I mean it, Karla. After the first of the year this can't continue. I've got a new job teaching at the law school. That's three nights teaching research and writing. I've talked to a fellow about referring some criminal clients. This guy says he can get me a fresh start in the business."

"Turning over a new leaf are you?" Karla said, her back to Darwin. She drew a circle on the wet glass and stared through it.

"People can change. Things can change."

"Teaching old dogs new tricks. The proof is in the pudding. Heaven knows, Mr. Darwin. Jack, you're a walking cliché." Karla sipped her gin. "Do you know how many times I've heard this new-leaf speech?"

"All right, Karla, you win."

"That's a good boy, Jack," Karla said, turning to face him now. She had deepened her tan at the parlor. "I think that's my cue to leave." Karla brushed by her husband and ascended the stairs to her room. She put on a bulky blue sweater, some jeans, and expensive Reeboks, then came down again. Darwin had spread some papers out on the kitchen table. He was drinking a gin and tonic, making notes. Karla stood looking down at her husband, wishing she could go to see David Avila at his Russian Hill apartment. He had forbidden her to come, but she wanted to defy him, to visit him anyway.

Darwin watched his wife leave the house, the gin entering his head, the smoothness of it like a caress, making his lips slightly numb. It was a happy feeling that lasted perhaps two drinks, and the rest was all letdown, even though it was hard to stop. Darwin had three weeks to prepare his first lectures, to study criminal law and procedure, to formulate examples and writing exercises. Darwin dropped his pen on the table and began to drink.

How could he have lost his own life so completely? Of course he had been lonely and in despair just after his parents were killed in the crash. It had made him sense his own mortality, and he had begun to mourn his youth, the childhood spent romping down in Burlingame, up in the Sierras, those surreally sunny days that were the flesh and blood of nostalgia. And there was the question of his resolve, his ability to stop drinking and reverse the current course of his moral decline, his ability to clarify his muddled thought, to rectify his anxiety. Darwin picked up his pen and tried to read law, then felt himself weaken inside.

As he sat there Darwin remembered one of Karla's special tricks. She used to practice it on him in restaurants, slipping off one of her shoes and rubbing her bare foot up and down his penis until he was hard, sitting there embarrassed with his boyish boner hidden under the table. She would caress him even as waiters and busboys came and went. Once in a pub on Larkin, Darwin had come, wetting his pants, sitting in the dark with his pants soaked, Karla's face shining at him through candlelight.

Darwin was alone in the yellow glare of the kitchen. All right, God, give me another bad Christmas. Then, Darwin thought to himself, let everything get better.

Karla sometimes told people that her black moods were an inheritance from her father.

That day she had one on Lombard Street in heavy traffic, the first warm traces of it on her cheek, and then the inevitable cool film of sweat tracking down her forehead. She drove to the bay and turned off into a Safeway parking lot, sitting quietly with the Mercedes running cool and clean while her hands shook and her heart raced.

A light rain began to fall through darkness and all Karla could see were the towers of the Golden Gate, its bulk looming through the black night, which seemed a perfect statement of her own being at the moment, a huge mass of something in the cold, an arrow pointed nowhere. She touched her face, then rolled down the window so that she could try to breathe. Moments later she found herself rifling the glove box and console for cigarettes, remembering then that she had failed to buy more when she had run out that afternoon.

Karla walked to the Safeway and bought cigarettes. She smoked one in the Mercedes, listening to hard rock music. The cigarette made her dizzy and her heart continued to pound.

When she could, she drove down Lombard and onto Russian Hill. She kept the window down, smelling the air and its cold salt tang. Huge rows of private condominiums rose on either side of her, the streets like canyons crowded by holiday shoppers. Men and women were walking their dogs, joggers flashed by in fluorescent gear. Windows showed traces of brightly decorated Christmas trees. Finally, on a cul-de-sac near Haven, she found a place to park and walked to a café she knew on Union where she sat near an electric space heater, ordered cappuccino, and smoked another cigarette. Whatever had happened to her was now over, and she could breathe again. When the waitress asked her to crush her cigarette, she dropped it in the cappuccino and walked out.

Karla went to Filbert and stood in the rain looking at the condominium where David Avila lived. There was a dull ache in her shoulders and her raincoat was soaked and the cold rain was wetting the ends of her long hair. She crossed the street and stood under the canopy of the building. She took off her belted coat and shook out the rain. Her heart was racing again, but not from anxiety. As she stood under the canopy, she could tell that the doorman inside was staring at her.

She opened the glass doors and went inside. She shook her wet hair and smiled.

"Yes ma'am?" the doorman said.

"Isn't this a night?" Karla said gaily.

"It certainly is," he replied.

Karla raised her head, giving the doorman a look at her sharp jawline and perfect neck. It was warm in the vestibule and her Chanel was evident.

"I'm so flummoxed," Karla said. "I'm here to see Mr. Avila but I can't remember his number."

"Does he expect you?" the doorman asked.

"He expects me. Oh yes."

"I'll buzz up," the doorman said. He reached for a row of buttons behind Karla.

"I'd like it to be a surprise," Karla said.

"I'm here to prevent surprises."

"Please," Karla said. "It would mean a lot to me. David and I are old friends." Karla moved close to the man. "Tonight I'm going to give him my Christmas present. It isn't something he expects, but he's going to be very glad to receive it. Do you know what I mean?"

The doorman eyed her. "I guess I do," he said.

"Just let me go up," Karla whispered.

"I could lose my job," the man said.

"I promise you won't. Thirty minutes from now Mr. Avila won't be thinking about anything except his Christmas present. And he'll be extremely pleased and very relaxed." Karla washed the doorman with a smile. "But if he has visitors, I could understand."

"Oh, there isn't anyone up there," the doorman said. He looked pained now, almost exhausted. "I suppose it couldn't hurt anything. But if anything happens, I could be in big trouble."

"You're a sweet man," Karla said.

"Number three-thirty. End of the hall."

"I wouldn't be surprised if Mr. Avila tipped you nicely this season."

"Okay lady," the doorman said.

He opened the glass door and let Karla pass. She rode an elevator to the third floor, walked down a plushly carpeted hall, and tapped on Avila's door. The corridors were wide and studded with sitting lounges, vases of fresh flowers, wide windows at the end.

Avila opened the door and blinked once. He stepped outside and stood there in jeans, safari shirt, tan loafers with tassels. Karla smiled at him and tried to kiss his cheek. Avila placed one hand on her chest. With the other he closed the door behind him.

"You've followed me," Avila said softly.

"Darling, don't be angry. I've had a very bad day and I needed to see you. Please let me come in."

"When did you follow me here?" Avila asked. Karla was trapped in his gaze, those piercing brown eyes.

"Do we have to talk here? Can't I come inside?"

"No. I told you clearly before."

"It's Christmas."

"How did you get in here? Did you just bat your eyes at the dummy in the vestibule?"

"I've never been to your apartment. Let me come in, David."

"I've explained this before," Avila said. "It's even more important now that we be discreet. Our devotion to this has to be absolute." Karla felt herself being tugged to the end of the hall, pushed down into the sill on two cushions. "Sit here and don't move. I'll be back for you."

When Avila returned he wore a raincoat and heavy walking shoes. Karla was lifted off the cushions and shoved down the hall to the bank of elevators. His hand on her upper arm was hurting her, but she said nothing, fighting back tears. They rode to the first floor and walked through the overheated vestibule under the frightened gaze of the door-man.

"Where did you park, Karla?" Avila asked.

The rain was coming down harder now.

"Up on Haven," Karla said.

"Let's go," Avila told her.

Rain had driven shoppers inside. They were alone, hurrying along the wet pavement.

"You're right," Karla said. "I followed you. But it isn't what you think. One day Jack and I had an argument and I felt lonely. It was early evening and I drove downtown to your office and parked in one of the garages along Crocker and went over to your building and stood outside the entrance. I wanted to see your face, that's all. I wasn't going to bother you and I wasn't going to interrupt your work or insinuate myself into your business at all. I had a terrible day and I wanted to see your face. Can you understand a thing like that?"

They were at a stop light, waiting to cross.

"Don't cry, Karla," Avila said harshly. "In the rain nobody could tell you were crying anyway."

"Don't be like that, David."

"You followed me, what's the difference?"

"I didn't know you walked home," Karla said. "Honestly I didn't. You began to walk and I walked behind you. I wanted to go up to you in the street and take you by the arm and ask you out to dinner, but I didn't. I kept walking behind you. I knew you wouldn't like that kind of surprise and I wanted to do what you told me, but I just kept walking. I don't know why. I thought for a moment you'd go into a parking garage somewhere and that would end my fantasy. But you didn't."

"And what is your little fantasy, Karla?" Avila asked her. They crossed the street and began an uphill climb toward Haven. The rain stopped suddenly, to be replaced by mist and wind. "Just explain to me your fantasy."

"I want to marry you, David. You know that. I've really tried with Jack. I know I can be a good wife, David. I just need a chance with someone I can understand. If I file for divorce from Jack, the lawyer says he can get a good settlement. And even if it isn't much, we could be happy, I know we could."

"So you followed me to the building?"

"It just happened. You never got in a car. You walked and I walked and then we were on Russian Hill."

"And tonight? What about tonight?"

They were skirting Hyde and a cable car clanged by. Karla tried to circle her arm around Avila's, but he broke free.

"One of my moods," Karla said. "I was home all afternoon and when Jack came home he started studying for his stupid law school teaching job and he was cold and distant and all at once I knew he really meant to divorce me, that this time it wasn't just one of his drunken proverbs. He was cold, David, and I can't stand it much longer."

At the top of Hyde they reached the cul-de-sac. Avila put Karla in the Mercedes and then got into the passenger seat beside her. The tinted windows were closed and it was warm and dark inside the car. Avila leaned over the console and kissed Karla on the mouth. He ran his tongue over her lips and kissed her eyes and put his hand around her neck, caressing her jaw with his thumb.

"I want you to understand something," he told her. He sat back in his seat, staring straight ahead.

"Of course darling," Karla said.

"We're going to take Jack for everything," Avila said. "We're going to have his house and his money. We're going to live in his house together and we're going to spend his money." Karla wanted to say something, but Avila covered her lips with his fingers. "I'm beginning to envision how this can happen."

Avila withdrew his fingers.

"Jack is going to file next month," Karla said. "We can be happy with what Rowe says he can get me."

Avila slapped her hard on the cheek. Karla fell back, striking her head on the window glass.

"David," she said gasping.

"You have to listen to me," Avila said.

"Don't hit me again," Karla told him.

Avila slapped her, low on the left temple. He had moved so quickly that Karla hardly saw him. She felt heat coming from her cheek.

"All right David, please," she said.

"Pay attention," Avila said.

"I'll pay attention."

"First, you've got to buy us some time. Play up to Jack a little. You know how to play up to him, don't you, Karla? Give him a reason to hope. A reason to delay filing for divorce. Be nice to him. He's a simple guy. He'll buy whatever you have to sell. Men do, don't they? Men buy what you have to sell? You sold men burial plots, didn't you? Well, we're going to bury Jack Darwin. We're going to bury him as surely as if he'd died. And after he's dead it will be you and me in that big house on Pacific Heights with the two-million-dollar price tag. It will be you and me sitting on Jack Darwin's trust fund."

"But we have enough, David," Karla said.

"Oh, I want it all, baby," Avila said. "Don't you want it all too?"

"I want you darling," Karla said.

"Then play Jack along for a while. When we've gotten rid of Jack Darwin we'll find ourselves a white beach and lie down on it for a long time. We'll spend his money. We'll spend a lot of it, won't we, Karla?"

Karla touched her cheek. It burned where she had been slapped. "Don't be angry with me, David," she said. She placed her forehead against the cool window glass and looked at the deserted streets, the rows of Victorian houses. She heard Avila open the passenger door.

"Don't come to my apartment again, Karla," she heard him say.

"I won't, David," she said.

"Things will change by spring," Avila said. "And don't be surprised at what happens."

Karla did not watch him go. She backed out of Haven and drove to Lombard, then on to Pacific Heights. She parked the Mercedes in the drive and went inside. Jack's papers and books were still spread on the kitchen table, but he had gone upstairs. Karla went to her bedroom. She could hear Jack in his bath next door. The water was running in the tub. Karla took off her wet clothes, dried herself with a towel, and put on a terry robe. She let herself into Jack's room and tapped on the bathroom door. When she opened it, she saw her husband in the tub, reading a book.

"I thought you were having dinner," Jack said.

"My friend didn't come. There must have been a mix-up."

"So, what do you want?"

It was the cold Jack. The sober Jack. Karla unbelted the robe and let it drop at her feet. Jack closed his book and looked away.

"This is stupid," he said.

"Oh, Jack, please," Karla said.

"Get away from me."

Karla looked at herself in the mirror, beautiful and naked, almost vulnerable. Beneath the tan on her face there was a red flush where Avila had slapped her. Her black hair was wet, clinging to her shoulders. "Don't be that way, Jack," she said.

"No more, Karla. I don't want this anymore. This whole relationship is a bad carnival, and I want off the roller coaster. I've decided what to do. I want to practice some decent law that helps people. I want to read and do some writing. For God's sake, Karla, I've lost all my old friends. I want some of them back. Our relationship ran them off long ago. So why don't you just go away?"

"Now Jack," Karla said quietly.

She walked to the tub and got in with Jack, squatting over his body. She splashed water on her legs, then her breasts, took the soap and washed between her legs, watching Jack watch her. She slipped her hand under the water and found his penis. It was hard, turned up toward her.

Jack closed his eyes. "No, Karla," he said.

Karla guided him inside and moved up and down over him. He turned his head and arched his back. It was over in a minute, Jack with his eyes closed. She got out of the tub and put on the robe.

"You are an amazing bitch," Jack said.

"This was for real," Karla told him. She found a comb and ran it through her hair, then kneeled beside the tub.

"The joke is on you, sweetheart," Jack said. "This doesn't change a thing."

"Why don't we spend Christmas in Tahoe?" Karla asked.

"You hate the cabin."

"I could try."

"Don't you remember how much you hate it?"

Karla got up and walked to the door. The bathroom was filled with warm mist.

"Let's give it a few months," Karla said. "At least until spring."

Jack picked up his book and began to read. When Jack finally looked at her, she went back to her room.

• • •

As a joke somebody had painted a Santa face on the watercooler. Vorhees ran some water in a paper cup and was drinking it when one of the squad secretaries came over and gave him a hug and said good-bye. After a female detective hugged him too, Vorhees went to his desk and finished the transfer paperwork. This time of year, there were parties on every floor, some impromptu gatherings, and the halls were full of milling people, senior officers from downtown, patrolmen, family members off the street looking for friends. It was one of those rare winter days when the sun was brilliant, and Vorhees had spent a lot of the day at his desk looking out the window, thinking about all his years chasing dealers, pondering guys like Vincent Alvarado and the futures they didn't have. He finished his reports, then signed the final transfer authorization. He went around to every desk and said good-bye to his buddies.

Then he rode the elevator to the third floor and found his new desk at homicide, another gray metal piece of junk that was too small for his long legs. The window was too far away to look out of, and was smudged with soot. A balding man approached the desk and put out his hand.

"Hey, I'm Tom Cooley," the man said.

"Amos Vorhees."

"I know. We're partners. Okay?"

"Okay, good," Vorhees said. There was an embarrassed silence as Vorhees offered him a seat. "I just came down to look around," Vorhees explained. "See how far away from the window they put me."

"You'll work your way up," Cooley said. "What you been doing all these years on the job?"

"Military police," Vorhees said. "Narcotics for ten years."

"Just so you'll know," Cooley said. "You being black and all doesn't mean shit to me."

"We'll do fine," Vorhees said. "And just so you'll know, you being white doesn't mean shit to me."

Cooley laughed. "You know what I mean? Maybe we'll get our own TV show someday." Cooley rubbed his nose. "I'm always saying the wrong thing. You'll get used to it."

Cooley led Vorhees to the squad lieutenant, who had an office in a glassed-in cubicle in the corner of the floor. She was a woman named Grace Lightfoot, small, pretty, with a bright smile.

"Sit down," she told him.

They shot the shit for a while, then Lightfoot took out a manila folder.

"Have a good week off, Vorhees," Lightfoot said. "Come back ready to go to work. I guarantee you a dead body on the street needing your expert touch. For a while I want you to let Cooley take the lead. Just follow him around and get a feel for the job. Don't get me wrong, I've reviewed your record and I'm happy to have you here. I just want you to work your way in gradually before you take off on full power." Lightfoot closed the folder. "Got Christmas plans?"

"My wife is pregnant," Vorhees said. "Her folks live down in San Jose. Maybe we'll go down and spend a few days. Mostly I'm going to lie around the house and watch the Forty-niners."

Cooley introduced Vorhees around the squad. Homicide wouldn't be so bad, he decided. At least the dead bodies wouldn't have needles in their arms. It was after dark when he got home. Upstairs he found his wife at work over barbecued ribs. Putting his arms around her waist from behind, he rubbed her neck and belly.

"I can't believe ribs," he said.

"This is a big day, Detective Vorhees," Alisha said. "I'm very proud of you."

"I met my partner today."

"What's he like?"

"He's fine. He told me that my being black didn't mean shit to him."

"Do tell," Alisha laughed.

"He meant it okay. He looked a little green after he said it, like oops, what did I say? The lieutenant is an Asian lady. Confident-like."

"Do we still get the week off?"

"All week. Call your folks. Tell them we'll be down day after tomorrow. We can spend a couple of days. Then I'd like to stay home. We can watch football and figure out those positions in your sex book."

"You have a dirty mind, Mr. Vorhees."

"It was you that bought the book," Vorhees said.

Alisha made a salad while Vorhees changed his clothes. He returned wearing jeans and a sweatshirt. He cracked a beer and thought about his father, who had disappeared from home when Vorhees was just five.

"The lieutenant said there'd be dead bodies waiting for me when I got back to work."

"Can we talk about something else?" Alisha asked.

Vorhees sipped some beer. "So, how are your mom and dad?"

"You're such a conversationalist," his wife said.

Darwin dreaded the day and he barely slept the night before, awake at dawn with the noise of anxiety in his ears.

He ate breakfast alone in the kitchen and drank a last cup of coffee on the patio where his mother had tended her roses for years. The bushes were dormant now. Looking at them, he pledged himself to tend them in the spring, when his life cleared itself, when he had reformed his resolve into something tangible. From where he stood he could see Karla's bedroom window, and he hated himself for wanting her again.

He drove across Nob Hill to a parking garage on Grant. The sky had taken on a gray winter dullness and the Saturday shopping crowds depressed him with their scurried gaiety. Inside the granite office building he rode an elevator to the eleventh floor. The receptionist nodded politely, perhaps recognizing his face. For years his father had paraded him around these halls, showing him off, letting the other lawyers see what kind of young boy Jack Darwin had become. He was genetic heritage at its best, a minuscule twist of DNA that would one day turn rich and successful.

A secretary led Darwin to a corner conference room full of books. Both men there were friends of his father, ready with file folders and portfolios spread on the polished mahogany table. There was a pot of fresh coffee, Danish, a box of Dominican cigars open. It was precisely eleven o'clock in the morning.

"Nice to see you, Max," Darwin said to the shorter of the two. "Tom, you too."

A metal imitation Christmas tree sat on a lamp table in one corner. Hidden speakers played carols. Both men remarked how well Jack looked. On the wall were portraits of the partners. Jack could barely bring himself to look at the photograph of his father in a suit and thin tie, probably taken in the 1950s, when life was very good. And life had been good to Tom and Max, as it had been good to Jack's father. They had been friends and colleagues most of their adult lives. They had played bridge together and drunk cocktails together at the Fairmont Hotel, or at the St. Francis bar, where there were dusty palm fronds lining the room and gilt-edged hookers who looked like magazine models. Now that times were not so good as then, Tom and Max were Jack's trustees, men in their seventies who looked over Jack's shoulder at the facts and figures.

Darwin took a cup of coffee and made small talk.

Max signed a document and slid it across the table. "It's the trustees' report, Jack," he said. "I think you'll find it both true and correct."

"I'm sure I will," Darwin said. Tom lit one of the Dominican cigars. He savored it, letting smoke hover on the table.

"What are your Christmas plans?" Tom asked.

"I'm going up to the cabin."

"How is Karla?" Max asked.

"Just fine, thanks," Darwin said.

"Seen an upturn in the practice?" Tom asked casually.

This was the part Darwin hated, an exchange of pleasantries that drew blood.

"Look, Jack," Max said, before Darwin could answer. "We may as well get this business started. The trust can't continue supporting your capital expenditures. According to our calculations the trust has advanced your business more than ten thousand dollars every month for three years. The trust has paid rent, office supplies, and even part of your secretary's salary. Of course, with the corpus in stocks and bonds and a bull market, we have no money problem doing that. Still, your father's will directs us to preserve principal and disburse when you're forty-five. If the trust were to be audited, we'd have a large problem."

"I know," Darwin said. "I appreciate all you've done."

"Come on, Jack," Tom said. "What can we do?"

"I'm going to get serious about my practice," Darwin told them.

"Really? This time?" Tom poured himself some coffee.

"I'm planning to get into criminal work. I think I know someone who can give me a jump start. I had some success in state court last month and I'm teaching next month to earn some extra money. It isn't much, but it will help."

"Have you cleared up your tax bill?" Max asked.

"I'm still a little behind," Darwin admitted.

"And then there are the stable bills for that horse," Tom said.

"My father's horse," Darwin said.

"Yes, of course," Tom said. "But the trust has paid four hundred dollars a month in fees since your father died. It isn't that we mind doing it, but it isn't strictly, shall we say, legal."

"I know. I do appreciate it."

"And then there is your membership at Olympic," Max reminded Darwin.

"I'll cancel it. I don't play golf anyway."

"Well, fine. That's a start," Tom said. Tom spent a few moments relighting his cigar.

"I'll see about the horse," Darwin offered.

"Let's see now," Max said, picking up a pen. "If you eliminate the horse and the Olympic you'll save a thousand or so a month. Maybe you can pick up your practice and get back to serious work."

Tom tapped his cigar against a thick cut-glass ashtray. He looked at the expensive blue ash. "What we're saying, Jack, is that we like and value you. We want the best for you. You just have to cut back until your practice picks up. I suppose the legal profession is crowded these days, isn't it? Why, when we started out, a degree from Stanford was worth its weight in gold. I don't mean to say we didn't work hard, because God almighty we did. Your dad and I used to work down here seventy or eighty hours a week, Sundays, holidays, all the rest. They were golden days, and we know the golden days are gone, Jack."

Max stood and walked to the corner window, looking out at the Embarcadero.

"I want you to understand something," Max said. "The trust won't, can't, pay your bills any longer. We've begun to fear an audit. And after all these years we can't lose our asses over this, can we?"

"That's the last thing I want," Darwin said.

"And Jack," Tom said. "Sell the cabin. If you want my advice, you can't afford a horse and a log cabin in the woods. I know it means a great deal to you for sentimental reasons, but you're practically facing a crisis here. And in a crisis, you have to manage in a panic mode. Sell the horse, sell the damn cabin, and don't look back."

Jack looked at the trustees' report. He felt a numb anger rising in his face. He knew they anticipated a divorce, financial disaster, newspaper headlines. He knew they couldn't help their attitudes. They were men used to boardrooms, country club dances, expensive bourbon at the St. Francis Hotel bar. Maybe Jack had started out as one of them, but he was no longer. Jack finished the report and signed it.

"I really have to go," Jack said.

"Call us anytime," Tom said.

"I suppose Christmas can be difficult for you," Max added. "I was hoping after four years the shock of your parents' death would be easier."

"It is easier," Jack said.

"We want to wish you and Karla a happy Christmas," Tom said, extending his hand. "Despite what looks like a hard attitude, we really mean it. As your dad would say, this is business. Nothing personal."

"Sure, I understand," Jack said.

Jack hurried out of the building and walked Union Square for thirty minutes, thinking about buying Karla a gift. He studied the decorated windows at Saks and Magnins, then went to the hotel bar at the St. Francis and ordered a bourbon rocks. He drank the bourbon slowly and listened to the carols and then he left and walked down Mason for two blocks until he came to Marge's. He stood outside the bar for ten minutes, watching people pass by, then went inside and stood at the crowded bar rail and ordered another bourbon rocks. He said hello to three lawyers he knew and stood talking to a CPA he'd met at Marge's years before, both of them barely able to hear above the din. When the crowd at the bar parted slightly, he saw David Avila at the far end of the polished oak jungle. Avila made his way over.

"Let me buy you a drink, Counselor," he said.

"Thanks, I don't mind," Darwin said.

"Bourbon rocks?" Avila said.

The bartender brought Darwin a fresh drink and he had one long pull of it. The alcohol was coming near to wiping away the memory of Tom and Max. What had been a dank hole of dread was becoming warm and cozy.

Avila ordered himself an Evian and lime.

"I need to thank you," Darwin told him.

"The drink is no problem."

"No, I mean about the case. Geronimo. I went to the law library and found *McLeod*. I made that argument to Hoffman and he bought it."

"He kicked your guy?"

"No, but he horse-traded a simple misdemeanor possession out of it."

"Did you deal with Nola?"

"Herself," Jack laughed.

"So, how do you like it? Being a hotshot criminal lawyer and all that rigmarole?"

"Oh, it's good," Jack said animatedly. "I'd like to do more. I mean, I think it's interesting."

Avila ordered another bourbon rocks for Darwin. Jack was feeling light and wavy now, whole and inconceivably happy. He could see himself as an oyster runner on the old Barbary Coast, a devil with the ladies, a man who always held the final black ace up his sleeve.

Avila paid his bill. "Call me the Monday after Christmas," he said. "I've got a guy who needs a good lawyer."

"You mean it?" Darwin asked.

"Sure, of course I mean it. We'll kick it around."

"Great, great," Darwin said.

"Have a nice Christmas," Avila said.

"You too, thanks."

"Going out of town?"

"Up to Tahoe, the wife and I."

"You married? I guess you are." Avila pretended to look at the wedding ring on Darwin's finger.

"Married four years now," Darwin said.

"Kids?"

"Not yet. How about you?"

"Not married, no kids. Not yet, anyway."

"Not yet," Darwin said. "Maybe you'd like to meet my wife sometime. We could have dinner."

"Maybe," Avila said. "My practice keeps me pretty busy. I never have time for social life."

"Good then, it's a done deal," Darwin said happily. "Absolutely, absolutely, absolutely."

Avila slapped Darwin on the back, then turned and walked out of Marge's into the late-afternoon gloom. Darwin placed both elbows on the bar and began to court his luck, the wife who'd decided to go to Tahoe after all, a new chance at practicing criminal law with David Avila. Maybe he was catching a wave and it would wash him somewhere safe.

Time to celebrate.

"Double bourbon rocks," Darwin sang out.

His SJ 8 was forest green, a rich magnificence of color, a LAWDOG vanity plate. He'd done his office in green as well, deep green carpet, tartan wainscot, pale green wallpaper. Green was hard and quiet, which was what David Avila liked about sex as well, hurting someone who was asking you to stop. Avila liked to watch his clients settle into the green. He could see them strain to hear something being whispered by the colors, something secret and just out of reach. It wasn't that green was the color of money, because it wasn't. Green was the color of ease and plenty, the cold color of old money, which wasn't really money. Old money was money that had ceased to bleed, money that had lost the putrid essence of its struggle. Avila couldn't help himself. Even the old Buick he kept at the apartment in the Marina was green. Light green, rusty, but green nonetheless.

On Christmas Eve the light went out of the sky early, leaving the clouds purple-tinged. One by one the streetlamps came on in the Marina near the apartment building Avila owned, just a few blocks off the bay. There were only four apartments in the place, three of which he rented to gays; the last he kept for himself, at least since the earthquake, when the last gay couple had moved away while repairs were being made. Avila kept it for reasons he vaguely understood, just a few suits of clothes in the closet, some jeans, shoes, and underwear. In the kitchen he kept a stock of inexpensive jug wine, and in the living room was a stereo and some CDs of older music, Limeliters, Kingston Trio, Frank Sinatra, even soft seventies rock. It was his pretend life, a place where he could bring women and put them in situations.

He had taken a taxi to the Marina docks. He walked two blocks up, one over, and went into the garage entrance on the back alley. The Buick started right away and he drove out through the Marina and caught Bayshore heading south. Traffic was light at first, then snarled on the south side of the city, then light again just out of South San Francisco. It took Avila only about forty minutes to get to the Holiday Inn at the San Bruno exit near the airport. He parked in the far visitors lot and walked into the lobby. Even on Christmas Eve it was crowded in the lobby, nobody taking any notice of him. When he got to the hotel bar he sat at the end and watched people come and go. The disco was very dark and a bored DJ was playing oldies on a bad music system. Only one woman was at the bar then, not good-looking, but drinking gin, occasionally smoking a menthol cigarette. When he caught her looking at him, he smiled. She was interested, sure she was. Avila could not believe his luck. It was almost never this easy. It was almost always hard, hard work.

Avila went to the rest room and washed his face and hands. He combed his hair straight back from his forehead. An air of calm came over him, as though he'd just gone inside a church. Out in the disco bar again, the woman was still there with her gin, only it was a fresh one. He brushed past her, then paused and turned.

"Listen, I'm sorry to bother you," Avila said. The DJ had taken a break, but it was still noisy with talk. "Could I buy you a drink? I mean that sounds so corny. And if you'd rather be alone, I respect that."

The woman blinked, thinking. She had on a gray business suit, white blouse. What was she, maybe forty? Avila smiled a sorry-I-bothered-you smile. He could tell the woman was on the brink.

"Sit down," she said.

Avila sat, half turned. The bartender was at the far end of the bar, arms crossed.

"I'm Arthur Carillo," he said.

"Jean," the woman said.

"My brother was supposed to fly in from Denver. I waited on his plane for two hours and when it came in he wasn't on it. The second Denver plane came and he wasn't on that either. I called his house and he said his son had broken his arm skiing and he couldn't come. I drove all the way down from Davis and here I am."

"That's too bad," the woman said cautiously. She took a good long drink. "What do you do, Mr. Carillo?"

"Computers," Avila said. "I guess everybody these days is in computers. I'm sort of torn between staying here tonight and trying to get back to Davis."

"Won't your wife be worried?" the woman asked.

"Oh, I'm not married. Never been married."

"Good-looking guy like you?" Gin talk, Avila thought.

"Not yet, who knows?"

Jean ordered a double gin and tonic. Avila had seen her drink two, which meant three or four. If they were doubles that would be six, maybe eight. Avila was nursing a single club soda. He wouldn't be ordering anything more.

"I bought a tree and everything," Avila said. "I even tried my hand at baking a turkey. My brother and I are close. Really close. He's got a kid, but he's divorced. His ex has the kid, a boy, at Christmas, so he's kind of down. I thought it would be great for the two of us to be together tonight. Maybe spend a couple of days playing tennis. Go fishing. Do boy things. I'm kind of disappointed if you want to know the truth. Now, we're both alone."

"That's too bad," Jean said.

"So, are you from around here?"

"Cincinnati, believe it or not."

It was perfect. An out-of-towner, too.

"You have kids?" Avila asked.

"Huh," the woman barked. "After two husbands I settled in to try life on my own." She finished her gin and tonic and waved for another. It had taken her about fifteen minutes to drink two ounces of booze.

"How'd you get stuck here?" Avila asked.

"I'm counsel for a little corporation back home. I've had depositions in Seattle for two weeks. I had a flight back through Minneapolis, but the airport was fogged out in the Midwest. The stupid airline told me I could get home through San Francisco. But they were wrong."

"A lawyer, huh," Avila said. "That's interesting."

"It's shit," Jean said. "You'd hate it."

"Well, whatever," Avila said. "Hey, listen. I'm starving. I haven't eaten since I left Davis at noon. You wouldn't like to go sit in a booth and have some shrimp would you? We could get a bottle of wine. I might as well just stay here as try to drive all that way home tonight. I wouldn't get home until dawn."

"I don't know," Jean said.

"Oh, you've already eaten, I bet."

"Well, why not?" Jean asked herself.

They sat in a dark corner booth. Avila ordered shrimp, salad, and a large carafe of wine. Avila told the woman of the endless round of sales conferences, softball games, twilight movies alone. Jean drank most of the wine, then wanted to dance to Johnny Mathis. By eleven, they were in the woman's room on the fourth floor.

The radio played old tunes. Avila took off his shirt and undershirt, letting the woman get a good look.

"I love your body," Jean said.

Avila kissed the woman delicately on the lips, ran his tongue over them. He put his hands on her ass. Her heart was beating fast now.

"Why don't you get in the shower?" Avila said. "I'll come in and join you."

Avila watched her go. He took off his pants and listened to the sound of running water. When he went into the bath he could see the form of the woman behind the frosted-glass shower panel, naked, washing herself. She peered through the glass, smiling, looking at Avila. Avila grabbed a big bath towel and opened the shower door. Jean was letting water run over her head.

"I haven't been with anyone for a long time," she said happily.

Avila got into the shower and closed the glass door. The big towel was growing wet and heavy.

"This isn't like me, you know," Jean told him.

"It's all right," Avila said. He picked up a bar of soap and washed her back, ran his hands between her legs, turning her slightly. Avila transferred the soap to his left hand and circled the woman's neck with his right arm, her throat in the crook of his elbow. He kissed her neck, her ears, the back of her head, running soap over her buttocks, pushing his penis lower, leaning his whole weight against her so she was stranded against tile.

"Arthur, I can't breathe," Jean said.

Avila arched her hard then, her feet nearly off the ground.

"Don't, please," Jean said. Avila tightened his grip, choking off her voice. The woman was on her toes, hands behind her, trying to break his grip. "Please," she said.

"Be quiet," Avila said.

He pushed himself inside her anus. Water was running over his face and he could feel the woman struggling against the pain, just off her feet, the weight of her forward against the tile, her hands trying to pull his hair. "Just be quiet," Avila said.

"Please don't hurt me anymore," Jean begged.

Avila banged her head hard against the tile.

She moaned a little and he banged her head again, a smudge of blood on the tile. Avila pulled back her head and looked at the gash, clean to the bone, a line of red trickling down between her breasts. He let her fall back against his body, then opened the stall door and let her go to the floor. She lay there on her back, eyes closed, naked, breathing softly. Avila washed himself thoroughly in the shower, soaping his hair, his body. He dried himself with a bath towel, then went into the bedroom and dressed. When he was finished, he used the towel to wipe all the bathroom surfaces, rifled the woman's purse for cash and credit cards, then left.

He hurried through the nearly deserted lobby and out to the parking lot. His Buick was in the near darkness, parked beside a hedge of oleander. You have to be lucky, Avila thought, sitting in the seat of the car. The smell of diesel exhaust filled the air with a biting acrid aroma and you could hear traffic noise thudding dully. The night was lurid with urban sprawl, spotlights roamed the hills, bouncing off the bottoms of scattered clouds. Jean had been pure luck, nothing like it. You have to be careful, but you need luck. Always luck. Over the years, Avila had visited the Holiday Inn six or seven times, pausing at the bar, never finding a woman he could approach. Now, on Christmas Eve, luck had come to him. Patience and luck. Avila decided to go to the Marina apartment and spend the night, not take a chance on returning to Russian Hill, where the doorman might remember him coming in late. On Christmas Day it would be easy to return home.

Avila drove south a few miles. At an exit to Millbrae he threw the woman's credit cards into a culvert beside the freeway. He took an off ramp and turned back north toward the city.

On the radio, Christmas carols. "Oh Come All Ye Faithful." "Joy to the World." Avila decided to call his mother in Los Angeles and wish her a merry Christmas, just for a joke. How long had it been? Five, six years? She used to ask about coming north to see him, but that was a long time ago. Three or four times a year Avila went to Los Angeles on business, but he had never bothered to see her. Sometimes he went by the house on Pico, but he never stopped. Why should he?

Night and cool wind. Christmas. To his right, warehouses and factories in South San Francisco, hills dark. Freighters and naval vessels on the south bay, hulks of dark gray with a sprinkling of lights. What would Jean do when she woke? She would call the manager and the police. She would go home to Cincinnati and try to forget the horrible thing that had happened to her at the airport Holiday Inn on Christmas Eve. She would worry about HIV. Sometimes when she was in bed at night she would find herself remembering the man who hurt her, whoever it was she had met in the disco bar. She would carry a tiny scar on her right temple, a souvenir. Sometimes when showering, she would have a touch of vertigo, a problem with her inner ear. She would lock her doors dozens of times, check and recheck them, listen for steps behind her, hear things. Each time she traveled she would have a premonition of danger and she would fear flying. It would affect her sleep, leave her with dreams, nightmares, cold sweats. She would regard men with distrust, even displeasure. It would be a long time before she drank gin and tonic alone in a bar, and late at night she would feel Carillo's hands on her ass, the crook of his elbow at her throat, and the heated pain of his penis inside her. No, she would not go for counseling. She thought of herself as too tough for such measures. She would gain weight, bite her fingernails, get up at three A.M. to watch TV. She would resort to nonprescription sleeping tablets, keeping a bottle beside her bed. Gobble them like corn nuts. She would carry the scent of Carillo around with her, totemic, palpable. Now on Avila's right was Brisbane, the baseball park, empty as a tomb on Christmas Eve. The light towers massed, shadowed like Peruvian idols. Impressive and alert, almost alive, spiderwebbed iron. Avila was driving fifty miles an hour, windows open. Christmas carols on the radio, clouds bumping on a hard northwest wind off the Pacific that was cold and smelled of salt and fuel. Black ghettos down by the bay. Hadn't O. J. grown up down there? Avila would like to meet O. J., share small talk, some professional secrets. After all, they'd come up together, up from the bottom where you could sense the muck dragging you down. How many bourbon rocks did Jack Darwin drink that afternoon at Marge's? They were doubles, some of them, just like the last two Jean had drunk at the Holiday Inn disco bar. Before Avila had left Darwin, he was already backslapping some lawyer or other, happy in his tweedy good-old-boy fashion, sharing a joke in the wood-paneled old San Francisco horseradish atmosphere. Jean and Jack, cock o' the walk. The TransAmerica Building, Coit Tower, half the bay flooded by dark, half empty of all color where the hills rose up in the East Bay, homes where the rich amassed fortunes and looked down, down. It was enough to make you puke. Avila beaded sweat, wishing he had done Jean once and for all. He wanted to go back and finish the job he had started, take her away from her future of sleeping pills and dreams and HIV scares, the future that saw her beginning to cry for no reason in the middle of a deposition as startled lawyers looked on shamefaced. Down through the belly of the city now. It Came Upon a Midnight Clear. O Holy Night. Jingle Bells. Now the James Lick in the Tenderloin, tenements dark, bars still open with their flickering neon welcomes, homeless in the streets, a few barrel fires. Arthur Carillo, David Avila. I'm David Avila. What is my mother doing tonight? Who is my mother fucking tonight? What dirty bum has she dragged in off the street to sleep with her tonight? What toothless mouth is she putting herself into? Down Franklin, through the Avenues, over Russian Hill, past the cable car station, flower stalls empty and dark, mile upon mile of row houses, apartment buildings, Chinese restaurants, Laundromats, liquor stores, garbage in the streets, lost boys in the streets, groups and gangs and seraglios. Vampires hanging out. Vampires sucking the blood of babies in the dark. The Beauty and the Beast. America. You could be anybody, do anything. Dare to dream. Now at Jack Darwin's house he saw its luminescence in perfect moonlight. Like a Moorish castle maybe, redwood roof, exquisitely manicured lawn, big eucalyptus leaning over, an arm of supplication. Karla with Jack in Tahoe. The house dark. Karla in Jack's bed, doing him, doing him. The American Dream. Who was running for President this year on that slogan? Shout the doctrine at the dark houses of the rich. Railsplitter to President. O Little Town of Bethlehem. Jack Darwin's big house in Pacific Heights. O Little Town. Joy. Avila felt the good kind of tired he felt after court, after lifting weights, after fucking a woman and making her hurt. Making her beg. O Holy Night, the stars are shining brightly. It is the night of our dear savior's birth.

**II**

*primo*

*n*ice office, Darwin thought. From lower Pine he could see a corner of the Bay Bridge and part of Treasure Island, even Coit Tower. It was a building from the twenties, made of gray stone, with ornate terra-cotta designs, cornices, some gargoyles over the entrance. The elevator was run by an old woman on a stool who chewed gum. Best of all, it was quiet and smelled of Lysol in the corridors, wet wax and a thin layer of dust. He had been shown into a corner office by a youngish woman in a dark blue skirt and white blouse. Darwin reckoned there were three rooms in all, a waiting and reception area, small library and a copier, Avila's corner office from which you could see both the Bay Bridge and Coit Tower. It had individuality written all over it, an office belonging to Avila alone, nothing mediated by committee.

It was noon and the Financial District was busy. From the eighth floor Darwin could see people milling around the Embarcadero park, eating their bag lunches, taking walks before heading back to work. The Pacific Exchange had opened after the holiday.

"Sorry about the noon meeting," Avila said, showing Darwin in and offering him a chair. Avila was eating a salad and a cup of yogurt with fruit. There were some oatmeal cookies on a plate to his right, and a small carton of orange juice with a straw sticking out. "I've got to be in court at one-thirty. A bail hearing in front of Laudermilk. Ever been in front of Laudermilk?"

Darwin said he hadn't. He'd never been in front of a federal criminal magistrate in his life.

"So, you want to do some criminal work?" Avila asked. Without waiting for an answer, Avila said, "Why, may I ask?"

"I need the money," Darwin said.

"That's fair enough," Avila told him.

"Is there any?"

"There can be. If you know what you're doing."

"I'd like to learn. I don't mean about the money. I mean the whole shooting match. I've been drifting for a long time. Civil law never seemed my life's work. To tell you the truth, I don't really know what my life's work will be, but it might be criminal law."

"Tell me," Avila said, "you didn't like the bullshit paperwork in civil cases, did you?"

"Didn't have the patience for it," Darwin said. "A lawsuit over five thousand dollars takes three years and fifty thousand dollars to settle. Besides, I don't have any big-name corporate clients to foot the bills."

"They don't anymore. Even the largest."

"I know. I can't blame them."

"I never did like the bullshit either," Avila said. "I love a case that begins and ends in six months, tops. No bullshit, not much paperwork. No tricks or gimmicks. Just me and the other guy across the table, trying to get the gun out of the holster quickest. You know, bang, bang, you're dead stuff."

"Yes," Darwin said. "It has the virtue of speed."

Avila finished his salad and ate an oatmeal cookie. Darwin declined a cookie.

"You work out?" Avila asked.

"No, not really. I go fishing. Do some walking."

"How was your Christmas?"

"Fine, tolerable."

"You and your wife in a cabin? Sounds terrific."

Darwin envied Avila his innocence. The Christmas in Tahoe had been terrible, bleak and unedifying.

"Well, my wife and I have some troubles," Darwin admitted.

"Sorry to hear it. I didn't mean to pry. It has nothing to do with anything."

"Just one of those things," Darwin said. "We got married at Christmas four years ago. My parents were killed in a plane crash in the fall. I was hurting and I thought she was there for me. I was vulnerable and she took up the slack." Darwin thought for a moment. "Perhaps I'm being harsh. My wife has qualities. She was a terrific businesswoman. I know she's tried to do her best. But we're very unlike. Very unlike. But, then, I'm starting to ramble."

"Listen, we better get down to business," Avila said, looking at his watch.

Darwin opened a legal pad. "You said you had a codefendant who might need somebody." Darwin watched Avila finish an oatmeal cookie. "You know, it amazes me, this process of finding clients."

"I got lucky from the start. I got a hold of a big CHP bust on the freeway and somehow got the bastards off. It hit the papers, word got around." Outside the window, a police helicopter went by low and fast. "If you want into this drug business, then let me give you some advice. Try to stick to dealers about halfway up the food chain. Street pushers don't have anything. You'll never even see the main men. What you want is wholesalers halfway up the chain who can afford to pay you up front, guys who don't give you any crap and who know the rules. Middle-level dealers know they can go down for five years and do their time, pay their legal bills. That's the game. A business really, just like any other. That means that lawyers like you and me get ten thousand up front, sometimes twenty thousand, and the dealer will do the time if he has to do the time, because in five years he comes out, four years with good time, and when he comes out he goes back into the business with his outfit. You hear a lot about the big guys, the Colombians, the Mexicans, the Hondurans, but they're a pain in the ass. Besides, it's dangerous working for them if you fuck up. Another thing, the IRS has started looking at lawyers now too, so don't juice up your books. You know, a lawyer cops fifty thousand dollars in fees for a few hours of bail work in magistrate court and maybe the IRS decides to come after him as a money launderer. Plenty of lawyers in New Orleans and Miami did money laundering. I knew lawyers in L.A. who ran two, three hundred thousand dollars through their trust accounts every month, put it in the bank, bought some Monsanto on margin, then bingo, sell it and the money is clean as a whistle. I don't advise you getting into that sort of business. It isn't legal. Stick with middle dealers. Guys you can trust. That's my advice."

"This may be over my head," Darwin laughed.

"I don't think so, Jack," Avila said. "I can call you Jack, can't I?"

Darwin blushed slightly. Outside a BART train rumbled by on steel rails.

"Sure, call me Jack. I just mean I don't know the rules. I don't know the courts and judges."

Avila pushed over a stack of books.

"Borrow these. One is a *Federal Defender's Handbook*. There's a copy of the Federal Rules of Procedure with some good annotations. The state trial lawyers have a handbook too. Pick one up. And when you get into this thing, don't let the district attorneys and U.S. attorneys think they can fuck with you. Never make a deal unless you get something back. Don't start off with talk about plea bargains. Those guys sweat just like you and I. Always go for separate trials if you've got two defendants. Government attorneys are lazy as shit, so don't stop fighting. Never waive a jury. Never waive a preliminary. File every fucking motion in town and when you lose ask for a reconsideration. Talk to the press whenever you can."

"You think I can do that?"

"Sure, you can do it."

Darwin picked up the books, a stack six inches tall.

"I think I'm going to enjoy this," Darwin said. It was a half-truth, the best he could manage.

"Here's your personal rules," Avila said. "First, attack the evidence. Then attack the witness. Then attack the police. Then lick the jury's behind."

"And about this codefendant?" Darwin asked.

Avila handed Darwin a sheet of legal pad with a name, address, and case number printed on it.

"Arthur Leroy Vine," Darwin read.

"My guy is Luther Lee Dokes. He's bad."

"What's the charge?"

"Possession of cocaine with intent to sell, what else? The DEA says your guy came to my guy and wanted to front out some coke, turn it to another guy across the bay. My guy says he didn't want to front the drugs but agreed to go half and half. My guy took the coke over to Oakland to your guy but they didn't make it any farther than your guy's apartment. Seems the buyer in Oakland was a snitch. The DEA busted them both when my guy drove up to your guy's apartment. That's how it works. Now you just have to figure out how to get your guy off."

"How do I get paid?" Darwin asked.

"You get five thousand flat," Avila said. "Whatever happens. Including trial. It isn't much, but it's the best I could do under the circumstances." Avila took out a leather-bound check register and wrote a check.

"Where did the money come from?" Darwin asked.

"Luther Lee gave me ten. I'm giving you half. It's legal, if that's what you're worried about. When you represent drug dealers you have to take their money. It's the American way. Everybody is presumed innocent, aren't they?"

"I guess they are," Darwin said. He looked at the check, his name, the figures. He had never thought of himself this way, getting money from somebody named Luther Lee Dokes. His father had explained that if you saw the money you weren't making enough. When you make enough, it went right into an account someplace. Money was clean until it touched your hand. It was the human hand that dirtied and bloodied money. "Innocent as heck," Darwin muttered.

"That's the ticket," Avila said. "Listen, I'd tell you more, but I want you to work this case up yourself. My guy, Luther Lee, he won't break. He'll do his five years if he has to and come out of jail and do five more later on if he has to do that. He's one of those middle dealers I told you about. He knows about minimum sentences and he won't flinch when the door slams. I don't know about your guy. Sometimes people get scared when they hear that metal against metal. You find out his story and see what he wants to do, then give me a call. You've got a magistrate hearing this Thursday in federal court. Bail, omnibus, discovery, the whole shooting match. They've got Arthur down in San Mateo at the county jail."

"San Mateo? Way down there?"

"Overcrowding, Jack. Ever hear of it? Taxpayers want all these bad guys in jail but they don't want to build any more prisons. They want drugs off the street but don't want to pay taxes. We could make cocaine legal, but that would put us out of business, wouldn't it?"

Darwin didn't know what to say. He didn't think he was a guy like David Avila, even though he admired his style. He admired the green wainscot, the plush green carpet, the way Avila held himself, like he worked out a lot. But as people went, Darwin couldn't see himself as a hard type. He didn't really know who he was, but he wasn't hard.

"I'll see Vine tomorrow," Darwin said.

"Sooner the better." Avila wolfed down an oatmeal cookie. "Tonight would be better. I told him you were coming down."

"I teach law school tonight," Darwin explained. "Monday, Wednesday, and Friday nights. Sundays I play cribbage down at Marge's. My life is a routine."

"Well, tomorrow night then. Check out the court file and remember your omnibus hearing and bail are Thursday afternoon at one-thirty." Avila stood and smiled, offered his hand. "Hey, welcome to the lonely fraternity. I hope it works out. I don't have a partner, and I could use somebody to take my codefendants on a regular basis. Maybe we could get something going."

Darwin took the elevator to the ground floor, then went outside and stood on lower Pine, deep in the Financial District. He was carrying the stack of books and his briefcase, trying to make sense of starting all over again in a practice new to him, criminal law, a field he barely remembered. What was left to him were a few Latin words like *asportation, malum in se,* the dusty remnants of a first year in law school that saw Darwin sitting in the back of huge banked classrooms, eating doughnuts and reading crosswords while far down in front a mindless hum substituted for what was supposed to be a thrilling lecture. Nobody had ever taught Darwin about people like Luther Lee Dokes or Arthur Vine, about street drugs, checks made out for five thousand dollars, scrawls that were at least partly cocaine. Jack remembered his own father had prided himself on never going to trial. Sure, he had argued the big appeals for Standard Oil and Union Pacific, cases that fixed the rules for railroad pensions, severance taxes that saved huge corporations millions of after-tax dollars. But this would be different.

Whatever Arthur Vine was going to be, he was certainly going to be different.

They led Darwin to the basement interview room of the San Mateo County Jail. Bare yellow walls, a single metal desk, two metal chairs. The room smelled of stale smoke and human sweat and you could hear sound seeping through the concrete walls, unnameable mutterings, cries, whispers, rogue screams. Darwin was quickly searched and he was allowed to sit alone for fifteen minutes in a small holding cell, one of ten in a long cold corridor, double rowed. There were no windows. Light fluoresced and revealed nothing.

Arthur Vine was ushered though the cell door, manacled, shack-led, and handcuffed. An officer shoved him into one of the metal chairs.

"Whuzz up, cuz," Vine said.

"I'm Jack Darwin. Your lawyer."

"You got a smoke?"

"I'm sorry. I don't smoke."

"Next time, bring me a fucking smoke."

Darwin took out a legal pad and sat down at the metal desk. Vine looked about twenty-five years old, maybe older, muscular, tired, his face wired up from jail time.

"Your arraignment and bail hearing is Thursday," Darwin told him.

"What about bail?"

Vine's face was like a newspaper photograph of itself. Grainy and half-focused.

"Judge will set bail."

"I want out of here, motherfucker."

"You being treated all right?"

"Oh shit, man."

Darwin was determined to settle in with Vine. He hauled him through the basics, name, background, arrest history, his family life. He had been born in Richmond and had grown up on the streets of the East Bay, right down on the waterfront, where things were always rough. Panhandling, odd jobs, dropped out of high school, old man ran off. Vine had an apartment near Fruitvale Avenue where he'd hung and sold small-time drugs to kids at Oakland Tech. He'd drop some drugs off, then buy wine and drink while watching TV, that's what he did. He killed time and time killed him. Vine told Darwin his street name was Primo. The high school kids called him that because his shit was good. Darwin could call him that if it made a difference.

"Send me some smokes, man," Vine said.

Some of the hardness had gone, out of need. Darwin told Vine he'd send some smokes in if he could.

"So what about Luther Lee?" Vine asked.

"What about Luther Lee?"

"What they say I do?"

"Tell me about the deal."

"Me and Luther Lee was fixing to barbecue, that's all, man."

"A barbecue?"

"Shit, man, Luther Lee he come over to my crib. I go out to see Luther Lee and Five-O was on the move. I didn't do shit. I don't know what Luther Lee he do. He don't talk shit with me, and I don't want to know. I got nothing to do with Luther Lee. Me and him was fixing to barbecue."

Darwin waltzed Vine through the arrest, piece by inevitable piece. They would talk and get sidetracked and Darwin would force Vine back on track, which would take about ten minutes. Vine complained about the food and the noise and the lack of smoke, and then they'd start over.

"Let's get serious, Primo," Darwin said finally. They had been at it for an hour, the jailer coming by twice to see if they were finished. "I have to know what happened."

"I told you, man, I didn't do nothing."

"I read the police reports, Primo," Darwin said. "I went over to the courthouse and read the information filed against you. The DEA took slightly less than two pounds of cocaine out of a charcoal sack that Luther Lee brought to your house. The science is all done."

"That was Luther Lee, man, I told you."

"Luther Lee handed you the sack?"

"Oh man," Vine said.

"Luther Lee handed you two pounds of coke."

"It wasn't me, man. I didn't know."

"Let's just say there was a buyer in the East Bay. Do you know the buyer?"

"Maybe it was some dude Luther knows."

"Some dude?"

"Just a dude. You know, a fucking dude."

"You've been stung, Primo."

"You got to be shitting me, man." Primo looked as if he might cry.

"No, your buyer was DEA."

"Oh shit, man," Vine said. "I was just doing the dude a favor, you know, man. Give me some shit! Shit, I don't know shit about toot and blow, man, I'm into weed. So, I do this dude a favor and here I fucking sit, man. Get me some shit! Everybody keeps saying get me some shit! And here I sit in this motherfucking place, man, that's cold."

"Look, Primo," Darwin said quietly. "Tell me the truth. You have to trust me on this. The truth is the only thing I can use here. The rest of it is crap and will foul me up."

"I heard that shit before too, man," Primo said.

"Think it over. Sit tight."

"*Sit tight, motherfucker?*" Primo screamed. "What the fuck you think I'm gonna do in here?"

"What I meant was, don't talk to anybody."

"Fuck no, I ain't gonna talk to nobody."

Darwin stood up to leave. "Hey Primo. I just wanted you to know that the buyer was a DEA snitch. That's the purpose of my visit down here tonight. And I wanted you to know you could trust me and tell me the truth. I'll do everything I can to get you out of this mess."

"Now I feel better," Vine said sadly. He placed his hands on the table. The handcuffs made a harsh clank. "What the fuck you gonna do about all this?"

"First," Darwin said, "I attack the evidence. Then I attack the witnesses. Then I attack the police. After that, I lick the jury's ass."

Primo smiled. "Well," he said, "at least you talk the fucking talk."


The Mezzanine at Ghirardelli Square overlooked ten acres of shopping. Karla sat in exquisite silence, looking down at the gray light, its elegant textures and tones, so many things to buy. A steady hum of cash changing hands met the bounce of windy glass. Gina cocked her head over a railing and raised a cup of five-dollar latte. She trained bodies for a living, sculpted lifestyles at a gym in the Marina.

"Okay," Gina said. "You look like you just swallowed the canary."

"It's that obvious?" Karla asked. The day outside insisted on being windy.

"I wouldn't say your glow is a secret. It's the first time I've seen you this way in a long time."

Karla stirred through her crab salad. She had shared her unhappiness with Gina, but she hadn't shared the news of David Avila.

"I suppose you're right," Karla said. "I'm going to make a break from Jack."

"Honey," Gina said, "he's the Golden Goose. Are you sure about this?"

"I've already seen a lawyer. Besides, money isn't everything, is it?"

Gina purred, a cattish laugh. "It isn't quite everything. But you wouldn't mind if I took Jack over when you're gone, would you?"

Karla studied the middle distance, colored banners, corporate logos. "Be my guest," Karla said. "I hope you like to read."

Avila brought cigarettes and chocolate, a carton of Kool filters and some Butterfingers. His man Luther Lee was turned out in prison orange, looking clean and rested. That would last about two days, more or less, and then the jail scene would grind Luther Lee down, just like it did everybody else. It depended on the noise, the food, lots of things.

Luther dug into the carton of cigarettes and loosed a Kool. He was tall and rawboned with a scar at the corner of his right eye. He dragged smoke in the way a drowning man drags in oxygen.

"What going down, David?" he asked Avila.

"They've got a snitch, Luther," Avila said. "Somewhere in the East Bay. Oakland maybe."

Luther Lee shook his head. He was young, but going gray. Avila knew he was smart and Avila liked him for being smart. That way you didn't waste so much time sifting through bullshit.

"I'm so fucking stupid," Luther said.

"Shit happens."

"So the snitch wires up with Primo and Primo talks to me and here I am."

"That's the way they catch the bad guys these days."

"Don't I know it, man."

"How's your brother?"

"Fine, man, for all I fucking know."

"He still in Seattle?"

"Drinks cappuccino, I hear."

"You're looking at five years, federal time."

"I can do that."

"You get fifty days every year. That puts you down to a little over four years."

"But you're going to beat this case, aren't you?"

"Give it a best shot, Luther, you know that."

"I can do the time, man, don't worry."

"You don't want to give them anyone, do you?"

"I ain't giving them shit. Don't ask me that shit question ever again, motherfucker."

"Everybody says that at first, Luther."

"I'm telling you."

"All right then. We play hardball."

"You don't know me, man."

"I know you, Luther. All my life."

"Yeah? Maybe so."

"I've got a lawyer for Primo."

"Some chump?"

"Better than that. I think the guy will stalk the case for us. File motions and that shit. We'll see what he turns up."

"Like what kind of stalking you talking about?"

"Maybe dig up our snitch."

There was a pillow-size window high up in the cell, an open space covered by hardened glass, wire mesh, and bars. A pigeon was cooing on its ledge.

"You're a smart motherfucker," Luther Lee said.

"But I don't know shit about Primo," Avila said. "Where'd you meet him?"

"He runs over to the city once in a while."

"He's pretty small time."

"He talks a good score time to time."

"Where'd you get the shit?"

"You know where I got the shit, man. Zack." Luther Lee lit another Kool. "You know the man. He's paying your fees, fucker."

"But I didn't know if he turned you the shit."

"Hey, they can't do my house, can they?"

"I don't know. Your house clean?"

"My house is always clean, man." Luther Lee dragged in some smoke. "Go up and see my woman, will you?"

"You still with Sarah?"

"For now," Luther Lee laughed. He leaned back in his metal chair, smoking with pleasure.

"They already searched your house, Luther Lee. They took all your guns."

"They legal. They don't mean nothing."

"They took a photograph of Sarah."

"I hope it do them some good."

"I checked the court file. We got Kelly."

"I don't know him."

"For a federal judge, he's okay."

"What does that mean?"

"He was appointed by Carter. Roman Catholic. Thinks defendants are presumed innocent."

"Tell Sarah come see me."

"She'll be here. I'll tell her."

"I don't like Butterfinger, man."

"Baby Ruth? Mars bars?"

"Bring me some Baby Ruths. Lots of nuts, that's what I like, man."

"You won't get bail, Luther. I'll try, but don't count on it."

"Who's the snitch?"

"I told you. I don't know. Let's let Primo's lawyer try to find out. Then Zack can play with it."

"You find out who the snitch is, man. We take care of that motherfucker."

"Luther, listen to me. You can't off a federal snitch. They may not need the snitch in court to make the bust good. It depends on how we do with our motions."

"Make it happen, man," Luther said.

"Let me explain," Avila said. "Unless there is something wrong with the search warrant, then the search is good. They found the dope. I've been through this secret-informant thing a hundred times and unless we can attack the search, you won't get to see the informant."

"We just need a name," Luther Lee said.

"We're talking about two different things here, Luther Lee. You can take out the guy, but you can't take out the search. I'm telling you it might not make any difference."

Luther Lee peeled the wrapper from his Butterfinger and began to crunch it.

"What's your cover?" Avila asked him.

"Selling cars in South San Francisco."

"Somebody speak for you on the job?"

"Guy named Harold. Bug-eyed white guy. Zack gives him a hundred a week."

"What about Sarah?"

"She do it."

"We need them both at the bail hearing."

"They be there."

"What if you get bail?"

"We'll have to see, won't we?"

"What does Zack want you to do?"

"You know Zack. He don't want nobody doing no time."

"You got your tax returns like I told you?"

"Sarah, she got the copies."

"Tell Sarah to bring the kid. Babies at hearings are always good. Bring the tax returns. I want Harold to speak well of you and bring his records. Are we together on this?"

"Same page and everything," Luther Lee said.

"You haven't been smoking that crack shit have you? You aren't going to go waxy on me are you?"

"I don't do that shit."

"One final thing. We might have to blame Vine at the bail hearing. He won't be around to hear it. We won't take that story to trial either. I'll explain it to his lawyer."

"You tell Primo he can fuck himself."

"Does Primo bang?"

"He say."

"What outfit?"

"Crip dudes."

"Get the word out we aren't fingering Primo."

"I can do that."

"I may want you on the stand at bail hearing."

"I can do that."

"How you love your son. How you sell used cars. How much you love your wife. How Primo is the man."

"Man, get me out of here."

"We'll try straight on."

"Zack, he get you the twenty thousand?"

"I'll use it up. You'll get your money's worth."

"I better, that's all I got to say."

Avila buzzed for the jailer. He was let out into the corridor.

"Don't forget, man," Luther Lee called to him. "I want those Baby Ruths. Lots of nuts, man."

Karla wore her hair braided. Designer jeans, Reeboks, a beige turtleneck and dark blue blazer that made her skin seem very tan. She wore no makeup. It was late morning and Jack had gone away after another brief argument, something she couldn't avoid.

That day, driving over the Golden Gate, Karla became afraid. It was not one of her black moods, but something dictated by circumstance. Her moods came and went like Pacific storms, though without their regularity, the fear taking shape inside her now a gnawing reality she couldn't shake. Her Christmas at Tahoe with Jack was terrible, silent and corrosive, Jack reading by the fireplace while Karla did crosswords and stared out the picture window at the ponderosa pines, wind-tossed and massive, covered by a blanket of thick wet Sierra snow. She would sit by the window and think about David Avila. She would hate Jack and his books, his chess sets, his quiet introspection, his ability to spend hours with his nose in some thick novel or other, a moth-eaten volume written in the nineteenth century. He had studied law, prepared his notes, and had taken long walks when the weather cleared.

She exited at Mill Valley and drove the beach road to Muir. Down on the beach waves were crashing, storm-big and heavily curled, pushed in from the Pacific on the header of another storm. Half an hour later she was at Stinson Beach, rows of restaurants on the waterfront, houses up in the hills behind, a quiet Sunday place for weekenders. She saw the green Jaguar parked outside the Breaker. Karla parked at the other end of the lot and went inside.

"I miss you," Karla said, sitting beside him.

It was an uncomfortable picnic table by a dirty window. Avila had ordered steamed clams.

"Where's Jack?" he asked her.

"He left this morning early. We had a small scene and he left. He really doesn't care what I do or where I go. I don't think I can hold him off anymore."

"He's my buddy now," Avila told her.

"David, what's going on?"

"I gave him a client. A drug dealer from the East Bay. Jack is happy now. He's onto something good."

"What are you doing?"

"Trust me, I told you."

"You just gave Jack a client?"

"And a check for five thousand dollars in fees. I thought he would pee himself he was so surprised."

"What good will all this do?"

It was sunny at the window and Karla put on her expensive Italian shades. She could see their reflection in the window, two beautiful people in a seafood shack on the West Coast, very chic and laid-back.

"You'll see, Karla. Just wait."

Karla had no appetite. She drank a diet soda and watched Avila devour the clams hungrily. She watched waves break over the coastline, throwing huge plumes of spray onto the rocks. It looked like a movie, didn't it? David looked so good, so real and clear, that she was almost able to forget the two hard slaps he'd given her.

"Jack has been to your office?"

"Of course. He went to court last week for his client. It was an arraignment and bail hearing. They usually do some basic discovery too. He was pretty good, I guess. Sober, argued clearly, seemed prepared. From what I heard, he did a good job. His guy didn't get bail, but it was close. I even gave him a stack of books to study."

"He took them to Tahoe."

"I know he's been studying on his own too."

"He's changing his life."

"No, Karla," Avila said. "We're changing his life."

"Stop it, David. You're scaring me."

"Let me have some fun, sweetheart," Avila said. "I gave him a case so I could watch him work. He'll do the research, argue the case, and I will sit back and use what he comes up with. It's an old trick. He's my stalking horse."

Karla felt the fear again, a tingle at first, working its way up her spine. It had all been so wonderful, meeting David at Marge's on nights Jack had been too drunk to remember anything, fucking David in backseats, there in the dark under Coit Tower with police cars passing by, meetings at an inn in Santa Rosa, everything a dream. Now something was happening to Jack and David, and Karla didn't know what it was, where it was leading. She wanted only to be with David. That and a lot of Jack's money.

"How did you spend New Year's?" she asked.

"Stayed home. Thought about you."

"That would be nice."

"I mean it, Karla. I see you and me in Jack's big house in Pacific Heights. We have money in the bank. We don't work and we take trips to white sand beaches together. You lie outside in the sun and turn black."

Karla closed her eyes and touched his hand.

"You promise me," she whispered.

They drove to Bolinas in the Jaguar. The hills were emerald green and horses grazed the valleys. They had cappuccino at an inn in town, then stood and kissed in the parking lot outside.

"Let's just get married," Karla said. "Jack is drifting further and further away. I can't hold him."

"You'll do fine. Put your mind to it."

"I don't think so. I think he's met somebody."

"No, I don't believe it."

"I think maybe he has."

"Why? What are you talking about?"

"He stays out until late, but he isn't drinking. He doesn't bother me anymore. It's just a feeling."

"Well, if he has, that makes our job easier."

Karla tried to kiss him but he moved away, looking at the hills behind Bolinas.

"My guy got bail," Avila said.

There was a wind now and Karla could barely hear what he was saying.

"I don't understand," Karla said. It was getting cold and Karla wanted her blazer, left behind in the car.

"My guy got bail. His didn't. That tells you something."

"Please, David. I need to know what you're thinking."

"No you don't. Not now, not really."

"I'd like to."

"It's all so simple. My guy got bail, his didn't. I have you, he doesn't. I'll have his house, his money. It's all so beautiful I can't believe it." Avila turned to face Karla. "It's all too beautiful, too beautiful. I have seven million dreams, Karla. Do you know how long it would take me to earn seven million dollars? I couldn't do it, dear. Not ever, not from fees on drug cases. Not practicing law in the gutter. Jack inherited his money, Karla. It isn't his. Not really. It might as well belong to us."

"Don't, David, please. This frightens me. You've asked me to be nice to Jack. I can't anymore. It's gone too far. It doesn't work. There is nothing left between us. If I try to talk to him, I provoke an argument, that's all. That's the only attention he pays me anymore."

"It doesn't matter, Karla. Our path is clear."

They waited for three couples to pass them in the lot, their talk loud with alcohol. Avila kissed Karla and walked her to the car, the low green Jaguar. He drove her back to Stinson.

That afternoon, she got in the gold Mercedes and looked at her lover in the rearview mirror, a tall, good-looking man standing near his green car, watching the clouds out over the ocean, his face in the sunlight, the clouds gray-tipped from a storm that would happen next week.

The morning rain made every street silver slick. Avila had lifted weights for an hour at the Turk Street Y, then run three miles. He was in the steam room doing sit-ups when Zack came in, wrapped in a terry robe.

"You'll die in that thing," Avila said.

They were alone. It was just after six in the morning.

"Good thanks," Zack said. "How *you* doing, asshole?"

They sat together on a tile bench.

"You did good," Zack said. His huge black beard was dripping wet already.

"How's Luther Lee?" Avila asked. He was doing sit-ups, counting through one hundred, heading toward one-fifty.

"Luther is great," Zack said.

"What's Luther going to do?"

"You tell me, you're the lawyer."

"Luther got anywhere to go?"

"Like Morocco maybe? Tahiti?"

"Why not? You know what I mean?"

Avila stopped his exercise. He used a hose to douse himself with cold water.

"Luther Lee knows what he has to do," Zack said. "He ain't going nowhere until we hear from you."

"I'll know in a month. There's a snitch in Oakland."

"I heard," Zack said. "That little fuck Primo."

"That little fuck Primo might crack. They have him down in San Mateo on Spaghettios."

"I had somebody talk to him."

"He begins to talk, I know his lawyer. I'll find out right away, let you know."

"He don't know shit about me."

"We hope, don't we?"

"It don't make no difference. Primo knows shit."

"Well, Luther is a man."

"That's the truth," Zack said. "Shit it's hot in here."

"They set bail at a hundred grand. I guess you know. We're lucky to get that. The U.S. attorney was howling about it anyway."

"Luther knows what he owes me. Your fee and bail. It's a load."

"I want to tell you it won't do any good to go after the snitch. This other lawyer will file some motions. We sit tight and see what breaks. Unless we turn the search, they don't need the snitch. You comprendo?"

"Turn the search, lawyer man."

"I'll call you."

"Yeah, I know. You'll call me." Zack wiped his beard with a towel. "Don't spend my twenty grand on hookers."

Avila watched Zack leave the steam room. He sat for a long time after that, until the first few men came in for their morning workouts.

Something good would happen soon. Darwin could sense it, feel it, touch it, taste it. It was in the air. The amazing thing was how it happened sooner than soon.

He had been teaching for a week when Dolores Hernandez happened. Maybe she was no reward for virtue, but she was indubitably there, and she was a reason to keep going.

During those first three sessions at the law school, Darwin could sense himself working well. He was well prepared, always comfortable in the classroom, even if he felt nervous inside. Darwin could write, and he could teach students how to write, he knew he could, and by the third class, even the most bored of them, the ones sitting in back the way Darwin used to sit in back, seemed to pick up on his enthusiasm and begin to pay attention. Darwin remembered his own legal education, how he'd looked down on it and wondered what he was doing in a roomful of Stanford hotshots, young preppies yearning to make big money in a profession chock-full of hotshots like themselves.

Then one cold and rainy Friday Darwin went into Frieda's after class for a drink and some Chinese food. He was sitting at a middle table nursing a bourbon rocks when Dolores Hernandez caught him staring at her. She was at the bar, only five or six feet away, too close for Darwin to pretend he was looking at something else. She turned to face him, elbow on the bar like John Wayne, then came over.

"I loved the problem you gave us," she said.

"Oh that," Darwin said, embarrassed. "It was the only funny case I remembered from my own law school. And it isn't even that funny, if you know what I mean."

Darwin had posed the problem of murder. During a tong war in the early history of Chinatown, a mortally wounded gang member had lain, bleeding to death, in a dark alley. Before he died, another gang member from a rival group had chopped off his head with a cleaver. In front of the California Supreme Court the defendant's lawyer had argued that his client had only accelerated the inevitable. Couldn't be murder, could it? What did the class think about that?

"Would you like to sit?" Darwin asked shyly.

She did, unaffectedly.

"Well," she said, "I'm dying to hear the answer."

"I shouldn't tell you," Darwin said.

"I won't tell," Dolores laughed.

"All right," Darwin agreed. "It won't make any difference to the writing assignment anyway. It's just a funny little puzzle." Darwin pushed away the bourbon. "I'm afraid one of the supreme court justices looked down at the defense lawyer with a slightly jaundiced eye. 'Speeding up the inevitable, Counselor, that's the *definition* of murder.' You can imagine the lawyer's chagrin."

Dolores laughed, rich, warm, magic to Darwin. She had big brown eyes and a cup of brown hair around her face. Something delightful entwined her. Maybe it was just his fancy, but Darwin hadn't felt this light in years. She was not young, maybe late twenties or early thirties. And here it was almost ten o'clock in Frieda's funky bar and restaurant on McAllister, Frieda watching them from behind the bar, one eye on a hospital drama on TV. A correspondence was in progress, something about bourbon, rain, a dark world outside a bright bar. For the first time in a long while, Darwin felt at ease with the world.

"Are you having something to eat?" Darwin asked.

"Just some fried rice," Dolores said.

Darwin meant it as an invitation, but it hadn't come out that clearly.

"You're very good in class," Dolores told him.

"You can't imagine how nervous I am. My knees knock so hard I'm surprised you guys can't hear them."

"It doesn't show at all," Dolores said.

"You're not a regular law student," Darwin said.

"I'm not?"

"I'm sorry, I mean you're older. More mature."

Dolores laughed. "I had to work a long time after college to save money."

"Are you from the city?"

"A little town in the valley, near Fresno."

"You'll do fine," Darwin said stupidly.

"What about you? What kind of law do you practice?"

"Born and bred San Francisco. I've done a little of this and a little of that. Right now I'd like to concentrate on criminal law. I guess you can tell most of my examples come from that field."

"It must be exciting."

"We'll see. I'm really just at the beginning."

"Maybe I've been watching too many lawyer shows on TV, but it does seem exciting."

"I don't want to mislead you. I'm no criminal-law guru. I've been drifting a little. And you know how it is when you drift. Things happen, but they really don't. There's a current taking you someplace, but it could turn out to be no place at all." Darwin sipped his bourbon. Was he rambling? "I have a wife. She drifted into my life, more or less. I don't know why I'm telling you all this. It sounds rather sordid. We're going to get divorced."

"I'm sorry," Dolores said.

Frieda brought over a plate of fried rice, a bowl of wonton soup for Darwin. Outside it was raining steadily, a drenching unrelieved downpour. Darwin must have talked for thirty minutes without stopping or touching his soup. When he finished, the soup was tepid. It was as though a dam had burst inside him and his life was pouring out through the breach.

Dolores Hernandez finished her rice and her soda. "Listen, I've got to go. It's kind of late and it doesn't look like this rain is ever going to quit. I'm not used to it. I'm used to warm and dry all winter!"

"Which way are you going?" Darwin asked.

"Out to the Avenues. It isn't a bad ride." Dolores was up, putting on her raincoat. "The bus leaves at ten-thirty, so I've got to move."

"Let me drive you," Darwin said. He looked down at his half-finished bourbon. He could see his face in it.

"I don't know," the woman said.

"I'm going that way. Pacific Heights. I'll drop you off."

"Sure, why not?" Dolores said.

They walked through the rain to Darwin's Volvo parked down the block on McAllister. The bourbon had settled in Jack now and he felt warm and in control, a little talkative, watching the play of rain on neon, patterns of light and dark against a blank sky. Too soon he was there, parked right in front of her place.

"I appreciate the ride," Dolores said.

Darwin could see a patch of white on the window glass where her breath had touched it. He wanted to touch it too, maybe with his forehead or an eyelash.

"Sure, no problem. I enjoyed talking to you."

"You okay?" Dolores asked.

"Sure, I'm okay," Darwin said.

Darwin heard her open the passenger door. She sat with the door open, rain splashing in.

"This is going to sound crazy," Darwin said. "I hope you'll forgive me in advance." Darwin was looking straight ahead down the avenue, rows of parked cars, stucco houses cut into apartments. "I wonder if you'd go with me to the aquarium on Sunday afternoon, maybe catch some dinner downtown after? Early of course." Finally Darwin brought himself to look at the woman. She was off somewhere, thinking.

"I wonder if I should," she said.

"I wonder myself."

"This isn't one of those student things?"

"I don't know what it is. But not one of those."

"This could really screw me up," Dolores said.

"No," Darwin said. "I mean, I know. I don't know."

She laughed softly. "That was pretty clear."

Darwin was relieved by the laugh. Whatever happened now, he was relieved by the laugh.

"I'm just feeling free," Darwin said.

"I like free," she said.

"I'm not crazy," Darwin told her earnestly. "I don't know what I feel and I don't want anything from you. Sunday is just a hard day for me. Long shadows and regrets, that sort of thing."

"Me too," Dolores Hernandez said. "Okay, pick me up here at two. I'll put in half a day of study."

She smiled and hopped out of the car and into the rain. Darwin watched her to the door, then inside, then drove back to his house in Pacific Heights. He did not know if he'd done right or wrong, or if he was somewhere in between. He doubted if something so pure could be wholly wrong. But whatever the facts of the case, Darwin knew how he felt. He felt like a bud about to open.

Same old Sunday night at Marge's on Mason Street, except that Darwin was not drunk. The cribbage players were there, and the loud braying lawyers, and the CPAs in their expensive suits and ties. Darwin and Dolores had gone out to the aquarium in Golden Gate Park, wandered around in eerie shadows for a couple of hours watching the sharks and barracudas. There were crowds of people at the aquarium, but they didn't bother Darwin. He had decided that Dolores Hernandez was genuine, that he didn't need to invent strategies to defend himself against her when she talked, or tactics to fend off possible harm. He felt as though he could relax and be himself. So, it wasn't the same old Sunday night at all, but a new Sunday night.

They were in a dark booth having dinner when David Avila came over.

"I thought I saw you over here, Jack," Avila said. "I hope I'm not interrupting."

Darwin shook his hand and offered him a seat. Instead of sitting, Avila leaned against the back of the booth.

"I was hoping to speak to you about a business matter," Avila said.

"Should I leave?" Dolores asked Darwin.

"Stay please," Avila said. "We'll talk in code. It won't take long."

"Sure you won't eat dinner with us?" Darwin asked.

"No, thanks. I've got a date."

"Okay, that's okay," Darwin said, relieved.

Avila slid into the booth on Dolores's side. "Did you get a trial date on your guy?" he asked.

"Mid-February. Motions due in three weeks. Is it always that fast?"

"Judges like to push. Some mean it and some don't. Kelly probably means it. But then he expects your client to cop a plea."

"How about your guy?"

"He's fine. We're on hold."

"Well, good," Darwin said, not certain if he should say anything else. "Is there something in particular?"

"My case is going to be three weeks behind yours, but I think we need to be on the same page. I'll call you with my trial date when I get it. My gut tells me the government will ask to try these guys together. I think we should oppose that on principle."

"So do I. By the way, I've read all the material you gave me. It was helpful, really. I think I've got a handle on my end."

"When do you see the evidence?"

"I made a date for next week."

"Look at it closely. Call me."

"I've already got a good idea about attacking the search. I've done a little research."

Avila sipped a glass of soda and lime. "Good. Try to tap into their snitch. It's the one thing that gets their attention. Otherwise, they think they own you. They'll grind you down if you don't find something to stretch them out."

"I've got a good idea, really."

"You wouldn't mind letting me in on it would you?" Avila asked.

"Well," Darwin said haltingly.

"I've got to powder my nose," Dolores said. She patted Darwin on the hand and Avila let her slide out of the booth.

When she'd gone, Avila said, "She seems nice. I'm sorry you're having trouble. I hope it works out."

"She isn't my wife. I'm sorry I didn't introduce you."

"Well, then," Avila said. "How about a bourbon rocks to celebrate last week?"

"I don't think so," Darwin said.

"I'm buying. Just one."

Darwin said okay, and Avila ordered a double. When the waiter brought it, Darwin tasted the drink.

"She is nice," Darwin said, taking more bourbon. "I hardly know her."

"Well, I hope it works out too."

"Thanks. It isn't what you think."

"Let's forget it. Drink up."

Darwin drank half the drink. He could sense the alcohol searching his head, finding a place.

"So, what about your idea?"

"My client says your guy came over to Oakland with the coke in a charcoal briquette sack."

"So?" Avila said.

"The cops moved before Luther Lee took out the black plastic bag inside. He handed the charcoal briquette sack to Vine and the DEA moved in. I've read some case law, enough to know that somebody looking at the transaction from outside couldn't possibly know that the cocaine was inside the charcoal bag. Nothing suspicious, nothing like probable cause."

"An outsider like a judge you mean."

"Like a judge," Darwin said.

"What about the affidavit the snitch filed?"

"Hearsay," Darwin said.

"They'll argue it was reliable."

"I'll argue they were guessing."

"Kelly will never buy it."

"I've read the cases. I've written half the brief."

"Listen," Avila said. "Argue they should have waited until the transfer came down to the snitch. Then they would have known for sure the coke was inside the charcoal sack."

"That's precisely the point."

"I like it. I like the way we think."

"Yeah, me too," Darwin laughed. "No probable cause to think the cocaine was inside a perfectly normal charcoal sack."

Avila took out an expensive gold-and-black fountain pen. He wrote down a number on a business card. "My home phone is unlisted," Avila said. "Call me anytime," he said.

Night driving to Pacific Heights, going by the Octagonal House, ablaze with cut-glass light. David Avila sitting inside the fawn leather interior, everything on the digital uptake. Avila felt digitized himself, everything in his body running softly in microbytes, split second, split-microsecond spurts of energy, clickety-click of atoms, molecules, his own DNA pointing toward Jack Darwin now, as if he'd just hopped down from an acacia in East Africa and was about to pounce. *Homo sapiens* against *Homo erectus,* not even close. Avila was a deep root in fresh volcanic soil, his muscles taut, the Jaguar engine blending smooth rhythms in near dusk, a black storm over the Pacific coming in, coming home, wind rising.

Karla answered the door in her bathrobe, opening it just a crack behind the safety chain.

Half choked by surprise, she said, "David?"

Avila had her open the door and he went inside. One frosty light in the kitchen showed through the dark and he could see out the patio doors to the deck, the shapes of roses, down to the bay below where a lighthouse on Angel Island pulsed circles against the cloud cover.

"Jack will be here anytime," Karla said, standing behind him.

"Get upstairs now," Avila said.

"What's happening?"

"Go. Do it."

Karla fled to her room, half backing inside, her heart pounding wildly. Avila came in and closed the door.

"Run a shower. Get in it."

Karla crossed the room and put her arms around his waist. She loved what was happening, the overtness of it, how it frightened her very soul. God, she thought, David looks so good in his black turtleneck and expensive tweed sports coat, jeans, loafers.

"God," Karla whispered. "We've got to be fast."

"Go run a shower," Avila said, kissing her hard.

Karla dropped her bathrobe and ran a shower in the bathroom. She stepped in, waiting. Through steamy glass she could see Avila drop his jeans, his coat, strip down his underwear and let them fall at his feet. He got in the shower behind her and she rested her head against the warm tiles while Avila draped his right arm around her neck and probed between her legs. She felt him hard against her back, and she could feel the muscles of his legs ripple against her own. Then he pushed into her from behind.

"You're hurting me a little," she gasped. She took a deep breath and tried to enjoy him.

"Listen to me," Avila whispered.

Water splashed on Karla's hair, ran down her body as the pain increased.

"I like this, honey," Karla said. "But shouldn't we use something?"

"It will be over in a minute," Avila told her.

Karla could barely breathe now.

"Can you go easier, sweetheart?" Karla said.

"Listen to me," Avila said. "Jack is down at Marge's right now. He has a woman with him. Nice-looking brunette."

Avila pushed hard inside her. Karla made a noise, a gasp, something to raise her against the tide of him.

"I'll be gone in five minutes. As soon as Jack comes through the door, call the police. Tell them your husband sodomized you against your will and beat you. Get the police out here quick. Lock yourself in the bedroom until they come."

"Oh God, David," Karla said. She was faint. David Avila tore into her like a madman.

"Listen, Karla," he said. "Tell it just like it happened. Only it was Jack, not me. He shoved your head against the tile. He hit you."

"No, please David."

"It's our chance, Karla. And it's the only chance you've got to get everything. I've seen his new girlfriend. She's a knockout. Much nicer in some ways than you. I think she's just right for him."

Avila used his left hand to bang her head hard against the tile. He came away from her and hit her with his fist high on the right temple, just above the eye. She began to fall but he caught her and dragged her from the stall, trailing hot water. He sat her straddled on the floor next to the tub. A bruise was appearing above her eye already. He hadn't broken the skin, but her forehead was welted and red.

Karla groaned, her head abuzz with images. "David . . . I don't know."

"Make sure they take photographs," Avila said. He began to dry himself with a bath towel. "When the police ask if you want to go to the hospital, tell them yes. Get a good rape exam. Make them do it, make certain they keep records. Tomorrow call Rowe and file against Jack."

Avila dressed hurriedly in the main bedroom. He came back into the bath and threw a towel at Karla. "Wash this bath towel as soon as you can. Right now, soak it with shower water."

"Do you love me?" Karla asked.

Avila pulled on his turtleneck. "Of course I love you. That's what this is all about, Karla."

Avila went into Jack's bedroom and was back in a few minutes. He leaned into the bath where Karla was sitting, dazed against the tub.

"It hurts, David," Karla said. "You love me?"

"Karla, Karla," Avila said. "I'm risking everything for you dear. Don't let me down."

Then he was gone.

They met late Wednesday afternoon. Darwin was staying at the Hilton near Union Square, and he walked down Pine just as people were heading away from work, making for the bus and BART lines, catching the trolley up Market. It had rained earlier in the day and it began to rain again as Darwin was walking and he was soaked because he left his raincoat in the hotel room. All the clothes he had were in the hotel room, one suit, some hurriedly packed slacks, a couple of shirts, two pairs of shoes, and a shaving kit. He hadn't been able to sleep for two days.

Avila offered him coffee and oatmeal cookies. Darwin took a cup and sat across from Avila, slumped.

"Are you all right?" Avila asked him. "You look a little ragged out."

"I'm sorry to call you like this. I just can't believe what's happening."

"Is it about the Primo case? Did Primo give you a bad time?"

"No, nothing like that. I filed the brief. I think I got their attention with my argument. I had a call from the U.S. attorney, some chap named Burris. He wants to talk. I don't know what about, but I'm going over there in a couple of days. I'll let you know."

"That sounds good. You could have called me. You okay?"

"No, this is more personal I'm afraid."

"More coffee?"

Avila poured Darwin his second cup. Darwin got up and stood at the corner window for a long time watching traffic move over the Bay Bridge. Lights in the East Bay were twinkling on, a dust of white edging up the canyons, turning the night a hazy purple shade. Darwin was so tired he felt as though he were dreaming. Hallucinations came and went and he made up imaginary conversations, he heard voices. He remembered being handled roughly by police, some kind of hysterical commotion behind him, then the rush of photographs, fingerprints, a nervous bourbon haze. He had been a little drunk, high on Dolores Hernandez. One minute he was happy, and the next minute it was over.

"You remember seeing me at Marge's Sunday night?"

"Sure, of course."

"Well, I went home about nine. I had another double bourbon after the one you bought me, but I was fine. Really. I went up to my room and began to get ready for bed. Brushed my teeth, grabbed a hot shower, started to do some studying. I had a class Monday night and I wanted to grade some research papers too, get ready for the next lecture. The next thing I knew, two cops burst into my room and arrested me."

"For God's sake, arrested you?" Avila said.

"Spousal abuse. Domestic violence."

"What? That's impossible."

"Domestic violence," Darwin said, still looking at the window, himself in reflection, right there in the middle of the gray painted city. "They took me downtown, booked me, released me an hour later on my own recognizance. Two cops drove me back to the house and let me get some clothes together, then put me on the street. I drove downtown and got a room at the Hilton. They issued me a criminal complaint for municipal court. Yesterday I got divorce papers from Herbert Rowe, maybe you know him."

"I'm sorry, Jack. This is really awful."

"I'm sorry to come up here like this. I didn't know who else to call."

"Don't worry, don't worry. What can I do?"

"Represent me in municipal court for one thing," Darwin said. He returned to the chair and sat across from Avila.

"Sure Jack, I'll be glad to. I've done a number of those cases in my time."

"You can't believe me, can you? It sounds too absurd."

"Well, tell me about it."

"I didn't do anything, David," Darwin began. "I've never struck Karla in my life. I never would. I never even raise my voice to her, and believe me we've had many arguments. It is just like I told you. I had dinner, a couple of drinks, went home to my room. I didn't see Karla when I came in at all. She must have been in her bedroom. When the police took me through the front door, I got a look at her. They were examining her. She was all bashed up. Big knot on her forehead, bruise over her right eye. The cops said she'd been sodomized in the shower. I'd come home drunk and raped her and beaten her. Just like that."

"Have you got the complaint?" Avila asked.

Darwin handed him the papers and Avila buzzed his secretary, who came and took them away for a file.

"Jack, I'll ask you just once. Did you do it? Tell me now or we won't speak of it again. You know it won't make any difference to my representation of you. None at all. And it won't make any difference to our professional friendship, our working together."

Darwin leaned forward in his chair. "David, I didn't touch her. I didn't see her when I came home. That's the honest truth."

"You didn't argue?"

"No argument. I didn't even see her."

"All right, I believe you," Avila said. "How do you explain her injuries?"

"I've thought about it for two days," Darwin said. "Maybe she picked somebody up in a bar, things got out of hand, and she couldn't face me without an explanation of her own. She had to have somebody to blame and she used me."

"Does she have a lover, Jack?"

"It's entirely possible. I wouldn't know, of course. I haven't paid any attention to her comings and goings for several months. I get the credit card bills. In my own mind our relationship is over. But Karla is a resourceful and manipulative bitch, take it from me. She's had a fight with another man and instead of panicking, she used her imagination to great advantage. She's put me on the street."

"I thought you went away over Christmas?"

"Oh, that," Darwin said. "I don't know why that happened. She has tricks. Sexual things. They make me crazy, some of them. I don't know if you understand. It was Christmas and everybody was happy. Fanciful baloney. I didn't want to be alone again at Christmas and so I fantasized that this time it would be all right."

"Have you talked to anyone about this case?"

"No, of course not. I'm not a complete fool, you know."

"I thought, well, maybe your new friend."

"Dolores? Never. Well, not yet anyway. She'll have to know sooner or later."

"Don't talk to her about the details, Jack."

"What about my Bar membership?"

"It's a misdemeanor, Jack. Relax, you're okay with the Bar."

"I feel so ashamed. Humiliated."

"Look, Jack," Avila said. "I want to level with you. The only person who knows the truth is your wife. I'd like to hire a private detective and trail her for a couple of weeks. If she has a lover who did this to her, she'll meet him. They always go back. Women have a hard time leaving men who slap them. It's well known. Even if the lover didn't do it, the information could prove useful to you during the divorce case."

"Speaking of which," Darwin said.

"Well, I don't do divorces, but I know some people."

"Thanks, but I know some people too. There's an old friend of my father. He'll be good."

"You're set then. What about a place to live?"

"First, what about fees?"

"Of course," Avila said. "As far as the detective is concerned, I know a good agency I can get for around three thousand plus expenses. That's for two weeks. They're competent and reliable." Avila poured himself some Evian water. It had gotten dark, and Avila switched on a table lamp. "As for my own fee in this, let's say fifteen hundred plus expenses."

"That's good of you, David," Darwin said. "Look, I'll make arrangements to get you paid this week. I'll have to get an apartment, I suppose. I can't afford every night at the Hilton. God, David, I can't even go back to the house I own. I grew up in that house. All my things are there. Everything my mom and dad built is there. I've got to get my house back."

"Take it easy, Jack," Avila told him. "You'll work your way back to the house. The house is yours, isn't it? You know as well as I that process takes time. I tell all my clients the same thing. A lawsuit is like going to the dentist for root canals. You see maybe twenty appointments ahead of you. You know there will be lots of pain. When you look at it, you think it will never end. Sometimes you get up in the morning and you can't leave your bed thinking about the appointments you have left. Crawl back under the covers. But eventually you keep your appointments. You persevere. You withstand the pain. Pretty soon it's over. You go outside one day and the sun is shining and the birds are singing and you start again."

"Do your teeth look good?" Darwin said.

Avila smiled. "I'm a damn good dentist."

"You'll enter your appearance in the case?"

"Today. I'll enter by fax and I'll get you on the docket and I'll get a continuance for as long as we need and then we'll find out what the police reports say."

"Can I send you a check?"

"Anytime. No hurry."

"You're a good guy, David," Darwin said.

"Hey, we're friends. I'll tell you the truth. You tell me the truth."

"I know," Darwin said. He was tired, but he felt somewhat relieved. He was no longer alone. "I didn't sodomize my wife. I didn't touch her. I've never hit her."

Avila got up and stood beside Darwin.

"I just had an idea," Avila said. "Why get yourself some dingy apartment? I own a little place over in the Marina. It isn't much, one bedroom, kitchen, living room. It's been vacant since the earthquake, but I've had it remodeled and just didn't let it out. You could stay there. I could run you up to the Hilton and we could get your clothes and you'd be set. Later, we can get you into the Pacific Heights place and you can bring all you need over there. It's a quiet place and really convenient. You can ride the cable car downtown to work. It's kind of a gay neighborhood. You don't mind gays do you?"

"Oh no, of course not. But it's too much to ask."

"It's nothing. I told you, it's vacant. The utilities are on, no sweat. Take it. Take it, Jack!"

"It sounds great," Darwin said.

"Go back to the hotel. Check out. I'll pick you up in an hour and take you over. You can go back to the Pacific Heights place all next week. You can make arrangements with the police department yourself."

"I don't know how to thank you."

"Just pay my fees!" Avila laughed, clapping Darwin on the back.

When Darwin had gone, Avila was alone with his thoughts. He made a mental checklist. Call Karla, lick her ear on the phone, warn her about the detective. Hire the detective, somebody cheap for a thousand or so.

Avila went to the Y on Turk Street and lifted weights for two hours. There he was, the new animal. Jumping down from the acacia tree, hot-breathed, eager.

It felt good to be so far ahead of the curve.


Call it survival or self-preservation. Call it the science of fate, or the fate of science. What Darwin called it was war, pure and simple.

That afternoon he was completely moved into the Marina apartment, an okay environment for a while, better than a downtown hotel room in San Francisco where room service breakfasts of cereal, cold toast, and bad coffee went for twenty dollars plus tip. He sat in the bleak and cramped space, studying his temporary divorce order, searching for handholds, loopholes, cracks through which he could slip a clutching set of fingers, perhaps an entire hand. An hour later he had made a list, and called his divorce lawyer, an old partner at Kline-James who had known his father for forty years, and who had handled all the local fancy-pants divorces for businessmen, celebrities, tennis stars from the East Bay on sabbatical from common sense. Twenty minutes after that, Darwin managed to close two Gold Card accounts, stop transactions on his money market funds and transfer them to a small savings and loan in Albany across the bay, then sell a couple of obscure mutual funds at a tidy profit. Whatever cash he could find he would stash. Whatever money he could hide from Karla he would hide.

About four that afternoon Darwin left the apartment. It was dismally gray outside, with a brisk chill blowing in from the bay, promises of rain, stutters of wispy white cloud hovering over the Golden Gate like a huge ice spider poised above its prey. That's it, Darwin thought suddenly, he would no longer wait to be devoured by whatever predator lay in hiding. At that moment, watching the ice spider, Darwin realized that his own father would have gone on the attack. "The best defense," his father had told Jack once, long ago, during one of Jack's vacations from Stanford Law when Jack had come home discouraged and tired, "is a tremendous forward motion and a lot of well-reasoned bullshit."

Darwin parked the Volvo in Safeway's lot and walked two blocks toward the beach. He waited calmly outside a boutique tanning salon, cappuccino machine against the window, a faint purr of money being spent stupidly. Shortly before five, he spotted Karla coming out the door of the parlor, a fresh tan shining conclusively against her skin, like a coat of warm paint. She walked around the corner and into a small cul-de-sac where she had parked the Mercedes. Darwin followed, taking care. It was not going to rain, and a sliver of sun slipped down over the ice spider.

"Hello, sweetheart," Darwin said to her back. "Fancy meeting you here."

Karla turned, surprised, for a moment off-balance. It meant a lot to Darwin, seeing the look of confusion and fear on her face.

"There's a court order, Jack, you goof," she said.

"I ought to put some bruises of my own on your face," Darwin said.

"Get away from me. I'll call the police."

"But you've already done that, Karla," Darwin said. "This is just a chance meeting, isn't it? I've been to Safeway. Now I'm walking down to the beach. We happened to bump into each other. A sudden affray. The woman is struck. Who could blame me? What more can happen to me than hasn't already happened?"

"I'm warning you," Karla said.

"Who *is* your boyfriend?" Darwin asked. "Is he a real estate salesman from Los Angeles? Maybe a rich dentist from Mill Valley? Did he beat you up or were you just having fun in the bathtub?"

"You're very simple, Jack," Karla said, gaining back some equilibrium. She was wearing designer running clothes, light pink top and bottom, pink lipstick, off-white Reeboks. Her skin was nearly black from the many tanning sessions, and even in Darwin's eyes she had begun to look faintly ridiculous.

"Oh, I know you, Karla. I know you inside and out."

"You think you do," Karla said.

"What am I doing here? Every Tuesday and Thursday like clockwork, sweetheart. You come down to the tanning boutique. You think I don't know where you go, what you do? After all, I read all the credit card bills, don't I? Your rose-buying days are over, honey. It's all separate property."

Karla opened the door to the Mercedes. She sat down in the driver's seat and lit a menthol cigarette.

"You've begun smoking again," Jack said. "Here I thought you'd quit."

"Good-bye, Jack," Karla said. She shut the door and started the engine, its low growl both sweet and menacing. The car had belonged to Jack's father, and he hated to see his wife behind its wheel. Darwin mocked Karla with a salute.

He walked over to the parking lot and got inside the Volvo. This evening there would be something of a sunset, leading to a dark night of rain and wind. Darwin could feel his heart beating wildly, keeping rhythm to some ancient instinct deep inside his body. Pushing up against Karla that way had been childish, almost stupidly silly. What had been important about the day was the hiding of money, the secreting of funds for his future, closing a few bank accounts and stopping the credit card hemorrhage. But pushing up against Karla had felt good, like maybe the way battle felt good.

Winter weather in long bleak stretches. Rain and early dark. There were headlines in the *Chronicle:* SNOW DUSTS BERKELEY HILLS.

Vorhees rode his desk for a week, summarizing autopsies, pecking at the computer. He did a backup canvass for a drive-by on Army Street, his own neighborhood. It was late afternoon on a drizzly Friday when he caught his first drama.

Cooley drove them to a rundown hotel on Gough. Through the

neighborhood, the Central Freeway ran on concrete pillars. Everything beneath it was treated with garbage and damp shadows, cars parked halfway on the sidewalks, liquor stores with their doors wide open, a neighborhood of poor pensioners, elderly widows, a few lonesome crackheads, and alcoholics. There was a narrow stairway between buildings, two corridors spread out, spiderweb cracks in the walls. In front of a door at the end of the hall a uniformed officer was standing with arms folded. Vorhees felt soiled just walking on the musty carpet.

"What have you got?" Cooley asked the uniform.

"One dead lady in the bath," he said.

"Who called it in?"

"Manager, down a floor."

"This is residential?"

"More or less."

"You know who the lady is?" Cooley asked.

"Not me. Manager says her name is Lisa Tracy. I might have seen her here or there on my beat but she doesn't ring a bell. She might hook part-time."

Vorhees followed Cooley into the apartment. Two grimy windows in front, a view of the Central Freeway, gray pillars, traffic noise like war being waged in Iraq. The room was tidy but there was a ground-in layer of grime over everything.

The uniform stood in the open doorway behind Vorhees.

"I didn't touch a thing," he said. "The manager used a passkey and said she was too scared to touch anything either. She said she was in here about thirty seconds."

"What's her name?" Vorhees asked without turning around.

"She's about fifty. Says her name is Violet. Apartment fifteen, sign on the door."

Vorhees walked to the kitchen and made notes. A narrow room with a gas stove, dirty refrigerator, Formica table platted with wine bottles, ashtrays, a loaf of bread going green.

In the bathroom they found the woman facedown next to the tub. She looked about forty, with gray stringy hair, sagging breasts, her head turned to one side like a bird, a questioning stare in her eye, the same stare Vorhees had seen on dopers who overdosed and didn't have time to get out the needle before dying. Cooley did nothing, just standing still eyeing the room, a bathtub on legs, homemade shower stall and its filthy glass door, a stool, sink. Women's clothes in a pile on the stool tank.

The uniform stood beside the bathroom door. "Oh yeah! I forgot," he said. "The manager heard the shower running. That's what brought her up here. Some water was leaking down to her apartment right below. She turned off the shower if that's a problem."

"No, that's fine," Cooley said. "You and your partner go door to door in this whole place and make a list of tenants. See what they know, what they saw, what they heard. Catch us a lead and I'll buy you a hamburger."

The uniform took out a notepad. "I forgot to tell you, the manager told me this gal washes dishes at a cafeteria on Market. The ME is on the way up here, about fifteen minutes."

Cooley walked to the shower, stepping over the dead body. Two paces to the shower, two paces to the sink, two paces back. The dead woman was on her stomach, so Cooley leaned over with a pencil and lifted some matted hair, pushed it back over her shoulder. Her right eye was blackened, oozing puss that had dried. Cooley got on his hands and knees and looked at the injuries, a gash on her forehead.

"Somebody banged her up good," Cooley said softly.

Vorhees had opened the medicine cabinet with his pocketknife. "She tricks," Vorhees said. There were a dozen condoms in the cabinet.

"Let's do this right," Cooley said. "You take care of the ME and I'll take care of the forensic crew. We both can chat with Violet."

"There's nothing much to steal here," Vorhees said.

"No, not much. No electronics. Maybe sex got out of hand."

"Wild sex doesn't usually involve banging somebody's head against a tile shower stall. She left a trail of blood on the tiles in there."

"He had her in the shower," Cooley said.

"She wasn't expecting it," Vorhees said, almost to himself.

"He came in peacable," Cooley said.

"He was a john?"

"Maybe. Maybe she had a boyfriend."

"There weren't any liquor bottles open."

"No big party. Maybe just a quick trick."

"Maybe she picked him up on the street."

"Let's hope somebody saw them."

"Son of a bitch," Vorhees said suddenly. He leaned under the stool and spotted a bright square of gold cuff link, the initial J engraved on its flat surface.

"Well, Lisa," Cooley said. "Maybe we can help you after all."

Vorhees put the cuff link in a plastic bag.

"You saw me pick this up, right?" Vorhees said.

"Lucky it wasn't a bloody glove."

"There's no such thing as a perfect crime."

The uniform stuck his head in the door.

"The crew is downstairs," he said.

"Five minutes," Cooley shouted. When the uniform had gone, Cooley said, "Look at this place. Whoever killed poor Lisa here dragged her out of the shower and put her down on the floor nice and easy. She didn't just fall that way."

"Spread her legs?" Vorhees asked.

"Maybe."

They stood together then, quiet, just looking. Vorhees tried to put himself back in time, back to when Lisa brought her man into the room and ran a shower. He took a second look at the medicine cabinet, condoms, a lady's razor, cold medicine, cotton balls. He walked into the living room and made some notes. Cooley was in the bathroom, under the tub, the sink, poking around in the bath towels. In the kitchen, Vorhees opened the refrigerator, checked the cupboards.

Cooley joined him in the living room.

"This wasn't about drugs or theft," Cooley said.

"No, not about that. I did that stuff for ten years, and this wasn't about that. Our guy was dressed up. Hell, he was wearing cuff links."

"Here's the plan," Cooley said. "I'll go downstairs and get the ME and the forensic crews started. You go down and talk to Violet and I'll meet the uniforms about the initial canvass. We'll recanvass later and then we'll canvass down where she tricks. From the looks of Lisa, I'd say she's been there since yesterday afternoon."

Vorhees followed Cooley down one flight of stairs. The halls were empty. When Vorhees knocked on number 15, a seventy-year-old face poked out the door. Inside, Vorhees noticed family photos on the walls and tables. The old lady sat in her easy chair and let Vorhees talk.

"I've just got a few questions," he told her.

"I know. I talked to the other officer."

"Just a few minutes. How long had Lisa lived here?"

"More than a year. She was a regular."

"Did anybody see her last night?"

"She comes in after dark. I hardly ever see her come in. Not last night either."

"Did you see a man here? Dressed up nice. Shirt and tie maybe?"

"I went to bed early. I always do."

"Did you hear any noise upstairs. A struggle maybe?"

"I told the other officer. I was asleep."

"The shower ran all day?"

"I guess it did. I didn't notice anything until late this afternoon. It started to seep through the ceiling."

"How many renters in the building?"

"Twenty-five. They come and they go."

"Did you know Lisa?"

"Only to say hello."

"Did you know she was a working girl?"

"Working girl? No, I didn't know. I don't want to know."

"This won't go any farther, but do you know if there are any more working girls in the building?"

The old woman thought for a moment. "I'd hate to say."

"Lisa would want you to say."

"Maybe Barbara, in ten."

"I won't breathe a word, I promise."

"Thank you."

"Did Lisa have a boyfriend?"

"Not that I know of."

Cooley tapped on the door and pushed inside. Vorhees introduced Cooley to the old woman and they spent ten minutes or so going over a list of the tenants. Life in the building, life on the street just outside. Lisa had a part-time job washing dishes at a cafeteria. No boyfriend. Tricked sometimes just for fun, and to earn a little money. Did she drink? Why not? Everybody drinks to make the time pass. Violet had a daughter in Mill Valley who came to see her sometimes, but Lisa never had any family visit. Did Vorhees want some tea? Cooley? Lisa had been on her stomach when Violet had come in, she didn't touch a thing, maybe the shower faucet. She knocked loud before she went in, poked her head inside, turned off the shower and called the police. It's hard here in the Tenderloin. You can't imagine how hard it is. Lonely too. Can't blame the girl.

It could happen to you.

Heavy morning traffic snarled the freeway. All the way down, Darwin thought about the old days, many of which he'd spent on horseback. He remembered Sundays when his dad would gather up the family into a woody station wagon and take them all to the Presbyterian church, Jack, his older brother, Adam, their mother, and then he would drive them down to the stables after the service so they could ride all day. His brother would get on the big gelding and Jack the small tame mare and they would gallop around the two or three hundred acres owned by the horse ranch, losing their dad, who rode his young colt named Traynor, the pride of the stable. A few years later Adam contracted meningitis and died, and something died in Jack's dad, and Jack too, and things were never the same again. As time passed, they stopped coming to the stable as a family, just as they stopped going to church, and pretty soon Traynor became Jack's horse, the one he loved.

Jack exited at Burlingame and drove into the hills on a paved county road. The ranch had been sold down to twenty or so acres, enough pasture for a few horses, some barns and an exercise arena. The ranch had riding privileges on ground nearby, but most of that was being sold off in parcels, the beginning of the end of open country in the hills, houses, condos, and strip malls right up to the foothills of the Montara Mountains. Driving up to the stable, Darwin could see Angel exercising a colt. Angel waved and came over to the Volvo where Darwin was standing.

"It has been a long time," Angel said. He was Mexican, a weathered man in a checked shirt and jeans. Darwin had known him for a long time, twenty-five years, more or less.

"Too long," Darwin said.

"You come to ride, Mr. Darwin?" Angel asked.

They began to walk beside a white fence. Darwin spotted some horses he'd never seen, an Arabian, two paints.

"How is Traynor doing?" Darwin said.

They stopped and leaned over the fence, watching horses eat hay. The weather had broken and the day was sunny with a hard blue sky.

"He's not so good," Angel said.

"How old is he now? Twenty-three or -four?"

"Twenty-four, Mr. Darwin."

"That's old for a horse."

"Could be," Angel said. "You come down to say hello to him?"

Darwin walked behind Angel to the stable. Inside he remembered its good healthy smell, the smell of horse flesh, leather, and grass. It was a smell he missed. How often had he come riding since his father's death? Maybe once a month at first, then once every two months after the trouble with Karla began. Traynor was in the fifth stall down, standing alone.

"His head is down," Darwin said.

"He's had a hard winter," Angel admitted.

"Does he get out?"

"I walk him some."

"He's crippled, isn't he?"

"A little, Mr. Darwin."

"Has he been down?"

"Twice this winter."

"I saw you'd had the vet out."

"He's an old horse, Mr. Darwin. I know how he feels. He's tired. He's had a good life, Mr. Darwin."

"Let me take him out. Walk him a bit."

Darwin led Traynor around the exercise yard, walking in circles for about ten minutes. Darwin felt sick and lost inside, Traynor walking slowly behind the man, head down, breathing heavily. Darwin remembered his brother riding the horse, both of them smart alecks, full of derring-do and vinegar. Back in those days Darwin couldn't handle Traynor. Darwin felt tears well in his eyes.

Angel came over to the exercise yard.

"You okay, Mr. Darwin?" he asked.

Together they walked Traynor back to the stable. Darwin spent some time rubbing down the horse, even though it hadn't broken a sweat. Darwin wanted to touch its flesh, feel the muscles and bones. The horse was a link to something Darwin cherished, something irretrievably gone, but still present nonetheless. Darwin finished the job, then walked outside and stood with Angel in the sun.

"What do you think about putting him down?" Darwin said.

"It's time, I think."

They didn't look at each other now. The hills were winter green, full of live oaks and chaparral.

"Give it a few weeks," Darwin said.

"I'll drive him to the vet myself."

"Don't throw him away."

"We can cremate him," Angel said. "If you like, I can bring you his ashes. Spread them in the hills."

"I guess it doesn't cause any pain."

"I don't think so, Mr. Darwin."

"I wouldn't want Traynor to have pain."

"He just goes to sleep."

"Good, good," Darwin muttered.

"Are you okay, Mr. Darwin?"

Angel had been in the sun his whole life, and his face was wrinkled and brown.

"I've been better, Angel," Darwin said.

"You going to get another horse?"

"Maybe. Later though. Not right now."

"Sure, Mr. Darwin. But maybe it would help you to get a young horse and train him up. We could train him together, like your dad and I trained Mr. Traynor."

"I've got some business first," Darwin said. "But I like the thought. Maybe we'll do it."

"It would be nice, Mr. Darwin," Angel said.

"Then count on it," Darwin told him.

Darwin drove back to the city and spent the afternoon putting things away in the Marina apartment. It was small, but it was clean and it seemed quiet. It had a television set and a working refrigerator, and he could walk down to the Marina and have lunch or dinner after work. Darwin decided it was time to quit drinking bourbon, and so that night he went to an AA meeting on the second floor of a Clement Street stucco. In the daytime it was a dance studio, but at night it was lined with tables and chairs with about seventy people inside drinking coffee and smoking cigarettes. Darwin didn't speak and he came home tired and depressed. He knew he was going to need all his strength, but he didn't know exactly how he was going to summon it.

.　　.　　.

Barbara Jean Ames was drinking vodka. She told Vorhees she had just gotten off work at a liquor store and smoke shop on Eddy and had mixed herself the first one, trying to relax. She let Vorhees look around and offered him a drink too. She said her feet hurt, and Vorhees sympathized.

"Did you know Lisa downstairs very well?"

"Lisa downstairs I didn't know. We said hello."

"You heard what happened?"

"Yeah. Pretty bad shit, huh? I might move."

"When the officers talked to you before, you said you hadn't heard anything at all. How about that? Maybe late yesterday afternoon."

"I'd have to tell you. I was drinking vodka."

"What did you know about Lisa?"

"She was okay, you know. Nothing special. She was nice."

"Look, we know she tricked."

"I seen her on the street."

"Down on Turk."

"She had a block or two. She wasn't a pro, if that's what you mean. I think she did it because she was lonely."

"The guy who did this to her, we think he was dressed up nice. That sound right to you?"

"Not really," Barbara Jean said.

"Lisa have any regulars?"

"Regulars? You got to be kidding."

"A boyfriend?"

"Honest, I don't know."

"The guy who killed her, he's a creep."

"I don't trick."

"He'll do it again," Vorhees said.

"I said I don't trick."

"Barbara Jean, he'll do it again. We'd like to stop him."

"I hear that."

"Anybody in the building close to Lisa?"

"Violet maybe."

"We checked on that."

"Lisa, she worked at a cafeteria down on Market."

"We checked."

"You talk to them, maybe they can help you out."

"Did you hear Lisa partying last night?"

"No, honest."

"Where's your turf, Barbara?"

"You going to hassle me?"

"No, honest."

"Turk and Eddy, down there."

"Don't get upset if I come back," Vorhees said. "We're going to get the exact time of death and then we're coming back."

"I work days," Barbara Jean said.

"You take care. Be careful."

Vorhees, out on the street, wasn't very far along. All he knew for sure was that Lisa didn't trick with men who wore French cuff shirts.

The plaque read: Johnny B. Burris, Asst. U.S. Attorney. They went out in the hall with two DEA agents, down a corridor, and entered a barren conference room, where the agents spread out the evidence on a table. Five of Luther Lee's guns were on display, two Glocks, a Smith & Wesson, a little derringer, and an automatic rifle. The cocaine was downstairs in the Federal Building property room, but there were photographs of the seizure, a single white brick displayed on a black plastic bag, an empty charcoal briquette sack, five thousand dollars in cash, a series of shots of the Vine apartment in east Oakland, Lee's two-tone Chevrolet.

Burris and the agents sat at the table and watched Darwin sift through the evidence, make some notes, copy the inventory. Burris handed Darwin a chemist's report and Darwin looked it over, saying nothing. Burris told Darwin they had no statements from either defendant.

Burris looked to Darwin like a used-car salesman, crew cut, smug and off-center.

"Your client is looking at a long jail term," Burris said. The DEA agents wore weapons and sat at the end of the table saying nothing. Both were young with long hair, one thin, one fat, both expressionless. "Vine could do himself a lot of good," Burris continued.

"You've read my brief," Darwin said.

Burris shook his head. One of the DEA agents took out a filter cigarette and began to smoke it, tipping ashes onto the corked floor.

"No chance," Burris said. "Listen, your guy gives us something, he can help himself out."

"I don't have any authority," Darwin said, stalling.

"Hey, we're just talking here."

"What does he have to do?"

"Start giving people up."

"And how does this deal work?"

"He works with us and we talk to the judge."

"What about a writing?"

"You mean a contract? We can't do that."

"We just trust each other, like that?"

"Look, guys like Vine are so full of shit you can't trust them. If he gives up some people, he'll get his deal."

"I think I should let the judge hear my motion."

"That's too late. You start the ball rolling, it's hard to stop."

"I've talked to Arthur a lot. He isn't the kind who'll sell people out. Besides, his hopes are up. I told him the arrest was no good."

"Didn't anybody ever tell you not to do that?"

"It isn't such a good idea is it?" Darwin said.

"Listen," Burris said. "Don't build up his hopes."

"I don't know where we are," Darwin told him. "First you tell me Vine is going to do five years flat. Then you say, oh no, it doesn't have to be that way at all. All he has to do is talk and talk, indefinitely, until you guys get ready to unleash him. Maybe he has to give up his mother before he's done. It's really hard to sell a proposition like that."

"Promise me something," Burris said. "Sound him out."

"All right," Darwin agreed. "Next time I see him, I'll ask him how he'd like to be a permanent snitch for the U.S. government, sell all his friends, his family, everybody he knows with no end in sight. I'll see what he says."

Darwin left the Federal Building and went to see his divorce lawyer, an old friend from better days. Darwin knew what people thought when he told them he hadn't touched his wife, hadn't laid a finger on her, hadn't even seen her. They smiled and clapped him on the back and said okay, whatever. Darwin hated telling it that way, it sounded so lame. But what could he do? It was the truth, wasn't it?

· · ·

They shared a surprise kiss at City Lights Bookstore on Columbus. Darwin had walked Dolores up and down the block, waiting for a seat or two to come open in a bistro where Darwin loved the cannelloni, where he knew the owner, who would make them happy. He wanted to impress Dolores just a little, and soon it became their joke, something harmless to toss back and forth as they strolled the block, looking at shops, people-watching. Darwin found himself reaching for her hand as they crossed the street and before he knew it they were holding hands like kids in love, which they weren't, but you couldn't have told it from looking. When they dropped by the bookstore Jack discovered they shared a fondness for Kerouac, his drunken lucidity, his theory that typing spontaneously could lead to good writing, his unabashed acknowledgment and embrace of the fast life, its momentary joy. Dolores told Darwin she didn't like the way Kerouac treated women. After all, he'd died drunk. But she did admire his experiment on the edge of experience, his friendships, his disappointments.

Then Darwin kissed her. He didn't know how or why he did it, but then, surprise of surprises, he kissed her softly on her full lips and she kissed him back, put her hand gently on his neck, touching responsively, without words.

They walked to Washington Square and sat on a park bench so they could look at the church.

"I've got big trouble," Darwin said.

Around them pigeons waddled, rubbernecked. The church in sunlight looked like a block of white granite.

"I thought as much," Dolores said. She was wearing a wonderful red tam that made her look like a child. "You seem worried a lot of the time."

"It's time I told you," Darwin said. "I'm living in a small apartment on the Marina. My wife filed for divorce. She's accused me of domestic violence. Somebody did put a bruise on her and a gash above her eye, but it wasn't me. Now she's living in my house, the house my dad and mom bought and where I was raised. I'm afraid my law practice isn't very successful and I'm facing a trial in municipal court on the abuse charge and I have to defend a divorce suit in state court. My money is tied up in trust and I'm not such a hot businessman."

"Oh my dear John," Dolores said.

"I've got to tell you the truth. It will sound like a lie. It always does. Every time I tell it. I never touched my wife. I came home one Sunday evening and twenty minutes later the police burst in my door and arrested me. Somebody had beaten her, but it wasn't me. Honestly."

Dolores put her arm around his shoulder. The air was cold and she was wearing a navy peacoat and Darwin had on his old camel hair topcoat.

"John, I believe you," Dolores told him.

"Simple as that."

"Yes, that simple."

"I've been going to AA. That's another thing you should know about me. I don't know if I'm an alcoholic, but I feel like one."

"It's a good thing, John," she said. "I didn't know but I'm glad you told me."

"I don't know why this is happening."

"You will get through."

"I keep thinking better times are just around the corner."

"They are, John," Dolores said.

"Yes, sure they are," Darwin said, hating to have spoiled the mood. "My lawyer says it's like going to the dentist. You endure the pain and then it is over someday. I don't buy it, but that's what he says."

"John, you're a gentle man. That's what I think."

"You like that?"

"I like it a lot."

"I'd like to be tough."

"I'm sure you do fine. The world is full of tough guys."

Darwin turned and kissed her on the mouth. It was a long kiss, full of tenderness.

They drew Deborah Mattingly on forensics, which was a good deal if you knew Deborah Mattingly. She brought the preliminaries down to Cooley at three on the dot and Cooley buzzed Vorhees over. Mattingly sat across Cooley's desk from the detectives, sipping coffee. Each of them had Xeroxes of the basic reports.

"Let's start with the ME," Cooley said.

"He dictated this and sent it up," Mattingly told them.

"Strangled, no finger marks," Cooley read. "Steady and increasing pressure, no palm prints either. Probably a choke hold of some kind. A bang on the head against the tile enough to render her unconscious. Superficial contusion and laceration over the right eye. Lots of blood, but no real harm."

"We assume it was a guy," Mattingly said. "Your guy was probably right-handed, got his arm around the throat, banged her head against the tile, choked her. It took a while too. When she's gone he relaxes his grip, holds her up with his left arm and gives her a shot with his right hand. It's her blood on the bathroom tile and there isn't a trace of any other blood. She had no signs of skin or tissue under the fingernails so she didn't have any time to fight back at all. It came as a complete surprise to her I'd guess. No blood elsewhere in the apartment, no fingerprints except for Lisa, not even any fibers that are worth a tinker's damn."

"Time of death?" Cooley asked.

"Three hours give or take between seven and ten on Thursday night. She had a little alcohol in her system, probably the last from one of those empty bottles you guys noted, but not enough to cause any intoxication. Nothing on the stomach to indicate she'd eaten anything, so I'd guess she didn't have dinner after work."

"The time frame is right," Vorhees said.

"Look, you guys," Mattingly said. "We went over that place with a fine-tooth comb. Bathroom tile, between the caulk, behind the sink. We opened the shower drain and dug out all the hair. It was all hers. Whoever did this to Lisa was very careful and not much in a hurry."

"You mean he enjoyed it. Planned it out."

"That's my experience," Mattingly said.

"Most guys are nervous when they pick up a trick," Vorhees said. "I don't mean the wino who finds twenty bucks, but the businessman type. You'd think he'd be scared to death, what with the wife and kids at home. Want to do it and get out quick. And here's a guy who doesn't leave a trace except for a cuff link. How did that happen anyway?"

"He planned it too well," Cooley said.

"Maybe the cuff links were in his pocket. His shirt. Maybe he wasn't wearing them." Mattingly shrugged, just thinking out loud. "Anyway, there's more," she continued. "The ME confirms she'd been sodomized. Probably the real thing too, no bottles there like that. But she'd been cleaned up. Probably in the shower this guy soaps her down and towels her off. Your creep washed her out. But there are tears on the anal wall."

"Very careful," Cooley said.

Cooley and Vorhees studied the stack of forensic photos, probably fifty in all, from every angle.

"Call the uniform," Cooley told Vorhees. "Have him do a second canvass and focus on the period seven to ten."

"I talked to Barbara upstairs," Vorhees said. "She said she was home that night, but she didn't hear anything. Said she was drinking vodka since five. That's probably true. Right now, I believe her. She's a part-time working girl too and I don't think she wants this guy out on the street. I think she'd level with me. She says Lisa didn't have a steady boyfriend or any regular tricks."

Mattingly stood and told them good-bye. She hustled down a corridor of cubicles and was gone.

"Do you suppose this guy drove a car, parked it on Turk, someplace close?" Cooley asked.

"It's worth a try," Vorhees admitted.

"We could check the records of parking garages in the area. Talk to the attendants."

"It's worth a try. We might get lucky."

"It's like Jack the Ripper," Cooley said. "Rich guy kills prostitute for fun. He enjoys it."

"So what do we know?" Vorhees asked himself out loud. "Guy with one initial of J. Right-handed. Very meticulous, even washes down his victim, probably takes a shower himself and dresses carefully. Knows what cops look for, so leaves no fingerprints or fibers. Lisa likes him, likes his look, and he has plenty of money so she lets him in, has a drink of vodka, then gets in the shower. Doesn't seem scared, doesn't panic, lets the guy in behind her. He gets her off her feet before she can react."

"Has he done it before?" Cooley asked.

"Yeah, why not. This wasn't a practice run."

"He's good at it. It's what he does."

"If he's this good at it, he's got to be good at something else."

"A professional guy. Somebody with brains."

"Let's check the files," Vorhees said.

Cooley and Vorhees spent two hours cross-referencing rape murders, sodomy murders, sex crimes of all kinds. In all that time they got only one good possibility, an unsolved sodomy robbery at the Holiday Inn near the airport. A woman named Jean Hobart from Cincinnati had run into a predator in the shower, lost her money and her credit cards, but hadn't lost her life. Choked, banged against the tile, both Cooley and Vorhees couldn't believe how close it was, and they wanted to pursue it, only Jean Hobart was back in Cincinnati and wanted to forget it ever happened. She'd learned her lesson, she was lucky to be alive. Besides, she was very drunk and it was dark in the disco bar. That evening, Vorhees caught up with her by phone. She told Vorhees she couldn't remember much, only that the guy was dark and muscular, pretty tall if she remembered correctly, the only problem being that she was very drunk on gin, and she'd kept drinking the whole evening, Christmas Eve. She thought he dressed nice and had good taste in wine and food. His name was Carillo, but that was probably bullshit. Arthur Carillo, at least that's what she thought he'd said.

When Vorhees reviewed the file on Jean Hobart, he found that a forensic crew hadn't even done a workup. Hobart had left town, not wanting to pursue the matter.

So, what did they have? A dark muscular guy, above average height, one initial J. It was quite a lot, really. Something would break soon, or this guy would do it again and get caught. They always did.

Cooley and Vorhees worked the parking garages around Turk and Eddy, then did some more computer analysis. But that evening they caught a murder-suicide out in the Sunset and a bad dope deal in Chinatown, and the next day a gas station attendant in Potrero. There were only twenty-four hours in a day, and they would have to work Lisa Tracy in where they could, when they had time.

It's what they called police work.

Uh, yeah, well, uh, hello, my name is John, I'm, uh, uh, an alcoholic. (A ragged chorus, Hello, John) I've never spoken here before. I don't know why. Well, I'm embarrassed. You know you never think it can happen to you. At least I never did. I don't know what to say. I've heard you have to hit bottom before you quit. I don't know if I've hit bottom, but I'm close. And it isn't what you think, either. It wasn't my drinking that made me hit bottom. (Murmurs) Well, I suppose it had something to do with it. But my wife is divorcing me and she's put me out of my house. That's why I'm here, I suppose. I've lived in that house all my life and I thought I'd live in that house for the rest of my days. Now my wife lives in my house and I can't go home again until things get legally straightened out. My business isn't very good. Maybe I'm in the wrong business, I don't know. But drinking never got in the way of my business, or at least I don't think it did. (More murmurs, nonthreatening) But when I married my wife it was probably drinking more than anything else that led to that, I mean, she let me drink and didn't say much about it. It was fun, or it seemed like fun then, and we drank a little bit together and I'd get going to drinking and I'd drink and drink and it seemed fun us being together and drinking and time passing and we went to Las Vegas and Reno and then we got married and it wasn't right. (Silence) What I'm saying is that I think drinking clouded my judgment. That's about it. Except that there's a lot of, well, you'd have to call it shit going on in my life, and I don't have the strength to face it and drink at the same time. That's why I say drink didn't cause some of these problems, because I don't know where they came from, but I know I can't face up to all of it if I drink, and that, as they say, is that. You can take it to the bank. (Mild laughter) A lot of the time I live in the past. I drink and think about the past, about my dad and my brother Adam who died of meningitis when I was fifteen. He was twenty-one. My dad couldn't get over it. None of us could really, but for different reasons. My dad couldn't get over it because Adam was the good son, the bright son, the one who was going to be like my dad. I couldn't get over it because I loved Adam and he guided me, took care of me. We rode horses on Sunday. That's what we did as a family, and sometimes even my dad had to work on Sunday, so my brother and I would go down and ride horses together. My dad thought he taught me to ride, but it was really my brother who taught me to ride, my brother and me riding down at some stables in Burlingame a long time ago now. (Murmurs) I've met someone new. (Murmurs of disapproval) Well, I know what they say. But I met her before I went to my first meeting over on Clement. She doesn't drink that I know of and we didn't meet through drinking or anything like that. I've told her everything. (Murmurs of approval) You know, we live in a paradise, we really do. We're already in heaven. It's just that things stand between us and paradise and we lose sight of how beautiful the earth really is, the natural world.

I guess I'm getting out of hand. It's just that I'm having a hard time and I'm getting out of hand. It's just that I'm having a hard time and I'm going to need my strength. I better quit now before I go haywire. (That was good, John)

Late-afternoon shadow cupped the office, a hundred lines running here and there. Darwin had brought Avila a check for fifteen hundred dollars, money he couldn't afford to spend on lawyer's fees, money he couldn't afford not to spend on lawyer's fees. He had debts everywhere. He was leaking money and his secret accounts were dwindling.

"How you doing now?" Avila asked him.

"Hanging in there. Dolores helps a lot."

"She's a pretty girl."

"She's a wonderful person."

"Where'd you meet her?"

"I'm embarrassed to say. She's in my research and writing class at night. Don't worry. The papers are graded anonymously. Besides, we're just friends. That's all."

"Well, good luck with her," Avila said.

Darwin handed Avila the check, pushed it across the desk and set it beside the Evian water.

"Where are we at?" Darwin asked.

"I've got the detective's report," Avila said. "I'm afraid he didn't turn up much. What I mean is he didn't turn up anything. Your wife had lunch twice in two weeks with girlfriends. She was no trouble to follow and she didn't meet any men. Period. The agency is good and can back every moment of their time up with written reports. I've made Xeroxes for you. His logs are pretty thorough." Avila handed Darwin a sheaf of written reports, an itemized billing. "You want to try two more weeks?"

Darwin looked at the billing. Twenty-eight hundred dollars including expenses. "Can I send you a check?" Darwin asked.

"Whenever," Avila said. "I paid the agency out of my trust account."

"I appreciate it very much," Darwin said. "I'll send you a check when I can free up some funds. But I don't think I can go for another two weeks."

"It probably doesn't matter, Jack," Avila said. "Your wife is too smart to get caught out now."

"Probably true," Darwin said.

"But look," Avila continued, "I need to go over the police report with you, Jack." Avila opened a short manila envelope and spread the contents, two or three sheets of stapled reports. "It's all in here. I've made a copy for you. For what it's worth, what your wife says happened to her, probably did happen to her. A welt on her forehead and a black eye. They did a rape test on her and confirmed tearing. They didn't pick up any fluids, probably because she showered. It isn't uncommon. Besides, it wouldn't be normal to do a sperm test when it's her husband that's accused. We can try to use that at trial. Anyway, it's too late to get an order on it at this time."

"What do you suggest?"

"Well, right now, it's your word against hers."

"I didn't touch her, David."

"I believe you, Jack."

"She's lying."

"Somebody beat her up."

"Could she have done it herself?"

"Look, we'd sound silly suggesting it."

"I won't make a deal," Darwin said.

"Don't worry. They don't make deals on domestic violence in municipal court. Not for ten years. The prosecutors up there are all women, tough as nails, dykes most of them. Hell, they don't have anything else to do but make men's lives miserable. They like what they do, for Christ's sake."

"I can't believe this whole thing."

"I've got an idea," Avila said.

"Anything."

"You've been sued for divorce. Get your lawyers to depose Karla right now. I'll get a continuance in the domestic violence case. If you can depose her soon, we can use the testimony at trial, if it's any good. Then you can get on the stand and tell the truth. Simple as that. I wish I could think of something else. That's why I hate these cases. There are never any witnesses and it boils down to us against them. You never know what's going to happen."

"We'll try to depose her then," Darwin agreed. "She's lying."

Avila asked about Arthur Vine. Darwin told him that the hearing on a motion to suppress in Vine's case had been scheduled for later in the week. Darwin loved the brief he'd written. Avila had read it, and told him it was great, one of the best he'd ever read. They agreed there was a chance the evidence would be kicked. Not much of a chance, but a chance. Wouldn't that be something? Another victory for Jack Darwin, criminal attorney.

At Gump's she shopped for mink. The fur made her shiver, a literal warm sexual throb in her legs. From a discreet distance, a guard watched while she strolled the aisles, examining muffs and stoles, the coats, jackets, vests, the mink, chinchilla, every piece poised in front of her like wealth. She caught the guard's eye and smiled as if to tell him she was a part of the fur world, an animal of another kind. Quickly the guard looked away, embarrassed to be caught staring.

She had spent the morning with Rowe, then had a late brunch, walked over to Gump's. The lawyer had received the notice of a deposition, telling her that she'd have to give testimony in three or four weeks. He'd assemble photographs of her injuries, collect police reports. "We'll be in tall cotton," he said, "when your husband is convicted." Karla embraced one of the coats, taking in its earthy smell. Then she took the escalator down to the ground floor and went outside.

Avila was waiting for her, standing under an awning on the street. He was wearing an elegant black topcoat and black beret. She had never seen him look so luminous. He was heavenly and she was afraid of him, afraid that fate would step in and separate them. That morning she had spent thirty minutes applying makeup to her faint bruise, now a gray smudge above her eye. It seemed a symbol of something profoundly exciting, an area of experience without emotional tone or complexity, yet strange and deep. She followed Avila to Sutter and caught up with him at the cable car stop. Karla sat down next to him.

"I've missed you," Karla said to him, across the aisle. The cable car went past the Fairmont Hotel, all its Christmas decorations gone now. "It's hard for me in that house all alone."

"What did Rowe say?" Avila asked.

"David, do you love me?"

Avila looked across at her, just a glance. "If it was up to me I'd take you right now. It'd be quick, but I'd take you right here. You have that kind of effect on me."

Uphill now, the cable car creaking along, the city spread out gray and vibrant.

"Jack is deposing me," Karla said. "Rowe is gathering all the police reports and photographs. He seemed to think the domestic violence charge would make a big difference."

"How big a difference?"

"He said it could settle the case."

"I don't suppose he knows where the money will come from?"

"He said he subpoenaed all Jack's records."

"The house is up against tax liens, isn't it?"

"Yes, I think so."

"Jack would never sell the house."

"I think he'd die first," Karla said. "Let's just give it to him."

They were at the edge of Chinatown. There were flower sellers on every corner, butcher windows full of flattened red chickens, upside down.

"Yes, perhaps he would," Avila said.

"Rowe said he could take a judgment against the trust fund. Collect later."

"The trust opens in ten years, Karla," Avila said flatly. For a moment, Karla wanted to trick David, shake her hair, gaze past his shoulder, off into the near distance of sexual adventure. But she couldn't force herself. Over Nob Hill was a view of Alcatraz, the cold blue bay, dozens of sailboats in slate gray weather. The wind was making Karla cold, David was talking, his eyes brown and fixed. "Do you want to wait ten years, Karla?"

"I could go back to work," she said distractedly. "We could be happy."

"Give Jack his house. Move out. Go back to work. Wouldn't that be lovely. Maybe we could raise some kids."

"You're doing so well, David," she said.

"This isn't about me, Karla. It's about getting what we want. You and me, we're alike. I know where you've been and I know who you are. We've come a long way, Karla, but we've a long way to go."

"I've done what you told me to do," Karla said.

They said nothing then, going downhill past the cable car barn, Russian Hill Park, the Marina below them. Hundreds of gulls wheeled and circled over the water.

"Karla, listen to me," Avila was saying. "There is all manner of law in the world. There are laws for Jack Darwin and there are laws for you and me. His money, how did he get it? Did he struggle for it? Did he sacrifice and work? What the hell did he do to earn his house in Pacific Heights, his stable full of horses, his Sunday nights at Marge's playing cribbage?" Avila touched her with his cold hand. "We're going to take it away from him, Karla. We have our own law, one he doesn't know exists. Our law is about struggle. Our law is about reality. When a guy like Darwin meets people like us, he doesn't understand the consequences. He may think that what he's got is some kind of God-given right, a kingship he's stepped into that can't be taken away. But there isn't anything in this world that can't be taken away. Nothing."

The cable car had stopped for passengers.

"David, you frighten me," Karla said. "I don't know if I can go through with this. What if something goes wrong?"

"There won't be a trial. You won't have to testify. Nothing will go wrong."

They reached the end of the line at Maritime Park. Joggers streamed by in fluorescent suits, fanny packs, the Pepsi generation staying in shape. Some bums were sunning themselves on benches down by the water. They got off the cable car and Avila bought cappuccino from a vendor. From a bench they watched Italian immigrant men playing bocce, the balls clicking crisply, hissing on wet sand and clacking together.

"David, listen to me," Karla said. She hadn't touched her cappuccino. "You know I love you. You know I hate Jack and I'd do anything for you. But Rowe says there is a chance he could force a sale of the house. Doesn't that mean anything?"

"There won't be a trial, darling, trust me."

"It isn't just that. What you did, it scares me."

"Didn't you like it a little?"

"Please, David, I'm serious."

Avila put on a pair of black suede gloves. He touched Karla on the cheek.

"In the shower, that was just a game," he said.

Karla put down her cappuccino.

"I liked it a little," Karla said.

"Good," Avila said. "I thought you'd like to know that Jack still has his special friend. A girl. A girlfriend."

"It doesn't matter."

"It might to Rowe."

"Of course, I forgot."

"Tell Rowe. Call him when you get home. The girl's name is Dolores Hernandez. She's one of his students. You'd think he could come up with something more original."

Karla buried her head in Avila's fur collar. "I've wanted you for days," she said.

"Listen to me closely," Avila told her. "I'm going to federal court today at one. I'm going to listen to Jack argue a case I gave him. Go home this afternoon and stay there all day. I want you to telephone Jack at his apartment and leave a message on his machine. He won't be home, but leave a message. He's teaching his stupid class tonight and if it's like every other night after class, he'll spend time with his girlfriend before going home."

"David, what's happening?"

"Just call him. I want you to leave a message that you'd like to meet him at the Aladdin Coffee House down on the Marina at about nine. Tell him you've decided he should have his house. Just say you'd like to talk about it."

"But David, how do you know what he does with his time?"

"Don't forget, I'm his lawyer. He's a man who tells his lawyer everything. And I'm his friend too. Jack is a guy who needs friends." Avila smiled and Karla tried to bury herself deeper into his collar.

"What if someone hears that message later?"

"I'll erase it. I have a key to his place, remember?"

"Why should I call him?"

"It won't matter, dear. If the police or anybody asks you, you deny you ever called. I don't think anybody will ask, but if they do, you never called. Simple."

The bocce players were laughing and shouting in Sicilian dialect. Avila touched her with his lips, just below the ear. A warmth roared through Karla and her breasts ached. Avila kissed her, put his tongue in her mouth, digging for something deep inside her, a thing he could touch whenever he wanted to touch it.

He checked, double-checked, cross-referenced, and re-cross-referenced NCCI and the California Crime Computer, as well as calling up every file he had on known rapists in the state, and in neighboring states. He and Cooley had about two hours a day to spend on Lisa Tracy and they tried to make both hours count. Twice Vorhees faxed Jean Hobart in Cincinnati and sent her photographs of men who had just gotten out of prison, men on probation and parole, men who'd been arrested and hadn't been convicted. It was a dead end both times, just like Vorhees knew it would be. Cooley recanvassed the Turk Street bars, video arcades, and encounter booths, checking on anyone who might have seen Lisa Tracy pick up her trick that Thursday night, but he drew a blank, just like Vorhees knew he would. They both arrived at the Friday staff meeting jacked up, tired and empty, with three more unsolved cases on their checklist, two drive-bys in the projects and an old woman in her apartment on Mason, maybe a suicide.

It was raining hard outside when they sat down across from Lightfoot, who had been reading their updates. Vorhees wanted to go home on time for once and be with Alisha, maybe grab a decent meal and spend some time with his wife as if they were having a normal life. When he switched over to homicide he thought maybe they could have a normal life, but the hope was fading. It was police work, pure and simple, and nothing could denature it. They discussed the drive-bys and got to Lisa Tracy.

"Anything new here?" Lightfoot asked.

Cooley reviewed their tracks, the canvassing, the parking garage records, checking crime computers. Lightfoot took them through the forensics and ME reports. In the meantime Lisa Tracy had been shipped back to Lovelock, Nevada, where her father was about to bury her.

"I talked to Lisa's dad," Cooley said.

"What's his story?" Lightfoot asked him.

His wife left him, he raised Lisa by himself. Lisa hung around Lovelock waiting tables and then when she was twenty took off to the big city.

"Boyfriends?" Lightfoot said. "Bad company back there?"

"Some high school boy, twenty years ago."

"He has a name?"

"Mr. Tracy doesn't remember."

"I suppose they have high school yearbooks."

"It isn't much," Cooley protested.

"You talked to the ladies on Turk Street?"

"Twice, sometimes three times. A few of them knew Lisa. She was a semipro. Kept to herself. We didn't hear anything that would help."

"No johns in fancy suits with nice cars?"

"They get all kinds," Vorhees said. "But nobody sticks out in their minds. I think they'd say. They're scared."

"They should be," Lightfoot said.

"I've been surfing the Net," Vorhees said.

"Turn anything?" Lightfoot swiveled in her chair and looked at the rain making greasy rivulets down the netted windows.

"Nothing that really fits," Vorhees told her. "I also faxed some photos to the woman in Cincinnati. She was drunk at the time and doesn't remember that much."

"She doesn't want to remember," Lightfoot said.

"Anyway, the photos don't fit. Besides, neither did the MOs."

"Look," Lightfoot said. "Our guy hasn't been caught yet. He's smart. He's cool. He's dangerous."

"I don't think he's in the system either," Cooley said.

"What about the fabled gold cuff link?"

"That's mine," Vorhees said. "I sent photos of the cuff link to the major jewelry stores in the city. I'm still waiting for somebody to recognize it."

"I'd hit that hard," Lightfoot said.

"I'll run it around personally. Why don't we give it to the newspapers?"

"Maybe he runs if it hits the newspapers."

"No, let's do that."

"It's worth the risk."

"Okay, the first of next week," Vorhees said.

"Let's sum this up," Lightfoot said. "We're looking for somebody with an initial J. Maybe dark and muscular. Maybe not. Not in the system. Cool and professional about it. Probably enjoys what he's doing."

"That's about it," Cooley said. Vorhees and Cooley exchanged glances and shrugged. "I tell you what I think," Cooley continued. "I hope he tries it with some lady who shoots his ass."

"Okay, you two keep on the computers," Lightfoot said, swiveling back to face them. "If you reach a dead end give the cuff link to the newspapers and hit the yearbooks in Nevada. Keep on the lady in Cincinnati until she remembers or wants to remember. I have a feeling we're going to need a break."

Cooley and Vorhees went to the lounge and bought sodas. Cooley washed his hands and face, sipping his drink while Vorhees stretched out on the sofa.

"Don't let it bother you, Amos," Cooley said. "We'll get this asshole sooner or later."

"I know," Vorhees said, eyes closed.

"You got images?"

"Images?" Vorhees said. "Yeah, how'd you know?"

"I used to get them too."

"It wasn't like this on narcotics," Vorhees told him. "Once in a while you see some guy in the street, but you know he had it coming. Even then it wasn't good, but I didn't get images."

"It'll pass." Cooley grabbed a paper towel and dried his face. "First couple of years I slept maybe four good nights. I got drunk quite a bit too."

"You think we're missing something?"

"Don't chew on it, Amos," Cooley said. "We're not missing anything. The guy who did Lisa Tracy was good. Or lucky. Or both. He'll fuck up and we'll get him."

"I think that's just it," Vorhees said. "It was too good."

Cooley combed what was left of his hair and put on a clean shirt. He put away his gun and locked his locker.

"Too good?" Cooley said finally.

"Just too damn good," Vorhees said.

"Whatever," Cooley said. "I gotta go home." Cooley splashed on some cheap cologne and put on a windbreaker. "My wife is making chili tonight. It's her idea of gourmet cooking."

"You think," Vorhees said, "anybody down at the Holiday Inn is holding back?"

"I don't think so," Cooley said.

Cooley waved good-bye. Vorhees remained on the sofa trying to rest his eyes, eradicating images. He had been told in training that the cases he investigated weren't personal, and that if he took it that way his behavior would get screwed up royally. He had a baby due in six weeks and he didn't want his behavior screwed up.

Fifteen minutes in detention with Arthur Vine put Darwin in a ripe mood. They were on the third floor of the Federal Building and Vine was tired, wanting to know how come Luther Lee made bail and he didn't. Darwin temporized, knowing the real answer, having little to say on the subject. Suppose, he told Vine, the magistrate had set bail at $150,000, as he did for Luther Lee—would that have made a difference? After that, things went downhill fast, Primo cursing Darwin, Darwin pacing the room trying to calm the guy, Darwin finally leaving as Primo continued to call him names. Going down the hallway, Darwin could only admire David Avila for dealing with this shit every day of his practice. You had to have something special in your blood to handle it. You had to see it as a game, a game the lawyer can never lose.

The courtroom on the fifth floor was small, with security cameras on posts, above doors, in nooks where you'd least expect them. The room itself was almost airless, nothing like the cavernous federal courtrooms he used to wander around in as a kid when his father would bring him down to show him off. Darwin could remember how his father used to exude pride like an aura. These days though, courtrooms were no longer a symbol of magnificence and power, but precisely the opposite, places of conclaves where secret ceremonies caused horrible harm to the people caught up in their clutches, all in the name of an abstract ideal. It was either that, or it was a circus, like O. J. and Menendez, worse than a circus because of the voyeurism involved.

Darwin was reading his brief when the judge was announced by the bailiff. Kelly was a trimly built sixty-year-old with flushed red cheeks and a mane of silver hair. He motioned for the attorneys to sit, and a deputy marshal brought Primo to his place beside Darwin. The courtroom was utterly empty and deathly silent, the air cleansed and dead, filtered dry.

"Good afternoon, gentlemen," the judge called. "I've read the briefs and I think I understand the issues. Mr. Darwin, it's your motion.

A motion to suppress. I think it's appropriate that you say a few words on the subject."

Beside Darwin, Primo smelled faintly of cat shit. He wheezed softly; Darwin suspected the onset of tuberculosis.

"Let me state the facts briefly, Your Honor," Darwin said, standing behind a lectern about fifteen feet in front of the judge. "My client, Arthur Vine, lives in east Oakland. On November fifth last year, he went outside to meet an acquaintance named Luther Lee Dokes. Mr. Dokes got out of his car and handed my client a sack of charcoal briquettes. DEA agents were across the street. The agents broke up the meeting and arrested both men. They were handcuffed by the agents, read their rights, and then the car belonging to Mr. Dokes was searched. Both men were searched. The agents did not ask permission to search either the individuals involved or the automobile. Neither man has made a statement to the government."

"And in the sack?" the judge said, smiling. "What did the agents find in the sack?" Kelly tipped his head, elflike.

"They found nothing in the sack but a black plastic bag," Darwin said.

"Excuse me, Mr. Darwin," Kelly laughed. "Didn't they find slightly less than two pounds of cocaine?" Kelly dropped a gold pen to his desk, plop.

"Oh no, Your Honor," Darwin said. "That was later. That was at DEA headquarters. Inside the charcoal briquette sack the agents found a black plastic sack wrapped with twine. The agents have said they didn't open the black plastic sack until later. It's in their reports. When they did open the black plastic bag, they say they found Baggies filled with white powder. Later, they had a lab do an analysis and they say it is cocaine."

"Not to put too fine a point on the facts," Kelly said.

"We'll take their word it's cocaine, for now."

"Just for argument's sake you mean?" the judge said.

The lawyers shared a laugh, Burris looking at Darwin.

"Fine, Your Honor," Darwin said. "Let's assume it's cocaine. It doesn't matter for purposes of my argument. What matters is the timeline. Luther Dokes parks in front of my client's apartment. My client comes out, says hello. The two men stand outside the automobile.

Dokes hands my client a charcoal briquette sack. DEA agents arrest both men on the spot. My client never opened the charcoal briquette sack. So it doesn't really matter what's in the sack, inside the bags, inside the Baggies, does it?"

"That's what I like," Kelly said. "A clear timeline. No barking dogs, no chauffeurs waiting at the gate, no shadowy black men chipping golf balls."

Burris and Darwin laughed at the same time. It was hard not to appreciate Kelly.

"I want to make my argument clear and simple," Darwin said.

"Go ahead," Kelly said. "You have my full attention."

"Let's keep clear. The agents arrested my client for possession with intent to sell. They then confiscated the charcoal sack from his possession, then they searched it at their headquarters. If that timeline is to hold, and if the arrest of my client is valid, it has to be valid solely because the affidavit filed in this case by an agent is both true and completely reliable."

"You say they're not?"

"I say this," Darwin told the judge. "The DEA agents should have searched the sack then and there." Darwin picked up a document. "I want to read part of their affidavit. 'Upon information and belief, Agent Stuart Van Landingham states that an individual identified as Arthur Leroy Vine will take possession of a quantity of powder cocaine on or about November fifth in the vicinity of his home, and so on.' " Darwin looked up at the judge. "That's it, Your Honor. The affidavit goes on to say they received their information from a reliable source. We know what that means. They had an informer or snitch."

Kelly picked up the case file. "We've got a codefendant here?" he asked.

"Out on bail," Burris said, standing.

"Same kind of affidavit on him?"

"Yes sir," Burris said.

"Does he have a motion on file?"

"Not yet, Your Honor."

"All right," Kelly said. "We'll get to him later. What is your point?"

"Add this affidavit to what the agents saw and you don't have probable cause for an arrest."

Kelly thought for a long time. "You think that *Rolfe* and *Lewis* and *Hagen* say that?"

"Yes sir, I do," Darwin said. "Here's what I think happened. The DEA talked to their informer and he told them he smelled a drug deal coming down. I think he had a vague idea about it. I think it's likely that the informant was part of the deal. But the affidavit doesn't say anything about a charcoal sack, nor does it say anything about Luther Lee Dokes. It's defective in that sense. But more importantly, the cases say that if an informer is an essential part of a drug transaction, then his accurate testimony is vital to probable cause and conviction both."

"Unless," Kelly said.

"Yes," Darwin said. "Unless the crime is apparent from the facts on its face."

"Obvious to the police agent observing it," Kelly said.

"Precisely," Darwin told him.

"And your argument is that it wasn't obvious."

"A reasonable inference from the facts is that two friends were meeting and might have a barbecue that afternoon. It may not be realistic in hindsight, but the facts are to be judged as a reasonable man would judge them at the time."

"They're charged with conspiracy too," Kelly said. "Does that make any difference to your theory?"

"No sir. To prove conspiracy the agent would have to prove an agreement. There is no mention of an agreement in the affidavit at all. The conspiracy charge alone would be even more invalid than possession."

"Mr. Darwin," Kelly said. "Your whole argument hinges on the charcoal briquette sack, doesn't it? Suppose Mr. Dokes had brought the cocaine in black plastic bags?"

"Same argument, sir."

"Even though black plastic bags are well known in the drug trade?"

"The DEA can handle that problem by getting their warrant to search. Then by doing a search. The agents here did an arrest before searching."

"Do you think the agents would have had probable cause to search these men after seeing the charcoal briquette sack?"

"Not on the basis of the affidavit they filed." Darwin put down his legal pad and looked at the judge. "Judge, all I'm saying is that *Rolfe* and the cases hold that an informant's affidavit has to be absolutely clear, detailed, and reliable. Otherwise, the government could fish every time they heard a rumor. It's part of the law handed down by the Supreme Court to tell the police what they have to do in order to use informants and undercover agents properly."

"You think there is no area for slippage in the affidavit?"

"Oh, sure there is," Darwin said. "Suppose an informant says that so-and-so is receiving a shipment of automatic weapons at his apartment. The DEA agents stake it out and see handguns delivered. No problem."

"Substantial truth then," Kelly said.

"The slippage there is taken care of because the agents saw a crime. In this case they didn't see anything at all. The sack could easily have contained briquettes. They should have searched first."

"Then you'd be attacking the search," Kelly said.

"And it would be invalid. What they really should have done is filed a detailed affidavit."

Kelly pushed his reading glasses high on his nose. "What do you have to say about all this, Mr. Burris?"

Burris looked chunky and pale, rumpled in his cheap suit. "First of all," he said, "the informant's information has to be reasonably reliable. The magistrate concluded that the information was reliable. The informant had information on a drug deal and right on time the deal happened, just like the informant said it would."

"He's arguing backward," Darwin said.

"Quiet, you!" Kelly said. "You've had your turn."

"Sorry, Your Honor," Darwin said.

Out of the corner of his eye, Darwin saw Avila in the far back of the courtroom, off to one side. Avila caught his gaze and nodded.

"It was Arthur Vine," Burris said, "who approached the informant. Our informant said they'd buy. On that information Mr. Van Landingham went to the magistrate and a warrant was issued."

"A search warrant," Kelly said. "Mr. Darwin is arguing that there wasn't any search."

"Everybody knows—" Burris began.

"I'd be wary of that argument," Kelly said, cutting him off.

"But Your Honor, my agents know that Dokes is a dealer. When they see him show up at Vine's apartment with a big sack, they know what's coming down. And it happened just like their informant said it would. All the Supreme Court requires is reasonable reliability. There is no way an informant can tell the magistrate, hey, look, the drug dealers are using charcoal sacks now. It isn't a fashion show."

"It sounds like your agents had a suspicion," Kelly said.

"No, they had probable cause to arrest."

"That's the rub, isn't it?"

"My agents were acting in good faith," Burris protested.

"Hold on a minute," Kelly told him. "The good faith exception validates an otherwise lawful search based upon some technical deficiency in the warrant. In order to use that argument, you'd have to admit a technical deficiency."

"Not admitting a deficiency, I can still argue that even if there is a deficiency, the execution of the warrant is valid if conducted in good faith." Burris looked back at his agent. "Your Honor, can I put Agent Van Landingham on the stand?"

"I'd object to that," Darwin said from his chair. Primo was breathing stertorously. "The only person we should hear from, if anybody, is the informant himself."

"That's not permissible," Burris said angrily. Burris sat in a quick huddle with his agent, five minutes of sibilant whispers. Primo tried to talk to Darwin, but he wouldn't listen.

"Would the court permit a short recess?" Burris said.

"For what purpose?" Kelly asked him.

"I'd like to talk to Mr. Darwin."

"Use my conference room," Kelly said.

The judge slipped off the bench and disappeared into his chambers, followed by the clerk and bailiff. A marshal came and stood behind Primo, one hand on his shoulder. Darwin trailed Burris into an oak-paneled conference room lined with books. In one corner was a coffeemaker, some golf photos, a single dead geranium in the sealed window. Down on Civic Center, through smoky glass, Darwin could see the homeless moving like ants among the barren trimmed sycamores.

Burris got a cup of coffee and stood at the window. "You know what's going to happen?" he said.

"No, what's going to happen?" Darwin said.

"Kelly might hear the informant and then he's going to uphold the arrest. The judge wants to shut your appeal down right here."

"Well, let's find out."

"If you make me use that informant on the stand, I'll see your guy never gets a break. Not at sentencing, not in choice of prisons, not anytime anywhere."

"Let's look at it this way," Darwin said. "Under the Federal Sentencing Guidelines, Vine is looking at five years, no matter what happens. If your informant gets on the stand, Vine does five years. If your informant doesn't get on the stand, Vine does five years. Now, what would you do in my place?" Darwin got up and went to the window and stood beside Burris, a big guy with knuckled hands, a guy who looked like he might have been a linebacker in high school, wound up doing law at UCLA.

"Look," Darwin said. "Let's do some business. It's Luther Lee you want. I know I'm right. Arthur Vine may be in a gang, but he's no dope dealer. He saw a chance to make a quick buck, that's all. He couldn't deal dope to the Dallas Cowboys."

Burris turned and laughed genuinely. "Maybe you're right," he said.

"Suppose we plea to simple attempted possession?" Darwin suggested.

"And Vine testifies against Luther Lee."

"No way. He won't do it."

"I'll have to check."

"Come on, it's simple."

"I still have to burn my informant."

"Maybe not. Who knows?"

"All right. Screw it. Simple attempted possession."

"No jail time. We're inside the guidelines on that."

"Fair enough. But I'll have to pass it through the big boss downstairs first. But it will pass."

The two men shook hands. They watched a trail of smoke rise from a campfire on the lawn of Civic Center.

"I'll tell Kelly," Burris said.

"You draw the journal entry?"

"Why not. It's just government work."

"How about an order for release on Vine?"

"Give me a break. After the plea hearing and sentencing, okay?"

"Sure, sure," Darwin said.

Burris placed a meaty hand on the window.

"You know," he said. "Sometimes I think there's just too much shit in the world for it all to go down the toilet."

Avila waited for Darwin outside the courtroom. Primo came out the door in handcuffs, followed by a marshal. When Darwin appeared finally, the two men shook hands.

"You look like the cat that ate the canary," Avila said. "I hope you don't mind my dropping by. I'm not checking up on you. I had business downstairs and I wanted to see how it was going."

"My knees are still shaking," Darwin said.

"I'm dying to know what happened."

"They're taking a plea. Attempted possession."

"You're learning fast," Avila said. "Congratulations."

"Look, you may not like all of it."

"I can handle it."

"The judge may make the informant take the stand. I argued they didn't have probable cause on the affidavit. It looks like they may go after Dokes."

"It can't be helped. Luther Lee is a big boy."

"Still, it looks like Luther Lee might have to do his time."

"Luther Lee made his case when he made bail," Avila said.

"You mean he won't appear?"

Avila shrugged. "It wouldn't surprise me. Luther Lee isn't really ganged up. He's more an independent. He isn't beholden to anybody except one guy higher up. And the guy higher up has no exposure."

They walked together down a long hallway to elevators. A security guard watched them pass.

"Can I ask you something?" Darwin said.

"Sure, anything."

"I just wondered if you'd had any word on the domestic violence case? I keep thinking some miracle will happen and it might go away."

"I'm sorry, no."

"I was just wondering."

"Look, how about dinner tonight?" Avila asked.

"Thanks, but I'm teaching class."

"That's right. I forgot."

"I'm enjoying it. The students are great. It keeps me occupied. I can't thank you enough for letting me stay in the apartment."

"When you get on your feet, I'm charging you rent."

"No, please."

"Hey look. It's just a joke. We're friends, right?"

Darwin swallowed hard. "I could use some friends. The girl you met. She's my friend."

"She's a looker."

"It's more than that. I like her."

They rode down to the first floor and walked outside under a light rain.

"Forget Luther Lee," Avila said, buttoning his raincoat. "Maybe when all this clears up we can go into business."

"That would be good. Maybe I'll get over the feeling that I'm on the side of the enemy."

"The enemy?" Avila asked. "You mean your clients? They aren't the enemy, Jack. You didn't invent the law. You've been put on this earth as a go-between. You see to it that the rules are applied to everybody, even Arthur Vine. We can't have a world without rules, can we?"

"You're right, I know. Still, my conscience is giving me a little, say, heartburn."

"What about meeting after your class?" Avila said.

"Sorry, but I told Dolores I'd stop by. I had a message on the machine that Karla wants to talk. I think I'm going to meet her tonight."

"Maybe next week then," Avila said, starting down the steps.

At the bottom, Avila watched Darwin trudge up the street in a light rain. Darwin was hatless, his raincoat pulled tight around him, towing a briefcase. Avila walked around the corner to the Y and changed clothes. He thought he might take a long run through downtown, then head out the Avenues on a bus. If he timed it right, he could have dinner, then be at the apartment by the time Jack and Dolores finished whatever it was they were going to do. It was exciting, dropping out of the trees like this, hitting the sun-stained savanna on top of things.

·    ·    ·

He thought of himself as good in class, nervous perhaps, but animated and prepared. His own law school experience had been terrible, an exacting period of boredom, repetition, endless hectoring ridicule, and because of these memories, he tried to involve his students, employ sleight of hand and humor and context, not trying to get them to "think like a lawyer" the way so many of his professors had put it, but to reason and calculate and examine, the way any good thinking person might reason and calculate and examine, making lawyers closer to human, not insects gnawing away at the recesses of doctrine and cant.

That night he was behind a long table with a lectern perched on top, staring at the huge banked classroom, a green blackboard behind him. The students had passed forward their research questions and a young woman had come to put them on the table. The light in the room was harsh and cold but Darwin felt comfortable.

"All right, one last thing," he announced. "Our next problem is ethical." There was a rustle of noise, a faint expectancy. "You are a criminal lawyer and you represent a client charged in a state court with burglary. The burglary was committed at nine o'clock at night, and your client wants to get on the stand and swear he was at a soda shop having a cherry phosphate. In fact, there are reasons to believe he wasn't in the shop having a cherry phosphate, and you have reason to think he committed the burglary. What should you do? Let him take the stand even though you suspect he's lying? Or not? What is your responsibility as an officer of the court? Suppose that I am asking your opinion as chief counsel and you have to write me a three-page memorandum of law by next class.

"The second part of the problem is this. Suppose he takes the stand and lies. You don't know it at the time, but later you find out to a certainty that his testimony is a lie. What should you do, either at the time of trial, assuming you learn then, or later, assuming you learn then?"

A boy in the front row raised a hand.

"You want cases and everything?" he asked.

"It would be helpful to have cases," Darwin said.

Darwin said good night and watched the students file out of the big room, one by one. He gathered his materials and rushed through the rain to Frieda's next door, ordered a diet soda, and sipped it at a table in the back. Ten minutes later Dolores hurried in and joined him.

"I'm a fine one to talk about ethics," Darwin told her.

"The papers are graded anonymously, silly," she said. "Besides, I'd do well no matter who the teacher was, isn't that right?"

"Sure you would," Darwin laughed.

Dolores ordered hot tea. "I want you to try to stop worrying about us."

"You think it will stop raining?" Darwin said.

"Not tonight," Dolores said. "In spring. It will stop raining in spring. Could we order out tonight?"

"I have to leave about nine," Darwin said. "My wife wants to talk to me about the house."

"That's wonderful, John," Dolores said. She looked beautiful and fresh to Darwin. "We'll have a quick bite and you can leave. It's okay."

"When all this is over, maybe we can spend more time together. By the way, I won a case in federal court today. Well, maybe I didn't win, but I made a nice argument and a client got a break."

"Tell me about it over dinner. That's wonderful."

"I know a Mexican place for carryout," Darwin said. "It's out on Geary. On the way." Darwin finished his diet soda. "I want you to know that I've been honest with you about everything. There isn't a thing I haven't told you."

"I believe you, John," Dolores said. "Now, could we get some enchiladas? Nine o'clock is only two hours from now. And I've got to read the disciplinary rules tonight, thanks to you!"

"I'm not giving you any hints either."

"Nobody asked you to," Dolores laughed.

God, Darwin mused, just to hear innocent laughter. It was music to his ears, the caroling of angels. He remembered the times when he and his brother Adam would laugh at the slightest provocation, gales of hilarity, all-night laugh sessions when their mother would enter their rooms and tell them to hold it down. Laughter like rain, no letup until spring.

At the Aladdin, Darwin ordered hot chocolate. Perched on a hill above the Marina, the coffeehouse was a perennial favorite and always full, especially after work on rainy Friday nights in winter.

After waiting ten minutes, Darwin found a table in the corner and sat down under a Boston fern that had seen better days. Outside, a cable car went by and discharged its few rain-sodden passengers at the Marina, then turned and went back uphill to Union Square. Darwin allowed himself to hope that Karla would relent, and all this trouble would melt into an obscure corner of his mind, where it would fester for a few months, even a year, and then would heal cleanly. In his reverie, he was a lawyer and a teacher and he had begun to live again, to breathe the air of freedom and responsibility, a thing he knew he had not been doing since the death of his parents four years before, or maybe even longer, since the time that his brother Adam died.

Darwin glanced at his watch. Karla was already half an hour late, but he wasn't surprised. Karla was designed to be late, it was in her blood.

He ordered a second hot chocolate and made way for a young couple to share his table. They ordered a carafe of wine, drank it, paid their bill, and left. Surely, when Karla came to the coffeehouse she would admit that she'd lied about the beating, and they would reach an accommodation. Darwin had steeled himself to the thought that this was going to cost him a great deal of money. Even so, he had found a new strength. He had spent hours studying criminal law, trial tactics, cases. On his own way to a new life, equipped with new knowledge. Perhaps it was too early to think about how Dolores Hernandez fit into his new life. His friends in AA warned him constantly to live in the moment, but the stirrings of his love gave him strength, a sense of contentment. How could something so gentle be wrong?

At ten-thirty Darwin gave up on Karla. He paid his check and walked five blocks through the steady rain, his disappointment like an anchor around his neck. Perhaps Karla had lost her nerve, perhaps her lawyer had counseled her to stay away, perhaps anything. Darwin tried to breathe deeply, exorcise his frustration.

Angel drove up from Burlingame in just under an hour. Traffic was heavy, slowed by rain. He had worked all day, groomed and fed the horses, eaten a quick dinner. He wasn't used to freeway driving, it made him nervous, and his sight wasn't what it used to be. It was after eleven when he found Darwin's apartment in the Marina.

He knocked twice, softly. Darwin opened the door and stood in pale light.

"Mr. Darwin," Angel said meekly. "It's me, Angel."

"Oh God, come in out of the rain."

Darwin stood in the tiny hallway in his sock feet while Angel dripped rain. He wore an old poncho, heavy boots.

"I'm sorry to come so late," he said.

Darwin helped the old man with his poncho and hung it on a peg. Angel was carrying a clay urn in his arms, about the size of a coffeepot.

"I went to your house," Angel said.

"I don't live there now," Darwin explained. "I'm sorry you had to detour."

"Your wife, she told me where to find you."

"You had to wait in the Marina."

"Just an hour or so."

"I'm really sorry," Darwin said.

They sat in the living room, Darwin on a sofa, Angel on a hard chair from the kitchen. Darwin had been polishing his damp wing tips.

"I didn't want to call you, Mr. Darwin," Angel said. "It didn't seem the right thing to do. I wanted to see you in person."

"Did my wife say anything else?"

"Nothing sir. She told me where you lived."

Angel placed the urn on the floor between them.

"So, it's done," Darwin said.

"Yesterday."

"Would it be all right to ask how it went?"

"The vet she is very good. Traynor went to sleep. There was no pain."

"That's good," Darwin said. "No pain."

"He was a good horse, Mr. Darwin."

"He had a long life."

"I remember him well, sir. When he was young he was a very strong horse. Do you remember him?"

"He had great spirit," Darwin said.

"Your father made a good choice in horses."

"My father was a fine rider. I used to ride behind my brother. Do you remember that?"

"Every Sunday for many years," Angel said.

"You're sure about the pain?" Darwin asked again.

"He was old, Mr. Darwin sir. He wanted to sleep."

Darwin sat quietly. What had Sophocles said? Judge no man happy until he is dead?

"You think horses are capable of happiness, Angel?"

"I am certain of it."

"They're marvelous animals, aren't they?"

"Better than men, Mr. Darwin."

"I wonder why that should be?"

"Perhaps men have too many desires."

"I think you are wise, Angel."

"I live around horses."

"Perhaps if more people lived around horses there would be better men."

"It is true, Mr. Darwin."

Darwin leaned over and touched the cold clay urn. He would take Traynor up to Tahoe and give him to the lake.

"I read a story once," Darwin said softly. "It was about war. About horses and mules floating with their legs broken in bloody water. It was a worse sight than the wounds of soldiers. Worse even than the deaths of children from cholera. Do you think that could be true?"

"Not of children, Mr. Darwin," Angel said.

"No, I suppose not." Darwin leaned back in his seat. "Tell the vet thank you. She did a fine job."

Angel pushed the urn toward Darwin. "This horse belongs to you, Mr. Darwin. He was a good one. You remember him like he was, young and strong. You come down to the stable soon."

"As soon as I can," Darwin said. "Maybe you could teach me to ride again."

"You get another horse, Mr. Darwin."

"I'd like to."

"I have to go home," Angel said.

Darwin helped him with the poncho. They stood in the open doorway together, rain slashing inside. It was a dreary neighborhood, stucco apartment buildings, alleys, cars parked off the street, two wheels on the sidewalks, a red glow from Ghirardelli Square like forest fires. It occurred to Darwin that he might just sell the Pacific Heights place and start over. Perhaps his desire for the house was impure.

"Be careful driving home," Darwin said.

"It is crazy on the freeway," Angel laughed.

"Crazy. Very crazy."

"You come to the stables?"

Darwin watched Angel weave his way through the parked cars, go around a corner. When he was alone, Darwin opened the urn and buried his hands in the ash and wept.

The weight room was empty, eerie and supernatural with denatured light. David Avila wore gym shorts and nothing else, pumping iron in silence. On a bench he did curls, five, ten, fifteen, switching arms, feeling the pain rise and subside, a threnody of pain. It was after eleven and the Y would close at midnight, time enough to enjoy the pleasure of pain. He would lift weights until he had obliterated his vision, until he could feel himself pass through to other worlds, to broad, nearly treeless savannas where tough grass and thorny shrubs hid danger. He did a set of overhead presses, pounding iron, hearing the metal ping as he dropped the weights to the floor, pushing himself up through more and more repetitions. His body was covered with a thin layer of sweat.

Zack came in through a door from the basketball courts.

"Hello, Counselor," he said.

There was an echo in the stillness. Avila finished a set and stood in front of the weight bench. Zack was off to one side, lumbering in a trench coat made from real leather.

"Nice coat," Avila said.

"They let Arthur Vine out of jail?"

"Not yet. Next week maybe."

"Do we have worries?" Zack asked. He stood motionless, running one hand through his black heavy beard.

"Some," Avila told him. "I went to the hearing. The stalking horse I hired did a good job. Maybe too good."

"He must have."

"How's Luther Lee?"

"He's hanging, man."

"His hearing is in two weeks. I filed a copycat motion."

"So, what's he supposed to think?"

"It's fifty-fifty. That's as good as I can do right now. If the government produces the informant, Luther Lee will go down. It's a technical thing."

"It's a fucking technical thing," Zack said.

"You want to hear it? Okay. Judge Kelly wanted to hear from the informant before he sent Vine to trial. That's because the cops didn't actually see the dope. The DEA didn't want Vine badly enough to produce the informant. They may want Luther Lee that bad. So now do you understand?"

Avila toweled his body.

"Luther Lee can do five years," Zack said.

"Of course he can. He may get his chance."

"It's your job to see it doesn't happen."

"Hey, I might get him off. But not if that informant testifies. You tell Luther Lee, will you?"

"Luther Lee will be okay."

"What are you saying, Zack?"

"Get the informant on the stand."

"Come on, Zack, you can't off a government agent."

"Fuck that," Zack said.

"Okay, so you want the informant on the stand."

"Make it happen," Zack said.

Zack's leather coat was shedding water, making a pool on the floor.

"Listen, Zack," Avila said, "I had to give over ten thousand to my stalking horse, just to see him run."

"Are you holding me up?"

"Do I have a gun, Zack?"

Zack buried his hands in the coat. Avila did a set of curls, both arms straining against dead weight. Zack took out a wad of hundred-dollar bills, counted out forty. He tucked them under a loose weight.

"Give me the informant," Zack said.

"You'll know in two weeks," Avila said. "If they don't put him on the stand, Luther Lee will walk. You'll get your money back."

"Fuck the money," Zack said. "It ain't the money."

"Okay Zack, it's the principle of the thing."

"I want the name."

"Don't think about offing the snitch, Zack. Don't even think it."

Zack headed for the door, then stopped.

"You're a smart lawyer you are," he said. "The way I see it, the world is full of smart lawyers. You know what that makes you?"

Avila dropped the weight bar. It hit the floor hard and made a loud echo.

"What does that make me?" Avila asked.

"Just like me," Zack said.

Avila laughed. "I'll take Luther Lee up to court next week. But you and me, Zack, let's not get into it."

"Fear is a good thing," Zack said. "It sets limits."

"You're a drug dealer, Zack," Avila said. "You know what that makes you?"

Zack waited. Avila slipped on a sweatshirt and came up to him, standing close.

"What does that make me?" Zack said.

"A valued client," Avila told him.


Creature of habit, that was Karla. Darwin knew it implicitly, and in following her to the tanning salon, he had acted on his knowledge, though it remained implicit. Only three days after commencing his surveillance did he finally admit that he'd been wasting his time.

Down on the Marina, Darwin had rented an anonymously gray Taurus from a local agency. He would park at the end of the block and sit in his rented car, waiting for Karla to emerge from her cocoon. She was easy to follow, driving the gold Mercedes in heavy traffic down on Bay Street, making her rounds, spending money and leaving an oozy trail of heavily commercialized wandering. She was a clock going around and around in well-oiled circles, Darwin in cadence right behind her—tanning salon, aerobics studio, flower shop, lunch on Ghirardelli Square with her only friend, Gina, over to the liquor store, coming out with a paper sack containing bottles of vodka, lime juice, mixers, menthol cigarettes. Darwin had her on radar, and she showed up in clear blue and green, but there was nothing, really nothing to see. Sometimes Darwin would cruise the Pacific Heights house in early evening and catch a glimpse of her on the back patio, staring at the bay as she waltzed her glass of vodka and lime around the porch, staring at the bay or at nothing, motionless as a drunken Buddha. Then Darwin would park at the end of the block and fritter away the night waiting for something to happen, but it never did. Darwin could have recited her routine in his sleep, it was that regular. And on the third day of his vigil, it dawned on Darwin that Karla wouldn't see her boyfriend in any of the usual ways or places. She'd learned her lesson. He would have to track her in a different way, using a different method.

Back at the Marina apartment, Darwin called his divorce lawyer, setting him to the task of collecting all the canceled checks from their joint accounts. They ordered copies of all her Gold Card receipts faxed to the lawyer. Darwin didn't go into his law office, didn't bother to trail her on her rounds. He returned the rental car. Two days later he had amassed three large boxes full of documents, canceled checks and Gold Card receipts that would account for one year in the life of his wife. A trail of money, the only trail that really counted for Karla.

Darwin bought a business calendar and began to go through the checks and receipts, entering the checks and receipts on each day. He listened to classical music for hours, making his entries, studying the form of his wife. He put her under his own electron microscope. He had to believe something would turn up, something like a whiff of rarefied air.

It was a new kind of battle for Jack. Stealthy. Surely he would catch a whiff of blood.

# III

# *the punishment phase*

Cooley and Vorhees caught the case on rebound from a squad that recognized the MO. It was early Monday morning and Vorhees had just walked in from his long weekend with Alisha, sleeping late, eating chili, going to the zoo.

When Cooley arrived a few minutes later he looked snappy in a new wool suit his wife had bought him with bingo winnings. They had a talk with their lieutenant and went over to the Avenues and parked crossways on the sidewalk in front of a yellow stucco single-story duplex with a concrete front yard and two tree roses in bloom on the porch. It had rained all weekend and the sky was blue, the air cold, so cold you could almost see your breath. Two women were standing by the front door with a uniformed cop, one older woman with her arm around a younger woman who was crying.

The uniform hustled over.

"She's inside," he said.

"You been inside?" Cooley asked him.

They talked in whispers as if they were in a funeral parlor, which in a sense they were.

"Just quick like," the uniform said.

"Did you?"

"I didn't touch anything."

Vorhees walked over to the two women and told them to hang on he'd be right out. The young one looked pale, as if she might faint.

Vorhees followed Cooley inside the duplex, down a short corridor, and into the main living room. It had a comfortable feel, low-ceilinged and cozy, light yellow wallpaper, potted plants, clinging ivy, a dining nook with a fridge. In the back there was a small bedroom, a bath. Plates of Mexican carryout leftovers were on a table in the dining nook.

"In here," Vorhees heard Cooley say.

Vorhees went down a short hall past linen closets, one bookshelf with a few textbooks on it, and a couple of vases of dried flowers. It was a nice place, he thought, a place that had "young woman" written all over it. He noticed that the bed in the bedroom was unmade, sheets rumpled, a coverlet thrown back. There was a picture of Christ above the bed, a shepherd tending a flock of lambs against the background of an ancient hillside, dark sun at right angles. Vorhees could see legs spread-eagled in the bathroom next to the tub.

Cooley was leaning over the corpse. She was a nice-looking girl, medium-length brown hair, olive skin, delicate hands. Both men stood in the bathroom and looked at each other, letting their eyes roam, visualizing. Vorhees had been taught to let himself go to the heart of a crime scene, not think until there was a reason to think. Right away he knew the girl was straight, not some part-time hooker off Turk, not that it made any difference. That part was simple. Vorhees told Cooley he'd be back, he'd talk to the women outside.

Vorhees asked the uniform to call forensics and ask for Mattingly. Both women watched him with desperate alertness. He went over and introduced himself. The older woman in her bathrobe lived next door, the younger was a friend of the dead girl. Vorhees took out his notebook and wrote down the name of the dead girl: Dolores Hernandez.

"I don't know anything," the older woman said. "I just let her use the phone."

The younger woman was Sandra. Vorhees felt sorry for her, all dressed up like a Catholic-school girl, dark blue wool skirt, white shirt, a gray vest with sprays of roses on its breast. She had a blue beret in her hands and was working it like prayer beads.

"I'm sorry, miss," Vorhees said. "Whatever you can tell me now will really help."

"Is she dead?" Sandra said.

"I'm afraid so. I'm sorry."

Sandra cried softly.

"I came by this morning," she said. "We go to law school together. I live down the avenues here. We walk over to Geary and catch the bus every morning. We talked Friday and she said she'd be waiting for me. I knocked and knocked and nobody came to the door."

"You went inside?"

"The door was unlocked. I thought that was odd."

"You went to the back?"

Sandra looked away, eyes brimming.

"Okay, this won't take long, Sandra," Vorhees told her. "You went to the back, you saw her?"

Sandra nodded, yes.

"You didn't touch anything, did you?"

Sandra shook her head, no.

"It's important to tell me if you touched anything."

"Just the door handle."

"You didn't see anything else?"

"No, I was scared."

"Sure you were," Vorhees said.

"Who did this?" Sandra asked.

"We don't know yet."

"I went next door and called," Sandra said.

This kid is okay, Vorhees thought. She's holding up better than anyone has a right to expect.

The older woman said, "She came over and asked if she could call. I've been with her all that time."

"You see or hear anything?" Vorhees asked her.

"No, I really didn't."

"No sounds of struggle? A fight? Furniture or something banging around? No screams?"

"No, I'm sorry. I didn't. And I was home all weekend."

Sandra sniffled, wiped her nose with a handkerchief.

"Who could do this to Dolores?" Vorhees said.

"Her folks are in Fresno. Near there. Who's going to tell them?"

"We'll take care of it."

"She was a law student. We go downtown."

"How long have you known her?"

"Just this semester. We're first year."

"How old is Dolores?"

"Oh gosh, maybe thirty. I don't really know."

"She have a boyfriend?"

"Yes. She wouldn't tell me much."

"It looks like she had dinner in there. Do you think she could have been having dinner with her boyfriend?"

"It could be."

"You know the boyfriend's name?"

"It was somebody from school. She was pretty quiet about it. I think it was kind of a secret."

"A secret boyfriend. Why would she have a secret boyfriend?"

"She was shy. I don't know."

"How did she seem when you talked to her Friday?"

"Fine. Normal."

"What did you talk about?"

"I saw her at school, lunch break. We don't have any classes together, but we see each other all the time. Just the usual talk. Riding the bus Monday morning."

"That's all?"

"We talked some about classes."

"She mention her boyfriend in the conversation?"

"No, no."

"How did you know about her boyfriend?"

"She'd tell me she had a date."

"You ever see her unhappy over this guy?"

"No, nothing like that."

Well, Vorhees thought, you'd be surprised about unhappiness. Sometimes people get involved and can't get uninvolved.

"Do you know her parents' names?"

"No, just mom and dad. Their photos are in the hall."

Vorhees took down Sandra's name and address. He wrote down the name of the next-door neighbor and let both women go. He started two uniformed cops on a neighborhood canvass and went back inside. Cooley was still in the bathroom.

"She put up a little struggle," Cooley said. He pointed to a broken cosmetic bottle, a towel rack on the floor. They had seen a magazine rack overturned in the living room, a sofa cushion on the floor. "She didn't last long, but she tried. There's a wet towel in the tub with blood on it. Maybe our boy got some blood on him too."

"She's a law student," Vorhees told him. "Her girlfriend came by to get her this morning. They were going to ride the bus downtown. The door was unlocked so she came in."

"The door was unlocked."

"Probably opened the door, let the guy in. Or maybe our guy went out and didn't throw the button."

Vorhees looked at the bathroom, yellow-and-blue paper, a vanity, a shattered towel rack on the floor. A tray of girl things on wall pegs, jerry-built and cheap. In the hall, Vorhees looked at mom and dad, two nice people in Sunday best. Cooley was in the bath, picking up a lock of the dead girl's hair with a pencil.

"Let's get Mattingly," Cooley said.

"She's been called."

"Our victim's been beaten up pretty badly," Cooley muttered. "There's a lot of blood in the shower stall. Her face is a mess."

Vorhees wandered into the small bedroom. There were no windows and it was claustrophobic. The way it looked, two people had been in bed. Something complicated was going on, but Vorhees couldn't tell what it was quite yet.

"He opened her right eye to the bone," Cooley called out.

Vorhees stood in the bedroom, absorbed in the photographs of country people, stuffed animals. The photos looked like brothers and sisters, kids with round faces, short haircuts, the girls in high school cheerleader outfits. There was a neat pile of girl clothes on the floor by the closet, a terry robe there too. There was a spot of blood on the robe, up near the collar.

Vorhees wandered into the kitchen and looked at the paper plates of leftover Mexican food, some rice, a ragged edge of enchilada. She'd had dinner with somebody else, that much was certain. Inside the refrigerator was all the usual stuff. He stood there for a while in the gauzy half-light of early morning, getting a sense of the place. Happy. Temporary. Cozy. Regular. Normal.

"See anything?" Cooley shouted.

"She had dinner with somebody. She had a secret boyfriend, maybe him. Mexican carryout. I think she was in bed with somebody too."

"Our guy strangled her," Cooley said loudly. "I'd bet on it. Killed her in the shower. Banged her head on the tile and made her pass out. Then strangled her. If I was a betting man, I'd say he sodomized her too. She was out when all that was going on. At least she caught that much of a break."

Vorhees went back to the bathroom and kneeled down with Cooley. The cut above her right eye was blue, with white bone behind it. She was a very pretty girl, long eyelashes, full mouth. Her mouth was closed and a crease of blood had dried on her upper lip.

"I saw a Rolodex out there," Cooley said. He walked around Vorhees, who sat down on the toilet and looked at the girl. Then he looked at the shower stall, no soap, no washrag, no shampoo. She hadn't been taking a shower at all. The killer put her in there for fun. Just like what happened to Lisa Tracy.

Vorhees went to his hands and knees and searched the floor for particles, anything. It seemed clean, except for some spots of blood near the body. Cooley came back inside the bathroom and the two men stood wedged near the door.

"I talked to Sandra, the girlfriend. There was a guy in her life."

"You think he had dinner here?"

"Yeah. I do."

"Slept here."

"For a while."

"You think a guy could sit down to Mexican carryout and then do this?"

"It's pretty cold."

"It happened to Lisa," Cooley said.

"He kills her in the shower. He cleans her up. He cleans himself up, piles her clothes neatly in the bedroom. He's so calm when he leaves he doesn't even bother to lock the door behind him."

"Just like Lisa, except Dolores put up a little fight."

"Just a little."

"Lisa didn't have the time."

"That's because she thought she was having fun," Vorhees said.

"Maybe the boyfriend has a last name that begins with J."

"Maybe he's a fancy dresser."

Cooley turned and did a walk-through of the kitchen and living room. He twirled the Rolodex.

"Maybe we'll get prints off the forks," Cooley said.

"Maybe we won't have to wait that long," Vorhees said. "She's a law student downtown. She's popular. She knows a lot of people. This girl was straight and people liked her. Somebody down at the law school knows about the boyfriend."

"Why keep him a secret?"

Vorhees looked at the print of Christ and his sheep.

"She was a good girl," he said.

They went out into the cold air. One uniformed cop was standing near the door. He told them he'd found only two people at home on the entire block, an elderly couple who didn't know from Adam. He said he'd canvass later in the afternoon and that evening when folks began to return from their jobs and errands. Squad cars had blocked the avenue and it was quiet, traffic noise on Geary, a helicopter overhead, wind in the phone wires.

"Sandra says Dolores was happy," Vorhees said.

They were waiting for Mattingly and her crew.

"Yeah?" Cooley said.

"Maybe having a secret boyfriend is a good thing."

"That's a thought."

At the end of the block a black Buick stopped. Vorhees could see Mattingly in the car, along with her crew, the photographer and fingerprint guy.

"We gotta call her folks," Cooley said. "You want to flip for it?"

"I'll do it," Vorhees said. "I've never done it. There has to be a first time."

"Let's go down to the law school. Peck around."

"I wish there was a good way to tell them."

"Who?"

"The parents," Vorhees said. "Another way to tell them."

"There isn't," Cooley told him.

"No, there isn't."

Deborah Mattingly walked down the street.

"There isn't any fucking place to park," she said.

"You remember the work you did on Lisa Tracy?" Cooley asked her.

"The bathing beauty on Turk?"

"The one."

"Yeah, I remember," Mattingly said, teasing back her red hair.

"I want you to do the same good work here," Cooley said.

"Okay, Detective," Mattingly said. "We'll spend some time here and send her off. You think it's the same guy?"

Cooley shrugged and Mattingly took her crew inside the apartment.

The two detectives got in their car. Vorhees rolled down the window and looked at the quiet block of row houses, tree roses, pigeons on eaves.

"You know," Cooley said, "when you were outside I checked her phone messages. Her folks called on Saturday and said they looked forward to seeing her on Easter. I guess that means she was dead on Friday night. It's enough to break your heart."

"Let's go," Vorhees said. "Let's get out of here."

Vorhees was in the registrar's office, a cold square of the world on a mezzanine above a central foyer. The woman across from him was about sixty, with frosted hair and a beaklike face that could frighten a professional wrestler. He had left Cooley in the dean's office, and a receptionist had walked him down to the office of Miss Farnsworth. Vorhees expected to have his knuckles rapped with a ruler any time.

"This is about one of our students?" she asked.

Wooden blinds covered the windows, and a computer on her desk purred green noise into the room.

"Dolores Hernandez," Vorhees said. "She's a first-year student."

"Of course," said Miss Farnsworth.

"What can you tell me about her?"

"Her records are confidential." Miss Farnsworth nodded slightly, as if she'd had the last word. "I'm afraid it is California law. You wouldn't want me to break the law?"

"Dolores Hernandez is dead. She was found murdered in her apartment this morning by a friend."

"Oh dear," the registrar said. "Oh dear, oh dear."

"So, I have to ask some questions."

"I see. I'm sorry."

"She was raped and strangled. It's a matter of some urgency."

"But there is still the law."

"Dolores Hernandez won't be needing her privacy rights," Vorhees said.

The registrar left the office for a few minutes. Vorhees waited in the striped light, listening to the computer hum. When Farnsworth returned she was carrying a large blue envelope. She sat down and punched something into the computer.

"What do you want to know?"

"Basic information on her application."

"Dolores Hernandez," she said. "Thirty-one years old. First-year law. She graduated from Santa Clara five years ago in art history and Spanish. She was a top student, working while she was in college. She had a small needs scholarship for her first two years down there. She did very well on the LSAT, top three percent. I'm looking at a little essay she wrote on why she wanted to go to law school." Miss Farnsworth sat in front of the screen, her lined face scratched by hazy blue light. "She did quite well first semester. Average in the upper eighties. That's an A here."

"Do you mind if I read her essay?" Vorhees asked.

Miss Farnsworth handed him the application materials and Vorhees read through the essay, about five hundred words of idealistic generalities. He studied a photograph of Dolores Hernandez taken during her college days, pretty and serious, a young woman looking into her future with bright eyes.

"What's her schedule now?" Vorhees asked.

"She has a regular load. All our first-year students take basically the same classes. Dolores takes contract law, torts, criminal law, and property. Both semesters are the same, with tiny variations. Let's see, she took an introduction-to-the-profession class first semester, and this semester she has research and writing at night. Some students take research first semester, then professions. It's fifteen hours in class, and a lot of work."

"A friend of hers said she had no outside job."

"Oh, I don't think so. We don't allow our first-year students to take outside work. I imagine some do, but on the sly, so to speak."

"You ever meet her?"

"I don't remember her," she said. "We have a thousand students. We're the largest daytime law school in the country."

"So, I'd be right in saying she was a good student. Good grades. Nothing unusual."

"I'm afraid that's all I know about her."

"Could you give me a list of her teachers and classes? We'll have to talk to some of the students."

"I'm sure our students aren't involved."

"I'm sure. Just to get background."

Farnsworth printed out a list of the classes and names of professors. Vorhees looked it over, classes midmorning to late afternoon, then an evening class on Monday, Wednesday, and Friday. Vorhees looked at the schedule, thinking back to the dead girl's Friday, classes midmorning, lunch on the veranda or in the cafeteria, maybe some studying at the law library. Maybe she hung around school until dark, went to her research class. Then she met her boyfriend and went home and got killed. Vorhees thanked the registrar and joined Cooley down the hall.

Cooley was leaning on a marble column, talking to a young man about twenty-four years old, wavy hair, V-necked sweater and suede coat.

"This is Stan," Cooley said when Vorhees came by.

Stan nodded warily.

"Stan goes to property class with Dolores," Cooley said.

"Hi, Stan."

"Hello," Stan said, flustered.

"You know Dolores Hernandez?"

"Sure, we go to property class."

"Oh yeah," Vorhees said.

"Stan says he was in research class with Dolores on Friday night, isn't that right, Stan?"

Cooley arched an eyebrow.

"Research and writing, yeah," Stan said. "Friday night she was there, front row center."

"Stan here says Dolores was okay Friday night."

"We sit in front," Stan said.

"Stan here gave me a list of people Dolores knew. Stan has been very helpful."

"Did you know Dolores well?" Vorhees asked.

Stan was shifting his weight, foot to foot.

"Nah," he said. "We just went to class together."

"Tell me about her," Vorhees said. "What was she like?"

"She was nice. Quiet. But she did okay in class. I mean she talked and stuff."

"You ever date her, Stan?" Cooley asked.

"I'm married," Stan said.

Cooley rubbed his face. "I'm sorry, Stan. We have to check the various angles."

"Sure, that's okay," Stan said.

"Did Dolores have troubles?" Vorhees asked. "Ever see her bruised, maybe depressed, tired?"

"No, nothing like that at all. She always seemed happy."

"What about boyfriends?"

"You mean around school?"

"She have any boyfriends?"

"She didn't have any boyfriends like that," Stan said.

"Like what?" Cooley asked.

"I mean, well. I mean people thought she was tight with Professor Darwin."

"Professor Darwin?" Vorhees asked.

"Yeah, you know. Research and writing."

Vorhees studied his printout. Research and writing, Monday, Wednesday, and Friday, five to seven in the evening. Darwin, adjunct instructor.

"What's it mean?" Cooley asked. "Getting tight?"

"They'd go over to Frieda's after class. Shoot the breeze. Drink coffee."

"That could get on a guy's nerves," Cooley said.

"Not on mine," Stan told him.

"Anything else?" Cooley said.

"Hey look," Stan protested. "I barely know the girl. I think it's awful what happened to her. She seemed okay to me. Real nice. We talked sometimes in class. Her real friend was Sandy Valerio. They were tight. Maybe you should talk to her."

"You think of anything else, give us a call," Vorhees said. He handed Stan one of his cards and the boy walked away, down the polished marble hallway.

The two detectives walked down the mezzanine stairs to the first floor. Behind them was a wide corridor banked on either side by sets of double oak doors. Students came and went all around them.

"What a prick," Cooley said.

"Stan? You mean Stanley is a prick?"

"Little fucking lawyer, that's what he is."

"Where'd you dig him up?" Vorhees asked.

"I got a list of classes. They let me go in and make an announcement. I have to give it to him, he was one of the few who raised his hand."

"What'd the dean have to say?"

"Gave me a printout and referred me to the registrar."

"The registrar is a beauty," Vorhees said. "But she did show me the girl's application folder. Wanted to be a lawyer to change the world."

"The first thing to change is to shrink the number of lawyers."

"You don't think the world needs all of them?" Vorhees asked.

"Ah, let's get out of here," Cooley said, heading for the glass doors to the patio and courtyard.

"A thousand a year," Vorhees called out.

"That's a lot," Cooley said.

They were parked in a red zone on McAllister. Sitting in the car, Cooley wrote out some notes.

"You call Fresno?" Cooley asked.

"Yeah," Vorhees answered.

"Go pretty bad, did it?"

"Very bad," Vorhees admitted.

"Look, I ran Dolores Hernandez while you were doing that. She came back clean as a whistle."

"I knew she would," Vorhees said.

"Just a nice kid from Fresno."

"Her folks are coming down tonight," Vorhees told Cooley.

"They know anything, you think?"

"I didn't have the heart to ask."

"We'll catch them at the station."

"There goes another night with my wife."

"Me too," Cooley said. "Not with your wife. With mine."

"Don't be funny," Vorhees laughed. "Six more weeks for Alisha. She's in that phase. Waddles around and everything hurts her back. I feel sorry for her."

They decided to kill time running another quick canvass on the Avenues up and down the block where Dolores Hernandez lived.

They'd attend the forensic meeting with Mattingly that afternoon, then both go home for a couple of hours before getting back downtown to see the kid's parents. They decided they'd catch this Professor Darwin after class, around seven. Maybe he knew something fresh.

Roses and more roses, two dozen long-stemmed red roses every week, week in and week out, delivered to the Pacific Heights house on Karla's account. Darwin charted the transactions on his calendar of events, Tuesday and Thursday like clockwork, and he had to wonder if Karla ever had delivered roses to that special someone. The idea struck him in bed one night like a spike of adrenaline. He had been up studying for criminal law and procedure, boning up for class, and he sat bolt upright and began to sweat.

The next morning he drove to Amy's Flowers in Ghirardelli Square, a boutique under a glass atrium. He waited as the owner served two customers.

"How can I help you?" the owner asked Darwin. She was a lively woman in a gray-and-pink smock, sun-lined face, body by Coppertone. "You look like you could use a bouquet!"

"I'd like to see some of your delivery records," Darwin said. "My name is Jack Darwin. My wife is Karla. I'm sure you know her."

"Oh certainly sir," she said. "I know Karla very well. She's an excellent customer."

"You have your delivery records, I presume?"

"Well, yes, we do," she said noncommittally. "But I'm not sure what this is about. I don't know if I should."

"It's about looking at your delivery records," Darwin snapped. "Just give me time to go through her orders. I'll sit in the back and be quiet."

"I don't know," the woman said anxiously.

"Look," Darwin said harshly. "There's a messy divorce going on right now. I'd be lying to you if I said there wasn't. I want to see those records. I'm doing you a favor coming to you like this. My lawyer suggested that he subpoena you and your records for a deposition. You'd have to come downtown and haul your records with you and sit around a law office all day on California Street. It could take the better part of six or eight hours. You'd have to close down, pack everything in boxes. I told him to hold off, that I'd do it myself as a courtesy to you and the shop. I know what it would be like shutting down part of the day. It's up to you, but I'm here to make things easy for you. You know how courts and lawyers can be."

It took the woman about five seconds to make up her mind. "Well, why not?" she said.

Darwin took a seat in her small rear office. The woman shuffled through file drawers, drawing up ten or fifteen carbon pads. Everything in black and white, six months back. The rest were at home, she explained. She'd have to get them and bring them down if it meant that much to Darwin.

It took Darwin an hour to go through the files. Hundreds of deliveries. Gladiolas to the hospital, flowers to rest homes, private residences, business openings. Mums to mom, daisies to sis, spring bouquets to Aunt Bee. But there was nothing from Karla to someone special. Darwin felt a flash of disappointment; then he thanked the woman, walked quickly through the square, and drove home to the Marina apartment.

Even in battle, not every patrol makes contact.

That afternoon Karla suffered a panic attack. She had been to see Rowe for a talk, mostly about money and her upcoming deposition, to review police files on the domestic violence case. Rowe told her he could postpone the deposition until March if it made her feel better. In his opinion, with a wife beater for a client, the other lawyer would make a nice, quick offer and it would be over soon. Besides, there was always a chance Darwin would sell the house, just to get out of his financial bind, and they could all get fat.

She rode down the elevator and walked out onto California Street and stood on the sidewalk surrounded by scurrying people. For a moment, she thought she might faint. Her ears buzzed as though she'd just been slapped. Images of car crashes slipped through her head, blood and carnage and severed limbs, and she knew she was having a panic attack.

She walked a block up California and went into an Irish pub. The bar was dark and smelled of ale. She used a pay phone in back to call Avila at his office.

"Karla, what are you doing?" Avila said coldly.

"I just wanted to hear your voice," she panted.

"Hang up. Don't do this."

"Please, David."

"What's happened?"

"Nothing has happened." Two Australian sailors were playing darts nearby, casting glances at her.

"Where are you?" Avila said.

"In a pub on California Street."

"What's happened?" Avila demanded to know.

"Nothing. I just felt sick."

"We'll meet tonight. Why not?"

"Oh God, thank you, David. I have to give testimony next month in the divorce."

"Is that all?" Avila asked.

"That's part of it."

"I told you. Trust me. Nothing will go wrong."

"I still don't understand you."

"Never mind that. Listen to me. I have depositions all afternoon at the Hyatt tomorrow. Down on the Embarcadero. Do you know where that is, Karla?"

"Of course, David."

"I'll finish up by five. I'll keep the room. Come up to the revolving bar on top around six. We'll have a drink and I'll fuck you all night long."

Karla heard the phone tick dead. But she could still hear David's voice in her head, an imaginary umbilical connecting her with something. Sometimes she heard other voices as well, angry voices welling up in her mind, accusatory, threatening. She made her way home and stood on the patio looking at Jack's roses. Karla hadn't made her bed for a week and she hadn't eaten a decent meal in twice that long.

She walked a vodka rocks upstairs and took a hot bath.

Dark clouds and cold wind, both men full of dread. The Hernandez couple had been to the basement morgue and were now waiting in Lieutenant Lightfoot's office. Grace had been talking with them, and when Cooley and Vorhees came in both of the parents were crying.

Mr. Hernandez was a prominent-looking man with dark curly hair, his wife small and tired from grief.

"These are the detectives I told you about," the lieutenant said. "Cooley and Vorhees."

Mr. Hernandez looked up. "Do you know what happened to my daughter?" he asked.

"Not yet," Vorhees told him. "Have you seen her?"

"Yes. Thank you for calling."

Vorhees thought the father was doing fine now. He'd hold up until he got back home, about the time of the first visit to the mortuary. Then it would hit him really hard.

"You'll find who did this," he said flatly. It wasn't a question, so Vorhees let it pass. The woman cried softly and steadily. The lieutenant got up from her desk and put an arm around her.

"Do you know anything that might help us?" Cooley asked the man.

"I don't think so," he said.

"What about an old boyfriend? Somebody that might have stalked her. Carried a torch, something like that."

"I don't think so," the man said. "Everybody liked Dolores."

"Did she work part-time here in San Francisco?"

"No, she had saved her money for school."

"Where did she work?"

"Down in Santa Clara."

"What about down there? Did she ever tell you about any trouble she might have had down there?"

"No, nothing. She worked at a travel agency. We visited her. There was nothing she mentioned. I think she would have said something to us."

"Was she troubled when you last talked?"

"No. She was fine."

"Any friends she talked about?" Cooley continued.

"Students. People she went to class with."

"A girl named Sandy?" Cooley asked.

"Yes. Sandra. They were close."

"And there was nothing in Santa Clara?" Vorhees added. "Anything. Any little thing that might help us."

"No, nothing."

"Did she mention seeing a teacher up here?" Cooley asked.

"No. Was she seeing a teacher?"

"I don't know, Mr. Hernandez. We'll find out."

"She was a good girl," the man said.

His wife could not console herself.

Lieutenant Lightfoot spent ten minutes telling the Hernandez couple how the investigation would run. Cooley and Vorhees shook hands with the man, then went down the hall and got a soda.

"Everybody's girl is a good girl," Cooley said.

"In this case, I think it's true."

"Yeah," Cooley said, shaking his head. "So do I."

Fatigue at five they called it, a forensic meeting with Mattingly's crew, Vorhees and Cooley, Lieutenant Lightfoot, all cramped under harsh fluorescent glare around a table covered with photos, charts, autopsy reports, diagrams, and lists of evidence. Vorhees had slipped home for a ham sandwich and baby report, changed his clothes, then come back in heavy traffic. The light outside Lightfoot's office was dim and unmodulated. Cooley was down to shirtsleeves, big half-moons of sweat under the arms.

"I declare this meeting open," Cooley laughed tiredly.

"Do it, men and women," Lightfoot told them. She was fingering photographs, a mental catalog.

"I'll go," Vorhees said. "Dolores Hernandez, thirty-one years old, no record. First-year law student. No witnesses on the first and second canvass. We have a picture of this that matches our picture of Lisa Tracy. Same MO, enough that both Cooley and I think the same guy did it. There was a struggle and we'd love some hair, skin, fingernails, anything you've got."

"It's all bagged and tagged," Mattingly said.

"Cooley retrieved the phone messages. One from her folks on Saturday morning. The Rolodex is in evidence, but we've had no time to get through it yet. There was twenty dollars and some change in her purse, all her credit cards were still there, or at least it looks like it. About four hundred dollars of electronics are still in the apartment. I think we can rule out burglary. We've got a line on a secret boyfriend, and at least one student says she's tight with a professor down at the law school. We think she let whoever killed her inside the apartment. Opened the door. That fits with our idea of the Lisa Tracy perp as some kind of gentleman. Nice clothes, clean-cut. Either way, she put up a little fight. Our visual search didn't turn anything."

Mattingly stood and walked around the table once.

"You can see the photos," she said. "The final autopsy won't be out until tomorrow, but the preliminary is here. She died Friday night. We'll have more later."

"Dolores Hernandez was alive at seven Friday night. A guy we talked to was in class with her until then." Cooley wiped his face with a wet towel.

"The ME says she was probably unconscious when she was strangled." Mattingly handed out Xerox copies of the preliminary report. "Somebody behind her with an arm around her throat. Like Tracy there were no fingerprint marks or palm prints either one. Takes her out of the shower, puts her on the ground, maybe sodomizes her after she was dead. What a thought." Mattingly finished her rounds and sat. "Tearing in the anal passage. Here's a good one. She had sexual intercourse, but no evidence of force or trauma."

"Fingerprints?" Lightfoot asked.

"Four good sets. We know two are hers. Sandra is on the door, we think. Two unknowns."

"She had dinner with somebody Friday night," Vorhees said.

"The unknowns are a thumb and forefinger. We're running them now. I put a priority on this."

Lightfoot studied some photographs. She passed them to Cooley and Vorhees.

"This is definitely number two," she said. "Are we agreed on this?"

Vorhees and Cooley said they agreed.

"I have a Christmas Eve friend I'm still picturing," Vorhees said.

"Right, our lady from Cincinnati," Lightfoot said. "You guys might try to figure out why Dolores let this guy in her house."

Mattingly only shrugged. "She knew the guy?"

"Makes sense to me," Lightfoot said. "I want to hear. I'm going to have to make a policy on newspaper stories pretty soon. They're getting curious." Lightfoot left the meeting room and said she was going home. Call her, she'd be back for a couple of hours in the evening.

Mattingly didn't have any fibers, and she didn't have any skin. It looked to her like the killer had cleaned the dead girl's fingernails. There was a good sample of semen if they ever had something to match it with.

Cooley and Vorhees went to the basement garage and got in their Chevrolet. They drove down Seventh to Leavenworth in the gray cold. Trash and newspapers blew through the streets and it was not raining.

Darwin missed her immediately. He came to class, looked for her face, it wasn't there.

He spent a few minutes shuffling his papers, handed out the essays from the week before, expecting Dolores to hurry through the door and take her seat in the first row, look up at him shyly, smile, look down—that quick acknowledgment that there was something special between them, a friendship in bloom. Ten minutes into his lecture she hadn't come, and twenty minutes after that he began to worry that she might be sick at home with nobody to care for her. He thought he would wander to Frieda's after class and telephone from there. If she was sick he could pick up Chinese noodle soup and they could watch some TV together. Despite lecturing, his mind wandered to the prospect that he might have someone to care for, to nurture, someone to give his thought to besides himself and his own problems.

The students held him after class with about a dozen questions. They crowded around, talking and joking, picking at his grades, asking for office hours when they could talk about their mistakes. When they were finished, Darwin went into the marble foyer of the law school, down the patio steps, and walked over to Frieda's. He ordered a hot chocolate, took off his topcoat and looped it over the back of his chair, but before he could make the telephone call two men interrupted.

"My name is Vorhees," one said, a tall black man with graying hair. "My partner here is Detective Cooley. We're with the San Francisco Police Department."

Darwin made way as the men stood on either side of him. The balding man had a florid face and pale blue watery eyes.

"What's going on? Is something wrong?"

Darwin thought about Karla. She was in his mind. Perhaps more charges had been preferred, something outrageous and false.

"Do you know Dolores Hernandez?" the balding man asked. "She's one of your students, isn't she?"

"Oh God. Is something wrong? Has something happened?"

"She wasn't in class tonight," the black man said.

"I know. Has something happened?"

"I'm sorry sir," the black man told Darwin. "But Dolores Hernandez is dead."

Later, Darwin would not remember having been told. A black curtain descended into his mind. He wanted to scream, but he was paralyzed.

"God no," he finally said. "Oh, God no."

"I'm sorry," the black man said.

"What happened? Where is she?"

Darwin sat down heavily.

"She was found in her apartment this morning," Cooley said.

"Strangled," the black man said.

"Oh dear God, no."

"You know her well?" Cooley asked.

"Where is she?" Darwin asked.

"Strangled, maybe raped," the black man told him.

Darwin walked into a long hallway full of smoke. For a moment he looked at his own hand on the restaurant table, and its forms and bones and sinews were x-rayed, the map of his nervous system displayed, the blood running like traffic on a freeway.

"No, no please," Darwin managed to say.

"Somebody she knew did it, we think," Cooley said.

They were on both sides of Darwin, standing over him, talking slowly, in and out of sequence, voices like mirrors in a hall of mirrors.

"Are you okay, Professor?" Cooley asked.

"I'm not, I'm not a professor," Darwin said. "May I see her please?"

"She mean that much to you?" Vorhees said.

"You two were pretty close, huh?" Cooley said.

"What are you talking about?" Darwin asked, looking at his hand on the table, bones blue, blood red, skin white hot from the X rays.

Darwin remembered being a boy once, placing his foot in a fluoroscope box at a department store, how the foot effervesced into something magic. "What are you saying?" Darwin asked quietly.

"I mean, she was just your student, right?" Cooley said.

"Oh please, don't do this."

"What are we doing, Professor?" Vorhees asked. "Are you going to be okay?"

Darwin put his head down on the table. From behind the bar, Frieda surveyed the men, her withered lizard face pointed at them in steady concentration. Darwin felt himself swim up against a tide. It was late at night and the tide was tugging beneath the Golden Gate, toward the open sea, toward the Farallones, where seabirds angled in and out over barren rock. The water was cold and Darwin wanted to sink under it, go to sleep. He buried his face in his hands and felt the salt of tears in his mouth. In his mind he was touching the skin of Dolores Hernandez, kissing her mouth softly, the way clouds might brush against clouds. Some students had come into the restaurant and were talking loudly, playing soft rock music on the jukebox. The Lovin' Spoonful, "Daydream."

"You want something to drink?" the black man asked him.

Frieda came over and left hot chocolate on the table.

"Here's something to drink," Cooley said.

"I want a bourbon rocks," Darwin said.

Vorhees went to the bar and brought back the drink. Darwin sipped the bourbon, felt the alcohol in his head immediately.

"I'm sorry, Professor," Cooley said. "We've got to have a serious talk with you right now."

"Go ahead," Darwin said. He held the bourbon on his mouth, tasting the alcohol, licking it.

"Dolores was in class Friday night?" Cooley asked.

"Yes. She was there."

"How well did you know her?" Vorhees asked. He sat down, asking the question over Darwin's right shoulder. "You were close I guess?"

"Look, we were friends," Darwin said. "I had dinner with her Friday night after class."

"Mexican carryout?" Cooley asked.

"Yes, yes. That's right."

"You were that close?" Cooley asked. "You went to your student's apartment for dinner?"

Darwin raised his hand. "Can't you tell me what happened to Dolores? Where is she? Can't I see her? Would that be too much to ask?"

"Was she alive when you last saw her, Professor?" Cooley asked the question in motion, now sitting down too.

"Yes, of course. Of course."

"What time did you leave her house?"

"Before nine. Just before nine."

"You're sure? How can you be so sure?"

Darwin gulped his bourbon dry and gestured to Frieda for another.

"How is it you're so sure about the time?" Cooley asked.

"I went to the Aladdin Coffee House in the Marina. I was supposed to meet my wife there at nine."

"Your wife?" Vorhees asked.

Darwin knew how it must have sounded, but he didn't care. Having dinner with a student at her place. Leaving to meet your estranged wife. He wanted to see Dolores. He wanted to see her again, no matter what.

"I'm separated from my wife," Darwin said. "I know how it sounds. I don't care about that now."

"Take it easy, Professor," Cooley told him. "We have to ask around, you know."

"Go ahead," Darwin muttered. Frieda brought the drink and Darwin drank half of it instantly. "Go ahead."

"So you left Dolores around nine."

"Just before."

"So you were at the Aladdin at nine?"

"Just after."

"When did your wife show?"

"She didn't. She never came."

"Oh, I see," Cooley said, looking at Vorhees over Darwin's head. "Well, can anyone verify your presence at the Aladdin?"

"Sure, lots of people. The waitress. A couple came in and shared my table. Why are you asking this?"

"Dolores was murdered Friday night. You were the last person to see her alive. You can see how we'd be interested."

Vorhees asked Darwin if he wanted his hot chocolate. Darwin told him to go ahead and drink it.

"Did you have sex with Dolores that night?" Cooley asked.

Darwin closed his eyes tightly. The bourbon was in his head, making a sound like oak trees in high wind. The detectives were close to him, pressing in.

"The professor was going to tell us if he had sex with Dolores Hernandez on Friday night." A voice, aimed at Darwin.

"Don't do this," Darwin said. "I loved her."

"Is that a yes, Professor?" Cooley asked.

"I was beginning to love her, for God's sake."

"So, yes, no, what?"

"What?" Vorhees echoed.

"Yes. I loved her. We made love that night."

"How long had that been going on?" Cooley asked.

"Going on?" Darwin managed to say. "You two don't know anything, do you?"

"Tell us about it," Vorhees said.

"There's nothing to tell," Darwin said, bourbon-angry now. "I cared about her. She was a wonderful person. We were friends."

"After the Aladdin, where did you go?" Vorhees asked.

"I went home. That's it. I went home. Look, could I see Dolores? Would that be too much to ask?"

"Pretty soon," Cooley said.

"You left her, she was alive?"

"I told you. Yes."

"Are you doing any other students?" Cooley asked.

Darwin tried to stand. Two hands on his shoulders stopped him. Darwin felt soft and invisible.

"Have her parents been told?" Darwin asked.

"We took care of it," Vorhees said.

"What time did you get home?" Cooley said.

"Ten-thirty. Something like that."

"Anybody see you late?"

"A stable hand from Burlingame came by. That was about eleven or so."

"Stable hand?"

"He brought me the ashes of a horse."

"Then you went to bed?"

"About midnight."

They were all silent for a long time. Darwin finished his second bourbon.

"You want to tell us about yourself?" Vorhees asked.

Darwin did a ten-minute version of his life.

"So, you're on pretty bad terms with your wife then?" Cooley asked.

"I've been on bad terms with her for a while."

"So, you left Dolores at nine. She was alive?"

"For God's sake yes."

"That's the story," Vorhees said.

"It's not a story. It's what happened."

"So, who killed her?" Vorhees asked Cooley.

"I don't know," Cooley said.

"Who killed her, Professor?" Cooley asked.

"I don't know," Darwin said.

Both detectives stood, as if on cue.

"Let's see," Vorhees said. "You'll be in your law office or at home this week?"

"Yes, of course."

"We'll be in touch."

"When can I see her?" Darwin asked, looking up at the two men now.

"Gimme a call tomorrow morning," Vorhees said. "I'll see what I can do."

Darwin sat alone in the bar for ten minutes. He wanted a bourbon as badly as he'd ever wanted a bourbon in his life. When the noise of oak leaves in a storm left his head, Darwin drove out to the Avenues and sat in his car in front of the stucco apartment where Dolores Hernandez had lived. For the second time in just a few days, Jack Darwin wept openly and bitterly.

Alisha made a mound under the covers. They were in bed, the windows full of darkness. Ocean wind clicked against the glass. Darkness stirred.

"You look like a peanut butter cup," Vorhees said.

"And your days are just as long as before."

"We're working a bad one," Vorhees said.

"Want to talk about it?"

"No, not really."

"You know what the psychologists say?"

"What do they say? Don't repress?"

"You used to rave about the drug dealers," Alisha told him.

The darkness was textured, woven.

"That was different," Vorhees said.

"In what way, dear?"

"You know, different. You can rave on about punks. This time it's a young woman."

"I'm sorry, Amos," Alisha whispered.

"It makes no sense."

"You'll catch the bad guy."

"Eventually," Vorhees said. "Say what you want. It really is a jungle out there."

Alisha shifted, touching her husband on the back. The phone rang. Alisha answered, then handed Vorhees the receiver.

"It's Cooley," Alisha said.

Vorhees took the phone.

"Hey, Amos," Cooley said loudly.

"It's late," Vorhees said.

"Listen, partner," Cooley said happily. "I just ran John Darwin through the computer. You won't believe what came back. The guy has a domestic violence case pending in municipal court. His wife says he got behind her in the shower and banged her head against the tile, then sodomized her against her will. That's what it says, Amos."

Vorhees sat up in bed.

"When was this?" he asked Cooley.

"Last November."

"He hadn't been getting along with her? Wasn't that how he put it?"

"I guess he did," Cooley said. "Sleep well, buddy."

Vorhees gave the phone to his wife. The electric clock on the stand said midnight, Cooley still doing police work.

"Something bad?" Alisha asked.

"Cooley still working the young woman."

"He needs to slow down."

"He's a great cop," Vorhees said.

"You both should relax."

"How can we relax?" Vorhees laughed.

Alisha pushed her hand under the cover.

"Let me help you," she said.

Overnight a tree rose bloomed in front. Karla clipped the pink flower, filled a vase with water, put the vase on the kitchen table. At the Hyatt, she had lost her anxiety. She had been centered, and when the doorbell rang she was ultrasurprised because nobody ever came to the Pacific Heights house, just the postman and a stableboy.

She opened the door a crack on its chain. A large black man introduced himself, showed a badge. Vorhees and Cooley, wanting a few minutes of her time.

She offered them coffee.

"Is this about Jack?" she asked.

She poured Vorhees a cup. They were standing in the kitchen, Karla in a workout jersey, sweatpants, tennis shoes.

"Indirectly," Cooley told her.

Vorhees went to the patio door and stood looking at the view of the bay, pale green hills, lots of sailboats.

"Is he in trouble?" Karla asked them.

"Not really," Vorhees said.

"I told the police everything," Karla said. "A long time ago."

"It isn't about that," Cooley said.

"Oh well then," Karla said.

"You and your husband," Cooley began.

"We're separated."

"He teaches at night, doesn't he?"

"I guess so. We talk through our lawyers."

"Were you supposed to meet him someplace Friday night?"

"No, where did you hear that?"

Karla filled Cooley's cup. Vorhees was watching the clouds bump in from the Pacific, like zinc-colored onion bulbs.

"Does he have a temper, ma'am?" Cooley asked.

"I guess like anybody."

"That night he beat you up, was that usual?"

"It surprised me."

"The violence of it, huh?"

"I suppose. It was pretty bad."

"It was just like the police report?"

Karla sat down at the kitchen table opposite Cooley.

"I thought this wasn't about that."

"It isn't."

"Then what is this about?"

"I suppose she should know," Cooley said.

"She should know," Vorhees said.

"One of your husband's students was murdered Friday night," Cooley said. "Her name was Dolores Hernandez."

"Oh my," Karla said. She felt an edge of anxiety now.

"She was murdered in a shower. Beaten badly."

"We had a fight," Karla said.

"In the shower," Vorhees said.

"Well, yes. You've read the report."

"He got you around the neck?"

"Yes."

"He choked you? Did other things to you?"

"Yes. It isn't pretty, is it?"

Cooley crossed the room and stood next to Vorhees. The view was excellent. Like a postcard.

"Your husband was moved out on court order?" Cooley said.

"Yes, he was."

"Where does he live now?"

"Down on the Marina," Karla told them.

Cooley read her the address they'd gotten from Darwin. She told them it sounded about right.

"You mind if we look around?" Cooley asked.

"I guess not," she said.

Karla followed them into the living room. The two men looked, but didn't touch a thing.

"Does you husband ever come around?" Vorhees said.

"He's come back twice to get clothes and personal things. It's arranged through our lawyers."

"No problems with him?"

"Not that kind of problem," Karla said. "We're in the middle of what they call a messy divorce. That always causes problems."

"I see," Cooley said. "He didn't mention it."

"He didn't?"

"You mind if we look in his bedroom?" Vorhees asked.

Karla led the way upstairs, down a carpeted hall.

Opening the door she said, "This is his room. We haven't shared a bedroom for a long time."

Karla stood outside the room while the detectives searched. She could hear them, opening drawers, closet doors, down on all fours crawling around. One of them opened drapes and the French doors.

Cooley stepped outside. He held a single gold cuff link, initialed D.

"Does this cuff link belong to your husband?" he asked.

"I suppose it does. I don't really know."

"Do you mind if we take it along?"

"I don't see why not," Karla said.

Karla led them downstairs and ushered them out. She returned to her room and put on her gym clothes, then a sweater over them, a pair of Gore-Tex pants. She tried to remember Jack in cuff links, but couldn't. She washed her face and hands and then remembered one night when he had worn cuff links, a simple blue stone in a gold setting, not the ones Cooley had shown her. They'd driven up to Reno, one of the many times they thought a short trip might salvage their relationship. Jack had gotten tickets to Rodney Dangerfield, but at the end of the show they'd had a fight at the casino, and Jack had gone to the bar, drinking heavily. She recalled him returning to the room on the tenth floor at Harrah's, standing at the picture window watching the lights of Reno flash and flicker, while she herself pretended to sleep, wishing he would crash through the window and fall to his death. Jack had mixed a drink at the refrigerator bar in the room and had slept upright in a chair. She remembered the cuff links, ovals of gold, ovals of blue stone. Not Cooley's cuff links.

Karla went outside to the gold Mercedes. She got in and sat quietly. Hadn't David told her that Jack was seeing one of his students?

.   .   .

They ate lunch at the Beanery Cafe, opposite and behind the law school. Avila had come from federal court, wearing a dark gray business suit. Darwin got there first and found a booth near the back, one of a row of seven. Avila ordered black bean soup and rye bread. Darwin was drinking iced tea, too nervous and sick to eat lunch.

"You look tired," Avila told him.

"I'm sorry to call on short notice."

"I understand," Avila told him sympathetically. "Were you able to see the girl?"

"No. They were okay about it."

Avila ate some of his soup. A few students drifted in and said hello to Darwin. It was a gray day, warmer, but windy. Darwin was working on zero sleep, a night full of crazy sounds.

"I'm very sorry about her," Avila said. "It's got to be tough."

"Very tough," Darwin said.

"Look, Jack," Avila said, "I've got to get back to court in forty minutes. I'm sorry to hurry you, especially now."

"No, I understand," Darwin said.

Darwin had been awake all night, pacing the small apartment, listening to the many voices directed at him. He held an imaginary conversation with his brother Adam, both of them very young, sitting in yellow lamplight over a chessboard, the pieces shiny, hummingbirds zinging here and there, darting at the feeder. Jack thought he might lose his sanity that night, but he didn't. When morning came he wished he had. It might be nice to forget his life, become another kind of human being, someone wheeled around an institution for years. Once during the night he found himself sitting in a chair with the urn between his legs.

"I was the last one to see her alive," Darwin said finally.

Avila finished his soup. A band of Hare Krishnas trooped by on Hyde Street, drums, tambourines, little finger cymbals ringing.

"The cops talked to you?"

"I told them everything."

"Okay, you have nothing to hide."

"They called me this morning. Early. They want to meet me at the apartment. I don't know what to do."

"What the hell. Meet them."

"I thought I should talk to you."

"I suppose they found out about the DV."

"But I didn't do that. I told you, Karla has a boyfriend."

"It's just a police report, Jack. Not to worry."

"What should I do?"

"Listen, Jack," Avila said. "I know you're upset. But you have nothing to hide. You didn't kill her. You cared about her. You saw her Friday night and she was fine. Is that about it?"

"Of course," Darwin answered, taking a deep breath.

"Then go talk to them. Tell them the truth."

"I just thought I'd check."

"Can you take a break soon?" Avila asked. "Go someplace and get some rest. Lie on a white beach?"

"Maybe get a white Bronco. Take a drive on the freeway?"

Avila smiled and said no, that wouldn't do. "Getting a Bronco is counterindicated."

Darwin decided to change the subject.

"How's Luther Lee and his case?"

"We're muddling along," Avila said.

"I hope you don't hold the motion against me."

"No, no. You represent your client. That's what you were hired to do. By the way, I have some other codefendants coming down the pipeline. You still interested?"

"Whatever pays," Darwin said.

"That's the spirit."

"They want to meet me after lunch."

"Go. What can it hurt?"

"I know. I just wanted to hear you say it."

Avila dropped a five-dollar bill on the table. They walked outside together and Avila watched Darwin trudge down Hyde. Avila used a pay phone to call Karla. She told him about two detectives who'd taken a gold cuff link from Jack's room. They spent five minutes reliving their evening at the Hyatt.

Hello, I'm John, and I'm an alcoholic. (Hello, John) This is very hard for me. I know this meeting lasts an hour, but I've only got time to say a few words, and then I've got to go. But I needed this meeting. It's really very hard for me to speak here. I've done it a few times, but it's never been harder than now. What I have to say is really hard because I had a slip. I drank two bourbon rocks a couple of nights ago. I feel sick inside. Ashamed—you know the routine, I guess. Last night I stayed in my apartment and watched some TV and thought about things, how my life has gone wrong and pretty soon I had it all figured out. I should tell you that after one bourbon rocks I thought about having another one and I had it right away, two big bourbon rocks in one sitting. Then I left the bar and went home and didn't have another one. I know you think that probably isn't true, but it is true. (Okay, John, ease back on the self-pity) You can't explain liquor to anyone who doesn't know how good it tastes and feels. I have it rationalized in my own mind, taking that drink. I'll tell you. Maybe I shouldn't. I know you'll think I'm feeling sorry for myself. Maybe that's true. But I have to tell somebody. Two of my friends have died just recently. (Murmurs) One of my friends was murdered Friday night. (Murmurs) She's dead and she was sweet and lovely and I cared about her and now she's gone forever. I know it's no excuse for drinking, but it's an explanation. I guess it's always been drinking that's kept me alone, but I thought of my drinking buddies, lawyers, businessmen sitting around tables playing cribbage and complaining about their lives, as my friends. They're what you guys, we I guess, call cronies. But two of my real friends did die and that's the explanation for why I took those two drinks. I guess I'm starting over, but the way I see it, and with the things I have to face now, it's going to be hard to stay sober every day, day after day, minute by minute, because right now I'd like to get drunk and forget everything. I can't because I have an important meeting in about thirty minutes and because I really want to quit drinking. I know it's something you have to do by yourself and for yourself, but the truth is right now I don't care much about myself. (Watch the pity, John) Anyway, I'm starting over and it takes one day at a time, but I don't know how I can face things without my friends, especially the one who was murdered. She was beautiful and good in every way, though I'm sure I would have discovered some blemishes if I'd known her longer. Everybody has blemishes, but we learn to accept them, get over them, even cherish them if they're not too bad. I'm sorry I can't stay here for the rest of the meeting, but I'm going to have my meeting and try to see my friend at the mortuary or wherever it is they have her. I can never tell you how much it hurts to have lost my friends. My old friend and I had lots of good times together and I'll never forget them. But my new friend and I were just beginning an experience. There aren't enough memories there. This is about self-pity, isn't it? But I feel sorry for her too, and for her family, and I don't know what to do. (One day at a time, John)

High wind and heavy traffic, on Mason Street they were going nowhere fast, Cooley driving.

"I faxed Darwin's photo to Cincinnati," Vorhees said.

"Dark and muscular he ain't," Cooley replied.

"It can't hurt," Vorhees told him.

They met the cable car coming uphill. They went over the hill and made the Marina, found a yellow zone on Leavenworth, and parked. They walked a block down and a block over to a series of small stucco apartment buildings, found Darwin's number and rang the buzzer. He answered in chinos and flannel shirt, tennis shoes. Darwin let them inside and the three stood in a low-ceilinged living room.

"This is it," Darwin said. "Look around if you like."

"You get to see her?" Vorhees asked.

"No. They've taken her home. I'm going up for the funeral. Thanks for trying, anyway."

"Her folks are very broken up," Cooley said.

"I know. I saw them downtown. I didn't get a chance to say anything. They were with a detective."

"Where's the Aladdin from here anyway?" Cooley asked.

"Just up from the cable car turnaround."

Darwin went to the kitchen nook and poured himself some diet soda. "Look, you guys," he said, "you don't think I had anything to do with her death, do you?"

"We have to check everything out," Vorhees said. "I'm sure you understand."

"Sure, I know," Darwin said.

"Mind if we hit the bedroom?" Vorhees asked.

Darwin pointed the way and stayed in the kitchen, standing at a little corner that divided the nook from the living room. Vorhees shut the door behind him, leaving Cooley to look around the living room. Vorhees could hear them out there, talking quietly, Cooley opening closet doors. Vorhees spent some time in the bath, just looking. Pretty soon, Cooley came into the bedroom. He opened some drawers, looked under the bed.

"I thought the guy was going to pass out when we told him about his girlfriend," Cooley said.

"It seemed like he took it hard."

"Or he's a born sociopath."

"Well, if he's crazy enough to kill Lisa Tracy and Dolores Hernandez, then he's crazy enough to put on a good show for us."

"Even so," Cooley said.

"I want to hear his explanation for the cuff link," Vorhees said, bending over to open a bottom drawer.

"It will be interesting," Vorhees agreed.

Vorhees opened a sliding closet door. He ruffled through a dozen shirts. He didn't find any with French cuffs, but he did find a cotton button-down with flecks of dried blood inside the collar, one tiny spot near the point. On the inside sleeve of an expensive camel hair topcoat he found a longish swatch of dried blood, about the size of a Tootsie Roll. Another dot the size of a nickel farther up the sleeve. The lining of the coat was green, the blood rust brown.

"Hey, partner," Vorhees said.

Cooley came out of the bath. "This guy is a dental freak. He's got one of those Water Piks. He must do a lot of smiling in court."

Vorhees unrolled the coat cuff. He showed Cooley the dried blood without speaking, then laid the dress shirt on the bed, collar out. The two spent another ten minutes going through more drawers, a suitcase in the closet, an overnight bag. Cooley went out to the car and got a black plastic trash bag for clothes.

"This guy is cold," Cooley said when he got back. "He's just standing out there drinking a pop."

"I still can't get over how he looked when we told him."

"Oh shit, he's a sociopath, pal." Cooley folded the clothes carefully, put them in the plastic bag. "He's lied to us twice already. He said he was meeting his wife. And he didn't tell us about his domestic violence beef. I count that as a lie."

"Let's get some guys going over the Dumpsters out back," Vorhees said. "Maybe canvass the neighbors about Friday night."

"Let me go to the car. I think we should have a DA at the shakedown. That's what Lightfoot says to do." Cooley left the room with the bag, and Vorhees could hear him saying something to Darwin. Vorhees gave it a minute, then went out.

"Well," Darwin said, "you're taking something?"

"Yeah," Vorhees said, "we're taking something. A camel hair topcoat and a dress shirt."

"Why? What's the matter?"

"There's dried blood on both."

Darwin seemed to stagger. "That's not possible."

"Hey, you cut yourself shaving."

"No, it's not possible."

"Why don't you come downtown with us?"

Cooley came back and stood in the entryway, door open behind him to marina noise.

"Maybe I should call my lawyer," Darwin said.

"Hey, we just want to talk."

"What about my clothes?"

"You'll get them back."

"I don't know. It can't be. Maybe if you'd let me look at them I could figure this out."

"Inside sleeve of the coat," Vorhees said. He headed for the door and stood just in front of Cooley.

"This is not real," Darwin said, mantra-like. "This is not real, not real."

"Come on Mr. Darwin," Cooley called out. "It won't take long. You'll be home before you know it."

Nola Gettes got the call at two. By three-fifteen she was outside the police gray room in the basement of the Hall of Justice reading a forensic summary and the police report on Lisa Tracy and Dolores Hernandez. Gettes could observe Darwin sitting at a metal table inside the gray room, sipping a diet soda. The light was so harsh you could almost see through the man's skin.

"By the way," Lieutenant Lightfoot said, "congratulations on your election."

"It was tight, wasn't it?" Gettes said, still reading.

Vorhees and Cooley came out of the gray room and joined them. They were in darkness, the brightly lit chamber behind glass like a crystal ball.

"I know this Darwin guy," Gettes said.

"He's a lawyer," Cooley told her.

"Yeah, I know. We had a case last year."

Gettes looked at Darwin, pale, tall, sandy haired, almost boyish, the stare of an impala stalked by a lion. He looked almost unconscious.

"Has he lawyered up?" Gettes asked.

"No," Vorhees said. "He mentioned that maybe he should call his lawyer, but then he forgot it."

"Read him his rights?"

"Not yet," Cooley said. "We've just begun to talk."

"Do it now," Gettes said. "Then hit him with the cuff link and let him have it hard before he can think about it."

"You hear us okay out here?" Cooley asked.

"Just fine, Tom," Lightfoot told him.

"It's fine," Gettes said. She turned to a stenographer she'd brought along. The steno was sitting on a chair, pen and paper in hand. "Lawyers can dick with tape. I'll go with the steno every time," she said.

Cooley and Vorhees went inside the gray room. The women stood in front of the glass, like at the aquarium.

"We'll just read your rights," Cooley said. "It's a formality."

Darwin sat quietly, eyes staring straight ahead. He looks pathetic, Gettes thought. If she'd been behind glass like that she would have been yelling for a lawyer, clawing up through the cops and the stenos for fresh air. What the hell was the matter with this guy anyway? Cooley finished reading from his rights card and sat down. Vorhees circled the room like a zoo lion.

"Run us through Friday night again, Mr. Darwin," Cooley said.

"I told you," Darwin said. "I taught class. Dolores and I met at Frieda's, then we went to her place and ate Mexican carryout. I left just before nine, went to the Aladdin, but my wife didn't show up. I went home."

"You say you saw a stableboy about eleven?"

"Maybe a little after."

"How long did he stay?"

"Only a few minutes."

"We know Dolores was murdered that night. Right in your time frame. The autopsy is pretty clear on that, Mr. Darwin."

"I've told you the truth," Darwin said.

Vorhees continued to circle, steadily clockwise, shifting back to counterclockwise. From behind Darwin, Vorhees pushed a plastic bag across the metal table.

"You recognize the cuff link?" Vorhees said.

Darwin made a motion to touch the bag but Vorhees stopped him. "Don't touch, sir," he said.

"Well, yes. It looks like mine. My father's I mean. I haven't worn those cuff links in years. I don't wear them. They're more or less keepsakes."

"Your father was Jack Darwin also?"

"John. My name is John. That was my father's name."

"So you don't wear these cuff links?" Cooley interrupted.

Vorhees began circling again. Gettes folded her arms, leaned her head against the glass to rest a little.

"No, I don't," Darwin said. "What's going on?"

"You know a woman named Lisa Tracy?"

"The girl on Turk," Lightfoot whispered to Gettes.

"No, I don't know any girl named Lisa Tracy," Darwin said, looking scared now. Not stunned anymore, but frightened.

"We found this cuff link in her apartment. She'd been murdered just like Dolores Hernandez."

Darwin sat back, mouth wide. "That's not possible."

"It was just after Christmas. Right down on Turk. You don't know her?" Cooley leaned into Darwin's face, nose to nose.

Vorhees came up behind Darwin, leaned in. "I found the other cuff link in Lisa Tracy's bathroom. You should have seen the place. Lisa Tracy naked on the floor, legs spread. Somebody beat and sodomized her. It was pretty sick."

"It can't be," Darwin muttered.

"Can't you do better than that?" Cooley said. "We're trying to help you here. Help you get things off your chest."

"No, no. Maybe I should call my lawyer."

"Here we go," Gettes whispered to Lightfoot.

"Anything you want, Mr. Darwin," Cooley said. "Is that exactly what you want to do?"

"I don't understand this. I don't know any Lisa Tracy. I haven't worn these cuff links ever. They were in an old jewelry box in my Pacific Heights house. The box had some of my dad's things, tie clips, his Phi

Beta Kappa key, some old pennies we collected together when I was a kid."

"Listen, Darwin," Cooley said. "Your wife says she didn't call you about any meeting at the Aladdin. How can you explain that?"

"She what? She called me. She did, she called me."

"She says she didn't."

"She left a message on my machine at home."

"I checked the machine, Mr. Darwin," Vorhees said. "There isn't any message on the machine."

"I don't know," Darwin said. "Please check again. Please."

"Maybe you went back to Pacific Heights to ditch some clothes. Maybe you wanted those cuff links at the house, not at the apartment where you lived. You dropped them off, but you noticed one was missing. There was nothing you could do then, was there?"

"This is ridiculous," Darwin stammered. "It isn't real."

"It's real," Cooley said. He rubbed a meaty hand over his face. "Come on, Darwin, think."

"I don't need to think."

"There's blood on the inner sleeve of your topcoat. Blood on the collar of a dress shirt. The guy who killed Dolores was right-handed. Are you right-handed, Mr. Darwin?"

"Yes, of course. Ninety percent of the people are."

"That's more like it, Darwin," Cooley said. "We want you to think along with us."

"This is ridiculous."

"You've got a drinking problem, Professor?" Vorhees said from across the room.

"I'm an alcoholic. I'm trying to deal with it."

Darwin turned his head, following the motion of Vorhees around twice.

"How did you know about that?" Darwin said after a while.

"That AA meeting you went to today. What'd you say in there? I always wondered about that." Cooley looked at the glass window. There were reflections in the glass, a haze of exploded white light.

"You followed me?" Darwin said.

"Let's stay on track," Vorhees said. "How long have you had a drinking problem?"

"You think I killed her?"

"Who?" Cooley asked.

"Who?" Darwin said, stunned. "Well, Lisa Tracy, who else?"

"What about Dolores?" Vorhees said.

"You think I killed Dolores?"

"Where did the blood on your shirt come from?"

"I don't know. How would I know?"

Gettes leaned over to Lightfoot.

"How long to run the blood on the coat and shirt?" she asked.

"Hernandez was O. We can type it in an hour. The DNA will take three weeks."

"Do a good job on the DNA. We've got enough to hold this ape right now." Gettes turned back to the gray-room window. "What about the cuff links? Could this guy have taken one back to his house?"

"Sure, no problem," Lightfoot said. "His wife says he went back at least twice to pick up some clothes."

"Well, the cuff link is *his* problem," Gettes said.

They looked at Darwin, the man with his hands flat on the metal table now, all emotion drained from his face. Lightfoot tapped twice on the glass.

Cooley said, "Okay, Darwin, stand up."

Darwin did as he was told.

"You're under arrest, John Darwin, for the murder of Dolores Hernandez. We've read your rights, and you understand them, don't you? We're going to handcuff you now. You'll get to call your lawyer after booking. I wouldn't say anything more right now unless you want to tell us about Lisa and Dolores. Of course, that would be voluntary on your part. If you want to get it off your chest, we could respect that. People sometimes feel better when they get things off their chest. Maybe you're glad it's over. It takes off the strain. You'd be free if you'd like to talk, free of your dreams, that is."

"Shut up, will you please?" Darwin said.

Vorhees cuffed Darwin, hands behind his back.

Gettes turned to Lightfoot. "I remember now. This guy beat one of my reversals this fall. I didn't think it would come back so soon."

Darwin and the detectives came out of the gray room, and the women watched them disappear down a long characterless corridor.

"Your guys did good," Gettes said.

Lightfoot walked Gettes to the elevator, watched her get on and punch up to one.

"Lawyers, lawyers," Lightfoot said to herself.

Headlines, Metro section, page 1: LAWYER CHARGED IN STUDENT SLAY-ING.

Avila put down the *Chronicle* after reading it twice. He was in a dim corner of the basement, Hall of Justice. In a holding cell he found Darwin in chinos, a flannel shirt. Darwin sat quietly, abstracted, like a puzzle with its pieces missing.

"Thank you for coming," Darwin said emptily. "I didn't know who else to call."

"Jesus, Jack," Avila said. The holding cell was almost too small for both of them. Avila stood and Darwin sat on a padded bunk. There were no windows, dim light, gum wrappers on the floor, cigarette butts. "It's in the afternoon edition."

"It's in the paper?"

"Late edition."

"I'm sorry," Darwin said. "You've got to help me."

"How'd you get in this mess?" Avila said.

"I told you," Darwin replied. "Somebody is framing me."

"I'll help you," Avila said. "There has to be some mistake. Tell me what's going on."

Avila turned and leaned on the bars of the holding cell. A blank green wall was four feet away, some bulletin boards, a locked blue iron door down the hall. Avila had never felt so alive, so keen, so up-to-date. It really was merciful, how genetics let things like this happen.

"Take me through this afternoon," Avila said.

"I met two detectives at the apartment. They looked around and found a shirt and a topcoat. They said there was blood on both. I don't know anything about it. They asked me to come downtown."

"You should have called me then," Avila said.

"I'm sorry. I was crazed."

"Okay, sure. I know how it is."

"When I got here, they put me in a room. Both of them questioned me. They showed me a cuff link they said came from an apartment on Turk where a woman had been murdered. I didn't know what they were talking about."

"They arrested you for Dolores Hernandez?"

"Yes. Dolores."

"So who's this woman on Turk?"

"I don't know, David. I really don't."

"You say anything to anybody?"

"Just the police. What could I say?" Darwin lay down on the bunk. "They think I killed Dolores. I never heard of this woman on Turk. I don't see how any cuff link could have gotten there, unless Karla and her boyfriend are involved."

"You admitted it was yours?"

"I told them about it. It belonged to my father."

"You want me to represent you, Jack?" Avila asked.

"Please, if you would."

"This sounds perfectly asinine, but we have to talk about fees."

"Yes, I understand. I have money. It's tied up in trust right now, but I have money."

"Let's say I charge you my standard two hundred, plus expenses. I'll bill it, no retainer."

"God, thank you, David. You have to get me out of here. I haven't killed anybody."

"Hey, I know you didn't, Jack, take it easy."

"You believe me?"

"Of course. No questions asked."

Darwin got up again. He was cold and shivering.

"All right," Avila said. "I'll get the state magistrate to arraign you as quickly as possible. They'll probably go to a grand jury. I'll talk to the papers if I can, we'll get a quick denial."

"What about bail? Can I get out of here?"

"Bail might be high, Jack," Avila told him.

"Can I put up the house?"

"Well, it's tied up in a divorce. I'm not sure the judge would go for that. Look, I'll read the basic police reports as soon as possible. But you have to be patient. You can't go to pieces on me and you have to trust me every step of the way. One thing I know is this, it's tough to defend a lawyer. They're always second-guessing you."

"You handle things. I trust you."

"It's easy to say, Jack."

"No, I mean it. You handle things. No second-guessing."

"First of all, don't talk to anybody in here. Don't talk to other prisoners and don't chitchat with the guards. They listen to everything and some jailhouse stoolie is always ready to sell you out to save himself a few years."

"You sound as if I'll be in here for a long time."

"I don't know," Avila said. "Bail is always difficult on a murder case. We have some things going for us in this case. Your family. Your name. Your long residence here."

"You didn't mention the evidence," Darwin said.

"I don't know what it is yet."

"I'm frightened, David," Darwin said. He swallowed hard, put his head in his hands.

"Take it easy, Jack," Avila told him. "You want anything? Can I bring you a chocolate bar?"

Darwin looked up and tried to smile. Avila pressed a buzzer for the guard.

"I'll see you in the morning," Avila told him.

He left Darwin in the dim cell, hands on knees, head down. Avila richly happy, loose through the forest, breaking into the brown savanna, wild with the taste of blood, prey scattered in thorny waste, the rich pure scent of death perfuming the scene.

She told people she came up the hard way, but it was just a publicity spin. In truth, she'd been born to run and she'd been running since she hit ground in law school at Berkeley, second-year president, *Law Review*, Order of the Coif, clerk to one of the most notable California State Supreme Court justices, just about the time the court turned right, some might say reactionary.

When she made her first try at district attorney, she was elected in a landslide, preaching against crime, advocating for women and gays, keeping her pedal to the metal. Her second election had been close, too close, and now she was on cruise control for state government, hoping that Jack Darwin and his two dead girlfriends would put her in Sacramento. She liked the sound of "Attorney General Nola Gettes." It had a nice ring. If there was a glass ceiling, Nola decided long ago she'd butt into it, see if it broke.

So when David Avila came into her office on the fourth floor of Civic Center courthouse, she put on her game face.

Avila said hello, sitting next to Vorhees, the detective on a sofa, with Lieutenant Lightfoot across the way in a wing chair. Avila was late, only about ten minutes, standard protocol.

"Anybody want coffee?" Gettes asked.

"Sorry I'm late," Avila said.

"Don't worry," Gettes told him.

"I appreciate the meeting," Avila said.

"I'll tell you up front," Gettes said. "I'm opposing bail."

"Come on, Nola," Avila said. "Jack Darwin is from a fine family. He owns his own home. He practices law here. Give him a break."

"He killed two women. With his money he's a flight risk."

"Oh, come on."

"He isn't living in his home. He's been thrown out by court order and the house is under the jurisdiction of the state court downstairs. Who knows how much cash he's got stashed in a Cayman Island bank."

"Nola, how about two hundred thousand?"

"Forget it, David," Gettes said.

Vorhees went to a buffet and got some hot coffee. They were sitting in a short circle around Gettes.

"What about discovery?" Avila asked.

"You can see everything," Gettes told him. "I've always had an open-book policy in this office. You know that. It doesn't change because the defendant is rich and guilty."

"You're so, well, sure about that."

"Tell him, Detective," Gettes said.

Vorhees took out a written summary. "The blood on the shirt and topcoat belonging to John Darwin came back a match with the type of Dolores Hernandez. Type O."

"So's half the blood in the street," Avila said. "What about DNA?"

"It's being tested," Gettes said.

"I want my own samples," Avila said.

"There's plenty," Gettes said. "You'll get your share."

"What lab are you using?" Avila asked.

Gettes named a firm in Silicon Valley.

"Let's not play games," she continued. "We have your guy in Lisa Tracy's apartment. We have your guy in the Hernandez apartment. It's his cuff link. He admitted it."

"You found the cuff link?" Avila asked Vorhees.

"Yes, yes. I did," Vorhees said.

"You found the shirts too, didn't you?" Avila said.

Vorhees nodded.

"Listen, David," Gettes said. "Your client isn't charged with the Tracy murder. Not yet."

"Let's go downstairs," Avila said.

They all went to a basement courtroom used to process new prisoners through arraignment. The room was about twenty feet square, grim and cold, with television cameras in four corners. Darwin was led in wearing prison orange, white socks, a flimsy pair of slippers. The arraignment lasted about fifteen minutes. It took a tired-looking magistrate about five minutes to read Darwin the information. Avila pled not guilty.

It was over that fast.

Imagine, Avila thought, being alone on the dangerous savanna in an orange jumpsuit. You wouldn't last long, would you?

Thirty-five years, thought Tom Fullerton as he drove down to the Hall of Justice. Blink and it's gone.

He remembered the morning Jack Darwin had been baptized in the big Presbyterian church on Nob Hill. Grand gray light pouring through the high stained glass, flooding gray stone and polished marble and walnut pews with an overpowering aura of . . . what? Grace or money?

Fullerton wheeled into the parking lot and told a guard his business, then found a spot far in the back of it, away from the bulk of the building near a chain-link fence topped by barbed wire. When he got out of his car he stopped to blink up at the security cameras. He wondered if God was watching now. If there was a God, one who'd let this happen to his godchild.

It took Fullerton thirty minutes to pass through the various checkpoints and security reviews. He found his godchild inside a small room, dressed in prison orange, white socks, sandals. It was enough to break his old man's heart. He embraced Darwin and they both sat, one man on each corner of a metal table. They leaned above cigarette burns and evil smells.

"I came as soon as I could," Fullerton told Darwin. "I've been pulling strings just to get here tonight."

"Thanks for coming, Tom," Darwin said. Darwin blinked, as if he'd been in the dark for a long time and light was hurting his eyes. "I want you to know I didn't do any of the things they say I did."

"I believe you, Jack," Fullerton said.

"No, wait," Darwin said. "I want you to hear me out. I know you've read the newspapers. Everybody reads the newspapers. So I imagine you've got the story. I'm a wife beater. I beat her in the shower and sodomized her. I killed a student of mine named Dolores Hernandez. Beat her in the shower and sodomized *her*. I'm some kind of monster."

"Jack," Fullerton interrupted.

"Hear me out," Darwin said angrily. "By now you know that the police found the blood of Dolores Hernandez on a shirt and coat in the apartment where I've been staying in the Marina. By now you know the police found one of Dad's cuff links in an apartment in the Tenderloin where a woman was murdered in her shower, sodomized and strangled. You've read all that?"

"Yes, Jack," Fullerton said. "I've read it. Is it accurate at all?"

"Oh, I imagine it's accurate," Darwin said.

"Then what are we dealing with here?" Fullerton asked.

"Tom, I want to ask you something."

"Anything, sure."

"I loved Dolores Hernandez," Darwin said. "I was just beginning to love her. Do you remember how that feels?"

Now, Fullerton thought, he was being asked to remember far back into his youth, the Stanford campus, a young blond woman studying anthropology, whatever that was. Fullerton remembered, sure. If you were human, how could you forget?

"I remember, Jack," Fullerton said.

"Well, I'm going to ask you to believe that I didn't kill her. I saw her Friday night. We made beautiful love for the first time. I left her home. She was alive. We'd planned on seeing one another in class on Monday. Look me in the eye, Tom, and tell me you believe me."

Fullerton's mind was flooded by gray light, the image of a tiny baby being blessed with paradise in return for a splash of holy water, a few ragged verses, a psalm, the witnessing of eternity.

"I believe you with all my heart," Fullerton said. "I never believed anything more in my life." Fullerton felt tears welling in his eyes. He took a handkerchief and wiped them away. He was too old for this.

"Then I need your help," Darwin said.

"Anything I can do, Jack. You can rely on me."

"This all started with Karla. Someone beat her and sodomized her. She has the physical scars to prove it. But it wasn't me. Probably her boyfriend. I've been thinking about this all night and all day for weeks. Now, with my dad's cuff link showing up in the Tracy apartment, it all makes sense. Karla's friend who beat her probably stole my cuff link. Killed Lisa Tracy. Broke into my Marina apartment and planted the blood evidence. They want my money, Tom."

"We have to go to the police. Have you told them?"

"Oh, of course. The police aren't going to do anything now that they've got their man."

"You've hired this David Avila?" Fullerton asked. "Wouldn't you like me to get someone older, more established?"

"I'm going with Avila," Darwin said. "I know him. He helped me once or twice when I needed help. Besides, this case isn't going to be won in the courtroom. I've figured out a way to find out who the boyfriend is and I've already started. Karla has left a trail somewhere. I know she has. Only I just have to find out where."

"We could hire detectives to follow her."

"It's been done, Tom. By detectives. I've done it myself. No, what I have in mind is a paper trail. But I've got to get out of here to pursue it."

"You mean bail."

"I mean bail. I've got to get out of here. I won't run and I won't hide. I need time, Tom. This is war, and I've got to be part of it."

"You drew Judge Gragg," Fullerton said.

"You know her, don't you?"

"Kline-James knows everybody," Fullerton said. "Let me get out of here and see what I can do."

They embraced and Fullerton went out to his car. Never before in his life had the city seemed so drab and lifeless, drained of meaning. If it was war Jack Darwin wanted, then Fullerton would be a soldier.

Eating jelly doughnuts and fast food, Vorhees had gained four pounds during his two months on homicide. He was at the Hall that morning by eight, eating more doughnuts, drinking coffee, sitting at his desk thinking about getting back on the basketball court, anything to stem his slide toward blimphood. His desk was now an L from Cooley's, and they had erected a glass partition to keep them away from some of the noise on the floor, a place where they could think, shift images, hack through the undergrowth of death. It was hot in their corner of the room, but that was the price they paid.

A squad clerk showed Henry Diehl to Vorhees. Vorhees said hello and gave the man a chair.

"Uh, thank you for seeing me," Henry Diehl said.

Vorhees offered him some coffee, but he turned it down. Diehl was a shrimpy friendly-looking man, bow tie, salt-and-pepper short hair, thyroid eyes, and dimples that worked at the corners of his mouth.

"You said you wanted to talk about Darwin?" Vorhees asked.

"Yes. I hope that's all right."

"Fine. Go ahead. Don't mind the doughnut."

"Sure, go ahead on the doughnut." Diehl was clutching a black umbrella. He twirled it around and around. "I just don't see how Mr. Darwin could have done this thing. I saw his photograph in the newspapers."

"I'm listening," Vorhees said.

"I'm not sure I should be saying anything. It is very personal." Diehl had a Castro Street lilt to his speech.

"Don't worry. I'm sure you're doing the right thing."

"Well, all right," Diehl said. "I go to AA meetings on Hyde Street. Jack Darwin is part of our group. He's new, but I've gotten to know him, I think, pretty well in a short period of time. That's what I mean about it being personal. Well, Mr. Darwin, I didn't know his name until yesterday, I mean, we just call each other by first names, you know, confidentially. Anyway, he got up in a meeting last Monday and he gave the most touching speech."

"Touching?" Vorhees said. "How so, touching?"

"Mr. Darwin said he'd lost two friends. I'm almost certain that he was referring to the young woman who was murdered. One of his new friends. If you could have seen him speak, you would have known how heartbroken he was, how upset. I'm sure he could not have done her any harm."

"It was that clear?"

"Yes. Very upset. I believe his words were that he'd lost an old friend and he'd lost a new friend. He was nearly in tears. I'm sure everybody in that room was near tears as well."

"Do you know anything about Darwin?"

"Well, no. His speech is all. That's why I'm here."

"Very affecting, huh?" Vorhees said.

"I can see you're not interested in the human side."

"Don't get me wrong, Mr. Diehl. But I traffic in concrete information. Evidence. If you know anything about Darwin's activities last Friday night, I'd be very interested."

"Of course I don't," Diehl said. "But if you'd heard him speak I'm sure you'd have understood how affecting it was. An AA meeting is hardly the place to tell an untruth. In fact, it is the one place where truth is almost certainly commonplace."

"Okay, thanks for coming in," Vorhees said. Vorhees knew he was being abrupt, but what could he do? He shook Diehl's hand and waited for him to go. When he was gone, Vorhees opened the morning *Chronicle:* D.A. OPPOSES BAIL IN LAWYER CASE.

Vorhees stared at the headline. Just for a moment, he wondered who the old friend might be who died. Could Darwin have meant Lisa Tracy?

The bail hearing began at one o'clock the next afternoon. Judge Gragg, the only black woman on the San Francisco Superior Court bench, was right on time, which was her style. Gettes, Avila, Darwin, court reporter, bailiff, two county sheriffs with automatic weapons and truncheons, security camera, high leaded windows letting in a little yellowish light on a now familiar scene for Darwin.

"I'll hear the state on bail," Gragg said, her voice echoing in the marble hall. "Nola, what do you want to do?"

"No bail, Your Honor," Gettes said, standing behind a lectern about ten feet in front of the bench. Gettes turned and looked at Darwin. "The charge is murder in the first degree. I think it's obvious Mr. Darwin is a very dangerous man, and shouldn't be out on our city streets. Besides, he has money, and he's a flight risk. He could wind up in Costa Rica living a life of ease. I don't think the people of California should have to live with that possibility as a part of their bargain with Lady Justice. I'd say in this case the flight risk is enormous, almost certain."

Tom Fullerton sat in back of the courtroom, last row on the right. There were perhaps five reporters, two TV anchors, fifteen or sixteen curiosity seekers up front. It wasn't the circus it was going to be.

Avila rose calmly. "Your Honor, my client requests a reasonable bail, as the statutes almost regularly require. Jack Darwin has been a resident of this city for his entire life. Member of a respectable family, a lawyer, officer of the court, his father a respected member of the society of lawyers in our city for many years. As a sidebar, Your Honor, Mr. Darwin has little available cash. His money is almost exclusively tied up in his family home and in a trust fund established for him by his father."

"Not the house," Gettes said, standing again. "It's tied up in a divorce. Maybe community property."

"That's not for certain, Your Honor," Avila said. "The trust is free and clear."

Judge Gragg lifted a silver pen for silence. "We won't consider the house. Assets must be clear."

"Nevertheless," Avila continued. "My client doesn't have so much as a traffic ticket in this city. He's an innocent man and he deserves bail."

"About this trust fund," Judge Gragg said.

Tom Fullerton, alone in the back of the courtroom, rose and asked to be heard.

"You are, sir?"

"Tom Fullerton," he said. "I'm a trustee."

"Oh yes," Judge Gragg said. "Kline-James, I believe."

"That's right," Fullerton said. "Mr. Darwin has a trust fund under my care that's worth at least two and a half or three million dollars. I manage it and I could guarantee its integrity."

"Very good, thank you, Mr. Fullerton," Gragg said.

Gettes rose quickly. "One more thing," she said. "The evidence in this case is very strong. Blood and other physical evidence link this defendant to the crime. This court would be taking a great risk allowing any bail."

"Anything more?" Gragg asked the parties. When nobody spoke

she continued. "The law requires me to balance the risk of flight with numerous other factors—the seriousness of the crime, the ties of the defendant to the community, and so forth. We've all been through this before. I find the serious nature of the crime is obvious. On the other hand, the ties of this defendant to the community are obvious too. I'm not inclined to authorize bond, but I will in this case. Bond is set at four million dollars." Gragg seemed to smile knowingly at Fullerton, then rose and left the courtroom.

"One minute," Fullerton said to the judge, before she'd shut her chamber door. "May I have a minute with Mr. Darwin?"

"Sure, help yourself," Gragg said, closing the heavy oaken panel.

Fullerton and Darwin sat in two juror's chairs, watched by the deputies. Avila sat at the defense table, shuffling papers.

"I'll have you out tonight," Fullerton whispered.

"You lied to the judge about the value of the trust," Darwin whispered back. Gettes was watching them now, eyes burning.

"Sure I lied," Fullerton said. "I thought she might try to wriggle out. Set the bail so high we couldn't make it."

"But I didn't want you to have to lie."

"I wasn't under oath," Fullerton said. "Besides, there are higher values than truth. Get out of here, and I'll see you tonight. You want to stay down on the Marina?"

"For now," Darwin said.

"I have to move fast now," Fullerton said. "Before Gettes gets a whiff of the stink."

"You know, Tom," Darwin said. "I'm surprised that Gragg even played her little game with you. I thought she'd deny bail."

"Kline-James gave her last campaign twelve thousand dollars," Fullerton said.

"I see, Tom," Darwin said.

"It's a war, Jack," Fullerton told him. "And I'm going to be one of your soldiers."

Judge Justine Gragg held a pretrial conference in her library on the third floor of the superior court at Civic Center. She was an imposing figure with a profound bass voice, not afraid to use it on attorneys who got out of line. Avila had been in front of her dozens of times, and it was late afternoon when he came downstairs to the library from a state

RICO hearing. When he came in, Gettes was sitting at one of the conference tables, along with her chief assistant. She was holding a cup of coffee, reading a magazine.

"How's it going, David?" she said without looking up.

"Nice to see you," Avila said.

"I want to give you the DNA results," Gettes said. Her assistant, a bearded veteran of twenty years on staff, handed a manila envelope to Avila. "Read it and weep," Gettes added.

"I can't wait," Avila told her.

"It's all there," Gettes said. "The DNA on the white shirt and topcoat belongs to Dolores Hernandez."

"We'll check it out," Avila said.

Judge Gragg came in. She took off her black robe and hung it over the back of a leather chair.

"Good afternoon, kiddies," she said. "I see we're going to trial on a case that's been in the newspapers every day for three weeks. Aren't we lucky?"

They exchanged laughter, informal greetings. A long window behind Gragg gave views of China Basin, Potrero Hill.

"Let me say one thing," Gragg told them. "There's been a lot of words printed in the newspaper, words out of the mouth of the district attorney's office. It isn't half a circus yet, but it isn't pretty either. I'm somewhat dismayed by the publicity." Gragg turned to Avila, smiled wryly. "Mr. Avila, I congratulate you on not joining the fray. You've been admirably restrained." Gragg turned back to Gettes. "But from now on I want all the leaks plugged and your collective mouth shut. Am I understood?"

"Let me say this about that," Gettes began.

"Just tell me you understand," the judge told her.

"Of course I understand," Gettes said.

"You'll try this case in my courtroom. Not on the streets. Frankly, I'm surprised Mr. Avila hasn't been in front of me before now to complain. I read the newspapers. The defendant isn't getting any breaks out there. I'm surprised a jolly crowd of citizens hasn't broken into his apartment and lynched him before now."

"You're exaggerating, aren't you, Judge?" the assistant asked.

"Mr. Paiewonsky, please," Gragg said. "I'll issue a formal gag order if I have to. I'd rather see this handled by agreement. Push me once and you'll have your order. Clear enough?"

Silence, unamused nods.

"I presume you've gotten together on discovery?" Gragg asked.

"We have," Avila said.

"First off," Gragg began, "let's establish a realistic trial date. And I mean realistic. How would six weeks suit you all?"

"Six weeks is fine, Your Honor," Avila said. "March, anytime later on."

"March twenty-five. Everybody okay with that?"

Silence again, Gettes making notes.

"Let's get the formalities out of the way," Gragg said. "Mr. Avila, do you have any notification of alibi or diminished-capacity defense?"

"No, Your Honor. I don't anticipate that."

"What about expert reports?"

Gettes looked up from her notes. "We have a forensic set and a formal DNA report. I've given both to Mr. Avila. The experts are named on the endorsement."

"We're going to have an expert run the blood," Avila said. "As soon as it's done, we'll file a notice."

"Do it fast," Gragg told Avila. "Say two weeks from today. Is that enough time?"

"I think so," Avila said.

Paiewonsky checked his notes. Avila knew that the assistant did all the hard work, then Gettes tried the case, went on TV, talked to the reporters. Every DA he had ever known had a Frankenstein breaking the big boulders.

"We may add one or two witnesses," Paiewonsky said.

"Do it fast. Two weeks," Gragg told him.

"I'll need time to file motions on them," Avila said.

"Speaking of motions," Gragg said. "I've studied the witness list and I see you have the defendant's wife listed. Isn't that going to be a problem?"

"Not at all," Gettes said.

"You're going to call the defendant's wife in a murder trial?"

"That's right, Your Honor."

"It's perfectly legal," Paiewonsky said.

"Thanks for the opinion," Gragg said.

"Mr. Avila, what do you say?" Gettes asked.

"I'll have a motion," Avila told her.

"Other motions, Mr. Avila?" the judge asked.

"A few, Your Honor."

"What kind, how many, evidence needed?" Gragg asked.

"Well, I think so," Avila said.

"Give me a general idea," Gragg said.

"We'll have a motion *in limine* on the defendant's wife. The others depend upon our DNA tests."

"That's it, Mr. Avila? A couple of motions? I'm very glad to hear it."

"We'll challenge the Lisa Tracy evidence," Avila said.

"That's the other murdered woman?" the judge asked.

"Yes. It isn't relevant, and it is highly prejudicial."

"Good, good," Gragg said. "That's going to be interesting. What kind of briefing schedule are we looking at?"

Paiewonsky took out his pocket calendar. "It would be good to have the motions by March five. We'll need, say, ten days to respond. Hearing in the late teens?"

"Mr. Avila," Gragg said. "Have your motions on file by March three. The government will have eight days. We'll hear the motions in my courtroom on the fifteenth. If you have evidence, get the subpoenas out and call me beforehand and we'll discuss the witnesses and tagging exhibits. Keep it simple, will you? Have your witnesses here and ready to go. I don't want these motions taking more than one day. On Monday morning the twenty-fifth I want everybody here for trial. If you're planning on a postponement, you'd better have a good, damn good, reason."

"Could I ask about cameras?" Avila said.

"No cameras, period." Gragg stood and poured herself some hot coffee. "Is anybody going to challenge me on this? I've a predilection against cameras in my courtroom. I don't have an articulated theory about why I'm against them, mind you. But as I read California law it's within my considered discretion to disallow them."

"The state has no problem with that," Gettes said.

Gragg said, "Nola, I've read your notice. You're really seeking the hard forty? That's the equivalent of death."

"That's right, Your Honor," Gettes said.

"Do you have something to say, Mr. Avila?"

"No, Your Honor. Their burden on the heinous issue," Avila said.

"The defendant has made admissions," Paiewonsky said.

"Those are for motions," Gragg said. "You have copies of his statements, David?"

"I've got copies," Avila said.

"Listen up, everybody," Gragg said sharply. "I want a trial, not a dog and pony show. I want my courtroom to be dignified. I don't want any theatrics." Gragg tapped a pencil on the desk, looked at Avila. "We've had some go-rounds, David. Please try to keep it under control, okay?"

"I'll do my best," Avila said.

"And Nola, you'll be trying the case?"

"Absolutely," Gettes told her.

"Paiewonsky second chair?"

"Correct."

"I want a list of all evidence on my desk at the time of the motions. And give me a list of the order you'll call your witnesses in. Naturally, you're free to scoot them around if things get fouled up."

"We know our order," Paiewonsky told her.

"And remember, kiddies," Gragg said. "It's about justice, not reputations."

They stood while Gragg finished her coffee, left the library room. Paiewonsky was smiling happily.

"How's your client doing?" Gettes asked Avila.

"He's okay," Avila said.

"Listen, you're not going to pull some psychiatrist out of your hat are you?"

Avila shrugged. "I have two weeks to name experts."

"Come on, David, if you're going for diminished capacity, we have a right to know."

"I'll let you know."

"Don't pull this crazy-man shit," Paiewonsky said.

"I won't disappoint you, Nola," Avila said, studiously ignoring the assistant.

"What the hell does that mean?" she asked.

"It's Mad Dog here I'm worried about," Avila said, gesturing to Paiewonsky.

"He is dangerous," Gettes laughed.

"He looks dangerous," Avila said.

"Seriously, David," Gettes told him. "If there's any plea, the time is now, the place is here."

"What would you suggest?"

"I don't necessarily need the hard forty. Plead to second-degree, give me some psychological problems, and he can do life and be out in twenty-five, maybe less."

"He won't do it," Avila said.

"My public waits."

"That's cold. I'll kick your ass."

"Tell me something juicy," Gettes said.

"Make me an offer."

"Come up with some theory. We know the guy had financial difficulties. He was going through a bad divorce. Maybe he was drinking too much. We'll drop the hard forty and he can do twenty-five years."

"You are hard."

"Come on, he killed two women."

"He isn't charged with killing two women."

"We know what we're talking about."

"I'll talk to him," Avila said.

"Only he has to come clean," Gettes said. "I mean, he really has to speak to the citizens of this county. Loud and clear."

"I wouldn't count on it," Avila said.

"Read the DNA report," Gettes told him. "Read it to your client. He's a smart guy. Tell him Lance Ito isn't on the bench and there won't be television cameras showing his pretty face."

"Now you've gone too far," Avila laughed.

"Call me, I mean it. I'm willing to listen."

Avila remained in the library after Gettes and Paiewonsky had gone. He drank a cup of coffee. Heaven could not be this good, he thought to himself. He could hear angels now, wings beating, angels coming to take his client away.

•   •   •

Hello, Karla.

Don't say anything, just listen. Your husband is out on bail, something I didn't count on. He might be watching you. He isn't as stupid as I thought. But he's looking at the hard forty. That means forty years in jail. He'll die in jail, Karla. He's a walking dead man. We'll have the house. With him convicted of murder, you can have the trust fund. Six million dollars, Karla. Do you know how long you can live in Mexico or Costa Rica on that kind of money?

Be careful. Don't call my office. I'll contact you when I can. Just remember, Jack isn't stupid. His old friend Tom Fullerton already lied for him in court. Trust nobody but your real friend, Karla. Your friend. Trust your real friend, six million dollars, Karla. All for us.

Hello, my name is Henry, and I'm an alcoholic. (Hello, Henry) You all know me here. I know you do. And I know you too. Most of you. I guess there are a few faces I don't recognize, but most of the rest of us are friends, and even the strange faces are friendly. I'm going to do something I shouldn't do. I'm going to tell you my name. (Murmurs) You probably know it anyway. Perhaps you do and perhaps you don't, but my name is Henry Diehl. I've been coming to meetings downtown here for three years now, and I've been sober the whole time. But I'm not up here to talk about me and my problems being gay and an alcoholic, and I'm not going to talk about my boyfriends and all the great times I had drinking when I was drinking. I'll do that next time. (Laughter) Right now I want to talk about one of our own, one of our friends, and his name is John. It isn't any secret what his name is either. After all, his picture has been in the *Chronicle* every day for a long time. And you all know what he's accused of having done. A woman was killed one Friday night a few weeks ago and he came to a meeting the following Monday. How many remember him getting up here and talking about losing two friends? (Acknowledgments) We all do. It would be impossible to forget what he said and how he said it. Well, I don't know too much about John, but I don't believe he killed that woman. It's a feeling, but if you heard him talk that Monday, how could you feel otherwise? What can we do? What should we do for one of our own? Well, that's why I'm telling you my own name. He lives in an apartment down on the Marina. I can give you his address if you want to drop him a card. I'm going to visit him today. I'm going to take him some books and a card. I know John had a slip, but I don't think he killed anybody. And I don't have a crush on him either. (Laughter) I just think we should help our brother. I feel it, he's a good person. Anybody who heard him speak here might feel the same way. That's why I've told you my name. Call me, do anything. Write him if you can. If you want to get together and talk about John, call me. Maybe we can do something to help him. Anyway, I'm through for now. I've got to get back to work. Next time I'll tell you a great story about when I got drunk in Petaluma and lost my car and didn't find it for two weeks. It's thrilling. (Laughter and applause)

A Pacific storm lashed the coast with steady rain for three days. It was said the storm had stalled, and that it might linger. In the East Bay a DEA informant named Perry Lehigh—street name Speckles—was killed, his body dumped in the San Pablo Bay, execution style.

Avila met with Darwin at the Marina apartment, murky blue light, characterless furniture, smell of moldy linoleum. Avila had worn extra cologne, just to give his client a whiff of life outside.

"How are you holding up, Jack?" Avila said.

Darwin was in chinos and flannel shirt, eyes red from lack of sleep. Muffled noise filtered in, radio sound, shouts, the steady hum of Marina traffic.

"I'm angry," Darwin said matter-of-factly.

"We've had the pretrial conference," Avila said.

"And?"

"Motions set for the fifteenth. Trial the twenty-fifth."

"God, they're going fast."

"I want it that way. I want you exonerated."

"What about our judge?"

"Gragg is okay. She stuck up for you. No cameras in the courtroom. Wants leaks plugged."

"I don't know her," Darwin said.

"She's tough but fair. She's black and she has a thing about people's rights. She thinks they have them."

"What rights do I have, David? Tell me."

Darwin was circling the tiny room. A note of angry desperation was in his tone.

"Jack, I know you're crazy over all this. But we've got to hang together here."

"I'm sorry, David," Darwin said. "It's just that I can't sleep. I haven't slept in three weeks. I'm in a war, but my opponent is invisible."

"That isn't any surprise, Jack," Avila said. "Try not to dwell on it."

"Karla's been endorsed as a witness against me."

"I'll keep her out."

"Can't you put her under pressure?" Darwin asked. "I've got to know why she's lied twice. There must be another man in her life. Somebody I don't know about. Somebody who did those things to her. If I could just talk to her, perhaps I could convince her to come forward. When she actually sees what's at stake here. What I'm going through."

"I'll call her lawyer," Avila said. "I promise you. I don't think it will do any good, but I'll try. For what it's worth, the DV in municipal court is postponed for now. Everything is on hold."

"I'm frightened, David. Really frightened."

"I know. Think about something else. Fight the feelings."

"The trustee of my dad's estate, Tom Fullerton. He's been really good about things. He closed my law office, negotiated a lease termination. He's freed up some trust money to help with expenses. I guess he's paying the temporary support order in the divorce case. Have you talked to him?"

"No, but I will if you think it would help. Is there anything else private to take care of?"

"No, I don't think so."

"We have our dates on pretrial. I'm busy with them now. I'm going to move to keep out the Tracy cuff links, and to keep Karla off the stand. I'll send you the briefs."

"All right. Thanks, David."

Avila opened his briefcase and took out the DNA reports. He asked Darwin to read the summary of conclusions.

"The blood on your clothes belonged to Dolores Hernandez," Avila said. "At least that's what the lab says."

"It was planted," Darwin said.

Avila stood too. "It's time to come to Jesus," he said.

"What? I'm telling you the truth."

"Come to Jesus with me, Jack," Avila said. "It's likely her blood.

You're going to have to explain to the jury what it's doing on your shirt and topcoat. Did that black cop plant it? Did things get rough at her apartment? Come to Jesus with me, Jack."

Darwin sat down heavily and buried his head in his hands. Classic, thought Avila. Just classic.

"I didn't kill her, David," Darwin moaned. "She was my friend. I cared about her."

"Let me give you a sample trial," Avila said. "They put on their case in about three or four days, keeping it simple. They call the two cops, the forensic tech puts on about three dozen photos of the crime scene. The autopsy reports from Tracy and Hernandez. They introduce your cuff link. They put on the DNA report and the statements you made in custody. They wait for you to get on the stand and then they contradict you when you testify you'd never seen Tracy and that you had a nine o'clock meeting at the Aladdin with your wife. You have no alibi, you are nailed by DNA and physical evidence. I hate to be blunt with you, Jack, but could you please come to Jesus with me now?"

There was a long difficult silence.

"I know what you're doing," Darwin said finally. "I know what you're doing and it's all right. A lot of clients lie or fudge the truth. You can see it all over them. O. J. never hit anybody. Never had a fight with his wife. Or they say they didn't read the contract. On and on until they finally admit they read the contract, they beat their wife. It's that time for me and you, isn't it, David?"

"Yes, Jack. It's that time."

"Well, I didn't kill either of those women. I made love with Dolores, yes. I left before nine to meet my wife. She never came to the coffeehouse. I've never heard of Lisa Tracy in my life. I didn't pick her up and kill her. Karla has an accomplice. He planted the cuff link. He broke in here. He's diabolical, David. I didn't beat my wife, and Karla knows I didn't. There isn't anything else and there isn't going to be any meeting up with Jesus. Never."

"All right, Jack," Avila said. "We need to do something about the DNA report. I need an expert, but it's going to run about ten thousand."

"I'll talk to Tom," Darwin said. "He'll okay it."

"I'll order the examination. Have Tom call me."

"I will, David. You know I will."

"What about witnesses?"

"There's me, for example," Darwin said.

"Character witnesses."

"I'll give you a list."

"Anybody else?"

"You have to break through Karla. You have to keep the Lisa Tracy evidence out of court. I haven't even been charged with her murder."

"It's powerful evidence, Jack," Avila said.

"It isn't relevant," Darwin said.

"They're going to argue it speaks directly to modus."

"I know. But somebody planted that cuff link."

"Jack, there's one other thing. The DA made an offer. I'm compelled to give it to you. She's willing to drop the hard forty in return for a plea. It would be second-degree, life, out in twenty-five. I have to communicate this. Think it over."

Darwin stood and commenced his circling motion. An animal in a cage.

"No, no," Darwin said. "I'm innocent. I'd rather die."

Avila clapped him on the back.

"Okay, my friend," Avila said.

Gettes was at her desk. Paiewonsky at her left, reading the Avila briefs and motions. Mad Dog had made some notes, and Gettes was digesting them, writing on a yellow legal pad while it rained and rained outside.

The receptionist buzzed: "A Thomas Merton Fullerton to see you. He doesn't have an appointment."

"All right," Gettes said. "I know who he is. Show him in."

Fullerton entered the huge corner office, an ornate old man, full head of gray hair, tweed suit, immaculate hands.

"Take a chair," Gettes told him. "I don't think we've formally met."

Fullerton wandered a bit, spying on things, then sat down in a leather wing chair across from Gettes. Paiewonsky eyed them from a desk in the left corner.

"I want to thank you for seeing me. No appointment and all. Something came over me. I just came up."

"It's a pleasure," Gettes said.

"Perhaps a mixed pleasure," Fullerton said. "I've come about Jack Darwin."

"Oh, I see," Gettes said.

Paiewonsky went back to the briefs, one ear open.

"Do you know who I am, Ms. Gettes?" Fullerton asked.

"You're a senior partner in Kline-James," she said. "I think we met once during the gas case. You're kind of on my shit list."

"Yes indeed. But I'm the lifelong friend of Jack Darwin's father. We practiced law together for forty years until he died tragically four years ago in a plane crash up at Lake Tahoe."

"Would you like some coffee?" Gettes asked.

"Can't touch it anymore," Fullerton said. "I used to sit in my office and drink twenty cups a day. Then my stomach went south."

"Occupational hazard," Gettes said.

"At any rate," Fullerton continued, "I've known Jack Darwin the son all my life."

"And what do you want to say?"

"Just that," Fullerton said, leaning forward. "I've known young Jack all my life. Since he was a baby. He'd come to the law office on Saturday with his dad. I've seen this boy grow up. I've seen how he handles himself. He isn't a murderer. That's what I want to say. He isn't a murderer. He couldn't be."

"Do you have any evidence in this case?" Gettes asked.

"No evidence," Fullerton said. "Not like you mean. I'm not here in any official capacity. I'm his friend."

"It must be embarrassing to the firm."

"Now wait a minute," Fullerton said angrily.

"Oh, I'm sorry I said that, Mr. Fullerton. But you're asking me to judge your friend. That's for the jury. Everybody who sits across the aisle from me has a lawyer, everybody is presumed innocent. And your friend has a good lawyer. I assume you know David Avila."

"I've spoken to him," Fullerton said. "But this is different. Literally. You're asking for the state to kill Jack Darwin. That's what forty years would do." Fullerton paused. "That's a heavy burden."

"I feel it, sir. I really do."

"I want to tell you a story."

"All right, sir. I'm listening."

Fullerton sat back. "One year, long ago, our two families went up to Bishop for an outing in the mountains. John and I had a couple of days off after a big contract negotiation and we took our wives and kids to the lake for fishing and hiking. That kind of thing. Well, little Jack had gotten a twenty-two rifle for his birthday and he brought it up. He took it out of the cabin with him. We didn't pay him any attention. Half an hour later he came back to the cabin crying like a baby, which he wasn't. Seems he'd shot a rabbit. Didn't kill it right off, just wounded it, and the boy had to watch that rabbit struggle and die. Terrible thing really. Boy cried all night and part of the next day. Put the gun away and I never heard of him using it again. One of those things that touch your heart and that you can't forget. He was a wonderful little boy."

Gettes sneaked a glance at Mad Dog, still busy.

"I appreciate that, Mr. Fullerton," she said. There was an interval in which Gettes hoped Fullerton would go away. "Darwin had a drinking problem, didn't he?" she said.

"Look, I'd rather not talk about that. I'll tell you one thing. Jack is a contemplative man. He has never been violent in his life, and I mean never. I've never heard him raise his voice to a soul."

"Isn't it possible he beat his wife?"

"I don't believe it. Never did."

"Good people do bad things, Mr. Fullerton," Gettes said. "Sometimes it happens. We can't explain it."

"I want to tell you something else."

"I really have to get back to work."

"Just a moment please," Fullerton said. "Dolores Hernandez was murdered on a Friday night. I had invited Jack to my house for an evening of Monday night football, some hamburgers, that sort of thing. He called me that evening and he sounded very upset. He said he'd lost two friends, that a very special friend of his had been killed and he wanted to stay at home. He said he'd just heard and he was finding it hard to adjust. Jack was short of friends, Ms. Gettes. You don't think he'd kill his friend, do you?"

"Do you have any evidence for me, Mr. Fullerton? You know I'm bound to take any exculpatory evidence to the judge."

Fullerton stood and extended his hand. They shook politely. "It isn't evidence I'm giving you," he said. "I'm begging for this boy's life."

"I understand, sir," Gettes said. "Let me think it over."

Gettes watched him leave. Sitting at her desk, she tried to concentrate on Mad Dog's scrawled legal notes. The first lines of his work read: "We can tear this to pieces. He's missed the main cases. See if you agree and we'll meet tonight. I see us getting the whole Tracy case in. Cuff links and all. And the wife won't get in. But her police reports will."

Gettes looked up, satisfied. She never liked to count chickens that hadn't hatched. But she had to agree with Mad Dog. It looked like a lock.

He discarded the small business calendar after a week's work. On the wall of his bedroom in the Marina apartment, Jack Darwin built his own calendar, a whitewashed space of plain wallpapered wall where he could track his wife down to the finest iota. Everything she did, everywhere she went, every piece of paper she generated. His lawyer had managed to get the phone logs of her long-distance calls, every toll call made to the Bay Area. Darwin spent all his waking hours plugging in the gaps in his knowledge of Karla, making up for the years he'd spent drinking in Marge's on Sunday night, not caring where his wife went or what she was doing.

He saw her buying roses, liquor, taking mud baths at a spa in Mendocino. When had she made that trip? Darwin drove to the spa and checked through the registration books, but he found nothing he could put his finger on. Perhaps she had met her lover there, but she had been careful. Even her Gold Card receipts showed nothing. Lunch and dinner. Mud baths. Tennis lessons. The time frame was right, and Karla had even told Darwin about the trip beforehand. Darwin went up anyway. It was a war.

Sometimes late at night, Darwin would sit in his apartment bedroom and look at his walls. A huge map of the Bay Area, another of Northern California. The wall calendar filled with tiny handwritten notes, numbered receipts. He had worn the year down to July, then to early August. He knew where she purchased gas. He knew where she had her hair done. He knew where she bought a gift card in the East Bay. The map was filling with red, yellow, blue, green squiggly lines, the comings and goings of Karla. Somewhere, Darwin had to believe, the lines would intersect, and her special someone would emerge, an afterimage of Karla's everyday life.

It wasn't that Darwin didn't believe in his lawyer, or trust the system. It's just that he didn't believe that his case could be won or lost in the courtroom.

About this time, Darwin decided he wouldn't do the forty years. It was a war, wasn't it? And in war, didn't somebody have to die?

Vorhees managed thirty minutes of full-court ball, running up and down the hardwood with some social workers, cops, two or three dope dealers gypping high school, Vorhees feeling his legs go numb as he let the younger guys speed around him for easy dunks. The church gym in the Western Addition was cold, and Vorhees started breathing heavily about ten minutes in, when he used to go thirty, forty minutes full blast without missing a beat. There was no shower in the locker room, so he went home and changed clothes, ate a quick ham sandwich, and was back at the Hall of Justice before two. The assistant DA they called Mad Dog was prepping him for hearings on defendant's motions that would take place in a few days, and Vorhees wanted to be a little early to go over some notes he'd made so that when the trick questions peppered him he'd be ready, he could take his time, tell it like it was, rather than giving a garbled version the defense lawyer could mangle.

When he got to his desk a DEA agent named Terry Burkholder was waiting, sitting on a metal chair in the cubicle, just inside the glass partition Vorhees and Cooley had erected for themselves. Burkholder was square-jawed and blond, with a long ponytail tied behind his neck with a rubber band, powder blue eyes, the kind of know-it-all smile that Sears employed to sell men's underwear. Vorhees thought he recognized the agent, but his memory was clouded by years and years of meetings with DEA agents, smoky rooms, clandestine settings, cars full of armed men wearing flak jackets. He shook hands with the agent and sat down. Vorhees was tired, his legs aching, his chest sore from the pounding for rebounds. Vorhees remembered being able to sit in the hot sun in Vietnam for six, eight hours, never break a sweat. Now he couldn't do thirty minutes on court.

"Hey, what can I do for you?" Vorhees asked.

"Have we met?"

"I think so, maybe. I don't remember the case."

"Okay, well. It doesn't matter. I went over to the narcotics squad but they pushed me up here. Maybe you can give me a line on something."

"Shoot," Vorhees told him.

"One of our informers, a small-timer named Perry Lehigh, well, that's what we called him, you know better, it wasn't, but anyway, he was one of our semipros in the East Bay and he was feeding us gang bangers over there one at a time, well, anyway, he got killed, dumped in San Pablo Bay. He was shot in the back of the neck once and then they took some quality time putting about eight more shots into his head, then put his eyes out with an ice pick. We have a problem with that, letting one of our semipros go down like that. It's bad for business."

"Yeah, I'm sure," Vorhees said. "But what can I do for you?"

"We've checked back through his activity. Maybe six months and more, just to see what he was doing that might have produced this. One of the cases was two guys who did a little cross-bay deal. One was a punk named Arthur Vine and the other was a cheese named Luther Dokes. You know these guys?"

"Oh yeah," Vorhees said.

"That's what they told me at narcotics. You were the man to see. We had Dokes in front of a federal judge ready to do five years. The lawyers pressed the judge to bring our informant into court. The U.S. attorney made a deal with Vine because he was a carpet stain, but with Dokes they had an in camera hearing, supposed to be secret. I suppose that's where Lehigh came in, because that's the last I heard of the case. Lawyers were Darwin and Avila. So, what about them?"

"One was *Jack* Darwin. For Vine. You may have read about him in the newspapers. The other is David Avila. Both city types. Hell, I don't think they're connected, but you never know. On the other hand, this scumbag Darwin sounds like he needed money and was drinking big-time. He was separated from his wife, beat her up, dating some student of his. Not a pretty picture. This guy Darwin might have let your man go for a price. It sure as hell wasn't Vine."

"What have you heard about Dokes?"

"He's connected to some midlevel guys in the city."

"You know them?"

"I could maybe find out."

"What do you think?"

"I'd look at Darwin, except he's going to San Quentin pretty soon."

"That bad?"

"That bad, I think."

"Anything else?" Burkholder asked.

"I don't think so. I'd like to help, but I don't have anything concrete. We talked to Darwin about his lady-killer instinct. I saw him in court beat a reversal on some guy, did a good job."

"You know this Avila?"

"Hotshot. Seems straight enough." Vorhees checked his watch, five minutes late for Mad Dog already.

"Hey, check it out if you can," Burkholder said. "I know you're busy. We all are busy."

"I'll sniff a little when I can," Vorhees told him.

"Our guy was okay," Burkholder said. "I'd like some definite payback."

"Whatever I can do," Vorhees said, extending a hand across his desk.

Vorhees watched Burkholder cross the squad room, trailing self-confidence. He gathered his notes and hustled downstairs for his meeting with Mad Dog.

At home that weekend, he continued putting together the baby room, a crib, some chests of drawers, a fresh coat of paint for one wall. He was reading the Sunday *Chronicle* after breakfast when he caught a single short paragraph in the Metro section, about fifty words if you counted the small print too, all about the death of a dealer named Arthur Leroy Vine, shot in the back of the head, eyes poked out with an ice pick.

Drug-related, the article said, but brutal.

The Ides of March had a nice ring, didn't it? Avila thought so. He was bursting with enthusiasm at his own power, the strength and resource he'd brought with him from Central Los Angeles, where, growing up, strength and resource were about all you could rely on to bear the immediate situation, or you'd die. Avila perceived a certain coherence in the struggle for existence, coming as it did straight to the heart of the matter. Avila in court, Avila in his office, Avila anywhere, could hear the clank of battle, genes in their little enzyme and protein shells collecting in rows for war, the glitter and rustle of death on a hot summer day.

It was ironic how nice Jack Darwin looked that day. He was freshly showered and groomed, dressed in a blue pin-striped suit, red power tie, black wing tips polished to mirror finish. Of course, he looked like he hadn't slept for a month too, eyes red, face lined, that faraway stare as though he'd been thinking about spending the next forty years in prison.

Avila sat down next to Jack outside the courtroom.

"How you doing?" he asked. "You okay?" Avila pretended professional concern. "You won't be saying anything today. I just want you alert and participating. Look alive, happy. Pay attention to the judge and look at her directly."

"I know what to do," Darwin said. "What about the DNA tests you've run?"

"Here," Avila said, taking a small manila envelope from his briefcase, sliding it across to Darwin. "Our expert says the blood belongs to Dolores Hernandez."

"I'm not surprised," Darwin said. "Somebody planted the blood. I didn't kill her."

"The blood, Jack," Avila said. "What shall I do?"

"Find the person who put it there."

"Give me a hint, a clue, anything?"

"Have you talked to Karla?"

"She won't talk about the case. It's her privilege. I called her attorney, but she won't budge. In my position, I can't badger her. It would backfire on us."

"She's lying, David. She's lying."

"Of course. I understand that."

They sat together for a while, Darwin reading the DNA printout results. It was cold in the hall, and a garish fluorescent light suffused the space, two wood benches. Avila watched Darwin lapse into what he called the tormented-cat routine. Once, when Avila was a kid, he had trapped a stray cat and put it in a small cage, poked it intermittently with a sharp stick. The cat fought for a long time, then lapsed into frustrated despair, barely moving, eyeing every motion outside with suspicion and rancor. That was how Avila saw Jack Darwin right now, sobbing with inner rage, impotent.

"Let's go, Jack," Avila said at last.

"Okay, sure," Darwin said quietly.

Only four reporters were in the courtroom, a number far below Gettes's expectations and hopes. She had been up in her office going over the briefs and arguments with Mad Dog for about two hours, and when she came down on the elevator she expected to be mobbed for interviews, expected to fight her way into court through a phalanx of flashbulbs and microphones. Instead, the halls were quiet, and she faced two questions, neither designed to put the spotlight on the district attorney. With no television and a virtual gag order from Judge Gragg, public interest in the case had waned. The masses had moved to another spectacle, another scandal, another story of death, an actor sneaking a gun on board an aircraft.

Besides the four reporters, there were maybe fifty or sixty people in the gallery, court groupies, a few lawyers killing time between divorce hearings, some friends of Jack Darwin sitting in the front row, Gettes recognizing Tom Fullerton and one or two others from the same firm. She sat down next to Mad Dog and studied the brief for a final time, going over her notes and outlines, taking stock of half a dozen cases she'd memorized. For a murder case, things were going very well indeed, so well that she knew she needed to knock on wood. There was no alibi, no psychiatric witness, no dubious claims of coercion, trickery, force or violence. Darwin's admissions were coming in loud and clear, and the DNA evidence was good as gold. It was a dream case, the case of a career, something that might put her ass in the attorney general's chair if she could catch some decent publicity and get a conviction. She liked everything about prosecuting, but she had never liked the death penalty. Deep inside, Gettes knew it was too final, that every case had loopholes, sidetracks, alleyways, subtle and not-so-subtle vibrations that could tip the scales of justice one way or another. And once you'd put a person to death, that was it, wasn't it? Maybe that's why she went for the hard forty on Darwin.

Mad Dog leaned over and whispered, "Don't let Avila take it to a personal level. I've had cases with him before. He can get under your skin."

"I know, M. D." Gettes said. "We'll cruise through this."

Judge Gragg came in and took her place on the bench.

"Are we ready, ladies and gentlemen?" she asked.

Two quick replies from Gettes and Avila, the judge reading through notes.

"Let's see if I understand you properly, Mr. Avila," the judge began. "You've got a motion on the prosecution effort to bring in the cuff link and any information whatsoever on the Tracy killing. You've got a motion to keep out the wife's testimony. You haven't got anything about alibi or diminished capacity, is that right?"

"Correct, Your Honor," Avila said, standing.

"Have you received the blood evidence?"

Avila told the judge he had. Darwin looked back to Tom Fullerton, catching his eye momentarily. Darwin looked away then, up to some windows high in the courtroom wall, semicircles of pale gray light, clouds, a few gulls.

"Do you have an expert to name, Mr. Avila?"

"Not yet. I'd like another week."

"I told you you had six weeks. No games."

"I understand," Avila said.

"No games. No expert reports, no expert testimony. That's the way it's going to be."

Gettes watched Avila work, smooth and organized, hard-looking with impassive, dark, heavy-lidded eyes that seemed smoky and dense. He spoke softly to his client, sifted through his notes.

"We have no expert now, Your Honor," Avila said.

"Very well," Gragg said. "Let's get to the motions. We'll take up the motion *in limine* first. You're asking the court to prohibit the defendant's wife from testifying?"

"Correct. The husband is privileged to keep his wife from the stand to testify against him in a criminal case. It is elementary law."

"Yeah, I've read the statute," the judge said. "I tend to agree with you."

"I'm gratified, Your Honor," Avila said.

Gragg smiled widely. "I've read your cases. The exception would be when a husband is accused of a crime against his wife. Is that not correct?"

"Which is not the case here," Avila said.

"But the wife has alleged a crime against her husband in another court?"

"There is a DV case pending, Your Honor."

"Is that relevant here?"

"No, Your Honor, it isn't."

"The district attorney says it is. There is a pattern involved in this case, isn't there? The whole point of the wife's testimony is that she was assaulted in exactly the same manner as the victim in this case. Or am I missing something?" Gragg turned her head slightly, pouring on sarcasm.

"You are missing something," Avila said.

"Oh really?" Gragg mused.

"This is a murder trial. The defendant's wife can testify against him in municipal court, where he is charged with domestic violence. But relevant or not, her testimony is not admissible here, where my client's privilege to prevent her from testifying against him is paramount."

"Even though it goes to method?"

"A wife can't testify against her husband. You've named the one exception and the statute doesn't apply."

"So we have to talk to the legislature?"

"Pretty much," Avila said. "The only relevant issue here is what happened to Dolores Hernandez, and the search for the truth about who did this terrible thing to her. My client's relations with his wife, whatever they were, are irrelevant to that search for truth. You let this testimony in and it will inflame the jury."

"There is a divorce pending?" Gragg asked.

"Yes."

"And the DV is pending as well?"

"Trial has been continued."

"We're holding our breath, then."

"Yes, I guess so," Avila said.

"And I can take it that allegations of abuse have been raised against your client in the divorce, is that correct?"

"Your Honor, I don't represent Mr. Darwin in that case."

"Do you know, Mr. Avila? I'm asking if you know."

"Yes, I think those allegations have been raised. And denied, I might add."

"And the wife made a police report in the DV case?"

"Yes, Your Honor."

Gragg tapped her pencil twice on the bench.

"What does the prosecution have to say?" the judge said.

"Your Honor," Gettes said, rising. "There is not a single shred of doubt that the testimony of Karla Darwin is relevant in this case. Her injuries are exactly the same injuries suffered by Dolores Hernandez and Lisa Tracy. Same bruises above the eye, same laceration on the forehead, same bruising on the neck, same strangulation, same sodomization. Karla Darwin can tell the jury what happened to her, and when the jury hears the forensic evidence, they're going to understand that what happened to Karla Darwin happened to Dolores Hernandez. I understand that these facts are open to interpretation. All facts are open to interpretation. That's why we have a jury in this case. I don't think the jury will be inflamed by the evidence. In our brief, we've given the court dozens of cases in which method evidence is relevant, some much more inflammatory than in this case. You don't have to be a rocket scientist to know that the wife's circumstances are relevant. That leaves the defense to answer the question why perfectly relevant evidence should be excluded from a murder trial. The people of California deserve a fair trial too. That's often overlooked."

"The people will get a fair trial," Gragg said.

"To read the defendant's brief you'd never know it," Gettes said.

"At any rate," the judge said, "I've read the statute on privilege and I've read the cases cited by Mr. Avila, and I'm of the opinion that Karla Darwin may not take the stand and testify against her husband. The statute allows the husband to claim the privilege. It's that simple."

"Yes, Your Honor," Gettes said, smiling at Mad Dog.

"But I like your other ideas," Gragg told her.

"We hoped you might," Gettes said.

"Your arguments on the police observations are on point," the judge said. "The police reports and records are not hearsay and they're relevant."

"Yes, Your Honor, we think so," Gettes said.

"Mr. Avila," Gragg said. "What do you have to say on this point? You haven't really briefed the matter."

Avila stood quickly, composing himself. "This is an end run around the statute," he said. "The net effect of allowing in records of the DV case is to let the wife testify against the husband."

"Oh really?" Gragg said. "I wish you had briefed the issue before now. I'll just have to take my chances in Sacramento. Anyway, the cases cited by the prosecution are solid. I'm going to let in the police reports and will allow the officers to testify what they saw in the home, and what was told to them by the wife. Also, the doctor's testimony and records about the rape examination come in. The statute only prohibits the wife from taking the stand. Are we understood?"

"Yes, Your Honor," Avila said.

"Now, ladies and gentlemen," the judge said. "We proceed to the second motion filed by Mr. Avila. You want all the evidence connected to the Lisa Tracy killing barred from this trial?"

"Yes, Your Honor. It isn't relevant and it would be highly prejudicial. It would place my client on trial for two murders."

"And the cuff link?" Gragg said.

"The cuff link is the reason. You'd be placing this defendant in an impossible position. He'd have no way to defend himself. It would automatically prejudice the jury."

"Ms. Gettes, what do you say?" Gragg asked.

"I say the defendant is on record as admitting the cuff link is his. He can explain his statement on the stand. He can sit silent. The law allows him to do that. But in the case of Lisa Tracy, not only is the method exactly the same as the case at bar, but we have a physical link to the defendant. To keep that evidence out would deprive the state of its right to use all its evidence. The cuff link isn't prejudicial in a *legal* sense. What Mr. Avila meant is that the evidence of the cuff link is damning, which is not the same thing as legally prejudicial."

"Mr. Avila?" Gragg said.

"This is a criminal case. If they were going to charge him with the Tracy murder, they should have done so."

"Well, Mr. Avila," Gragg said, "I'm going to overrule your motion. Frankly, I don't think it's even very close. The cuff link and all the police reports on Lisa Tracy come into the case. Take me up later. You will anyway."

"All right, Your Honor," Avila said.

"If that's it then folks, thanks for being so brief. I appreciate it. I'll see you on the twenty-fifth."

Gettes rose and watched the judge go into her chambers. Darwin and Avila conversed briefly, then left together.

"Christ that was easy," Gettes whispered.

"Avila missed everything," Mad Dog said.

"He doesn't have much."

"Even so, that was weak."

"Strike two, then."

"Almost three," Mad Dog said.

"I can't believe he led us down the path to Karla Darwin. He spent his whole brief worrying about the wife's privilege. We couldn't have broken that privilege in a million years. What was he thinking about? Had he forgotten the police reports, medical observations, the stuff with the hospital staff? Surely he knew there would be a fight about all that."

"Maybe he's cashing it in," Mad Dog said. "I smell a deal."

"God I hope so," Gettes said. "These murder cases give me a pain in my neck."

Mad Dog closed his briefcase. "Yeah, me too."

"And I thought you didn't have a heart," Gettes told him.

"It isn't that," Mad Dog replied. "There's a lot of work in a hard forty appeal. That's all."

Forest Hill was quiet, the big house empty. Tom Fullerton was in his easy chair reading the newspaper after a long day in what had been a week of long days. He read a few lines, then stopped and wondered if he would ever retire, or if someday he would be found slumped behind his desk, a drop of white spittle at his lip, his heart permanently silent. Half a dozen of his lawyer friends had gone like that, at the end of a hard day, weariness over some contract or other turned into demonstrable death. More than drowsy with age, Fullerton was unhinged at missing the first day of Jack Darwin's trial because of the press of work. And when he read about the composition of the jury, he found himself amazed and angry, disappointed that he hadn't been there to exchange the occasional sympathetic glance with Jack, who would turn his head shyly and look, his face full of anguish and lost hope.

Four blacks, three Hispanics, two Asians, three whites, a mix of alternatives, and even these jurors had not been sequestered. Fullerton dropped the newspaper into his lap and roused himself from the deeply wrinkled Mexican leather. The house seemed to creak in the wind and a fire guttered in the fireplace where his wife had left it after she had gone down to the Peninsula to visit her aging mother in a nursing home. And now he was alone in a house worth a million, a partnership downtown worth seven figures, hosts of plaques, testimonials, a shelf full of unread books, investments that took up twenty inches of print-out on his accountant's computer.

Fuck this, Fullerton thought to himself. He put on his topcoat.

It was pitch-dark and cold outside. A freezing wind whipped the cypress trees, the dimly lit suburban streets snaking downhill into distances unperceived. He got into his new Cadillac and drove to Pacific Heights in fifteen minutes, taking about five minutes to find a place to park within walking distance of Jack's house.

He stood in front of the Pacific Heights house where John had lived, a man with rough grace. He must have been hard to share a house with, impossible to cultivate almost, and yet there had been an imposing freedom to him, a freedom that did not feed from others. Fullerton aimed the arc of his memory back and down, toward young Jack and his brother, Adam, clear that Jack was the artistic and sensitive one. No way Jack Darwin was a killer. No way.

Fullerton swung onto the flagstone path. Back in the good old days they'd played basketball in the drive, the kids shouting for the ball, both little boys against older men who towered over them and laughed. He remembered the smells of roast pork and bock beer, hamburgers and red onion, the boys rose-faced in the summer cold and wind. There had been a time—what—twenty-five years ago when Adam had stepped on an upturned rake and sent the rake's teeth into the sole of his tennis shoe, blood blooming there like a flower, and little Jack darting to his brother's side and withdrawing the rake, little Jack with the bloody spear in his right hand, almost crying but not quite letting himself cry for fear it might alarm or disgust his big brother, who was old enough to understand and assimilate the pain, but who was still surprised. Not the actions of a killer.

The doorbell rang. It startled Fullerton, who had pressed it himself.

Karla opened the door until the night chain snapped tight.

"I'm sorry," she said, confused.

It was the smell of vodka, unmistakable and deep. Fullerton sensed another aroma, maybe fear. He had some nerve coming over to Jack's old house, didn't he?

"Tom Fullerton," he said pleasantly.

There was music in the house, Tony Bennett. Karla seemed to stumble from the door. Fullerton could see her skin above a black turtleneck sweater, hot and brown, the product of tanning parlors and unguents.

"You're Jack's friend?" she asked. "I remember you."

Fullerton shoved his way inside without being asked. He knew the house as well as he knew his own house, left and up two steps to the library and den, down two steps to the breakfast area, out to the patio. Behind Fullerton, cold air rushed inside through the open door. Fullerton remembered Scrabble parties in this house, barbecues and poker games and New Year's Eves where the guests were drunk and good-natured and everybody drove their own cars home and cigarettes were openly smoked and the women were elegant in gowns and red lipstick. After Jack had married, he and his wife had been to the Darwin home just twice. There had been an attempt at friendship, some ersatz gaiety, but it had become clear that Karla was a different breed. Had she actually resented Jack's money, his social standing? Tom Fullerton didn't know. He felt as though he'd let Darwin down, his own unconscious snobbery. Maybe he'd never given Karla a chance.

"Do you mind?" Fullerton said. He tapped the door shut and it clicked gently closed.

"I haven't, I don't know you really."

"I haven't been in this house for a long time."

"Long time," Karla said.

Fullerton saw a vodka bottle in the kitchen. He went down and found a glass and poured himself a finger without ice. He put the glass to his nose and smelled the liquor. Karla stood above him in the alcove, imperious and slightly drunk.

"You never liked me," Karla said impetuously. "None of you did."

"I never knew you," Fullerton said.

"That's a likely story."

Fullerton walked to the patio doors and stared at the bay. He poured more vodka into a fresh glass, slashed tonic in from an open bottle. He walked the drink to the stairs and handed it to Karla on the palm of his outstretched hand. A confessional drink, he thought, if that's what it turns out to be. Drink of the blood.

Karla hesitated and then snatched the drink angrily. The sleeves of the turtleneck were rolled to her elbows. She wore black spandex tights.

"Offerings to the bereaved widow," Karla said.

Fullerton watched her drink greedily.

"Jack wouldn't hurt a fly," he said. "And he isn't dead yet."

"You're so . . . ," Karla said. Hesitation in her voice, a search for words. "I don't know."

Fullerton was warm in his topcoat.

"That's an interesting choice of words," he said.

"I'm going to own this house," Karla said.

"Really?"

"You think you know everything? You don't."

Fullerton walked up to the den and library. The fireplace was full of smoke. Karla swept past him and collapsed into a leather sofa. Her drink was nearly gone.

"I know Jack didn't kill anybody," Fullerton said. "I'm surprised his wife isn't more of a help at this time."

"You don't know what he did to me."

"I've heard. It's hard to believe."

"He was drunk."

"I've been drunk with Jack. He's a pussycat."

"Some pussycat," Karla said. She closed her eyes and dropped her head into a sofa cushion.

"Suppose you tell me," Fullerton said.

"I'm not supposed to," Karla told him.

"Amazing how that cuff link appeared, isn't it? I saw a photo of it in the newspaper and I didn't even connect it to Jack. I mean he hadn't worn those ever. How do you suppose they turned up in the apartment of a dead woman on Turk?"

"You get what you deserve," Karla said.

Fullerton walked to the mantel and picked up a portrait of Jack as a child, a skinny shard of a boy with a dust of freckles on his nose. The light was amber, a slice of Lake Tahoe in the distance like a rose. Are there no more happy lives?

"It must get lonely in this house," Fullerton said.

Karla was silent. Fullerton thought she might be asleep.

"Don't you worry about me," she said at last.

Fullerton put down his drink, untouched. The music had gone off and the fire was sputtering dead.

"Jack never touched you, did he?" Fullerton said.

The drink spilled from her hand as Karla nodded down into her own breast. Fullerton went up the bedrooms and saw the unmade bed, clothes strewn willy-nilly. Some pill bottles were on the dressing table. Hideous wallpaper with fake pearls. There was nothing left of his golden memories now except the memories themselves.

Fullerton left the house quickly, sick of being there. Karla snored softly on the sofa. For a long time Fullerton stood on the flagstone path studying the house as a vivid dark swirled around him. He needed to do something more for Jack. If nothing else, he would be in court every day. Beyond that, what could he do?

Mad Dog called it an "off jury," an unpredictable jury, a favorable jury, a jury full of twists and turns, rocks and rolls, but every time he and Gettes thought about it mental smiles came into their heads. Mad Dog himself had spent a good part of the morning in front of the off jury, waltzing a street cop named Wilson through the DV investigation and reports, making it short, trimming the examination to two hours instead of the five days it might have taken Ito and the O. J. prosecution. Now he was sitting quietly as Gettes examined Amos Vorhees, glancing at the jury, trying to exact some measure of comprehension. Were they paying attention? Did they have that faraway bored stare? Once in a while he made some notes for redirect, but mostly it was a piece of cake, Vorhees being smooth and professional and prepared.

Mad Dog made a row of six dots on his legal pad, then made another, jotting down personal characteristics under each dot. Of the four blacks, three were paying full and complete attention, one woman on the far end near the judge nodding as the morning went on. He wondered if Gragg would pounce on her, administer a feisty lecture, or drop some No-Doz down her blouse. The three Hispanics were women, sitting in the same file, and Mad Dog noticed they often exchanged quick conversational gossip during lulls in the testimony, sometimes during the reading of case reports, probably talking about their kids, who would be on *Oprah* that afternoon, some silly shit the judge ignored. The rest of the jury looked like any jury anywhere, and Mad Dog reserved judgment. One thing was for sure, Mad Dog was surprised he'd gotten any Hispanics on this jury, what with the victim being a Mexican American. You would have thought Avila would have used up his preemptories knocking them off. But he didn't, and now Mad Dog had his beloved "off" jury, one that was going to send Jack Darwin to San Quentin.

Gettes finished up with Vorhees.

"That was great," Mad Dog told her when she sat down.

"He's a good witness," Gettes said. "Smooth as guzzler's gin."

They had gotten it all in, the Tracy evidence, the cuff links, all the photographs of her bathroom, even a used towel. Mad Dog thought Gettes might let out a huge howl of satisfaction right there in the courtroom, but she didn't. From the bench, Judge Gragg asked Vorhees if he needed a break. The black detective told her he didn't. He was ready to go.

"Your witness," Gragg told Avila.

Mad Dog watched Avila collect his notes, study them for a moment, letting the jury see how deliberate and calm he was, how careful. Building drama, becoming the focus, whatever. Over the days through jury selection and the preliminary witnesses, the audience had dwindled to a select twenty or thirty, three or four reporters, some groupies, lawyers, friends of Darwin, the Hernandez people from Fresno, one old railroad man from Lovelock, Lisa Tracy's dad. Just behind Darwin, in the first row, was Tom Fullerton. Mad Dog remembered him from his visit to Gettes, the plea he'd made for Darwin's life. It was touching, and Mad Dog wondered if Fullerton would haul ass over to Quentin to visit Darwin for forty years.

"Anybody ever tell you that you look like Karl Marx?" Gettes whispered to him during the silence.

"I'll take that as a compliment," Mad Dog said.

"I'm going to see if they'll take a plea," Gettes said. "Surely they'll want to dodge this bullet."

"You'd think," Mad Dog said distractedly.

For a full fifteen minutes they listened to Avila drag Vorhees through his background, his years of growing up in the Western Addition, his tour of duty as a marine cop in Vietnam, the long climb through narcotics all the way to homicide detective. Mad Dog thought Vorhees was untouchable. Despite Verhees' attraction as a witness, Mad Dog noticed the black woman juror nearest the judge dozing again, head forward, steady small snores. What the hell, let Avila pile up the credentials for them if that's what he wanted to do, and let the black woman sleep. The juror nodded awake, jerked, nodded down, the process endless, eyes fluttering, shut, open, shut, open, and then slept soundly for five minutes. Mad Dog remembered a murder case during which the foreman had slept almost all the time. It must have made for wonderful deliberations later. Even Mad Dog had to admit this was boring.

Avila said, "Now let me ask you—has any white person ever called you a racial bad name?"

Mad Dog stiffened immediately. Gettes tapped his arm and put a pencil to her yellow pad. Mad Dog shook his head, no, he wanted to see where this went.

Vorhees glanced at the judge. Mad Dog had coached him to wait five beats before answering any questions. The judge raised an eyebrow and looked down at Gettes.

Vorhees fidgeted.

"Yes, I've been called names," Vorhees said.

"What kind of names?" Avila asked.

"All kinds. Racial epithets. You name it."

"Give me a list."

"Nigger. Coon. Bunny. Spearchucker."

"That's been the case most of your life?"

"That's correct."

"It bothers you?"

"Of course."

"Ever retaliate in any way when you were called those names?"

Gettes wrote a note on her pad: "We stop?" Mad Dog made a split-second decision to let it go on.

"I had some go-arounds in high school."

"You mean fights?"

"Yes. Fights."

"Anything else?"

"I had to do it again in basic training."

"In the marines?"

"Yes."

"And in Vietnam?"

"Only once. Gunfire directed our attention away from racial differences."

Great, Mad Dog thought to himself. There was mild laughter in the audience. Juror two near the judge was fast asleep, snoring gently.

"Are you headed somewhere specific?" Gragg asked Avila.

He said he was.

"Would you say you hate white people?" Avila asked. "After all, you've been through a lot, haven't you?"

Vorhees looked at Mad Dog. Five empty beats.

"I don't hate whites," Vorhees said.

"You've got a problem with them?"

"I don't like being called nigger, if that's what you mean."

Avila changed his direction.

"How long have you known Officer Wilson?"

"Off and on, five years. I don't know him personally. I know who he is."

"He's a black cop and you know him."

"That's right."

"Now, Wilson took the DV report from Karla Darwin?"

"He said he did."

"Did you talk to him about the DV case at any time?"

"Of course. I interviewed him in connection with my own investigation of the defendant."

"When was that?"

"Right after we ran the name Darwin in the computer."

"Before you went to the Darwin house?"

"Yes, just before."

"He described the Darwin house?"

"Yes."

"He'd been all through the Darwin house, hadn't he?"

"Of course."

"You said you were alone when you found the cuff link in the Lisa Tracy bathroom?"

"I wasn't alone. Detective Cooley was nearby."

"You found it alone though?"

"That's right."

"And did Wilson give you the cuff link?"

Judge Gragg took off her glasses and looked around the court-room wearily. Mad Dog wrote a note: "Let him answer." Five beats.

"Absolutely not," Vorhees said.

"You didn't plant that cuff link?"

Mad Dog note: "Do it now."

Gettes rose. "This is one of the most outrageous fishing expeditions since Jonah," she said.

"I can connect it up," Avila said.

"Come up here, people," the judge told the lawyers.

At the bench Mad Dog and Gettes surrounded Avila.

"You're going to connect it up?" Gragg asked.

"I can do that," Avila told her quietly.

Mad Dog said, "Mr. Avila is out there alone, Your Honor. I'd like to see him connect it, but I don't think he can." There was an audible murmur in the audience.

"You people sure?" Gragg asked Gettes. "I'm ready to shut this down."

"Be our guest," Gettes told Avila.

They returned to their tables. Gettes leaned over to Mad Dog and said, "What's he got?"

"He's got shit," Mad Dog said. "Bank on it."

"I can see headlines," she said.

"You know," Avila said, "that the defendant did not live at his home during the Tracy murder?"

Vorhees said, "That's correct."

"Then how could the cuff link arrive at the bathroom floor of the Tracy apartment?"

"The record is clear. The defendant returned to his home on several occasions to retrieve clothes and personal effects."

"That's it? That's your theory?"

"He had the opportunity to return, leave the cuff link. He realized he had only one. He left it. He never expected to be arrested. They never do."

"Officer Wilson didn't give you the cuff link?"

Five beats.

"Absolutely not," Vorhees said calmly.

Mad Dog doodled a hangman's noose on his legal pad.

"Turning to another point," Avila said. Avila stood behind the lectern, searching his notes. Mad Dog noticed the sleeping juror jerk awake, surprised to find herself in court.

"We're waiting," the judge said.

"Yes, Your Honor," Avila replied, walking in front of the lectern. He leaned on it from the side. "You've emphasized the distinctive nature of the crime committed against Lisa Tracy, haven't you?"

"That's correct."

"Very distinctive?"

"Very."

"Ever seen a crime like it?"

"Yes. The crime committed against Dolores Hernandez."

Avila blanched. Slam dunk, thought Mad Dog.

"But any others? In your experience."

"Yes. One other."

"Tell us about it."

"A woman named Jean Hobart was assaulted at the Holiday Inn down at the airport last Christmas Eve."

"Same style?"

"Yes sir."

"Did she die?"

"She didn't. She was lucky."

"You ever solve that crime?"

"No sir, not yet."

"Did you connect it with any suspect?"

"No sir, not yet."

"You wanted to solve that case, didn't you?"

Five beats, Vorhees looking at Mad Dog.

"Of course I wanted to solve it."

"That was your first case on homicide?"

"It was my first, basically."

"Couldn't solve it, could you?"

"Not yet."

"It bothered you, not being able to solve it?"

"It bothered me. Of course. Not being able to solve a crime always bothers you."

"Doing good work is how a detective advances, isn't it?"

Five beats. Nothing from Mad Dog.

Gettes wrote: "This is ridiculous." Mad Dog made a big X on his notepaper.

"That's one way," Vorhees answered.

Oh no, thought Mad Dog. First mistake.

"What other ways are there?"

"Doing good work, that's what I meant," Vorhees stammered.

"That's not what you said."

Vorhees shrugged. "There is some politics."

"Like the politics of race?"

"Not that I've noticed."

Avila smiled. "Very diplomatic. I think we all know what you mean."

"Objection," Gettes said automatically.

"Sustained," Gragg croaked. "Musing out loud is not permitted, Mr. Avila."

"All right, Your Honor," Avila said. Turning to Vorhees now Avila said, "I'll ask you this clearly. You saw a chance to solve a big case and get in the headlines, didn't you? You took your chance by conspiring with Wilson to plant that cuff link, didn't you?"

One beat, four short of optimum.

"Absolutely not," Vorhees said.

"Wilson had the opportunity to steal a cuff link from the Darwin home, didn't he?"

"He had an opportunity."

"Plenty of time to steal that cuff link."

"Ask him."

"I'm asking you."

Gettes stood. "This question is asked and answered. Besides, Mr. Avila did have a chance to ask Officer Wilson that question and he didn't do it."

"I'll do it on my own time," Avila said.

"The question has been answered," Gragg said. "You're done here, Mr. Avila. Unless you've got something concrete."

Avila stood at the lectern, taking refuge in his notes. Suddenly he left the lectern and strolled directly toward the sleeping juror.

Looking straight at juror two, Avila said, "Your Honor," in a booming voice. The juror jerked awake again, eyes wide and confused.

Avila locked his stare on her. "Madam, we've just had very important testimony elicited here. It would have been wonderful if you'd been awake to hear it."

"Enough, Mr. Avila," Gragg said. "Do you want a mistrial? Is that what this charade is all about?"

Avila stared at the juror, then turned and walked to the lectern, putting his hands on his hips.

"Not at this time," Avila said. "I have nothing further," Avila continued, sitting down.

Judge Gragg took off her glasses and looked at juror two.

"Madam juror," the judge said calmly. "I know it has already been a long three days. The morning wears on and on. Please try to maintain attention to the testimony. Very important matters are at stake. If you continue to sleep, I'll have to excuse you for an alternate. All right now, let's take a fifteen-minute break. You folks go refresh yourselves."

Mad Dog followed Gettes into a corridor between the judge's chambers and library. Gettes was biting her fingernails nervously, even though there was nothing left to chew. Mad Dog was happy, on top of the world.

"That was okay," Gettes said. "A good morning's work."

"That was great. Avila was hopeless."

"I think they're going to plea," Gettes said.

A few reporters hovered near the chamber door, hoping for an interview, any tidbit.

"You think I look like Karl Marx?" Mad Dog asked.

"Karl Marx? No, you don't look like Karl Marx. Karl Marx had style. You're just a mad dog."

RACE CARD.

Vorhees folded the *Chronicle* in half, smoothed it, dropped it on the floor at his feet. He sat on the edge of the bed in boxer shorts and T-shirt, staring at the folded newspaper. He placed a hand on his left knee and traced the course of a pulpy gray scar. The knee hurt at times, during heavy rain and cold weather, after basketball, always during a long walk or run.

Behind him, Alisha came into the room.

"Amos baby, don't let it work on you," she said.

"Read the story. It's in print."

"It isn't vital."

Vorhees picked up the newspaper, unfolded it, read the headline again. RACE CARD.

"They made it sound like I said the department was a racist department. I never said that. I said there were other factors in promotion. Like luck, seniority. Like some political suck. But I never said anything about racism."

"I know, Amos," Alisha said.

"And that lawyer, Avila," Vorhees continued. "He missed the whole point. It wasn't that I could have planted the cuff link. Me and Wilson. It's always been the timeline. Let's say Darwin wears a pair of cuff links when he's killing Lisa Tracy, then he goes back to his house and wants to leave them there one day when he's picking up some other things. He finds out one is missing. Why would he put the other one back? Maybe he would. Maybe he's a massive fucking ego freak. Maybe he thought he lost it someplace else. Maybe anything. But Avila missed the point."

"I guess, lucky he did," Alisha said.

"And another thing," Vorhees said. "I'm a big believer in correct style. It's a very distinctive thing. I said it on the stand today. Style is like a fingerprint. Guys get addicted to their drugs and they get addicted to their style. They like ski masks. They like Glocks. They like Quik-Trips at three in the morning with a sawed-off shotgun. They do their style time and time again. I've got a computer full of styles, modes of operation. If I'm such a big believer in style why didn't the lawyer Avila go after me on the style of that guy down at the Holiday Inn? Some guy, dark and muscular, tall. Not Darwin, not that time. But same style. Avila missed the boat."

"Baby, I want you to get some sleep," Alisha said. "I'm glad to see you raving like this, but it's time to get to bed. It's your last chance to sleep for six years, Amos. And when our daughter turns sixteen you won't sleep for another four or five years when she's out with the captain of the football team. You'll be sitting up in a rocker beside the door. I know you will."

"Basketball team," Vorhees said.

"All right, captain of the basketball team."

Vorhees turned and embraced his wife. She was big and he was careful with her.

"What'll we name her?" he asked.

"We could do African," Alisha laughed.

"Kwanza," Vorhees said.

"Or Irish. Colleen."

"Baby, I love you," Vorhees said.

"You're a good cop, Amos," she replied. "Forget the newspapers."

Alisha went to the bathroom and Vorhees lay back on the bed. Streetlights outside cast a pale yellow glow on the windows. In the morning Amos Vorhees would get up early and put the folded *Chronicle* in his marine combat trunk along with his dress blues, some battle photographs, a fatigue outfit, and dozens of letters he'd received in Vietnam from his mother, yellow paper now, wrinkled by the humidity of a faraway place. The afternoon *Chronicle* and its RACE CARD headline would become another aspect of the war he thought he'd left behind.

Fullerton brought iced tea to the patio. It was cool in late March, and they were wearing jackets, neither of them wanting to be inside while it wasn't raining. Darwin took his glass of tea and sat on a wooden bench beside a row of dormant roses. There were Norfolk pines in the near distance, and a monkey puzzle tree down the hill. He could see shake-shingle roofs and miles of green.

"Your lawyer is almost a joke," Fullerton said. "Let's do something to stop this."

"I could cop a plea," Darwin said.

"This race thing is ridiculous."

"What about the planted cuff link?" Darwin said, almost to himself. "I didn't think he'd accuse that black cop and his uniformed pal. It doesn't hold water."

"I could file something," Fullerton said. "I've got an old friend named Sandy Mooney. He's a crackerjack criminal lawyer. We could ask for a continuance, substitute Mooney. Let's ask. Go on record."

"Not yet," Darwin said. "I told you I'm working on something at the apartment."

"Jack," Fullerton said. He had been pacing in aggravation, wearing a hole in time. "I'm seventy-six years old. I want you to take something from me without asking any questions." Fullerton was holding a manila envelope. He handed it to Darwin, then pretended to look at his backyard, a swing set, tree roses, a dog run without any dog inside. "It's quiet here, and I've had a good life. I have no regrets. I love my wife, but she's ill, Jack. She can't remember things. Her mind is going. It's only a matter of time."

"I'm sorry, Tom. I didn't know."

"There's fourteen thousand dollars inside that envelope. It was my money, now it's yours."

"But Tom," Darwin said.

"I said no questions," Fullerton told him.

"All right, Tom."

"You're like a son to me. My only son."

Fullerton showed Darwin to the door. Then he made a small fire in the fireplace and had dinner with his wife.

Running clean was how Mad Dog described their case. They were in an alcove behind the judge's bench watching the audience come into the courtroom, some reporters, a few of Darwin's friends, stragglers, people in out of the driving rain. It had been decided that Gettes would take Cooley through the discovery of the Hernandez body, then let Darwin's transcribed statements be read to the jury by Mad Dog.

"Keep it short and sweet," Mad Dog whispered.

"Just like we rehearsed," Gettes told him.

They took their places behind the prosecution table. Judge Gragg entered and called the session to order, Cooley slouching up to the witness chair in lime green sports clothes, like some car salesman out of the mid-seventies. Too much polyester for me, Mad Dog thought, too much cologne, but he was a perfect picture anyway, you had to love him, how could he lie?

Gettes led Cooley through his career. She let him talk about his plaques and awards, his kids. Mad Dog called it buttering the stale bread.

"And what time did you arrive at the victim's apartment?" Gettes asked Cooley.

"Just after nine," Cooley answered.

"Refer to your notes if you wish."

"Okay," Cooley said.

"What did you find when you arrived?"

"Two women were standing in front. There was a uniformed officer standing guard as well. He told me he'd seen the victim inside."

"Did he say if anyone had touched anything?"

"He told me the place was secure."

The officer had testified already, and Gettes was just traversing old ground briefly.

"Did you go inside?"

"After we talked to the two women."

"They told you what?"

"One was the victim's friend at law school. She said she'd come by to meet the victim and go to school. The other was a next-door neighbor."

"What did you see when you went inside?"

"There was some sign of a brief struggle. A couple of magazines on the floor. Chairs disarranged."

Gettes showed Cooley a diagram of the apartment. He confirmed its accuracy.

"And did you examine the rooms of the apartment?"

"Yes. By that time Detective Vorhees had come inside. We both did a search and examination."

Gettes spent thirty minutes confirming all the details of the police reports.

"And you were the first detective in the bathroom?" Gettes asked.

"Yes, that's right. I went in first. Vorhees came in and we looked around, and then Vorhees went to the kitchen to make his inventory."

"And you examined the body?"

"Yes. I did."

"Tell us about it."

Cooley led the prosecutor along a carefully prepared path, a complete description of the murder scene, the position of the body, an inventory of evidence. For Mad Dog, looking on, it was as sweet a presentation as he'd ever prepared. In all Gettes took twenty minutes with Cooley on the inventory at the apartment, ten minutes on the canvass, another fifteen minutes on the interview with Sandra. It was a nice tight display put on in under two hours, and Mad Dog knew they were running clean then. Gettes toured the lectern once, allowing the jury to see her powder gray business suit, her prim white blouse, the simple gold butterfly on her right lapel. She was cooling the jury down; then she was going to let Mad Dog drag them through the real shit.

"Do you know what the word 'heinous' means?" Gettes asked.

"Yes, I think I do."

"Explain please," Gettes said.

"It means violent and brutal."

"Was this a heinous crime, in your opinion?"

"Objection!" Avila said.

"What about conscienceless?"

"Objection, Your Honor," Avila said.

"Overruled," Gragg said.

"Thank you," Gettes said. "Now, Detective Cooley, do you think Dolores Hernandez was the victim of a heinous crime?"

"Yes. Absolutely."

"Why? Please tell the jury."

"Dolores Hernandez was attacked in her home. She was forced to the shower, her clothes ripped from her body, probably after she was partially unconscious. A cut was opened above her eye that went almost to the bone. She was put in the shower and battered still further. Numerous other bruises were on her throat, so she was strangled. And all this time she was being sodomized. Then strangled."

"She would have known what was happening?"

"For much of the time, yes."

"Have you seen other crimes like this?"

"Yes. The Lisa Tracy murder is exactly like this."

"Have you ever spoken to a law student named Gilhooley?"

Cooley took out some written notes. He reviewed them for a few moments. "Stan Gilhooley told us that Dolores Hernandez was seeing a professor, Jack Darwin. He said she'd been in class Friday night before she was killed, and that she'd been at a bar and restaurant next door to the law school after class. Apparently Darwin taught the class."

"Did you interview the defendant?"

"Monday evening."

"What did he tell you?"

"He told us that he'd had dinner with Dolores Hernandez on Friday evening. The dinner took place at her apartment. He said he left a little before nine to keep an appointment with his wife at a coffee-house. He said he got home shortly after ten-thirty."

"Did he say what he was doing between nine and ten-thirty?"

"Sitting in a coffeehouse called the Aladdin in the Marina."

"Waiting to meet his wife?"

"That's what he said."

"Did he meet her?"

"He said she didn't show up."

"And he got home when?"

"After ten-thirty, before eleven."

"How was his mood during your interview on Monday?"

"He was upset."

"Did he admit his relationship with the victim?"

"Not right away."

"What did he say?"

"He said they were friends."

"And then?"

"Later he told us they'd had sexual intercourse the night the victim was killed."

"He finally admitted to sexual intercourse with Dolores Hernandez?"

"Yes, finally."

"And then?"

"And then he ordered a bourbon rocks."

"Objection!" Avila shouted.

"Nice try," Gragg told Gettes.

"Withdrawn," Gettes said, smiling at the jury.

Mrs. Hernandez sobbed in the gallery. Gettes walked slowly to the prosecution table and sat down beside Mad Dog.

"Let's take a break," Judge Gragg said.

"Perfect," Mad Dog whispered. "Two hours, including a sob break or two."

Darwin ate lunch in the judge's library. Gray tuna salad, wilted pickle, potato salad, some iced tea in which the ice had melted, two Oreo cookies. Darwin could tell it was raining outside because people came and went in the courtroom dripping water. He could hear Dolores's mother sobbing in his head, one more fearful image added to all the others.

Avila joined Darwin a few minutes later.

"Rough, huh?" Avila said.

"It's terrible."

"We have until two. You want to talk?"

"Sure," Darwin said.

"I've had a second lab report just come back from the expert. He can come in and say their procedures are shaky. But these lab guys down in the valley are the best."

Darwin explored the tuna sandwich with a plastic fork. He was down to about three hours a night sleep. He had lost ten pounds and was getting sore throats every week.

"What do you think?"

"They'll put Vorhees on to take him through the blood collection at your apartment. Then they'll put on their forensic DNA man."

"What about Karla? Have you talked to her?"

"She won't bite. The police reports were bad enough. I'm afraid if we got her on the stand she'd really hurt you."

"Why is she lying?"

"I don't know, Jack. We've got enough to worry about without her testimony coming in."

"Have you talked to Tom?"

"Sure. He's been good about the money. You're all set and the house is being taken care of, taxes paid. He put up the DNA test money. Gettes tabled a deal this morning."

"What kind of deal? I didn't do it. Tell her that."

"Gettes will drop the hard forty for a plea."

"I can't do it, David. I didn't kill her. I didn't. I loved her. Somebody planted the cuff link and blood. For God's sake, help me."

"You know I have to communicate the offer."

"Sure, I know. Thanks."

"Jack, you're sure?"

"I'm sure," Darwin said, pushing away the metal tray that sat in front of him. "Karla was lying about the domestic violence incident. This has to begin with Karla. Please talk to her somehow."

"I can try her lawyer again."

"One other thing, David," Darwin said.

"Okay, Jack."

"Attacking the black cop," Darwin said. "It doesn't sit well with me. He doesn't seem the type."

"The type?" Avila asked. "God, Jack. You know my style. Attack the evidence and the police. It's all we can do. You said it yourself, somebody planted that cuff link, the blood. It might as well be the black cop. He's all we've got."

"It just hurts, that's all."

"It's what we have, Jack."

"Who's doing this to me, David?"

"I don't know," Avila told him.

"You don't believe me, do you?" Darwin said.

"It doesn't matter whether I believe you or not, Jack. You've been a lawyer for as long as I have. I can tell you I believe you and I can urge you to tell the truth, but in the end it doesn't matter what we believe or say to one another. All that matters is that we're on the same page and that we move the jury our way."

"But the truth is out there somewhere," Darwin pleaded.

"The only vein I see exposed is Amos Vorhees. He looks solid all right, but I've got to show some reasonable doubt somewhere. It's amazing that Judge Gragg let me go as far as she did. Probably had to do it because she was black. That leaves only you, Jack. Do you want to testify?"

"I want to. I have to."

"All right then," Avila said. "You get on the stand and let the jury take a good long look at you. You tell about your life, your family, your background. You tell them about your feeling for Dolores Hernandez. We'll make it clear to the jury who you are, what you stand for. We'll put on Tom Fullerton to speak for you too. We'll spend the next three or four nights preparing for your testimony. By the time you get to the stand, you'll be ready. We'll tell the jury that no matter how much blood evidence there is, you're not a killer. We'll give them a choice between their heads and their hearts."

Darwin managed a brief smile. He was light-headed from lack of sleep.

"One other thing, David," Darwin said.

"You name it."

"I wasn't wearing the camel hair topcoat the night I had dinner with Dolores."

"Yes, we've talked about that. I had my investigators talk to all the people at the Aladdin. Nobody can remember you specifically. It was crowded, a lot of people came and went. We tried."

"My stable hand came to see me that night."

"And?"

"He might remember my blue suit."

"I thought you'd undressed."

"I had on blue pants."

"It's a long shot. Not much."

"Yeah, I know. I have a lot of time to think."

"Try to hang in there, Jack," Avila said.

"How many more days until they're done?" Darwin asked.

"One, maybe two. They've got the DNA lab tester and maybe the stenographer who took your conversation at the station house."

Darwin stood up.

"We'll be done soon," Avila said.

"For better or worse," Darwin told him.

"Try not to think that way. I know it's hard."

Darwin watched Avila go again.

Twelve came that afternoon. Headed by Henry Diehl, who sat on the aisle behind the defense table, Fullerton next to him, they took up seats and stood as Darwin was led into the courtroom. Darwin seemed shocked to see them standing.

"Who are those people?" Mad Dog asked Gettes.

"You know Fullerton," she told him. "Believe it or not the rest are from Darwin's AA group downtown."

"Now I've seen it all."

"You can say that again," Gettes whispered.

The bailiff called court to session and a DNA expert was sworn.

"Bring this in under thirty minutes and you're a genius," Mad Dog told Gettes.

She looked at her watch, took a deep breath.

Behind the lectern she spent fifteen minutes on the credentials of the expert, another ten on lab certification. In an even five minutes more, Gettes had nailed Darwin with DNA.

"Short recess," the judge said.

Gettes walked to the prosecution table and dropped her notes, Mad Dog tapped his pencil.

"You're amazing," he said.

"The jury loved my look, didn't they?" Gettes said.

Of the twelve, only Fullerton and Diehl remained in the courtroom.

"I've seen you every day," Diehl told Fullerton. They were sitting in the silent courtroom, on uncomfortable wooden seats. Diehl introduced himself and the two men shook hands.

"I've known Jack for many years," Fullerton said. "His father before him, as they say."

"I've only known Mr. Darwin for a few months," Diehl said.

"You're from his group, aren't you?"

"All of us are," Diehl answered. "We're his temporary support group."

"Jack told me. I know he appreciates you folks coming."

"I'm not a courtroom groupie," Diehl said.

"No, I didn't think you were."

"I don't think Mr. Darwin did it."

"I don't think he did either," Fullerton said.

"I wish I could do something."

"I've been thinking the same thing."

"It's strange," Diehl said. "I expected a trial to be more, well, helpful. I don't know why I say that."

Fullerton was silent.

"All this evidence," Diehl said. "It seems so cut-and-dried. Everything piles up and then the man disappears underneath it."

"I'm going to get a sandwich downstairs," Fullerton said. "You want to join me?"

"Sure," Diehl told him. "I could eat something. I skipped lunch to make some calls at work."

"Let's go, then," Fullerton said. "Maybe you could tell me why you think Jack didn't do it."

They left the courtroom and stood beside a bank of elevators.

"You think you can tell a killer by looking?" Fullerton asked.

"A cold-blooded one? Yes, I think maybe you can."

The elevator door brushed open.

"I think I couldn't maybe. But I think I could tell who wasn't a killer. That sounds odd, I suppose."

"That's just it, isn't it?" Diehl said enigmatically.

Late-afternoon sun patterned the wall. Avila abandoned the lectern, stood just behind Darwin, his hand on the defendant's left shoulder.

"The tests you performed," Avila asked the Silicon Valley expert, "don't say anything about who killed Dolores Hernandez, do they?"

"No, that's not my testimony."

"You don't know who killed Dolores Hernandez, do you?"

"No, I don't. The test says that the blood in the defendant's apartment is that of Dolores Hernandez."

"Just answer my question."

"The answer is no, I don't know."

"You don't know then who killed the victim?"

"Let's not get sidetracked," Judge Gragg interrupted.

"No, let's not get sidetracked," Avila said. "In fact, there are many ways your tests could be wrong, aren't there?"

"There are some inaccuracies possible."

"Not enough DNA to sample is one?"

"Not enough DNA, that's right."

"And you sampled two small stains on a topcoat and a shirt?"

"Correct."

"Were the samples too small?"

"No, I wouldn't say so."

"But smaller than you'd like?"

"Of course. But not too small."

"How many probes did you get in the samples?"

"Three."

"That's a small sample, isn't it?" Avila asked.

"Somewhat."

"Weren't larger samples available at the crime scene?"

"Not that I know of."

"Weren't you aware of a bloody towel at the victim's apartment?"

"Oh yes. That. I've seen that."

"What about it?"

"It had been soaked in water."

"And that makes the samples of blood contaminated?"

"Yes. Heat and ultraviolet could contaminate a sample as well, if that's what you're aiming at."

"That's helpful. Water and sunlight."

"That could contaminate a sample, yes."

"You were aware it was raining the night of the killing of Dolores Hernandez?"

"I wouldn't know."

"I'm telling you," Avila said harshly.

"If you say so," the witness replied.

"And if Detective Vorhees took the shirt and topcoat out into the rain it would contaminate the samples?"

"It could."

"But you didn't talk to Vorhees about the samples, did you?"

"No. I examined the sample. It seemed fine to me."

"And another possible error is documentation, isn't it?"

"Of course. We take every precaution to avoid that."

"Don't labs have to be tested by outside institutions before they are certified to run DNA tests for the state of California or anybody else?"

"All the time. Our lab procedures are tested regularly."

"How often?"

"Twice a year."

"That's because DNA testing is highly volatile?"

"What do you mean?"

"Subject to errors, foul-ups, mistakes."

"Yes. It's delicate. Every lab has an error rate. The rate is factored into the tests. We do several tests in order to further decrease the possibility of error."

"But errors occur."

"Of course."

"Many more than one in three hundred thousand?"

"Objection!" Mad Dog shouted.

"Sustained," Gragg said.

"But errors occur," Avila said.

"They can."

"Was this a blind test?" Avila asked.

"No, of course not."

"That means you tested samples found in the defendant's apartment and you already knew you were looking for Dolores Hernandez's blood, didn't you?"

"Well yes. Of course."

"That doesn't affect you? Make you prone to see gremlins?"

"No. I don't see gremlins."

"You were paid by the prosecution to find the blood of Dolores Hernandez and you found it. Already knew what you were looking for."

"Is that a question?" Gragg interrupted.

"It didn't affect the results," the witness said.

"But a blind test would be preferable?" Avila said.

"Objection," Gettes said. "No foundation."

"Overruled," Gragg said wearily.

"It might be preferable," the witness said, "if we were looking for the defendant's blood at a crime scene. That wasn't the case here."

"There are many other ways for DNA testing to go wrong, aren't there?"

"Not many."

"Mislabeling or mishandling in the lab?"

"Yes, that can happen."

"You ever heard of lab contamination?"

"Of course."

"That's different from environmental insult?"

"Yes, that's different."

"Explain that to the jury, sir," Avila said.

"Lab contamination results when reagents or other substances found in the lab come into contact with the blood sample."

"Such contamination can create a false positive, can't it?"

"Very rare."

"But when you amplify DNA it can be contaminated?"

"Certainly."

"Now explain all these possibilities to the jury. Rain can contaminate a sample. That's environmental insult?"

"Yes."

"Lab procedures can go wrong?"

"Yes."

"Lab contamination can ruin a test?"

"Possibly."

"What about the chain of custody?"

"Well, you need to make sure of the integrity of the sample."

"That means that somebody could plant a sample on the crime scene. Or plant it in the defendant's apartment or home. You'd never know the difference."

"Objection!" Mad Dog shouted. "Pure speculation."

"That's not the question," Avila said. "I asked if it was possible."

"I'll let you go on, Mr. Avila," Gragg said.

"And then," Avila continued, "you have to compare a test result with some hypothetical base population. Your base data could be wrong, couldn't it?"

"Not likely," the witness said.

"I asked you if it could be wrong," Avila said.

"Possible. That's why we certify the integrity of the base-population data."

"And who was your contact at the police department?"

"Detective Vorhees," the witness said.

"Ah, Vorhees," Avila said. "He's the man who collected the blood samples at my client's apartment while his partner was in the other room. He's the man who found the cuff link at Lisa Tracy's apartment while his partner wasn't looking?"

Mad Dog stood quickly. "Is that a question, Your Honor? Or a soliloquy? An irrelevant and prejudicial speech?"

"Stop please," Gragg said from the bench. "If you have a question, Mr. Avila, please ask it. No more sermonizing."

"This DNA evidence, it's all speculation isn't it?" Avila asked.

"Not at all. It is science."

"Indeed," Avila said, placing both hands on Darwin's shoulder. Darwin tried to face the jury. "It's a newfangled test based upon probability."

"No, it's not," the witness said.

"And out of all this mumbo jumbo, you still don't know who killed Dolores Hernandez, do you?"

"Oh, objection, Your Honor," Gettes said.

"The witness never said he knew that, Mr. Avila," Judge Gragg said.

Avila left the lectern. "Your Honor," he said, "I move that the entire testimony of this witness be stricken on the ground that it is incompetent."

Judge Gragg put her glasses on the bench.

"Objection Your Honor," Gettes said, standing. "Counsel saw the pretrial order. He had his chance to examine the blood evidence. Nowhere did he object then, and I think he's out of order now."

"Inside my chambers, please," Gragg said.

Henry Diehl sat forward, trying to ease the strain on his back. He was tired. He'd been sitting on wood for six hours.

"What's going on?" he asked Fullerton beside him.

"A lawyer is calling nine-one-one," Fullerton said.

"Huh? I'm sorry?"

"The defense lawyer has no strategy. He's trying to invent one on his feet."

"That isn't good, is it?"

"Not in my book," Fullerton said.

"You've been a lawyer how long?"

"Forty-four years."

Darwin was looking back at them. Dark circles under his eyes, bags.

"You think she'll knock out this witness?" Diehl said.

"Not in a million years," Fullerton told him.

Fullerton leaned forward with Diehl. He shaped his hands into a prayerful attitude. This is for you, Jack, Fullerton said to himself.

In fifteen minutes the lawyers were back. Judge Gragg trailed in later. She sat on the bench, making notes.

"Ladies and gentlemen of the jury," she said. "I cautioned you at the commencement of this case that the lawyers and I would have occasion to hold conferences in private. We've had some already, both in front of the bench and in my chambers. We discuss legal issues in these conferences. These matters are not by law for the jury. We confer in private not to exclude you, but because they are technical questions of law and the lawyers need to be free to argue their cases. You are here to decide the facts and then apply the facts to the law as I instruct you. What we did just now in my chambers was to decide the merits of the legal motion of the defense to exclude the DNA witness and his testimony." Once again, Gragg took off her glasses to emphasize her point. "I've decided to overrule the motion. First, the question has to be asked, is the expert a qualified expert? I think he is. Secondly, we must find the expert opinions he expressed are supported by scientific reasoning or methodology. I find that they are. Finally, we must ask if the expert opinion is based on reliable data. I find that it is. And finally, I must inquire whether this expert's opinion is so confusing or prejudicial that it should be excluded. I don't believe it is. I think the jury can understand it easily. I trust you not to be confused or prejudiced by the opinion as expressed. Simply consider it for what it is. And Mr. Avila, is that clear to you?"

"Yes, I think so, Your Honor," Avila said. "But I take exception."

"I'm sure you do," Gragg said. "Now, do you have any more questions at this time?"

"Not at this time."

"Ms. Gettes, what about you on redirect?"

Gettes held a whispered conference with Mad Dog. She walked slowly and deliberately to the lectern.

The witness sat waiting. "Do you remember explaining the DNA molecule to me in my office?" she asked him.

"I certainly do."

"Would you relate that explanation to the jury?"

"Sure," he said. "No problem. Let's say the molecule of DNA is a neighborhood of brick homes. All of the homes are somewhat alike in structure, roofs, doors, windows. Each home has rooms inside it. Now, all the houses together are the chromosomes. The rooms inside the homes are genes, and each brick is a nucleotide."

"And scientists can analyze that structure?"

"Surely."

"And this is solid science, not hypothesis?"

"Absolutely."

"And the rooms in the houses you analyzed, they belong to Dolores Hernandez?"

"To a mathematical certainty."

"And that certainty is?"

"There's a one in three hundred thousand chance of a random match. Otherwise, it's her blood."

Gettes left the lectern, took a single step toward the jury box. "I think I understand that," she mused. "I certainly think I do." She turned to Avila and Darwin. "Your witness."

Avila searched his notes.

"Nothing more," he said.

"Ms. Gettes?" the judge said.

"At this time," Gettes said imperiously, "the prosecution rests, Your Honor." She put a hand on her hip, posed, let the jury contemplate her serious nature. She sat down next to Mad Dog and snapped her briefcase shut.

"That's it then?" Mad Dog whispered. "Everything but motive and common sense."

Gettes watched the jury, all eyes on Jack Darwin.

"Details," Gettes whispered back. "You never said if you liked my new spring look."

In Los Angeles, Avila had specialized in sociopaths. He knew them, dealt with them, represented them in court. They were his people, blood of his blood, flesh of his flesh. L.A. was a city filled with sociopaths, of course; it bred them like tropical fish. Even straight people could be mistaken for sociopaths, lying their way into situations and then lying their way out. Avila would meet them all the time at the county jail, and he would let them tell lies to his face. He listened to their lies for weeks, stories changing form like ghosts. Weeks would pass and Avila would visit and revisit his client until the lies became quiescent, and then he would plead his client guilty to some charge or other, it hardly mattered, Avila not knowing or caring how the lies connected to the truth, or whether there was a difference. Avila studied his sociopathic clients and learned from them, from their inability to discern their own self-interest, the joy they took telling lies. Avila had learned what lies were worth telling. He prided himself. He thought of himself as professional.

They were in the bland gray hall, Darwin looking pale in a dark blue suit. Darwin held his trial notes in two hands as if they were a Bible. Defendants often made notes, how quaint! Perhaps Darwin thought his words would save him, that each recorded day of his suffering would render him immune from final judgment. It amused Avila, this devotion to words and meaning, as if life *had* meaning. What an irony that his new client had no lies available. Lies had covered him, made him suffocate.

"We start tomorrow," Avila said. "When I finish my opening you're taking the stand."

"Did you see Angel?" Darwin asked.

"I spoke to him briefly."

Darwin waited hopefully.

"Did he say anything?" Darwin asked finally.

"He can't help us, Jack," Avila said. This was a lovely way to put it, almost true. Not a lie really, but transparently viable. "I'm sorry as hell, Jack," Avila said. "But calling him to the stand won't do anything but convince the jury that we have nothing to say. My strategy is to use your character to convince the jury that you couldn't have done these terrible things. We let them hear you loud and clear. We've got five hours of good testimony right now. When we're done, the jury will know you, like you, understand you. Then I'm putting on Tom Fullerton to speak for you. I can't think of anyone better, can you?"

"No, he's known me all my life," Darwin said. "Is there any word from Karla?"

"No, Jack. We can't count on her."

"But she's lying. I know she is."

"But even that wouldn't change the blood evidence."

"She has a lover. Somebody."

"She's been tailed all over."

"They won't believe me, will they?" Darwin asked hopelessly.

"Sure they will," Avila told him.

"No they won't."

"Look, Jack," Avila said. "Don't think that way. You need to look ready and eager to tell your story. You need to get on that stand and act like what you are, an innocent man, a man who has been wrongly accused. You need to exercise a little outrage that this is happening. You need to look that jury right in their twenty-four eyes and tell them down to your guts that you didn't do it, and you couldn't do it, that something terrible has happened, but you're not responsible. I'm going to pave the way for you in opening, but after that you've got to take the handoff and run across the goal line. You crack on the stand and give the jury reason not to believe you and they won't. I've seen a lot of juries in my time and they listen to the defendant, pay attention to you. They want you to be innocent! They really want you to be innocent. Can you get on the bandwagon with me, Jack?"

"Sure, I'll try," Darwin said.

"Hang in there, then," Avila said. "We've rehearsed this enough. Go over your notes. Be ready. Don't let Gettes put you over without a fight."

It was full dark by the time Avila reached his Jaguar parked in the Hall of Justice parking lot. He drove up Seventh Street to the YMCA and lifted weights for an hour, did some stretching, then undressed and waited in the sauna. Fifteen minutes later Zack entered and sat on a redwood bench down from Avila, up a level.

Avila poured a cup of eucalyptus oil–laced water onto the heating coils. The chamber filled with hot steam. Zack sat wrapped in a bath towel, sweating profusely. His face turned swarthy.

"Jesus, you're boiling me," Zack said.

"You whacked them both," Avila said. "You whacked the snitch and you whacked Vine."

"They had it coming," Zack huffed. "How can you stand it in here? I'm getting out."

"Vine wasn't part of the deal and you weren't supposed to whack the snitch. It's dangerous."

"Word gets around you fuck with us, you're dead," Zack said. "It's good PR."

"It wasn't part of the deal," Avila said.

"You want more money, is that it?"

"It isn't about the money."

"Then, what's it about?"

"I'm in a drug case and the two principals get whacked. That's my problem, Zack. I gave you the East Bay guy, that's okay, you know his name. You shouldn't have whacked him. Vine was stupid."

"He was a nothing," Zack said. "His people will remember."

"He wasn't totally ganged up," Avila said.

"Look," Zack said, huffing. "I'll take care of you. You'll have five grand at your office this afternoon."

"All right, Zack," Avila said.

"Hey, nobody gives a shit about Vine."

"I hope you're right, my friend."

Zack stepped off the redwood bench. The steam was clearing.

"Don't ever think we're friends," Zack said.

"I'm as close as you'll ever get," Avila said.

"You're a fucking lawyer," Zack said. "That's all."

Zack left the sauna and stood just outside in front of a narrow glass window. Avila could see him standing in the harsh glare, rubbing himself with a face towel. Now that Avila was no longer dealing with L.A. sociopaths he would have to recategorize his clients. Maybe Zack was a predator. After all, that's what Avila told himself he himself was, a predator. Avila was one of the first maybe, a loner, a predator. But now the predators were running in packs, like Zack. It made a person feel cold, but it was the truth.

Five hours and ten minutes by Mad Dog's watch. Gettes thought it might have been longer, given the rigors of emotion Darwin suffered through trying to make himself look innocent for the jury. By Mad Dog's reckoning it was unintentional and mundane. He had started out cocky and outraged and wound up like a dishrag. For a brief moment juror two had slept during the "love story"—as Mad Dog called it— while another had yawned twice, yet another caught himself glancing at the gilt clock high on the wall above the audience. The day tended to drone on and on like that, a regular daytime drama. During hour three his facade had cracked badly, though Mad Dog acknowledged it could have been a show cooked up by Avila to elicit sympathy from the jury, Avila being a smart cookie and general courtroom Svengali. After all, Darwin had nothing going for him but his own blue blood and character, which, as Gettes put it, "wasn't that fucking hot to begin with." During the break, Gettes and Mad Dog went to the judge's small law library and conference room just behind chambers and drank a couple of diet sodas. The city outside was shrouded with cold mist and they could barely see Civic Center, all the bums and panhandlers massed at the corner of McAllister, where somebody was giving a talk.

Mad Dog had trimmed his beard, trying to look like Che, not Karl Marx.

"We going long or short?" he asked Gettes.

Mad Dog sipped his soda, set the can on a window ledge. It had been five years since he'd had a cigarette, but he wanted one now. "I wish I had a damn cigarette," he said to his own reflection.

"Those people are in the front row again," Gettes said. She was flipping through a bar journal.

"There are twelve of them," Mad Dog said.

"They come and they go. Sometimes there are only seven."

"You see Sandy Mooney out there?" Mad Dog mused. He was sure somebody was smoking an unfiltered Camel in the room next door. He could smell it, his nose was impossible to fool. "He's an old labor and criminal lawyer."

"The name's familiar," Gettes said.

"He defended all the labor guys on the waterfront way back when. He must be seventy."

"Fits right in with Fullerton, then."

"Don't sell him short," Mad Dog cautioned.

"How do you *know* these things?" Gettes laughed. "I mean really, how do you frigging know these things?"

"Clairvoyance," Mad Dog said. "Plus, I been up here a long time."

"So what's he doing here?"

"Observing. He's been in back for a week."

"I didn't see him," Gettes said.

"I saw him."

"That's why you're the Dog," Gettes said. "What's he doing here?"

"He's on Fullerton's payroll would be my guess. Scouting for errors on appeal. Avila won't do the appeal. It'll be Mooney."

"Okay, I can deal with that," Gettes said. She joined Mad Dog at the window, looking down on Civic Center, stunted sycamores, like rows of gallows.

"Civic Center," Mad Dog said. "It's a mess."

"Graffiti and bonfires."

"Sign of the times," Mad Dog mused.

"Say it ain't so, O Mad Dog," Gettes laughed.

"Time to go," Mad Dog told her, draining his soda.

Down on Civic Center, chains of gray smoke drifted. Even through the heavy plate glass you could almost smell rubber burning.

"Let's do the short version on Jack Darwin," Gettes said.

"You tired?" Mad Dog asked.

"Not really. Let's get the jury out of here. Let them do their work."

"All right by me," Mad Dog said.

They walked into a corridor that separated the courtroom from judge's chambers. An armed guard stood beside the door where lawyers came and went. Mad Dog had been doing trials for twenty years, since before the time of metal detectors, bomb scares, and armed guards. There had never been a civilized way to conduct a murder trial, but it had been better than this.

"I'm going to jump around on him," Gettes whispered.

The guard nodded. He had his hand on the butt of an automatic pistol, holstered.

"Thirty minutes, more or less," Gettes said. "Spin him, make him deny everything. Look at the jury and shake your head every once in a while. Avila will kill us for it, but it will be noticed."

"You're the boss," Mad Dog said.

They went inside the courtroom. Five minutes and the judge came in, called order. Darwin took the stand looking tired and stoop shouldered. Gettes took a chance and stood in front of the lectern in her smart outfit, leaning against it slightly. Here I am, she thought, smart gray tweed, ruffled blouse, perky blue string tie.

"Dolores Hernandez was your student, wasn't she?" Gettes began. Mad Dog had counseled her to start in the middle and work her way out.

"Yes, she was," Darwin said, surprised. His voice was light as dust in moonglow.

"Who knew you were sleeping with her?"

"I wasn't," Darwin stammered. "I mean, we were friends."

"You told police investigators that you'd had sexual intercourse with Dolores Hernandez the night she was killed."

"Yes, yes that's true. I did. But you misunderstood."

"Yes or no. You were sleeping with her?"

"Once. The first time."

"Now, who knew you were having sex with her?"

"Nobody knew. How could they?"

"But people knew you were seeing her?"

"I don't know what people knew."

"A student named Stan Gilhooley knew, didn't he?"

"I don't know. How could he?"

"That's how you came to be interviewed, wasn't it?"

"That's what I'm told," Darwin flashed.

"Other students knew you were seeing Dolores Hernandez, didn't they?"

"I don't know what they knew."

"Students would come into Frieda's and see you together, wouldn't they?"

"They could have."

"And it isn't ethical for a professor to date a student, to sleep with her, is it?"

"Objection," Avila said.

"I'll allow it. If he knows." Gragg raised an eyebrow at Gettes.

"It isn't ethical, is it?" Gettes said. She sneaked a glance at the jury, smiled.

"I don't know. I didn't think."

"It that an answer?" Gettes said.

"What I mean is, I didn't grant her favors. I wouldn't do that."

"There is a law school student and professor handbook isn't there?"

"I think so."

"Have you read it?"

"Not all, I don't think."

"Objection," Avila said again. "This isn't relevant."

"Character is an issue here or will be. So are motive and state of mind." Gettes looked at Mad Dog, who frowned.

"Overruled," Gragg said.

"Is it ethical?" Gettes said.

"Perhaps it isn't. I didn't plan to meet Dolores. I was a very part-time temporary adjunct faculty member. You make it sound as if I were a full professor. I wasn't. We were friends. She was special. I needed friends then."

"In the direct examination you talked a lot about the cuff link found at the Tracy apartment. It's your cuff link, isn't it?"

"No, it belonged to my father. It's a keepsake."

"You told Detective Vorhees it was yours."

"I inherited it, yes. I don't wear it."

"Its mate was found in your house."

"Probably," Darwin said.

"We could call a witness who has seen those cuff links at your house in Pacific Heights."

"Yes, all right," Darwin said.

"It's your cuff link then?"

"Yes, I told you. I think it is."

"How did it get inside the Tracy apartment?"

"I don't know. Someone placed it there."

"You're the victim of a conspiracy?"

"Yes, absolutely. I need time to prove it."

"How did the blood of Dolores Hernandez get on the topcoat and shirt in your temporary apartment?"

"Objection," Avila said.

Judge Gragg looked up. "On what grounds?"

"It assumes facts," Avila said.

"Oh, please. Rephrase the question, Ms. Gettes."

"All right," Gettes said. "How did that blood get in your apartment?"

"I don't know if it is her blood," Darwin said. "I don't know how it got there."

"Someone planted it there?"

"It has to be."

"You're the victim of a conspiracy?"

"Yes, absolutely."

"A racist police officer did it?"

"I, well, I don't know. My wife has a lover. I cared for Dolores. When I left her apartment she was alive. I didn't kill her, for God's sake. I couldn't kill her."

"You heard a police officer read a report of the domestic violence incident that involved you and your wife?"

"Yes, I heard," Darwin said quietly.

"You've testified you didn't hit her."

"I didn't."

"So, what? Where did her injuries come from?"

"Somebody else hurt her."

"You never did?"

"No. Never."

"Your wife is lying?"

"She is. She must be. I know she is."

"You're the victim of a conspiracy."

"She's lying, I know that."

"Detective Vorhees is lying."

"I don't know exactly."

"The lab expert from Silicon Valley is lying."

"I didn't say that."

"You've never been in Lisa Tracy's apartment?"

"Never."

"Someone planted your cuff link there?"

"Yes. It has to be that way. I know it sounds crazy, but you have to believe me."

"Where were you between nine and eleven the night of the murder of Dolores Hernandez?"

"I've told you today. I went to the Aladdin Coffee House to meet my wife. She called and left a message and asked to meet me there. She never came. Then I went home."

"But your wife isn't going to testify, is she?" Gettes asked.

"Objection!" Avila shouted.

"Come on," Judge Gragg told Gettes. "You know better than that. A privilege is involved. I want the jury to ignore the question. From now on, please play fair, Ms. Gettes."

"Sorry, Your Honor," Gettes said.

Mad Dog tapped his pencil. Ten minutes to go.

"You have a drinking problem, don't you?" she asked Darwin.

Gettes studied the jury. Awake. Studious. Serious.

"Object," Avila said finally.

"Grounds?" Gragg asked.

"Not relevant. Not asked on direct."

"Overruled," Gragg said.

"Thank you, Your Honor," Gettes said. "Now answer the question, Mr. Darwin."

"Yes. I have had a problem. I'm taking steps to deal with it."

"You were drinking the night your wife says you beat her?"

"Uh, yes. Just two bourbons. But I never touched her."

"But you were drinking that night?"

"Yes."

"You have financial problems, don't you, Mr. Darwin?"

"They can be solved."

"But you have financial problems?"

"Some. I'm working them out."

"You're involved in a divorce?"

"Objection," Avila said. "My client can't comment on another lawsuit."

"It's public record, Mr. Avila," Gragg said. "Overruled."

Gettes took a step toward Darwin. He looked pale and drained on the stand, smaller than his real self, as if he'd been shrunken under vacuum sealing, then reconstituted. "You're involved in a divorce?" Gettes asked.

"Yes," Darwin managed to say.

"In fact, you were ordered out of your home in the domestic violence case?"

"Yes. But I didn't do anything."

"Let me see if I understand this," Gettes said. "Drinking problem, financial worries, messy divorce . . ."

"Objection please," Avila said. "Badgering."

"Move on, Ms. Gettes," the judge said.

Gettes turned and faced the jury. "You killed Lisa Tracy, didn't you, Mr. Darwin?"

"Oh no. I didn't. Please."

"You killed Dolores Hernandez, didn't you?"

"No, God no. I cared for her."

"You beat your wife, didn't you?"

"No. That's not true."

Gettes smiled at the jury. Sadly, she thought.

"That's all, Mr. Darwin," Gettes said sternly.

She sat down next to Mad Dog.

"We're going home for the day," Gragg told everybody. "We shall recommence tomorrow morning at nine-thirty."

The courtroom emptied slowly, two bailiffs leading Jack Darwin out the side door.

"You went over thirty minutes," Mad Dog said.

They were alone, one deputy sheriff at the back of the courtroom.

"Five minutes," Gettes said. "Give me a break."

"It was good," Mad Dog said. "I liked that last smile."

"They loved me. They really loved me."

"But Darwin was okay. He held up."

"Yeah. I almost feel sorry for him."

"The sobbing parents were great."

Mad Dog wanted a cigarette.

"I wish I had a butt," he said.

"And I wish Darwin would plead," Gettes said. "Even now."

"Don't think about it," Mad Dog said. "You're only the messenger, not the message."

Two beautiful days in a row surprised everybody in the city. Darwin and Fullerton were sitting by a window at a Chinese restaurant on Clement Street, having dim sum after a hard day of trial. There was a high wind raking the city, but sun made it seem warmer than it was, which was something of a psychological perk.

"It's over at trial," Darwin told Fullerton. "Avila has made a hash of everything he's touched." Darwin placed a stack of yellow pads on the Formica-topped table. He sipped some of his green tea and watched shoppers along Clement, old Chinese carrying baskets of bizarre vegetables, kids with backpacks coming from Catholic school down the block. It was late in the day and already shadows were beginning to circulate like the wind currents. "I've been keeping trial notes. Notes of everything that's happened since we began pretrial. It's funny, but Avila started me on this criminal-law kick. He gave me volumes to study. Trial tactics. Case law. Procedure. The whole nine yards. I used criminal-law examples to teach my class at school. And what he's been doing is shoddy."

"I've asked Sandy Mooney to sit in at trial."

"I saw him back there."

"We'll appeal. We'll fight to the last breath."

"I'm on Karla's track."

"You know," Fullerton said, "I went to see her. She'd been drinking heavily. I think she's falling apart psychologically. She was hardly coherent."

Darwin fiddled with a fried wonton. The waitress brought another pot of tea and Darwin refilled their glasses. He could see his own reflection in the plate glass, a hovering image. He'd lost weight and he looked exhausted from lack of sleep. Now, with time running out, he was working on his charts until three or four every morning. He was up to November, the year running out and he hadn't found anything concrete. Three or four times he'd run up to Marin, checking out an anomaly in Karla's movements, but it hadn't turned out. More and more he was beginning to doubt his own method. Maybe the secret someone would remain a secret. Maybe the war would be lost after all. Darwin looked away from his own image and said, "I don't think there's going to be time for Karla to crack. You're on the stand tomorrow, and then there's final summation and then the case goes to the jury. We're only talking about two days tops."

Fullerton took a deep breath. Darwin remembered him as a young man, curly black hair, Thomas E. Dewey pencil mustache, flashing gray eyes. Now he looked old and worn out, overworried about his ailing wife.

"Do you still have the envelope I gave you?" Fullerton asked.

"You know I do, Tom," Darwin said.

"Pack some things for tomorrow," Fullerton said. "Get a briefcase of things you want to take. Keep it minimal. Only what's vital to you. Carry it with you to the courthouse. Keep it with you tomorrow. Meet me outside the elevators at lunch break."

"Are you thinking what I think you're thinking?"

"You're my godson," Fullerton said. "My only son."

"Don't involve yourself, Tom," Darwin said. "You've already lied about the trust. That's bad enough. I can run on my own."

"No you can't," Fullerton said. "That's precisely the point. None of us can make it alone."

"Tom, your life. Your career. Suppose we finish up tomorrow at noon. There could be closings in the afternoon and instructions the next morning. I'm supposed to call in to probation every night at ten. Somebody will know I'm gone by then at the latest. Besides, where could I go?" Darwin had been forced to surrender his passport and driver's license as a condition of bond. He was driving illegally anyway, but it was a risk he'd been forced to take occasionally.

"I've worked it all out," Fullerton said. "At the first break after closing and before instructions to the jury, you meet me at the elevators on three. Let's say no more about it. Remember, keep your briefcase with you at all times."

"Tom, what have you been doing?"

"Being a soldier," he said.

·     ·     ·

Vorhees ate a stale ham and rye in the basement cafeteria of the Hall. From the machine his sandwich cost two dollars, the room refrigerated by processed air, bathed in filthy blue light. Cooley came in wearing a rumpled gray suit.

"Where you been?" Vorhees asked him.

Cooley slumped down looking very tired.

"I got your note," he said. Cooley unbuckled his shoulder holster and placed it on the Formica tabletop. "This thing is hurting me under the arm. Maybe I should adjust the strap."

"Trial over?" Vorhees asked.

"Tomorrow. The evidence is all in. I think Avila is calling a character witness. Then it goes."

"Hey," Vorhees said. "My wife just had a baby."

"Way to go," Cooley said, smiling. "Congratulations. What kind of baby we got?"

"Little girl."

"That's great, Amos," Cooley told him. "How are they? They okay?"

"It went perfect. They're both fine. Healthy."

"Got a name yet?"

"Dierdre," Vorhees said. "Dierdre Elaine."

"I like it. That's nice."

"My mother's name was Dierdre." Vorhees bit on stale ham, hard bread. "She raised me in the Western Addition."

"That's great, Amos, really."

Vorhees tossed down a crust of bread. He wished he could offer Cooley a cigar, but he'd been too busy to buy any. First he'd been in trial, then on a case, then at the hospital. Now he was a father, and all kinds of strange thoughts were in his head. Mostly he wondered if he should remain a cop. What if he were killed?

"You look bushed," Cooley said. "Been up all night?"

"Yeah," Vorhees said.

"Go home. Get some rest."

"Got to go back to the hospital. Lightfoot gave me two days off."

"Lightfoot is okay."

"Yeah, she's fine."

Cooley went over and poured some coffee into a paper cup.

"Something eating you, Amos?" he asked.

"You got some radar, partner."

"Spill it."

"A guy named Arthur Vine got killed last week." Vorhees squeezed shut his eyes. "Up in Hunters Point."

"Should I know this guy?"

"No. He's an old case from narcotics. A punk. Not even ganged up. But he had hopes, you know?"

"So what about him?"

"I don't know. That's just it."

"Punks get killed all the time," Cooley said.

"But he's matched up with a dead DEA informer who got it over in the East Bay."

"I don't follow," Cooley said.

"Avila and Darwin represented those two guys. Last year a drug case came down in the East Bay. Vine sells to some informer, and Luther Dokes, an independent dude from the city, delivers dope to Vine in Oakland. Both of these guys are now dead. A DEA agent named Burkholder visited me a couple of weeks ago, asking if I knew anything about these guys. He was covering his informer who was facedown in San Pablo Bay with his eyes poked out. Now Vine is dead. Darwin represented him."

"Well, that's bad. What's the connection?"

"The lawyers forced the government to produce the informer in a secret hearing. Then the informer shows up dead."

"You think Darwin did it for money?"

"I'm not thinking about it real hard."

"Who's got the Vine killing?"

"Not us. Squad sixteen I think."

"So let them worry about it," Cooley said.

"Yes, but Burkholder came around again."

"He's pissed about his informer still?"

"You can see his point," Vorhees mused.

"I don't see how you can leverage Darwin now."

"Maybe if he looks at the forty years long enough, he'll give somebody up."

"It's a thought," Cooley said.

"Still, I don't like Darwin for it."

"Sure you do," Cooley said. "Guy drinks too much. Has expensive taste. Beats his wife. Money draining out his asshole like shit. He fucks his students. He takes a few bucks to name an informer. It makes sense."

"I don't know," Vorhees said. "A guy named Henry Diehl came to see me once. Just a guy, bow tie, Castro Street type. He's part of Darwin's AA group. I don't know why, but the guy impressed me. Sincere, you know. Real serious. Said Darwin told his group he'd lost two friends. One of them was Dolores Hernandez."

"Yeah, and the other friend was Lisa Tracy," Cooley said. "You don't know how these guys are. He gets drunk and probably doesn't even remember Tracy. Drunk, goes up to her place, does her, stumbles home."

"And the cuff link? Something isn't right about that."

"Yeah, he lost it."

Vorhees tossed the sandwich at the trash bucket.

"I gotta go to the hospital," Vorhees said.

"Hey," Cooley said, "I would have eaten the leftover."


Fifty minutes on the stand and Tom Fullerton wished he'd never agreed to testify. He thought Avila did a reasonable job on direct, but the man they called Mad Dog dragged him through every money and drinking trouble Darwin ever had. It was humiliating for Fullerton to recite the intimate details of Darwin's failed law practice, his dreamy devotion to Sunday night drunken cribbage at Marge's, how the trustees had to advance money from the trust. It was worse than terrible, and Fullerton didn't have the heart to listen to closing arguments.

He stood outside the courtroom, watching through a tiny port-hole window as Gettes pranced and made her speech. Sandy Mooney stood next to him, pacing back and forth.

"You did your best, Tom," Mooney told him.

"They crucified me," Fullerton said sadly. "It was worse than I'd imagined. You'd think I have enough experience to make a better witness."

"Let's get drunk," Mooney said.

"I'm going to wait for Jack."

"Just one, then. For Jack."

"No thanks, Sandy," Fullerton said. "But I appreciate your sitting through the trial."

"They'll nail him, you know," Mooney said quietly.

"Yeah. It looks that way."

In the courtroom, Gettes was in front of the jury box showing them a DNA chart.

"It was too easy," Fullerton said. "Too damn easy."

"I'll review the transcripts," Mooney said.

"Does he have a chance on appeal?"

"Not much," Mooney said. "You never know."

"That bad?"

"What's his defense?"

"That's just it. It was too easy."

"We'll go talk to Jack when this is over." Mooney swung on his tweed topcoat.

In the courtroom, Gettes was holding a gold cuff link, exhibiting it for the jury. Darwin's head was up, but his face was ghostly pale. Fullerton thought about the little boy who'd shot a rabbit, the little boy who cried all night about what he'd done, the little boy who bravely pulled a rake from his brother's injured foot, a mild little boy with a freckled face and crooked teeth and a big happy smile. You had to be astonished at the things life could do to a person.

Summation for Avila took slightly more than forty minutes, give or take some time he spent shuffling papers, staring wisely at the jury, the woman who had been asleep paying special attention to the man who had embarrassed her. Darwin felt a lucidity come over him as he listened to his life story, a feeling akin to out-of-body experiences he sometimes read about in tabloid headlines at the checkout stand. It was two o'clock in the afternoon, and Judge Gragg had made everyone work through the standard noon hour lunch break, trying to move things along. When Avila finished, he stood behind Darwin for one last time, hands on the defendant's shoulders, giving the defendant over to whatever blind Ladies of Justice might balance things out in the end. Darwin took a deep breath and tried to touch each juror with his eyes, knowing it was futile now, knowing that he was going to take another path. He had become a guerrilla warrior in his own mind, and he would rather die than submit to the processes that had so inexorably ground him down, processes that had seen the deaths of a woman he loved and a stranger intimately tied to him. What was the definition of murder he'd learned in law school? Accelerating the inevitable?

Darwin gathered his briefcase and told Avila he was going to grab a bite to eat with Fullerton. Judge Gragg adjourned court for the day, instructing the parties to return at nine sharp the next morning to give the case over to the jury. Darwin hesitated briefly, looking at the huge ornate clock high above the courtroom. Then he went out to the hall and saw Fullerton waiting for him at a bank of elevators at one end.

"This is it," Fullerton said calmly. Darwin glanced around the crowded hallway. It had been a long time since reporters had besieged him with questions, harsh lights flashing in his eyes, the inevitable minicam for "on the scene" reporting at eleven. "Let's ride down a floor together," Fullerton continued. "You get off at two, and I'll ride on down to one."

"Are you sure about this, Tom?"

"It's all arranged," Fullerton told him.

" 'Arranged,' what do you mean 'arranged'?" Darwin clasped his briefcase closely to himself. It contained the remaining checks and Gold Card receipts for the previous November and December, a huge trial notebook he'd compiled, plus a copy of the trial notebook for Fullerton, along with a journal of what Darwin referred to as his "plague year." "I thought I'd get my Volvo and just start driving. Maybe head up to Santa Rosa and get a room."

"They'd find you in twenty-four hours," Fullerton said. The elevator door whisked open and Fullerton almost had to shove Darwin inside. Before they were going down, Fullerton said, "Go down the stairs to Van Ness. Cross Van Ness and go to Fulton between the art museum and opera house. You'll see a New Age deli near the freeway. Go inside it and there's a side door you can't miss. The side door opens onto a Park and Pay lot. You'll see a gray Chevy van. Get inside."

"Tom," Darwin whispered.

"Be quiet, do it."

"Do you have the keys? Is it safe for you?"

"There's a driver."

The elevator door opened to a crowd waiting for a ride. Fullerton pushed Darwin out. Darwin had a moment, looking back at his father's old friend, his own godfather, a man who'd served the law his entire life. Darwin shoved a copy of his trial notes at Fullerton, who took them with a look of profound sorrow on his face. Darwin turned and hurried down the back rotunda stairs and out into the traffic of Van Ness. It was a preternaturally beautiful day for early April in the Bay Area. A few puffy clouds, light winds, almost warm. Darwin did as he had been told, walking up Fulton between the marble buildings of Civic Center toward the flyover and an area of grim tenements. He found the New Age deli on Fulton near Ash, and went inside, then through its side door. Sure enough, a gray Chevy van was in the lot. It was an old car, with rust spots under the doors, a cracked taillight, worn, almost bald tires. Darwin walked to the passenger side and looked in the open window.

Angel nodded slightly, almost embarrassed. "Hurry now, Mr. Darwin," he said. "Get in and please hurry."

Darwin took his seat and closed the door just as Angel started the engine. They turned into Van Ness traffic heading for the freeway south.

"Angel, what are you doing?" Darwin said.

"Mr. Fullerton and I have had a long talk," Angel said. "Please do not worry about me. I am a very old man. It is one of the benefits of being near death. It makes you feel free. Besides, I know you did not do this terrible thing."

"But you can't get involved. Just drop me off near my apartment."

"You don't understand, Mr. Darwin," Angel said. They were on an up ramp in traffic, just about to join 101 in progress. "Mr. Fullerton and I have known you since you were a very small boy. We are the only ones. Your mother and father, bless them, they are dead and cannot speak for you. Your brother too is gone. We *know* Mr. Darwin. They say the child is father to the man. We *know*."

"Where are we going?"

"The horse farm. There is a cabin in the hills."

"I'll leave as soon as I can arrange it."

"You are seeking the murderer, no?"

"Yes," Darwin said.

"You will seek him from there."

Darwin looked at the bay, its pastel loveliness, and beyond the bay, outlines of the coastal range, San Jose, the rosy late-afternoon sunshine petaling down.

"I'll stay for a short while," Darwin said. "If I can't find the man, I'll leave."

Angel seemed a shrunken version of the man Darwin had known for so many years, white hair, wispy gray-black eyebrows, darkly lined face. Perhaps it was true, Darwin thought, that old age was liberating. Perhaps old age puts one closer to the wellsprings of life.

"This old van is like me," Angel said, smiling. They were in the slow lane, going fifty.

"We'll have to fix that cracked taillight," Darwin said. "We wouldn't want to get stopped by the cops, would we?"

"No, Mr. Darwin," Angel said. "That would not be good."

Darwin did not make his ten o'clock probation call. The sheriff's office telephoned the judge at home. Cooley and Vorhees were called, and the trustee Fullerton. By eleven, an APB had been issued for California. "Like flies on shit," Cooley said, "all the airports and bus terminals and car agencies are being watched." The two detectives were in court at nine the next morning, sitting near the back, rafts of reporters present, making notes. The jury was ushered in and Judge Gragg took her seat.

"Ladies and gentlemen of the jury," she began. "We all are confronting a very unusual situation today. You don't need me to tell you that the defendant's lawyer does not know where the defendant is, and he has not contacted Mr. Avila. Today, it was to have been my duty to instruct you in the law and send you off to deliberate. You were to make factual findings, apply my instructions to your findings, and hopefully return with a just verdict. You may wonder what will happen next. The lawyers have spent time with the court this morning, reviewing California law on this subject, and it is my belief that the answer is clear. We will proceed to judgment. All of the witnesses have been heard, all of the documents admitted into evidence, all the experts' reports read and analyzed. You have seen all the witnesses and have been able to evaluate their demeanor and credibility. The defendant was present too, and his lawyer had ample opportunity to cross-examine every witness and object to every piece of documentary and physical evidence. There is, therefore, no reason not to go forward. The sole question remaining is—what inference should be drawn from the absence of the defendant today? Here is the answer to that question. I will give you no instruction whatsoever regarding the absence of the defendant. Your decision should be based upon the facts that you have heard already, and upon the instructions I am about to give you concerning the law as it is applied to those facts. It is my firm belief that you have enough evidence to make a rational judgment about this case based solely upon that evidence. Perhaps your judgment will be somehow affected by the defendant's absence. But use your common sense. Now, let me proceed."

"I'm surprised the bastard didn't run before," Cooley whispered to his partner.

"He'll turn up," Vorhees said. "Sooner or later."

Clear weather, cold wind, blue days. They met at the Rex on Union Square, where Avila rented a room for depositions. Karla parked at a garage on Post, paused in her walk to shop at an antique store, then went to the hotel. Karla drank a cappuccino in the boutique café, then walked the back stairs to the room. The room itself was quietly dark, luxurious in an understated way, shades drawn. A smell of lavender and chocolate. She could hear the shower running, and Avila opened the door.

"I've been crazy," Karla said breathlessly. "Jack is gone. He's run away. I'm afraid."

Avila touched her, the way she'd dreamed he would. He pulled her inside the room, shut the door, ran his hands under her sweater and felt her nipples harden.

"They'll find him soon," Avila said. "If they don't, we've just lost six million dollars in the trust fund."

Karla slipped out of her skirt and panties. She felt weak and sick.

"I wish I thought they'd find him," she said.

Avila backed her against the wall. He was hard, and his skin warm. She closed her eyes tight.

"He has balls," Avila said. "But they'll find him. Do you know where he might have gone?"

Karla used the wall, moving. She was slick inside, her knees shaking.

"Let's take a shower," Karla said.

"Yes, a shower," Avila said. "We really shouldn't be taking this chance. Jack might be down the hall." Avila smiled to himself. He loved taking chances.

Karla was naked and she could smell her own readiness. Avila led her to the shower. He undressed and they got under the water together. Karla felt herself being arched back, hot water flooding her face. Avila covered her breasts with his hands, and she felt pain inside.

"David," she said.

"Shut up," Avila said urgently.

"David, please."

"Shut up, will you?"

"Don't be so rough."

"You like it."

"Please," Karla said.

Avila pushed her against the tile. For a moment, Karla thought she would lose consciousness.

"We did it," Avila said.

"David," Karla gasped. "Did you kill those women?"

Karla felt him throbbing inside her. She wanted to utter a cry, but she had no breath.

"That's it, baby," Avila said.

"Yes, that's it."

"This is how I like you," Avila said.

Avila worked her into a corner. Steam filled the bathroom and Karla felt herself being lifted from the floor as starry bits of red cluttered her vision. She put her hands on the tile to balance herself. She was light as a feather, floating in steam and pain. It was like birth or death, like flying through strange dreamscapes. One of her fingernails broke on the tiles.

"This is how I like you," Avila said.

"I know, David," she replied.

"We'll be together with Jack's money," Avila said.

"I know, David."

"This is how you like it," Avila said again.

"I know, David."

He let her down suddenly. She was nowhere then, alone with him.

# IV

# *the least of my brethren*

*t*he morning *Chronicle* trumpeted the news! ABSENT SHOWER KILLER GUILTY!

Angel had driven into Mountain View and brought Darwin back the paper. He sat in the toolshed where he was staying and read it through. Manhunt. Bail system under review. The system fails again. Long bars of striped sun fell on the dirt floor, bits of straw mixed with horse dung. On the walls were old tack, horse-grooming equipment, buckets. In one corner was a cot, just beside the blacksmith tools. It smelled of oak trees, horse flesh, the powdery earth of dry chaparral country.

Darwin was down to one month's worth of receipts and he had begun to lose hope. He spent all day poring over his trial notebooks, preparing the faxes he would send to the district attorney, Fullerton, anyone who would listen. He had prepared one fax already and had taken a chance on driving over to San Jose to send it from a public print shop, his heart in his mouth all the way. Every time he looked in the rearview mirror he saw a highway patrol car. Every time he took an off ramp he expected to hear a siren. But it didn't happen. The newspapers were full of speculation that he'd been able to flee the country. The talk shows had him in Honduras, Costa Rica, Mexico. There was talk of Asia too, Tibet, where Darwin would be living in a monastery disguised as a monk. In truth, he was hiding out on the back forty acres of a nearly defunct stable and riding academy, out in black-jack oak, being fed a diet of canned stew, potato chips, sandwiches of peanut butter, bologna, tuna fish. In his mind, he knew it was a matter of time before he'd be tracked down and captured. In that sense, he already considered himself a dead man. There was a certain freedom in the notion. It must be the same as getting older. Deep inside he felt a kind of religious calm, mixed with reasoned anger, and a devotion to Dolores Hernandez that drove him every day.

Day dissolved into night, night into morning. The world revolved on its axis, and Darwin studied his check stubs, his Gold Card receipts. Karla's special someone was there.

The baby had lustrous skin the color of maple syrup. Vorhees would sit next to the crib and ogle her, pull faces, gurgle, bubble noises from the side of his mouth, poke rattles in the air like a crazed shaman, even then in the act of defining himself as a new father, home tired from a long day, his arms over the crib rails, while the nursery bathed in crepuscular northern light. Alisha would take long baths while Vorhees watched his daughter sleep, and when she woke, he would hold her while she cried, and soothe her, coo to her like a pigeon until she slept again, her tiny hands curled up near her tiny face, both tiny feet like surreal reproductions, too small. Vorhees would listen to her breathing, while shadows climbed the nursery walls, dark clouds of shadow against the faint pink walls, movement on the polished wooden floor. Alisha had erected a festival of mobiles in one corner, and Vorhees learned their movements.

And sometimes his mind filled with an imaginary headline: SHOWER KILLER TO DIE.

Shower killer running, Vorhees thought to himself that night, while the baby slept. He sat quietly, hearing Alisha in the kitchen making dinner, her comforting domestic sounds like a veneer against the rush of faraway traffic, Pacific wind against glass. On impulse, Vorhees put on a pair of decent slacks and a sweatshirt, an old sport coat with patched elbows. He found a pair of sneakers and put them on and went into the kitchen. He stood behind his wife, wrapped his arms around her.

"I've got to go downtown for a little while," Vorhees whispered. He touched his wife's ear with his lips.

"Oh, Amos," Alisha said.

"I'll be back soon."

"I'm almost finished here. It'll get cold."

Vorhees tried to lick the goulash spoon.

"The baby is asleep," he said. "She'll be fine until I get back."

"It's not the baby," Alisha said. "What is it with you now? Another case, or what?"

"That shower killing thing," Vorhees said.

"It isn't your fault," Alisha said.

They'd been through this before, more than once. Vorhees could feel her anger, the way her back stiffened.

"No, it's not that," Vorhees told her.

"Then what is it?" Alisha asked.

She had dropped the stirring spoon and was standing stiff-backed and ruffled.

"It's something else," Vorhees said.

"Like conscience?"

"I told you no," Vorhees said. He released her and stood arms to his side.

He left her that way, facing the stove. It took twenty minutes to drive downtown and park in the lot beneath Civic Center. In another ten minutes he had walked over to Turk Street, just down from the YMCA where AA groups held meetings in an older brick building. Vorhees climbed wooden stairs between two buildings and entered a long, narrow room dense with cigarette smoke. He stayed in back, leaning against a wooden pillar, and listened to one meditation, a few talks, one confession, all related with humor, lamentation, recantation. It struck Vorhees as witty and good-natured, without self-pity or recrimination.

In time, he spotted Henry Diehl perched on a metal chair in a far corner of the room near a table piled with doughnuts. Diehl was a wiry terrier of a man with salt-and-pepper butch-cut hair, a tweed suit, bow tie. He was dapper in an old-fashioned way, with a cherubic face and dainty hands. When he smiled, dimples creased his cheeks.

Vorhees listened to the final meditation, a prayer in which the collective members asked God for the strength to live one day at a time, for the wisdom to know what they could change and what they couldn't. Vorhees watched as Diehl circulated, shaking hands, talking to members. Finally they caught each other's eye, and Diehl came to the back of the room.

"I know you," he said happily.

"Detective Vorhees."

"Yes, Detective Vorhees," Diehl said. Diehl dropped his voice to a whisper. "Are you having some personal difficulties, Detective?"

"No, nothing like that," Vorhees said.

"You're sure now?" Diehl asked. "These are people who can help. People who are very understanding of these matters. You know we have a separate branch for police officers and their families?"

"No, thanks, Mr. Diehl," Vorhees managed to say.

"Would you like a doughnut then?" Diehl asked. "I just love the ones with pink sprinkles, don't you?"

"No doughnuts, thanks," Vorhees said. "In fact, my wife is waiting goulash and French bread for me back home. She thinks I work too hard, too much. Maybe she's right."

"Yes, she probably is," Diehl said brightly.

"It's crowded for nine o'clock," Vorhees said.

There were perhaps forty people standing in discrete groups, finishing their coffee and cigarettes.

Diehl turned and looked.

"In California," he said, "bars are open until four. They close for a few hours and reopen at eight. If you're of a mind, you can buy a bottle to carry you from four to eight, which is what I used to do on weekends. A lot of people do. I did. My drink was vodka, believe it or not. I hated the taste. It made me gag. But you can mix it with anything. Grapefruit juice, Tang, mouthwash if you want. You'd be surprised how many serious drinkers choose vodka at the end. Besides, it's cheap."

"I suppose it is," Vorhees said.

"You look a little lost," Diehl said. He smiled at a couple going out. "Would you like to sit down?"

Diehl pulled two metal chairs together. Vorhees sat knee to knee with Diehl.

"This place used to be a billiard emporium," Diehl said.

"You can see the indentations in the floor from the tables," Vorhees noted.

"You're very observant."

"I guess that's my job. Observe."

"There's another meeting in thirty minutes," Diehl said.

"Oh really?" Vorhees said stupidly.

"Your wife is waiting."

"Yeah. I should go pretty soon. I guess you'd like to get home yourself?"

"Not me," Diehl said. "I'm staying. I'm doing three meetings tonight. It's Friday after work, and believe me, I used to get wound up on Friday nights. Hard week, just got off work, hey, why not get drunk for three days and nights? You know the syndrome, don't you?"

"I guess I do," Vorhees said.

"Are you all right?" Diehl asked.

It was cold and drafty in the hall. An uninterrupted row of windows in front were banging in the wind.

"You care to talk about Jack Darwin?" Vorhees asked suddenly.

Diehl lifted his head, eyes bright.

"Sure," he said. "But I've told you what I think."

"You went to see him during trial?"

"Many times." Diehl was holding a paper cup full of coffee. He sipped it once, carefully. "I took him books. We played chess. We talked. I found him a very intelligent and sympathetic man. That's what I know about Jack Darwin."

"I'm just curious about his two friends," Vorhees said when Diehl had finished. "You came to my office and told me he'd been upset about losing two friends. I haven't been able to get that out of my mind."

"I know what you're thinking," Diehl said. "You think the second friend who died was Lisa Tracy."

"It occurred to me."

"You want to know if he told me anything about it?"

"I'm not working a case, Mr. Diehl," Vorhees said. "Or at least I'm not working the Jack Darwin case anymore."

"You think he killed both women, don't you?"

"I think he did."

"But you're not sure?"

Vorhees thought for a moment, bit his lip.

"You deserve the truth," he told Diehl.

Diehl went for more coffee, pausing to say good-bye to a dozen people, one an elderly woman in sweat clothes. He walked the coffee back and sat down.

"And the truth is?" he asked.

"The truth is, I don't know what to think."

"But you're not sure about Jack Darwin?"

"Look," Vorhees said. "I'd like to know about the other friend. That's all."

"It's a horse," Diehl said flatly.

"A horse?" Vorhees said.

"The other friend was a horse. I spent hours with Jack. Talked, talked, talked. Sometimes I'd just sit with him for an hour and he'd talk to me about his life. The things that were wrong, the things that went wrong but shouldn't have, the things that he knew were wrong but couldn't prevent. He also told me about the good things, the things that were right and good, and the things that should have been good, might have been good, but weren't quite right, but could be. I think you know his folks were killed in a plane crash up at Tahoe four years ago."

"Yes, I think I knew that," Vorhees said honestly.

"Don't get me wrong," Diehl continued. "Jack wasn't completely alone. The friends at his father's law firm have been wonderful. Even his lawyer was good to him. His lawyer let him have the Marina apartment when he was evicted from his Pacific Heights house. Well, the other friend Jack was talking about that day in the meeting was a horse. He had ridden the horse as a teenager. It belonged to his father, and his older brother helped train the horse. The weekend Dolores Hernandez was murdered, the horse was put to sleep."

"A horse," Vorhees said under his breath.

"Jack told me about that whole weekend," Diehl said. "He'd been with Dolores at her apartment. They had takeout Mexican food. He went home that night and a stable hand brought the ashes to him in an urn."

"Now I remember Darwin mentioning that."

"Yes. He'd just gotten home a few minutes earlier. Friday night. The stable hand drove the urn of ashes up from Burlingame and brought it to Jack. Even though things were bad in his life, this hit Jack very hard. I think it represented the last vestige of another life he'd led years before. His time as a young boy with an older brother he adored. The mother who adored him. He lost his brother, then his parents, then the horse. It seemed to him that things were crashing down all around him. When he came to that meeting at noon on Monday, he was speaking of Dolores Hernandez and the horse with affection and regret. They were both his friends, and he thought he'd lost everything."

"Do you know what time the hand came by?"

"Late, I imagine," Diehl said. "Elevenish."

"Eleven?"

"Around there."

"This stable hand spoke to Darwin that night?"

"Oh yes."

"Went into the apartment?"

"I imagine, yes. Why?"

"It wasn't mentioned at trial," Vorhees said.

The hall was empty now, deserted as a midnight bus station.

"I've got to make more coffee," Diehl said. "We alcoholics are permanently oral fixated."

"Do you know how I could contact this stable hand?" Vorhees asked.

"His name is Angel," Diehl told him. "That's all I know. The stable is down in Burlingame, off a country road up by the reservoir. I wish I could be of more help, but that's about it."

Vorhees stood. He felt hopelessly embarrassed.

"Is there any chance you could help Jack?" Diehl asked.

"I don't know," Vorhees said.

"I wish I knew what was on your mind."

"I wish I did too," Vorhees replied.

"What about Jack? Can you help him?"

"I'm thinking things over."

"Thank you, Detective," Diehl said.

Vorhees got home to goulash and French bread, eating with Alisha in the nursery while they watched the baby. The baby woke at four that morning and Vorhees fed her, walked her for thirty minutes, drifting with her toward dawn.

Friday night drive time—Mad Dog on foot up Van Ness Avenue in light rain, messy rain, head-down rain that soaked the hatless man, his beard, dripping down the back of his collar, between his shirt and the old overcoat he refused to throw away, so old it made him look like a refugee. Funny, Mad Dog thought, that's what he was in a sense, a refugee, taking on the nothingness of the world with his Polish roots, gruff, determined, hard-bitten and sentimental, the schmaltzy odds-against man alone in the hip capital of West Coast America. What a pink elephant! Stopping for a light at Eddy, Paiewonsky recalled the faint blue tattoo on his mother's right forearm, a mathematical formulation that somehow epitomized her life, reducing her to a jagged rubble of memory and melancholy. Oh, way out of place was Mad Dog, a Jew from New York working in the foothills of the Sierra Nevada. From the first, Mad Dog thought he'd stand out like a sore thumb, or worse, but he didn't. He'd tried seventy-six cases to hick juries, then moved over to the district attorney's office in San Francisco County with something of a reputation as a tough guy with criminal defendants, hard to fool, no-nonsense, down-to-earth, simple as pie, salt of the earth. He lived alone. He did not vacation. He listened to Mendelssohn on Saturday nights, and he did not drink, and he did not smoke. He had no number tattooed on his right forearm, but he might as well have.

When he got the fax, he read it carefully, alone in the office. Something resonated inside his head and for a long time he sat in his office, looking out the window at gathering rain. It was another cold Friday night, and here was a fax from beyond the grave. He knew it was Darwin speaking to him. It had to be!

He went four blocks up to Buffalo Cody's, a tourist trap where the district attorney's office drank after work on Friday nights. When he walked inside he saw that Gettes herself was presiding over steam beer, baskets of peanuts, plates of barbecued chicken wings. It was a cavernous place themed to "old San Francisco," photos and memorabilia on the walls, horse harnesses, fire hats and hoses, buffalo heads. Chinese building the railroad for Crocker, Huntington, and Stanford. Booths lined three sides, and in the middle were a dozen wooden tables.

Mad Dog sat down opposite Gettes at a wooden table.

"You're five or six behind," Gettes said laconically.

Mad Dog took off his overcoat and shook out the water, used a paper towel to dry his hair and shaggy beard. It was past seven, and the Friday night after-work crowd was already thinning, heading home for more drinks and TV. When he was reasonably dry, Mad Dog went to the buffet in back and got a plate of wings, a glass of iced tea. When he sat back down, Gettes was saying good-bye to several lawyers and investigators on staff. He drank some of his tea, tasted the wings. The room was very dark, highlighted in spots by beer signs flashing on and off.

Gettes finished and drank some beer.

"I hate this place," Mad Dog said tonelessly.

"What don't you hate?" Gettes said.

"Mendelssohn," Mad Dog answered. "Warm woolly mittens. Kittens. Brown paper packages tied up with string."

Gettes laughed heartily. She ordered another steam beer by raising her mug and waving it side to side.

When the beer came, she dusted off the foam with her finger and drank it half down. "You know," she began, "we've been coming down here after work for years, and I've only seen you here once or twice in all that time. You're not antisocial are you?"

"Yes," Mad Dog said.

"That's it?"

"Yes," he replied.

"I can't believe you. No girlfriend? No wild sex life you've got cataloged on video? No skeletons in the closet? There must be some kind of fire burning in old Mad Dog's belly?"

"There isn't," he said.

"I can't believe it," Gettes laughed. "Then something must be on your mind. It's raining shit outside."

Another lawyer said good-bye. Glazed eyes, tie unknotted. All that was left of the Friday crowd were tourists who didn't know better, or who had read the guidebooks and believed them. Mad Dog tasted a wing, tossed it down in disgust.

"Something is on my mind," Mad Dog said. "It's the Darwin lawsuit. The case."

"Yeah, I wondered," Gettes mused, tasting her steam beer.

"It bothers me," Mad Dog admitted. "I was thinking on the way over here how many murder cases I've done. Over fifty. I even did one where a guy chopped up two women with an ax."

"You could say Darwin chopped up two women. Brutalized a third. I mean, you could, if you wanted to think of it that way."

"I guess I could. I guess I could think of it like that."

"But?" Gettes said. "But? There's a but in here somewhere isn't there?"

"But," Mad Dog said. "I always thought money could buy justice. It's my one conviction left after all these years. Now it doesn't seem true."

Gettes laughed heartily. "But Darwin had one of the best."

"Yeah, I've tried cases with Avila before. Nothing too devastating, but he's good."

"But?" Gettes said. "But?"

"But look," Mad Dog told her. He leaned over the table, establishing some personal contact. "In twenty years of doing this shit I've never heard of a lawyer in a murder case deferring his opening statement. If there's one thing I know about a murder case, it's that you've got to get out of the gate fast, get the jury's ear, counter the prosecution's case, plant some expectation in those twelve pairs of ears, make them bleed for your client, make him the victim. Don't let the prosecution take the ball and run with it."

"Mostly I agree with you," Gettes said. "But, hey, everybody has their own style."

"You can make it how you like. But deferral isn't good strategy. Avila waived the preliminary. Then he drops the opening statement until all the prosecution evidence is in? How bad is that?"

"It isn't grounds for appeal, Maynard," Gettes said heartily.

"Look, I know deferral isn't grounds for appeal. But I've never seen a murder case go down the jury's gullet so smoothly. Like Darwin was this little canoe going over Niagara Falls, oops, and it's busted up on the rocks a thousand feet down. Sayonara."

"I gave him a chance," Gettes said. "He could have pled out. Done his twenty-five years. He could have had a ripe old age in Sonoma, picking peaches. But he didn't. What more could I do? Darwin didn't have anything. Quit worrying."

"I'm not worrying," Mad Dog said.

"I've never seen you so, well, agitated before," Gettes said. "Why start now, after twenty years? It's all part of the job."

"I'm not worrying," Mad Dog said angrily. "You talk about twenty years. Do you know how many trials I've done up here in twenty years?"

"Lots," Gettes giggled. "Oodles, gobs. Heaps."

"And in all those trials," Mad Dog interrupted, "I've never seen a lawyer wake up a juror in open court. It isn't done. Every year you guys send me down to trial tactics school in L.A., and one of the lessons is this: You don't wake up a sleeping juror. Leave it to the judge. You wake up a juror it sets them against you forever. If the judge does it, then nobody gets blamed. The juror stays awake, hates the judge, but not the lawyer. Not the client. It isn't done."

"Avila lost his cool," Gettes said. "He made a mistake."

"Not him," Mad Dog said firmly. "Not Avila."

"Why not Avila? He was in over his head."

"Oh sure," Mad Dog sighed. He was resting on his elbows, eye to eye with Gettes. "I told you, I've been up against Avila before. He doesn't lose his cool unless it's planned."

"Oh come on," Gettes mocked. "He's a drug lawyer. Maybe he was in over his head after all. Maybe he didn't have any defense, maybe he was tired, maybe he was pissed off. Maybe he wished he was asleep the day he woke up the juror and lost it. Besides, none of that is appealable either."

"I'm not worried about what's appealable."

"I thought you weren't worried."

Gettes finished her glass of steam beer and attacked some barbecued chicken wings. Mad Dog was cold, getting colder in the drafty pub. The rain had dampened his dress shirt, which was sweat-damp already.

"You read Avila's briefs, right?" Mad Dog asked.

"Sure, you know I did. A dozen times."

"You like them?"

"Not much," Gettes admitted. "We talked about it."

"Yeah," Mad Dog said. "It was fun then. Getting those bad briefs and taking them apart. The brief on the relevance of the Tracy evidence, it was junk. We tore it apart. It missed the main point and a lot of cases."

"We would have won the motion anyway," Gettes said. "We had the MO on the wife to support the Tracy motion."

"How well I know," Mad Dog said. "But if you keep out the Tracy evidence, you keep out the MO evidence on the wife too. We didn't charge him with Tracy, so we dragged it in anyway. I can think of a dozen arguments to keep it out. Avila didn't make them in his brief. It was a lousy brief."

"So, what am I supposed to think?"

"You're supposed to think . . ." Mad Dog stopped. "Well, you're supposed to think that Avila could have done a better job. Think about the brief he filed on the wife's testimony. Avila files a motion to keep out the wife. That's a given almost. The privilege is solid. But he doesn't mention the domestic violence reports, the police interviews, the physical evidence. What ultimately happened at trial was worse than the wife coming in to testify, because all the bad stuff came in and there was no cross-examination. I can think of a dozen arguments why all that evidence shouldn't have come in, but Avila didn't even mention it in the brief. I remember us sitting there and licking our chops because he'd forgotten about the physical evidence and police reports. So a cop got on the stand and testified as to what the wife told him. Darwin got the worst of all possible deals on that one."

"Look, O Mad Dog," Gettes said soothingly. "We talked about that one, didn't we? We had some case law on the physical evidence and police reports, right?"

"But we didn't have to use it. The wife stayed off the stand but her evidence came in anyway."

"The testimony was relevant, Mad Dog," Gettes reminded him.

"Sure, it was relevant. I'm not saying it wasn't relevant."

"Then what are you saying?"

"I don't know."

"You're being a bore," Gettes laughed. "I liked the old Mad Dog better. I liked the dog who had big sharp teeth and once he latched on he didn't let go. That's my old Mad Dog."

"Maybe that's what I'm doing," he said. "Maybe I'm not letting go."

Gettes thought for a long time. "Well, maybe you should let go then," she said.

"You want me to let go? You want me to hold on? Which is it going to be, Nola?"

"You're getting testy, O Mad Dog."

"And another thing," he said. "Avila didn't open his mouth in the three weeks before pretrial. The newspapers were hounding us every day and Avila didn't make one single statement. It was all over TV, every night, how many times a night? You were interviewed how many times? Twenty, thirty? Where was Avila all that time? You think Johnnie Cochran would have dug a hole and disappeared while his client was being tarred and feathered on Channel Nine? They might as well have held a public hanging."

"Well, I thought about that," Gettes admitted. "My theory is that he didn't want to publicize himself as a loser."

"That's a cynical theory."

"You buy it?"

"Not really," Mad Dog said.

"On what theory?"

"For the client, there's got to be a story you can tell. For the lawyer, bad publicity is much better than no publicity."

"You'd have fired a barrage?" Gettes asked.

"Sure, that's what I would have done."

"Shown your face on TV?"

"That's not all," Mad Dog said. "I would have fought hard for a change of venue. I would have walked into court one day and piled up a stack of newspapers a foot high. I would have shown the judge the publicity against my client and I would have asked for the trial to be moved, far away. Down to Bakersfield, L.A., anyplace where my client's face hadn't been seen twenty times a day. Avila didn't make the effort, didn't file a motion. Hell, in a murder case you've got to open every loophole and try to wiggle through. About all you can do for your client is give him a chance on appeal. And the change of venue was a loophole Avila didn't even try to open. Not an inch. For my money, those jurors read the newspapers and watched TV all day before the trial. They knew Darwin before they walked into the courtroom. And Avila didn't even take it to the judge."

"All right," Gettes said, "you've got a point."

"There are other things," Mad Dog said.

"Oh, other things?"

"I've made a list. It's on my office desk."

"Oh great," Gettes said. "Why don't you have a beer? I've granted you this last point."

"I don't drink."

"What do you do for fun?" Gettes asked. She glanced at her watch. More tourists came in and gawked at buffalo heads. "I mean really. What do you do for fun on your days off?"

"I have so many," Mad Dog grunted.

"You're a damn good lawyer," Gettes told him.

"Thanks," Mad Dog said sourly.

"No, I mean it. You're a damn good lawyer."

"What does that mean?"

"Nothing. Just that. It's just that you need to have some fun. Take a week off and go someplace and sit in the sun, find yourself a woman to, well, relate to."

"You think that's my problem?"

"Well, I don't know," Gettes said. "We all have our itches."

Mad Dog took a deep breath. He was thinking about his wife, seeing her face in the flashing beer signs, her mad dark Jewish Bohemian face, locked in her artist's world, hearing voices, listening to the world's slander, the invitations to die. And one day the voices triumphed, that constant din of iniquity. Mad Dog found her in the bathtub with her wrists slashed, water rinsed by crimson. It was the only time in his life that Mad Dog had cried.

"I'm going home," he said.

"That sounds ominous," Gettes said huskily.

Mad Dog shook the water from his topcoat. Now he was decidedly cold. What did he yearn for that was just out of reach? What indefinable something beckoned him?

"There are other things about the case," he said. He stood, throwing the topcoat over his right shoulder. "I made a list. A dozen things that stink. I sealed it in an envelope. It's on my desk with your name on it."

"For God's sake," Gettes hissed. "Don't let anybody get ahold of it."

"Read it, okay?"

"You're serious about this, aren't you?"

"Maybe I've been prosecuting too long. Maybe you're right about me being a good lawyer. Maybe too good. Maybe I couldn't tell real life from a soap opera, I've been at it so long. Maybe there isn't anything to me anymore."

"Look," Gettes said. "I'll read it. Why don't you take a week off? You've got it coming."

"Read the list. I'm serious."

Gettes leaned across the table and grabbed his coat cuff. "What's this about, dreary old Mad Dog?" she asked.

"You'd laugh," Mad Dog said.

"No, I promise."

"It's about justice," Mad Dog said quietly.

A long measured silence. "I'm not laughing," Gettes said. "You think I don't worry about justice?"

"I don't know, Nola," Mad Dog said. "I've never known what you're serious about."

Gettes dropped her grip on the coat cuff.

"There's a me inside this bullshit," she said.

"I always thought there was. I just didn't know. Now I'm wondering if there's a him inside David Avila."

"I'll read the list," Gettes said. "Only you have to promise me you'll keep this to yourself for now."

"Deal," Mad Dog said. He pulled on his overcoat, the one that made him look like a refugee. "I'm thinking of getting out of the business."

"Don't do that," Gettes said. "You're in a phase. We lawyers get in phases. You grind and you grind and pretty soon you lose sight of what you're grinding for. Sometimes on wet Fridays after work it seems like there isn't any point. You think about it long enough and you think you'll quit. Don't let it get you down."

"Avila threw the case," Mad Dog said.

"He made some mistakes."

"Read the list."

"I will, O Mad Dog," Gettes told him.

Mad Dog left the Buffalo and trudged all the way to his walk-up apartment in an anonymously gray building just south of Japantown. He got out of his wet clothes and put some Mendelssohn on his ancient phonograph, then sat in a pool of lamplight and let the music wash over him, substitute for rain. What Mad Dog had left of his beautiful Bohemian wife was a faded photograph, a young woman on a pilgrimage to Israel, standing in front of the Temple, its golden dome peeking from behind her beautiful black hair, a smile exploding like starshine from another universe. Mad Dog touched her face with his fingers, then put the photograph back in the desk drawer where it belonged.

He remembered he hadn't told Nola about the Darwin fax.

. . .

They argued on Sunday, he said she said over pancakes and syrup, with nobody able to get the last word. In the middle of the argument, the baby woke and began to cry and Vorhees went to the nursery.

Alisha followed him. "It's Sunday, Amos," she said, arms akimbo, standing in the doorway like a guard.

"I know it's Sunday," Vorhees replied. He held the baby on his shoulder. "I'll be back in three hours, tops."

"You're a father. Being a good cop is part of being a good father. It's a package deal to me. It's the Darwin thing, isn't it?"

It was a special Sunday in April, sunshine borne on a light breeze, a few puffy clouds over the Berkeley hills, a sudden emerald stillness that had captured the city with its warmth.

"It's not the Darwin *thing*," Vorhees complained. "I don't have a Darwin *thing*."

"That lawyer accused you of planting evidence."

"I've given that over."

"Then what?" Alisha said. "I don't ask much of you. But I would like a Sunday morning."

The baby stopped crying. Vorhees kissed her on the forehead, laid her gently back in the crib. He eased his way around Alisha and made it to the bedroom, Alisha on his heels. Sitting on the bed, he put on his shoes and socks, watching his wife pace back and forth.

"I know you've been cooped up," Vorhees said. "I appreciate it. I love you for it. I know how you must feel."

"Then what? Why can't you do this on department time? Why do you have to do it on our time?"

"It's all department time. You knew that when you married me. It was explicit."

Alisha sat next to her husband.

"This isn't about power," she said.

"I know," Vorhees said.

"I get lonesome."

"I'll be back in three hours, tops. Maybe less. There won't be any traffic on Sunday morning."

Alisha put her arms around him, sneaked her nose into the corner of his neck.

"You were up all night," she said.

"The baby," he told her.

"Not the baby. Something else. Until you tell me different, I'm thinking it's the racial thing. The thing that lawyer did to you on the stand. You tell me you've given it up, but I think it's in there digging at you. You said it yourself. You've been called nigger all your life."

Vorhees went to the closet and put on a windbreaker. He stood at the windows and looked down at the deserted, sun-swept street.

"One time in Vietnam," Vorhees said, "I was doing guard duty on a firebase fly-in zone. Choppers came and went all day long, all night too when the firing wasn't too bad. Every chopper had about five wounded. One day I was down in one of the underground bunkers the docs used as a preliminary operating room. They'd bring in the serious cases to work on them before getting them out to base hospital down country."

"Amos, honey," Alisha said.

"No, it's all right," Vorhees assured her. "Charlie was all around us. Lobbing in mortars in the day. Coming up to the wire at night. There was so much noise you couldn't hear your knees knocking. I was in the bunker, dust so thick you couldn't breathe, when this black marine jumped down the sandbagged stairs and held a shotgun on the docs. He was high on pot, crazy eyes, the whole nine yards. I guess he'd snapped that night. He told the docs he was going to off everybody, then himself. There wasn't time to do anything. I had my hands full with bandages and couldn't get near the guy. He kept waving the shotgun around and screaming he was going to off everybody. One of the docs, a captain, turned around and looked at him. 'Get that fucking nigger out of here,' he screamed. Simple as that, didn't even think about what he was saying, just told me to get that fucking nigger out. I dropped the bandages and walked over to the marine and he looked at me for a minute, then he put down the shotgun and out he went. I followed him up the stairs and we stood in the open looking at the mortars coming in. Then the marine stumbled off into the night and I never saw him again. Maybe he got it that night, I don't know. What I remember is that doc telling me to get the nigger out of there. Just like that."

Alisha came over to Vorhees and looked at the street.

"That's a heavy load, Amos," she said.

"It's funny about the doc," Vorhees said. "He must have saved five or six black marines that day. Up to his armpits in their blood all day. Black marines. The doc was working his tail off all day and all night saving their lives."

"I don't know what you're talking about, Amos," Alisha said finally.

"Stuff in my head."

"If this trip means something to you, go ahead. We'll be here when you get back."

"We'll take the baby to the park."

"That sounds fine," Alisha said.

The car was at the bottom of Potrero, a station wagon wedged between two Audis. He drove the southern freeway for a change of scene, skirted the foothills, then cut off on a country road above the San Andreas Reservoir. It took him fifteen minutes to find the stables, parking near a redwood cabin surrounded by corrals and outbuildings. Vorhees was told that Angel was down by the barn with some horses, working on tack. The land ran uphill to groves of oak trees. Vorhees found Angel sitting on a bucket, drawing a huge awl through pieces of worn bridle.

"I'm Detective Vorhees," he said to the old man.

"Oh yes," Angel said, standing stooped, offering his hand. "It is my pleasure."

"Go ahead with your work," Vorhees said. "I won't take much of your time."

Angel sat down and drew a thong of leather through the bridle.

"It's nice down here," Vorhees said aimlessly.

"It used to be."

"You don't mind talking about Jack Darwin?"

"No, I don't mind," the old man replied. "What has happened to him? Will he be in jail?"

"They'll find him," Vorhees said. "I don't think he's okay now."

"I read the newspapers. This thing. You think he did these things they say he did?"

"I think so," Vorhees said.

"I don't believe it," Angel said softly.

The sunlight was bright, and Vorhees had to shade his eyes. He could smell dust and horseflesh.

"You knew Darwin a long time?" Vorhees asked.

"Since he was a boy."

"I don't suppose you'd like to tell me about him?"

Vorhees breathed the deep animal smell of the barn, hay, dust, earth. You didn't get that in the city for all the diesel, concrete bereft of smells. Lonely for smells. Vorhees wondered if a man could lose his sense of smell, being without it for so long. He remembered the aroma of Vietnam, but that was war. Angel drew a needle through a leather strap, tied it down, and snipped it with scissors.

"What is it you have, Detective?" Angel said.

"I have concern," Vorhees said.

"Yes," Angel said, spitting on the leather coupling. "The boy Jack Darwin was quiet and unassuming."

"He was happy?"

"How could I know? Who could know?"

"I suppose that's right," Vorhees said. "You know he was convicted of the killings."

"Only one," Angel said.

"One, yes."

"He did not do it."

"You think he didn't do it?"

"I know," Angel said quietly.

"How could you know?"

"I knew the boy."

"Father to the man," Vorhees said.

"That is well put," Angel told him, looking up from his work.

Vorhees glanced at his wristwatch. One hour and counting. What was he doing here?

"Did you see Jack Darwin the night of the murder?"

"I drove to his apartment in San Francisco," Angel said. "I made a mistake and went to his home, but his wife told me he didn't live there anymore. It took me a long time to find his new home, but I found it."

"Mind telling me about it?"

"There is nothing to tell. It was raining and he opened the door. I took him something important, something that has nothing to do with this thing. We talked for a few minutes and I left."

"That's all. You talked about the horse?"

"You know about the horse?" Angel asked. "Yes, we talked about the horse. Mr. Darwin was very fond of the horse."

"How did he look?"

"You mean, was he upset? Of course. He loved the horse."

"I mean, what was he wearing?"

"This is important?" Angel asked.

Yellow butterflies whisked through the pasture. Two egrets were poking through horse dung.

"It might be," Vorhees said.

"He was soaked with rain. He was wearing a white shirt and dark blue pants."

"Dress pants? Like a suit?"

"A suit, yes. Dark blue with pinstripes. I can see Mr. Darwin in my mind's eye right now. His clothes were wet."

"You remember clearly?"

"He was sitting on the sofa. A newspaper was spread out on the floor and Mr. Darwin was polishing his shoes. They were black shoes. He told me that his father had taught him to polish his shoes every day. He was polishing his black shoes because they were wet with rain."

"Blue suit, black shoes," Vorhees said to himself. "Did you see his topcoat?"

"No, not the topcoat. I saw his suit coat over a chair in the kitchen."

"You're sure about the colors?"

"My mind is clear."

"I have to go back to the city," Vorhees said at last. The old man got up from his bucket and leaned on a railing. "Did anybody ask you about Darwin? A lawyer? Anybody?"

"Oh yes," Angel said. "The lawyer telephoned me here. He asked if I knew anything that might help Mr. Darwin."

"David Avila. Was that the lawyer?"

"Yes, that was his name."

"He asked you that? In those words?"

"Those were his words. How could I forget them?"

"His exact words?"

"Those were his words," Angel said.

They shook hands and Vorhees went up to the office and got in his station wagon. He took the Bayshore home, more traffic, but he made it in thirty minutes. He spent the afternoon in Golden Gate Park with Alisha and the baby. It was hard, but he managed to switch off his cop mind and turn on his dad mind. Late that night his cop mind switched back on and it kept him awake. He fed the baby at four and watched the sun rise and tried to formulate whatever it was that was buried in his consciousness. Something transparent but real.

Darwin watched the detective go into the main stable office, then walk down to the barn. His heart raced wildly and he broke a sweat, thinking of the consequences to Angel. For a moment, he thought he would walk calmly downhill and give himself to the black detective, avoid anything terrible for Angel. Hope against hope that the detective would let the old man alone.

The bulky black detective talked to Angel, who was sitting on a bucket in the sunshine, a beautiful April Sunday the old man was using to work his leather.

The two men talked politely as Darwin continued to watch, his forehead against the shaggy wood. To his surprise, the two men rose and shook hands, the black detective walking away as if he had no care in the world. Angel glanced quickly up the hill to the shed, then went back to his work.

Darwin decided then that he would complete his work and leave as soon as possible. He would walk somewhere, try to catch a bus, steal a car, become a fugitive. Anything would be better than being trapped in a tack shed, dragging Angel down with him.

A black man watched Avila from across the room. Rows of dumbbells between him and Avila, a rack of iron, two weight benches. Avila was naked to the waist, wearing warm-up trunks, dark blue sweatpants, no shoes or socks, just Avila and the cold iron and the cold room and the curious stare of the lone black weight lifter. Avila snapped off fifteen right arm curls with a sixty-pound bell, then fifteen more on the left, allowing the iron to drop from his hand with a hefty noise on the floor. The sound of the dumbbell reverberated, echoed, died away.

On the far side, a door opened and Zack appeared in black chinos, black turtleneck, heavy black beard flecked with gray. He looked at the black weight lifter, and approached Avila, who was halfway through another set of power curls. The light in the room was densely fluorescent, a shower of invisible particles.

Zack stood to one side while Avila finished his set.

"I'm in a hurry," Zack said.

Avila did fifteen, another fifteen, and dropped the dumbbell at Zack's feet. He spit phlegm at the spot.

"We need to talk, friend," Avila said.

"So talk," Zack said. He watched the black man run through twenty pull-ups on an overhead bar, sixteen, seventeen, then twenty, on through his routine. "So fucking talk, man," he said.

Avila turned and walked through a swinging door, Zack just behind. Down a narrow corridor single file and down a flight of narrow stairs, across the empty and darkened basketball court, high windows full of nameless whispering sounds. Through another small door they came to the racquetball courts, empty for the night. Avila opened a short wooden door and Zack followed him inside. Avila flipped a switch and the court was flooded with brilliant light. Zack stepped to the middle of the court and Avila tapped the door closed. Wood and human sweat.

"They're both dead," Avila said.

"So I heard," Zack said.

Avila walked tight circles around Zack, pacing like an animal in the zoo, right, then left, then right, left again. Circles around and around. He paused to look at Zack, who was paring his fingernails with a knife.

"You fucking offed a DEA informer," Avila said.

"What's your point?" Zack asked. He snapped shut the knife and put it in the pocket of his chinos. "Is there a point?"

"Then you offed Vine."

"You have a point?" Zack asked again.

"You fucks offed a DEA informant."

"We fucks didn't do shit," Zack said. "So what, anyway?"

"We fucks didn't do shit," Avila said. "We fucks didn't do shit."

"You're losing it, man," Zack said, trying to circle around the pacing Avila.

"No, fucker," Avila said, looking Zack back to the middle of the room. He faced Zack, who was maybe an inch taller.

"What do you want to say, man?" Zack asked.

Hard stare at Zack, scary: "This nigger Vorhees called me at the office today."

"The detective?"

"No shit," Avila said.

"What'd he say?"

Avila paced another circle around Zack. Half-moon one way, half-moon back, very scary now.

"He asked if I had a minute to talk," Avila said. "Just like fucking that. Could I spare a minute?" He said it was about Perry Lehigh, the DEA informant."

"The DEA fuck," Zack said.

"Yeah, well, this nigger knows I turned the informant's name to Luther Lee. That's where you fucks come in."

"DEA fucks get killed all the time," Zack said, his head turned to watch Avila behind him.

"I told you not to do it," Avila said.

"I don't like the tone, man," Zack said.

"You want me to tone it down?"

Avila turned to one side and kicked Zack in the stomach hard. Zack went to his knees, then hands and knees. Zack stayed down there for a minute or two, catching his breath.

"I'll fucking kill you," Zack finally said.

Avila kneeled near Zack's head, whispering into an available ear. Zack was hacking now, sweat on his forehead.

"You fat sack of shit," Avila said. "You goddamn fat sucking sack of pig shit."

"You're dead," Zack said. Zack lifted his head.

"Say that again," Avila told him.

Zack snorted.

"Please say that again."

Silence. The overhead light buzzed, like insects.

"Who do you think you're fucking with?" Avila asked. "Some punk like Arthur Vine?"

"I didn't do Vine," Zack said. "I'm getting up." Zack got to his feet, slumped slightly. "I didn't do Vine." Avila was pacing again, around and around.

"You think Vorhees is stupid?"

"I wouldn't know," Zack replied.

Zack in black, like a shadow. Zack, red-faced and huffing.

"Hurts, doesn't it?" Avila said. "Next time it will be your stupid fucking face." Avila took a deep breath, held it for the count of ten. "Who did Vine?"

"Luther Lee, who else?" Zack answered.

"How hard is that to figure out?" Avila asked. "You know it. I know it. You think that nigger doesn't know it. You think those DEA fucks aren't out there trying to find some payback for their informer? What's going through that simple fucking head of yours?"

"So, what is it, man? What's your point? It's done."

"Undo it then," Avila said.

"Sure, undo it. Just like that."

"Take Luther Lee off. Before they talk to him."

"I can't take off my main dude," Zack said.

"Vorhees is coming to see me tomorrow. Luther Lee will be next. They'll finger him for Vine and sit on him until they put both of us away. You're next in line for the DEA puke. Use your head."

Zack opened his mouth to speak, then stopped. He looked at the small wooden door, five paces away. Avila moved, let him look.

"I can see you thinking, Zack," Avila said. "Give it a try."

Zack licked his lips.

"You can't let your people get taken down," Zack said. "It's that simple, man. Luther Lee did Vine on his own. The DEA setup was payback. As for Vine, who cares? That stupid little fuck came over here to Hunters Point in his tan Camaro like he owned the place. They went down to the Point and Luther Lee capped the fucker. What can I say? I guess Luther Lee wanted to send his own message. He sure as hell didn't clear it with me. Maybe he thought the DEA would turn Vine on the case even without the informer. Who knows? Shit, don't ask me about Luther Lee because sometimes he does his own thing. I ain't his mamma, am I?"

Avila closed his eyes. "These clowns can add two and two, Zack. When they add two and two they get you and me. You dig it?"

Zack tried looking at the ceiling.

"It's just business," he said.

"When I see this Vorhees prick," Avila said, "I'm going to give him Luther Lee. If that gets back to Luther Lee, I'm going to come after you. No ass kicking, no warning. No more mind games, tricks, dicking around. I'll come after you, pure and simple."

"Luther Lee, he won't know jack," Zack said.

"Whatever it takes to get Vorhees off my back, I'm going to do it."

"You got my permission, man," Zack said, trying to smile.

"I'm so fucking glad," Avila said. "When the cops go after Luther Lee, you're going to have to whack him."

"He's my main dude, man."

"Whack him. Do it."

"He can hack it, man. He won't give you up."

"He is a dangerous dude."

"I can't whack him, man."

"You whack him, or I whack you both," Avila said.

"They won't connect you, man," Zack protested.

"They already have."

"They're just fishing for shit," Zack said.

Avila shook his head and made for the door. He opened it and went into the hallway and waited for Zack to duck through. They went into the next room, stood in the middle of the dark basketball court.

Zack was across the center line, arms folded.

"I hate to whack Luther Lee," he said.

"Two days."

"All right, man," Zack agreed.

"It's your only choice."

"You'll hear from me," Zack told him.

Zack walked across the empty court and left by a swinging door in the corner of the vast hall. Avila stood at center court, stripped to the waist, barefoot, not noticing the cold. He was not afraid, but he felt the pressure.

Rush hour at the foot of Pine, Cooley parked in a red zone. Streets slashed by shadows. Streets engulfed by people. Streets agog with commerce, explosions of finance.

"Don't be long," Cooley said sarcastically.

Vorhees closed the passenger door. "Wait for me please," he said through the open window.

Inside he caught the elevator to six, went down a carpeted hall, introduced himself to a receptionist who looked as if she wanted to go home, raincoat over her shoulder, hat, bag, briefcase all piled on a coffee table. She buzzed Vorhees down a passageway and Vorhees heard the door shut behind him. Avila was at a desk, standing but not offering to shake hands. Vorhees took a leather chair. He could see a slice of the Bay Bridge out one corner window, stolid and gray against a blue background.

"I can't talk about the Darwin case," Avila said.

"I appreciate that," Vorhees replied. "I didn't come about the Darwin case. I think I explained that over the telephone."

"Okay, I get you," Avila said, sitting finally. "What's on your mind?"

"You represent a fellow named Luther Lee Dokes?" Vorhees asked.

"Sure," Avila said. "He's on the federal hump."

"Got a trial date?"

Avila rifled his calendar. "Early June. The fifth."

Vorhees was looking at Avila. Up close, he was big. Big hands, broad shoulders, somebody who lifted weights a lot, not an amateur. Vorhees had seen hands like those before, hands with the cartilage between knuckles broken into carbuncles and mounds, a person who banged his hands against a tatami mat for hours, hands like stone.

"Well," Vorhees continued, "a guy named Perry Lehigh got killed over in the East Bay last month."

"I heard about that, didn't I?"

"He was an informant for the DEA. He came down on Luther Lee and Arthur Vine."

"I heard he got it in the East Bay," Avila said. "Is that your concern?"

"Arthur Vine is on my list," Vorhees said. "I knew him and Luther Lee from the old days in narcotics."

"Jack Darwin had Vine," Avila said. "You knew that, didn't you?"

Vorhees studied the man's eyes. Nothing there, black as night and motionless. Like photos he'd seen of Bosnian kids who'd been in basements for three years listening to shells burst overhead.

"Now that you mention it," Vorhees continued, "Arthur Vine got killed too, up in Hunters Point. Both Vine and the DEA guy got it in the neck, eyes picked out. You know how it is with criminals, they have a way of doing things, like you and me roll out of bed on the left side. The way they have of doing things maybe they like so much they can't stop doing it that way, no matter what. They don't think about it while they're doing it, they just do it. Maybe some of them enjoy doing it, who knows? Maybe some deep psychological shit is swirling in their heads while they're doing it. Anyway, Lehigh and Vine got it the same way, in the neck, eyes pecked out. Puncture wound all the way into the forehead. Kind of an amateur lobotomy, with extras."

Avila sipped some Evian. There was a plate of oatmeal cookies on the desk beside him.

"I guess," he said, "your theory is one guy killed both."

"Sure, I think so. It's like that shower killer thing. Some sick fuck grabs a girl and drags her into the shower. Maybe she gets into the shower with him because she thinks they're going to have fun. Maybe he drags her into the shower. However it works, they're in the shower and he grabs her around the neck like they're playing games, but he keeps choking her until she gets scared. Maybe he gets her off her feet so she can't fight him and he bangs her head against the tile so she gets a little tired. He's right-handed and he keeps his right arm around her throat while he does his work behind her. He enjoys that too. Then when he's done, he strangles her. Maybe cleans her up afterward because he's a sick meticulous fuck. That's how we got this guy, because he couldn't help doing it his way. Just like this guy killed Lehigh and Vine. Because he couldn't do it any other way. Imagine sick fucks like that who can't help themselves. Sick, isn't it?"

Vorhees stopped, like screeching to a halt in dead silence. His talk had burned rubber all the way to nowhereville. Avila was quiet, looking out the window.

"I can't talk about Darwin," Avila said finally.

"Yeah, sorry. I was just telling you about MO, how you can spot a sick fuck from his style."

"What do you want to know?" Avila said sullenly.

Muscles at work in Avila's jaw.

"The DEA thinks somebody set their agent up."

The office was nearly dark, but Avila made no move to turn on a lamp.

Vorhees continued: "There was a closed hearing in front of Kelly a few weeks ago."

"I know, I was there," Avila said.

"Lehigh came in and testified on the search affidavit. At the end,

Kelly overruled your motion and set the case for trial. I imagine that pissed Dokes off royal. He's looking at five years because of Lehigh and Vine."

"I represent Dokes," Avila said, hands folded. "I couldn't say anything about it one way or the other. I know Dokes isn't stupid, if that's of any help. Maybe you should talk to him."

"How much did Dokes pay you for defending him?"

"You know I can't discuss that."

The room had become powdery blue with evening light. Light leaking away from the windowpanes.

"Does Dokes have a higher-up?" Vorhees asked.

"Same answer. You know my position."

"I was in narcotics for ten years. We've been on opposite sides more than once."

"Yeah, I recognize you."

"I know Luther Lee too. He's been on my sheet twice, but we couldn't get around to him. He isn't ganged up, I know that. But he's major. I guess I'm just talking out loud."

"Go ahead and think," Avila said. "It's your nickel."

That's better, Vorhees thought. Muscles in Avila's neck working now too.

"What I think is Luther Lee has a main man," Vorhees said. "They don't see how they can survive a world where DEA informants are taking them down for five years at a stretch. It chops time into too many fragments, you know? Anyway, Luther Lee gets cranky and kills the informant. Then he gets out of control and kills Arthur Vine, pokes the guy's eyes out and dumps him in Hunters Point, so anybody reads the newspapers they get the message. It's a pride thing, you know?"

"I'm listening," Avila said.

"Anyway, I'm just wondering who Luther Lee's main man might be, if you know?"

"Sorry," Avila said. "You know my position."

"Listen, I don't mean this personally. But a lawyer like yourself, you might have to file a motion to bring an informant into court, just part of doing business. But a lawyer can't want somebody whacked, just like that. I just want you to know I understand your position, how it could be difficult. Maybe we could work something out."

Avila tore at Vorhees with savage eyes, burning holes in the space between them.

"There's nothing to work out," Avila said.

"I was wondering if Luther Lee still lives up in Diamond Heights with his old lady and brother?"

"Listen, I can't talk about Luther Lee. But he lives up there."

Full dark in the room now, scary as hell, with rays of light splashing in from the reception area.

"Maybe I should come to the point," Vorhees said.

"Maybe you should."

"I want you to bring in Luther Lee. I want to talk to him downtown at the Hall of Justice. When would be a good time for you?"

Avila sipped Evian. He switched on a desk lamp.

"Bullshit," Avila said.

"That's a good attitude."

"Get out now," Avila said.

"You're refusing? Just so I know."

"You heard me," Avila said.

"A DEA agent named Burkholder will be around. It's only a matter of time."

"This conversation is over," Avila said.

Avila stayed seated while Vorhees rose. He looked out the windows at the empty streets, the cold blue sky.

"If Luther Lee runs, I'll look to you," Vorhees said.

Avila stood.

"Out now," he said.

Vorhees took the elevator down and found Cooley in the Chevrolet, reading a paperback primer on yoga. Vorhees got into the car and they sat in their red zone, watching stragglers go home.

"Where you fucking been?" Cooley asked.

"It took longer than I thought."

"Well, I hope you're happy," Cooley said. He opened a page of the yoga book. "Look here, you think a guy could get into that position and enjoy it?"

"It looks complicated," Vorhees admitted.

"I gotta take my physical in two weeks," Cooley said.

"Now I get it," Vorhees told him.

"I'm ten pounds overweight. That's with the charts they use for old guys like me. Rose says this yoga can get you cranked in no time."

Cooley showed Vorhees the photo of a woman pretzeled into an amazing contortion.

"Lay off the doughnuts," Vorhees said.

"So, you happy?" Cooley asked, snapping the book shut.

"You got to help me with this."

"How am I gonna help you with this? Darwin is on the run and they'll get him. It's making you crazy."

"I told you," Vorhees said. "Darwin was wearing a blue suit and black shoes the night of the murder. I can prove it. I've got a witness. He didn't wear the camel hair topcoat, and when he got home he was soaking wet all over, just from walking to his apartment from where he parked."

"Maybe he wore it. Some guys got no taste."

"Darwin has taste. You've seen his clothes. You've seen how he carries himself. This guy wouldn't go anywhere in a blue suit and camel hair topcoat."

"You got the blood on his shirt and coat," Cooley said. "Not to mention the cuff link."

"Yeah, the blood," Vorhees said. "You know who owns the place where Darwin was staying? The apartment on the Marina? You know who gave him a place to stay after he was kicked out by his wife?"

"Okay, I'll bite," Cooley said.

"*David Avila,*" Vorhees said. "A guy named Henry Diehl told me that. The other friend who died, the friend we kept thinking was Lisa Tracy. It wasn't Lisa Tracy. It was a horse. Some nag Darwin used to ride as a kid. I guess it broke him up when they put the horse down."

"Avila owns the Marina apartment?"

"Weird, isn't it?"

"So, what went down up there?" Cooley asked. He started the engine and they rolled south toward the Embarcadero, heading over to Market and the police garage at the Hall of Justice. "I mean, what did Avila say about the informer?"

"He said, bullshit."

"Just like that."

"I'm quoting him. Maybe I pimped him a little."

"Very distinguished conversation."

"Something was clicking inside him, Tom. He looked half loony up there."

They bumped across the tracks on Market.

"I haven't been sleeping," Vorhees admitted.

"Baby up all night?"

"Once at four, then again at dawn."

"She'll chill out pretty soon."

"You know something else?" Vorhees said. "This guy Tom Fullerton said Darwin never wore cuff links. He said he saw a picture of them in the newspapers and didn't give it a second thought because he hadn't seen them in so long. Didn't even remember them. Darwin said he had them as keepsakes because they were his dad's."

"Yeah, then how did they end up at Lisa Tracy's?"

"I don't know. But I know I'm going to see Luther Dokes."

"Let's just be careful," Cooley said.

Cooley drove without speaking. He parked inside two acres of other vehicles, behind chain-link fence topped with barbed wire, scoured by security cameras.

He put two hands on the steering wheel. "All right," Cooley said. "I'm definitely interested."

"I'm glad to hear it," Vorhees said.

"You know we have to do this on our own frigging time?" Cooley said.

Vorhees said, "Yeah, I know it, Tom."

Karla vomited vodka and Seconal into the bathwater. She sat quite still, head full of vague revulsion, then eased herself out of the tub, standing in the middle of the bathroom naked, unable to look in the mirror. Nothing in the undergrowth of her experience had prepared her for this, an intimate collapse without precedent. She stepped into the shower and ran hot water over her body until the residue washed down the drain. She got out and wrapped herself in a towel.

When the doorbell rang she was in the bedroom, pulling on a sweatsuit. She put on some sunglasses and went downstairs.

Through the front peephole she saw two detectives, one large black guy with graying hair, another short and balding with a florid face, dressed in what might have been a leisure suit out of the seventies. She let her head fall against the door and thought about not opening it, but she knew the gold Mercedes was parked in the drive, not ten paces away from the front door. Brilliant sunshine flooded the scene outside, too bright for Karla to stand. She slid the chain from its grooved latch.

"Good afternoon, Mrs. Darwin," the black man said.

"Hi," the other said quickly.

Karla unlatched the chain and eased the door open. She tried to remember last night, the night before, nothing coming to mind.

"What is it?" she managed to say.

"Do you mind?" the black man said ambiguously. "I mean, could we have a moment?"

"I've told you everything," Karla said.

"This won't take a moment," Vorhees said.

Karla was sick, hungover sick, nothing left to vomit. A knot had tightened in her stomach and her throat hurt from ten minutes of dry heaves. Despite not having eaten for two days, she felt no hunger at all.

"What do you want?" she asked.

"It's about the Lisa Tracy murder," Vorhees said. "We think there's something in the house that could help us enormously. If it's no trouble."

"Please, Mrs. Darwin," Cooley said. "It's about that young woman who was murdered on Turk."

"I thought you solved that," Karla said.

Her hands were ice cold. Why were they so cold?

Karla opened the door. She felt weak, supporting herself on the jamb, one hand on the doorknob. She was like a tightrope walker suspended above an abyss, wind whistling in the canyon below, legions of ghosts calling to her from far away.

Vorhees stepped inside and Cooley eased around him.

"We'd like another look in your husband's bedroom," Vorhees told her politely.

"Is that legal?" Karla muttered.

"Sure, with your permission," Vorhees said.

"All right, go ahead," Karla said. "Just go ahead and get it over with and go."

Karla descended the three steps to the kitchen. When she looked back she saw both detectives watching her curiously, the shorter one tugging at the holster under his arm, the tall one like some Easter Island idol. Jesus, Karla thought to herself, just go upstairs and leave me alone. She walked to the kitchen counter and placed two hands flat on its cool surface. There was a vodka bottle inches away, beckoning. She wanted to pour a drink, but she was afraid to do it while the cops were watching her. She heard them go upstairs, open Jack's door. In a few minutes they came down again and stood in the foyer above her.

"We'd like to take along this jewelry box," Vorhees said. "If that's all right. We could leave a receipt."

Karla turned and looked.

"Jack's jewelry box? Okay, go ahead. Just go."

"Thanks, Mrs. Darwin," Cooley said.

"Yeah, thanks a lot," Vorhees said after him.

Behind black sunglasses, Karla shut her eyes. She heard the front door close.

She was not supposed to, but she went to the phone and dialed the Marina number. She left a short message for David, trying to remain calm and distinct. With that out of the way, she went back to the kitchen and poured herself a vodka and grapefruit juice and walked the drink out to the patio and looked at the bay below her.

Oh, soothing blue bay.

Roses in bloom. One dark red Mr. Lincoln.

A light breeze in her black hair.

Portugal. Pink castles and dusty gray cacti.

A bad boy, deep inside, hurting her.

David, where are you?

They walked over from Jackson Square, Mooney and Fullerton with paper bags containing the remains of their lunch, corned beef on rye, cartons of cole slaw, pickles from a deli on the Embarcadero. It was a warm day in early spring and they'd eaten their sandwiches sitting on a bench in the square, surrounded by pigeons and secretaries. Mooney had drunk a sixteen-ounce can of Rainier ale, tossing the empty can in a garbage bin on the corner nearest his office. Mooney had a three-person law firm in a squat brick building on a corner of Battery Street, about two blocks from the piers. When they got to the office, Mooney lit a short black cigar and sat in a chair in front of a plate glass window looking down on the street. Fullerton took a footstool and perched on it near the window too.

"I know what you're doing," Mooney said.

Mooney was wearing a dark green three-piece suit that might have been thirty years old, lapels a foot wide, three-button vest, polyester material, pants with flared cuffs. Fullerton wore his "late Reagan" outfit, jeans, flannel cowboy shirt, expensive lizard-skin cowboy boots.

"What am I doing?" Fullerton said, bemused.

Mooney handed him a cheroot. Fullerton lit it with a wooden match.

"You're paying my fees out of your own pocket," Mooney said.

"What makes you say that?"

"Deny it to my face, you old fart," Mooney laughed.

"Ah, what's the difference?"

Down on Battery, a city bus roared away.

"I guess there isn't any difference," Mooney said. Mooney had reddish gray hair, adorable Irish eyes.

"Did you get the transcripts I ordered?"

"Last week. I read them twice. In fact, I had them scanned onto the computer."

"You have a computer?"

"My secretary does," Mooney said.

"So what's your opinion?" Fullerton asked him.

Mooney sighed, breathed out smoke. "You want the long version or the short version?"

"Are you billing me now?"

"Hell no." Mooney laughed gruffly.

Fullerton rose and waltzed his cigar around the office. Model sailing ships, photos of the thirties waterfront, a bookshelf full of books about maritime and labor law. A framed photo of Dashiell Hammett.

"Then give me the long version," Fullerton said.

Mooney walked to a glass cabinet and poured himself a snifter of brandy. He walked back to the window and watched the people on Battery Street.

"So what do you think, Sandy? Really."

"Relax," Mooney said. "You wanted the long version, you're going to get the long version. I've given this a lot of thought, how Jack got into this mess. What happened before he was arrested. What happened during trial. How did he run into David Avila, do you know?"

"He said they had a case together."

"A drug case?"

"Yes, I think so."

"This Avila is a drug lawyer. Don't get me wrong, he has a good reputation in trial. But he hasn't done many murder cases, I don't imagine."

"I don't know," Fullerton admitted.

"I'll tell you what I think in two words," Mooney said. "Short version first."

"What's that?"

"It stinks," Mooney said.

"It stinks?" Fullerton said. "What are you talking about?"

"This case stinks, simple as that."

"If you don't like the fact that Jack is running, just tell me."

"No, you old fart. It isn't that." Mooney sipped some cognac. "The whole case stinks. Front to back."

"Well, I'm all ears," Fullerton said.

"What do you know about search and seizure law?" Mooney began rhetorically. He held the snifter up to the light and studied the brandy. "It isn't like good cognac. It's an ambiguous area of the law, full of gaps and episodes. You remember the old days, when the cops would come into the union halls and root around for stuff, tear things up, destroy records on some pretext or other? That was the old days, of course. Nowadays the pretexts are more deliberate and you have to know your way around the rules. When I read Jack's notes the other day, I discovered his lawyer sent him up to the Marina apartment to let two detectives search the place. Just like that. Avila didn't concern himself with the search very much. Now, if one of my union boys had told me the cops just wanted to look around his apartment, see what they could find, I would have been over at his place standing in the doorway with a baseball bat, over my dead body kind of thing. Evidently Avila told Darwin to go over and let them in. What could it hurt? And another thing, those same two cops were at the Pacific Heights house earlier. Karla let them come inside and search his bedroom. That's when they found the other cuff link."

"Karla gave them permission."

"I'm not telling you for certain that was a bad search. But I never would have sent Jack Darwin up to his apartment in the Marina to let two cops search the place for evidence of a murder. And I'm telling you there would have been hell to pay in court before that cuff link would have been admitted into evidence. I would have filed a motion challenging Karla's ability to give permission to search. There would have been motion practice that was loud and ugly. I searched the transcripts and there isn't any mention of the issue at all. Avila didn't attack it."

"Is that grounds for appeal?"

"Mooney says no," he replied. "That's the hell of it. It's washed away, gone, unappealable." Mooney sipped more cognac. "I can always argue the effective assistance of counsel, but it's hogwash, everybody knows that. You've heard the law. The defendant is entitled to effective assistance, not brilliance, not infallibility. Avila is an experienced lawyer. If he shows up in court sober and sits in a chair, it's usually effective assistance. But practically, you have to expect more of Avila than that. Even though Jack wasn't living up in Pacific Heights, it was his property. He owned it. He'd lived there all his life. He had the right to come and go and get his things when his divorce lawyer called in advance. In my opinion, he had an ongoing privacy interest in his bedroom, at least. Besides, those two cops had plenty of time to request a search warrant if they had probable cause. You could show they didn't know what they were looking for, and stumbled across the cuff link. What I'm saying is there was ample ground to challenge the search in court. Any lawyer worth his salt would have done it. And no lawyer would have told his client to let those cops snort around the apartment in the Marina. It doesn't wash, Tom."

"The cuff link hurt him, Sandy," Fullerton said.

"You said he never wore them," Mooney said.

"Jack didn't wear them. I never saw him wear them. Not in the five years his mother and father have been gone."

"Avila didn't make much of that in trial either," Mooney said.

"And he didn't ask me about it on the stand."

"He should have. I would have. Hell, any lawyer would have brought that out. When all you've got is reasonable doubt, you have to bring up every little thing. And something else. Suppose you walk up to a sleeping juror and yell boo, embarrass the shit out of them in open court. That's what Avila did, Tom. And that's not lack of insight. That's bullshit. It has the reek of malice."

Fullerton crushed his cheroot.

"I was in court for that one," he said. "But it isn't anything to appeal, is it?"

"Hear me out," Mooney said. "You remember the composition of the jury? Four blacks on that jury and I don't see where Avila used any peremptory challenges. Hey, back when I was defending labor organizers we used to try to get blacks and Orientals on the jury, but the prosecution always challenged them. We'd wind up in court with twelve fat white burghers, squinty bastards with red cheeks and the smell of wurst on their clothes. As soon as they called a black to the box, the prosecutor was up with a challenge. You know they can't do that anymore. But I ask myself, here is Avila thinking about pulling the race card out of his sleeve. He's going to attack a black cop on the stand, call him a liar and worse, and what does he do? He lets four blacks go on the jury without challenge. Besides that, his race card was bullshit from the get-go. I watched those black jurors while Avila was grilling Vorhees, and they weren't a happy bunch. They knew what was coming down, and it wasn't good for Jack Darwin."

"Poor strategy," Fullerton said.

"You can call it that," Mooney told him. "It doesn't make a pretty picture. Gave his client up to bad searches. Didn't challenge any blacks on top of his race card. Didn't even have the jury sequestered. Don't forget that one, Tom, that's elementary textbook strategy. And then there was the speaking motion on DNA."

"I thought that was pretty hopeless," Fullerton said.

"Hopeless," Mooney scoffed. "In open court he attacks a credible DNA expert? What does that accomplish? Avila forced the judge to rule from the bench. What does she do? What can she do? She winds up giving the jury a lecture on how tight the expert testimony has been, how good the lab they chose turned out to be. It all reemphasized how good the DNA evidence was in the first place. Avila couldn't have done a better job with that expert if it had been his own witness. The time for that motion was pretrial, where if you lose at least you don't lose in front of the twelve people who have your client's fate in their hands." Mooney twirled the last of the cognac. "Days were when I could drink these all afternoon, then start on ale at night."

"And fall asleep at eight," Fullerton said.

"On top of some gorgeous blond bimbo," Mooney laughed.

"You wish. The good old days."

"That's the gospel," Mooney said.

"Does Jack have any chance?" Fullerton asked after a short silence.

"You know what we've been talking about up here isn't any ground for a decent appeal. Trial tactics. Lawyer screwups. Mistakes. It isn't anything to carry up to the next level. I can make up something in the appellate brief, but those old men in Sacramento aren't going to buy it. I'll have to attack Avila, try to get a new trial. That's the best and only strategy I can think of right now. I hate to do it to a fellow lawyer, but I have no choice. Your boy Darwin wrote *some* brilliant trial notes."

"There's a life at stake here," Fullerton said.

Fullerton stood at the big windows looking down at Battery Street. The city had changed so much, he was thinking. Lawyering had changed, everything had changed. He was old, but he hadn't felt old before now. Still, he decided he'd fax Gettes his thoughts.

At the foot of Bay Street, Cooley stopped for coffee at a convenience store. Vorhees remained in the car, sifting through the contents of the jewelry box, an oblong of withered leather with a faded gilt JD on top. He fingered the pieces, piece by piece, one by one:

Phi Beta Kappa key, dated 1932. Two circular riding medals from the Vallejo State Fair, date none, old though, tarnished bronze with green mold on back. Two pairs of plain gold barred tie clasps, scratched. Two baby teeth, slightly yellowed. One gold wedding band, inscription inside, L to JD with love. A second plain gold wedding band, inscription inside, JD to L with love. An Indian head penny. The faded photograph of a cabin, front porch, side view, hummingbird feeder besieged by hummingbirds, blurs in sunshine.

Cooley came back with his coffee.

"It's goddamn cold," he said angrily. "Sixty-five cents and the coffee's cold."

Vorhees closed the jewelry case.

"It's all old stuff," he said quietly.

"Oh yeah?" Cooley said.

"Old stuff. Had to be his dad's."

Cooley picked up the case and looked through it.

"Okay, so you're right about this one," he said.

"Makes you wonder, doesn't it?"

"I suppose it does," Cooley said.

"Well, does it, or doesn't it?" Vorhees asked. "Darwin comes to his house at Pacific Heights and takes his dad's two cuff links out of the box, puts them on, goes over and kills Lisa Tracy. Sometime later, he comes back to the Pacific Heights house and puts one back into the box. Doesn't he think that maybe the other one is in Lisa Tracy's house? And besides, he says he doesn't wear them. It looks like this jewelry box is all old stuff, mementos, things that belonged to his dad. Baby teeth, for God's sake. And it's never brought up in court. What kind of shit is that?"

Cooley swirled his cold coffee.

"Jesus, it's a nice day," he said.

"Are you listening to me?" Vorhees asked. "Darwin takes two cuff links out of the box, puts one back? When did he do that? Why would he do that?"

"Okay, it doesn't make sense," Cooley said. "I agree with you. I have all along."

"We didn't find a French cuff shirt at the Marina apartment."

"He ditched it."

"It wasn't in the Dumpsters out back."

"He's too smart for that."

"I suppose so," Vorhees admitted. "What are we going to do?"

"We already burned our lunch hour. You happy?"

"I think it's time to talk to Lightfoot," Vorhees said.

Cooley pulled onto Bay, going east. They were eating city bus diesel for two blocks.

"Did you get a look at the wife?" Cooley asked. "She isn't doing real well, you ask me."

"Sick-looking all right," Vorhees agreed.

"Just got up at noon."

"Didn't wash her hair."

"What the hell," Cooley said. "Her husband is on the run from a murder charge. How should she be doing?"

Vorhees put the jewelry case on the seat between them.

Hello, Karla.

Oh God, David. It's you isn't it?

I told you not to call the Marina number. I'm sorry you called it, despite my having told you not to. There are risks we should not take. What is wrong with you, dear?

David, the police have been here.

Police?

A black detective and his partner.

Cooley and Vorhees.

I think so.

When? Make this quick, sweetheart. Calling the Marina apartment is a very stupid thing to do.

This afternoon. Please don't be angry with me, David. I'm so confused. Confused. I've been having trouble, David. Please understand that I've been having trouble every day.

What did the police want, Karla?

They wanted to search Jack's bedroom. Again.

And you let them?

What could I say? They came inside before I could think. What could I tell them? How would it look?

All right. Shut up and tell me. They looked in his bedroom, did they?

Yes, David. What else could I do?

You gave them your permission? You told them to go ahead and look in his bedroom, just like that?

Yes. What could I do, David?

All right. That's fine. What happened then?

I don't know. I mean, I went downstairs to the kitchen and they went upstairs to the bedroom. When they came out of his bedroom they were carrying one of the jewelry boxes from there. It was an old leather one.

The one with Jack's initials on it?

I don't know. I think this one belonged to his dad.

His dad?

Yes, it was an old one. He kept junk in there.

Did you talk to them, Karla? Did you say something to them, you stupid bitch?

No, please, David. Don't say those things.

I'm sorry, dear. I'm just upset. Did you say anything to the policemen?

I need to see you. I miss you and I'm afraid. I think I know what you're doing.

What am I doing, Karla?

You killed those two women.

Jack killed those women, dear. Haven't you been reading the newspapers? I think Jack is dangerously ill. I think he's a sociopath. I don't think he has a conscience. I think he's fooled you. I think he's fooled a lot of people in his time. He's sick, Karla. Don't forget that.

I need some end to this, David. Things seem like they're whirling around me so fast. I can't stand the way things are anymore. I'm falling apart.

Did you talk to the police, Karla? Did you say anything to them about us? About me? What's going on in that simple head of yours? Why can't you keep focused, dear? Why can't you keep your mind on the things that are important to you and me? You lack focus, dear.

I don't know what's important anymore, David. You'll have to tell me.

What's important, Karla? Why, you and I are important, and the money. The police can't hurt you, Karla. The only thing that can hurt you are those things in your own head.

How can I forget Jack when two police come to my house and search his bedroom? What were they looking for? Why did they take his dad's jewelry box?

Did you talk to them, Karla? Answer me.

No. I let them in. I went down to the kitchen.

That's all? You're sure?

First I told them I didn't have anything more to say. I didn't want to let them in, but they both stood outside and I didn't know what to do. I let them go into the bedroom, that's all. I didn't say anything about you or about Jack or about anybody. I just went down to the kitchen. I want to go away. I want us to go away together.

Maybe *you* should go away, Karla. Take a vacation. Go to Mexico. Go to Cancún and wait for me.

Why can't we go together? I need to see you.

I can't leave now. I have cases. I have things that need to be taken care of. We have the rest of our lives to be together. But we have to stay focused.

You killed those two women. I know you did.

Don't be ridiculous, Karla. Jack killed them.

How could you?

Don't be ridiculous, bitch.

I can't stand this.

This is for you and me. You're missing the point.

What if they come back, David?

The police?

What if they come back?

You're sure the jewelry box belonged to Jack's dad?

Yes. I've seen it before. Jack showed it to me one night when he'd been drinking. There were old things inside it. Medals, some baby teeth. Junk like that.

Brown, with initials JD on the front in gold?

Yes, that's it. How did you know?

Never mind, Karla.

Did you take a cuff link from the box? Is that what you did? I'd have been a fool not to see it. Answer me, David. I need to know. I think I know, but not knowing is killing me.

Killing you? It isn't killing you, Karla. Not yet. Just remember that everything in the world happens for a good reason. Nothing is left to chance. Keep your mind focused and trust in me to do everything that needs to be done. You trust me, don't you, Karla?

David.

Karla?

David, I'm afraid. I've been afraid every day and night for three months. I don't sleep and I can't work out and I'm so alone. What have you done?

Karla, be quiet. Just fucking be quiet.

Please, David.

Be quiet. Let me think. I have things to do this week, Karla. But next week we'll be together, I promise. Maybe we can go up to Mendocino again and sit in the mud. You remember when we went up to Mendocino and sat in the mud, don't you, Karla? Would you like that? Or maybe we could fly down to Cabo and meet there. We could get condos next to each other. We could watch the whales. Maybe they'll have some whales in the ocean down there.

I don't know what you're talking about, David. I'm so confused. I'm having bad dreams, David.

I'm talking about us being together.

Why did the police take that jewelry box, David?

I think they're going to charge Jack in the Tracy killing. Whatever it is, it doesn't involve you. Just keep your mouth shut. I think you should leave the country for a while. I could meet you someplace.

I think it does.

Does what?

Involve me. It involves me.

No it doesn't, Karla.

I can't live like this anymore, David.

Maybe you won't have to.

We've got to talk.

Can't you wait a week, dear?

I don't think so. You killed them, didn't you? Those two women. You killed them?

Maybe we can meet in the city.

Please call me, David.

Maybe I will. Turn on your answering machine and if you hear from me, erase the message. Can you do that?

All right, David.

I'll talk to you soon. I love you.

I don't know what to do.

Don't worry. You won't have to live like this much longer.

The click hurt her physically. It hurt her ear, like being slapped. Her head ached and she felt dirty, as though she had just come through a raging desert sandstorm and had been scoured of her skin. For a long time she sat on the sofa with the phone in her lap, thinking not about David, but about Jack. The house was quiet as always, and she could not get a picture of Jack out of her head, Jack in a narrow cell, bathed in cold gray light, shrouded in light. Although Karla's vision was dulled, Jack appeared mummylike, withered and dry. The gray light that enveloped Jack created a one-dimensional caricature of Jack, a figure sunk in concrete.

Later, she rose from the sofa and walked upstairs to the family room. It was a small, cluttered space, disused for years, containing a sewing machine on a table, an ironing board, metal bookshelves filled with scattered books and papers, file folders, photograph albums, vases full of plastic chrysanthemums, jelly jars packed with odds and ends, buttons, pennies. In a space beneath the single bed she found a trunk and opened it, taking out the chrome-plated .32 automatic, loaded, on safety. She held the pistol and sat on the single bed in the dusty light of the afternoon. She put her tongue on the cold metal of the barrel and tasted it, licked it and licked it, like a mother cat. She closed her eyes and ran the barrel of the weapon around the orbits of her eyes, then around her lips twice.

She had a picture of Jack.

She had the picture of a bottle of Stoly's.

She put down the gun and began to shake.

The pollarded sycamores were green in leaf. Gettes noticed them walking over to the state bar association on Franklin Street, and she noticed them again as she was waiting in a third-floor lounge. As she waited, she couldn't help thinking about that second "mystery fax," traced to a print shop in downtown San Francisco. Could Darwin be that close? She was standing at the heavy windows, looking at the sycamores, noticing them in leaf, and when she turned back a young man named Monroe scuttled into the room. By his side he held a manila envelope, low against his hip.

"This is sort of irregular," he said.

Monroe had blond hair, a cowlick sticking up in front. A row of capped white teeth gave him a puppetlike appearance. "I mean, very irregular."

"Don't worry about it," Gettes said. She smiled tartly, very forgiving and motherly.

Gettes knew Monroe a little. He had worked on Democratic Party fund-raising for years, and she had met him at coffees and swishy cocktail parties in downtown hotels. Part of the gay coalition, deep into cash-and-carry politics.

"If anything comes out about this," he said, "I'll probably lose my job. I wouldn't want to lose my job. It's a good job. I wouldn't want to lose it."

"I promise you," Gettes said, still smiling. "As soon as I look this over, it's going right into the shredder. Faster than greased shit."

"Beg your pardon?"

"Well, I'm destroying it as soon as I read it."

"I'd appreciate that," Monroe said.

He looked around at nothing, then tapped the manila envelope against his right thigh. Desperado and all that.

"Just remember this," Gettes told him. "No matter what happens, and nothing will happen, your name will never come up. You have what's called, I believe, complete deniability as far as I'm concerned. Besides, this involves criminal justice, not politics. You have my word this isn't political."

"We hear so much about scandal," Monroe said.

"This isn't scandal," Gettes said. She used her confidential tone. "How'd you get this so fast?"

"Everything is on computer," Monroe said. "It's on disk. I just call it up."

"I'll destroy the printout, rest assured," Gettes said again.

Monroe caught her with his blue eyes. He looked as though he wanted to say something memorable, but then he turned and fled up a flight of stairs to his right. Gettes gave it five minutes, then went down the same flight and outside. She took her time going from Franklin Street to the War Memorial Opera House, but she found Mad Dog sitting on a park bench beneath one of the pollarded sycamores. She sat down beside him and he gave a start of surprise.

"Penny for your thoughts," Gettes said, putting the manila envelope on the bench.

"You'll need more than that," Mad Dog said. "Well, what about it?"

"Oh, Monroe was anxious to please. Like a puppy dog with his new toy."

"You have that effect on gay men," Mad Dog said.

"Please," Gettes told him. "I've got a torrid sex life nobody is privy to. Not even you, Mad Dog."

"I'm salivating," he said.

"I'm glad you've got back your chutzpah."

"Mendelssohn," Mad Dog said.

"I bet you got laid over the weekend."

"That's my business," Mad Dog said. "You read my memo cover to cover. That's what you did with your weekend."

"Between the sheets," Gettes laughed. "I told you that's where I was."

"Well, here we are," Mad Dog said.

Gettes read the first two of five sheets of printout. They were short, triple-spaced paragraphs. A section of ledger, one line for office use only.

"Okay, here we go," Gettes said. "David Avila. Born 1964, Los Angeles, California. Mother Sandra L., father Diego P. Went to community college in Santa Monica, graduated from San Diego State. Worked his way through private law school in the San Fernando Valley as an usher in a theater, busboy, odd jobs, lawn care. Mediocre grades, looks like to me. Got a job in the late eighties with a small firm in downtown L.A. called Poole and Roberts, doing mostly criminal work. Municipal court stuff, DUI, whatever the cat dragged in. Looks like he didn't join any specialist sections of the bar, kept up his dues, no mention here of any writings, articles, that shit. Two years later he is in private practice on his own with an office near Wilshire. Only one complaint, from a legal secretary named Sylvia Dorning. Hey, this is interesting. She was a legal secretary for the small firm Avila worked for in L.A., and her complaint was made a month after he left the firm and opened his own practice. Maybe he was fishing off the company pier. Anyway, the complaint was withdrawn later. No action."

"Where can we get ahold of the complaint?" Mad Dog asked.

"Ethics committee," Gettes said. "I don't think we're going to get ahold of it. I don't have any friends on the committee, and I wouldn't ask if I did."

"I think the substance we can get," Mad Dog said.

"The substance is in here," Gettes said. "Nothing specific. It just says the secretary was sexually harassed on the job. There aren't any referral notes and there probably wasn't even an investigation. Ten years ago they didn't take this stuff very seriously. I wonder what games our boy played with dear Sylvia?"

"Rough games," Mad Dog said.

"Let's not jump the gun," Gettes said. She folded the printout sheets together and put them in her purse. "I promised to destroy this stuff, but we can sit on it for a while. I don't know what you expect to do with this stuff anyway. It's just idle noise, isn't it?"

"Maybe I should call Sylvia."

"Why not? It can't hurt. Are you crazy?"

They got up and began to walk toward Civic Center. They were in and out of street crowds, a juggler, two fiddle players, and a one-man band. Mad Dog tossed a quarter to the juggler.

"Don't call Sylvia," Gettes said. "It isn't our job."

"Whose job is it?"

"Maybe the police," Gettes said.

Stopped at a light. Mad Dog walked over and bought a frankfurter from a vendor on the corner.

"You going to eat that?" Gettes asked.

"I thought I would."

Mad Dog shoved a third of the hot dog into his mouth. "We got a notice of appeal on Darwin," he managed to say through the bread and meat.

"Who's doing it?"

"Sandy Mooney," Mad Dog said. "He was sitting in back of the courtroom through most of the trial. I have a feeling he was anticipating this outcome. He's good. Tough as a boot."

"Tough as you?" Gettes asked.

They crossed the busy street beside the art museum.

"Tougher than me," Mad Dog said.

"That may be," Gettes said. "But he still doesn't have an appealable issue. And besides, what appeals court will give a fugitive a break?"

"What about the faxes?"

"Your faxes aren't appealable stuff," Gettes said.

"You're still not convinced, are you?"

"Convinced of what?" Gettes asked. "That Avila threw the case intentionally? What earthly reason could he have for doing that? If you want to know what I really think, I think the guy was bored with the case. He took it for the money and he ran away from Darwin because it was a sure loser. I think he did shitty work and it's kind of a tragedy for Darwin, but I think justice was done in the long run. I think Darwin killed those two women, and he's stupid not to have taken my deal when he had the chance. I can see Avila pleading with him to take the deal and then getting tired and bored and doing a shitty job on the case. It happens. It happens all the time."

Mad Dog finished his hot dog.

"No shade of doubt?" he asked her.

Gettes turned slightly, profile left.

"A shade," she said.

"I thought so," Mad Dog told her before they went back to work. "I thought so, I did."

Incoming incoming, someone shouted down the hall, a turn of phrase that made Vorhees flinch subconsciously, his mind switched to Vietnam, bright flaring mornings on parapets with the sun blasting through shattered forest. He'd spent most of two tours in Da Nang, which you'd mistake for Disneyland except for the beer and dirty magazines, but he'd been up-country three times to free fire zones, riding in on big Hueys, being put down in the middle of the incoming. It was a place where "incoming" had real meaning.

"Here you go, Vorhees," an aide said, angled around the glass cubicle of his office.

Vorhees grabbed a thin piece of fax paper, read the blurry print: "Sexual harassment claim against David Avila, made by Sylvia Dorning, Poole and Roberts, Los Angeles, CA, 1989—kind of makes you wonder?"

Cooley rounded the glass enclosure.

"Hey," he said. "Lightfoot in five minutes. You want some shitty coffee?"

"Check this out," Vorhees told him, handing over the fax. "It just came in from a mysterious stranger."

Cooley squinted at the document.

"Deep throat, huh?" he said.

"It's a complex and odd world," Vorhees said.

"So, who did send this?"

"We could make some guesses," Vorhees told him.

"You're serious," Cooley said. "You don't know?"

"Who hates Avila? Who cares about Darwin?"

"You got me," Cooley said. He took a printout from his jacket pocket and handed it to Vorhees. "I got my own," he said, amused. "It's the crime computer on Avila."

"I thought you weren't interested."

"I said I was interested just a little."

"Some mysterious juvenile beef," Vorhees said. "File closed, not expunged." Vorhees looked up at Cooley. "Do we know how to bust into juvenile records in Los Angeles?"

"Maybe," Cooley admitted.

"Then a battery charge by Sylvia Dorning, dismissed."

"Now that's interesting," Cooley said.

Cooley had a paper cup of coffee, and he finished it leaning on the glass partition. They went down a long hall together and into Lightfoot's corner office. The lieutenant was behind her desk, eating an afternoon bagel with cream cheese, drinking a diet soda. A tough-as-nails Asian lady with a Glock on her right hip. Vorhees stood in the corner by a hat rack and Cooley pulled up a metal chair.

"What have you two clowns been doing?" Lightfoot asked.

"I don't follow," Cooley said.

"I just got a mystery fax on the Darwin case," she said. "I thought we were all finished with that one."

"I just got a mystery fax myself," Vorhees said. "You want to hear it?"

"Me first," Lightfoot told him. "I have some professional concern about this Darwin case. Yesterday you guys asked me for meeting to go over some problems with this case, a case I'm thinking is solved. And now I get a mystery fax. You wouldn't happen to know what is going down, would you?"

Vorhees and Cooley exchanged meaningful glances.

"I'm waiting," Lightfoot said.

"I guess I should talk," Vorhees said. "Look, Lieutenant, we don't know about the faxes. Really. We haven't had time to make any guesses. But we went to Karla Darwin's house yesterday. We did it on our own time too."

"Lunch hour," Cooley said.

"Oh my, lunch hour," Lightfoot said.

"And anyway," Vorhees continued, "we went to the house in Pacific Heights. What can I say? Cooley was tagging along, but it was mostly my deal. The lady was home, but she looked pretty ragged, like maybe she just got up with a large-scale hangover. She went down to the kitchen and took a loving look at a bottle of vodka before telling us we could go into Darwin's bedroom and look around. So we went upstairs and looked for the jewelry box. We had permission, Lieutenant. Clear and unequivocal. And as far as the jewelry box goes, you can tell it didn't belong to Jack Darwin, but to his dad. It had family mementos, some baby teeth, a photograph."

"And what does this have to do with anything?" Lightfoot asked.

"It's just this," Vorhees said. "I find it hard to believe that Darwin would wear cuff links from that box of mementos. His friends say he never wore them. He says he never wore them. And the timeline on the cuff links is bad. Do you suppose he'd wear the cuff links to the Lisa Tracy killing, then sometime later go over to the Pacific Heights house and drop off one cuff link? Maybe he's sentimental. Maybe he did it, but I can't believe it because he isn't stupid."

"You're saying you believe somebody planted the cuff link at the Tracy killing?"

"I guess so," Vorhees said.

"And what about you?" Lightfoot asked Cooley.

Cooley frowned. "My partner might be right."

"That's what you've got?" Lightfoot said.

"I don't think Darwin was wearing a camel hair topcoat the night of the Hernandez murder," Vorhees told her.

"Is that so?"

"Look, Lieutenant," Vorhees said. "I drove down to Burlingame to talk to a stable hand who saw Darwin the night of the Hernandez murder. He told me Darwin was wearing a blue suit and black shoes. He remembered it clearly. I believe him."

"You're making some kind of fashion statement here?"

"This guy wouldn't wear a camel hair topcoat with a blue suit and black shoes."

"You think he wouldn't?"

"That's right," Vorhees said. "I think he wouldn't."

"Do you have evidence?" Lightfoot asked. "Or should we just call up *GQ*?"

Vorhees looked at Cooley.

"Not yet," Vorhees admitted. "But then I got a fax ten minutes ago, just like you did." Vorhees handed over the fax to Lightfoot.

She read it once quickly. "And who's Sylvia Dorning?" she asked.

"She's a legal secretary in Los Angeles. Somebody David Avila worked with when he was first in private practice."

"Okay, Detective," Lightfoot said. "Who's the author of our secret faxes?"

"We just started thinking about that," Vorhees said. "But I just faxed a photo of David Avila to Jean Hobart in Cincinnati. I'm waiting to hear back from her."

"Now that would be evidence," Lightfoot said.

"There's another thing," Vorhees told her. "I talked to a friend of Darwin's named Henry Diehl. He's an AA member down at the group where Darwin started attending meetings. He said Darwin was genuinely distraught when he heard about the Hernandez murder."

"No white Bronco, no evidence," Lightfoot said.

"I think it's evidence," Cooley said.

"So do I," Vorhees acknowledged.

"I'm glad to see the partners are scratching each other's backs," Lightfoot joked. "So let's have a share-and-tell. My little fax hot off the wire is a list of about fifteen things wrong with the Darwin defense. It reads like a legal brief of all the screwups and blown opportunities. It's done in handwriting on plain paper, no headings. It looks like somebody smart sat down on midnight oil and this is what they came up with. You could say it's an indictment of David Avila. That is, if you thought this kind of thing was evidence."

Vorhees took the fax from Lightfoot and studied it for a few minutes, then handed it on to Cooley. Lightfoot finished her bagel, then got up and walked to the window and looked down at acres of parking lot, chain-link fence, a ribbon of freeway and bridges.

"Do we have the wrong man on the run?" she asked. Silence. "And who is our deep throat? And why is he sending us these faxes?"

"Darwin?" Vorhees said.

"I've got one problem," Cooley said. Lightfoot turned. Cooley looked down at Vorhees and shrugged haplessly. "Only one person had access to Darwin's bedroom. And that's his wife Karla. You're telling me she killed Lisa Tracy and planted the cuff link? You're telling me she killed Dolores Hernandez? All that bad shit to get rid of her husband? You can't sell that to me, and I'll buy damn near anything. There has to be another player."

The three of them toyed with their thoughts.

"Lieutenant," Vorhees said finally. "I'd like to go down to L.A. and dig up Sylvia Dorning."

"You want to go to L.A.?" Lightfoot said.

"I'd use my own time," Vorhees answered her. "Use my own nickel too."

"Forget your own time and nickel," Lightfoot said. "Take next Friday away from the office. Cooley, can you run the work on your own? If we've got the wrong man on the run, let's find out. At least we need to *find out*."

"Hey, I got a printout," Cooley said. "The Dorning beef was a charge in L.A., but it got dropped. Sexual battery. Avila had a juvenile record too. Can we get at it?"

"I could take a look-see," Lightfoot said. "Juvenile records have been known to leak out onto the floor occasionally. It's kind of tricky."

"I'll leave Friday morning," Vorhees said.

They spent five minutes going over plans, then Cooley and Vorhees went back to their glass enclosure. They had just sat down when an aide handed Vorhees another incoming.

"It's from Jean Hobart," Vorhees told Cooley.

"Oh yeah?"

"It says, 'It looks like him, but I was drunk.' "

"Half a loaf," Cooley said glumly.

"Damn, I should have done a photo lineup," Vorhees said. "That might have nailed it."

"She's told too many people she was drunk." Cooley said. "It would never stick. She's telling the truth. She doesn't know for sure."

"You're probably right," Vorhees admitted. "You want to come with me to visit Luther Lee Dokes?"

"Do I have a choice, partner?"

Vorhees unholstered his Glock. He set it on the table between two stale paper cups full of coffee.

"He might run," Vorhees said.

"Great," was all Cooley replied.

Zack lit a number, inhaled the smoke deeply. He could see the green Jag just ahead, its LAWDOG license tag, one lane over on Pine going west in traffic. It was his second number of the morning, by now his head tight and his lips dry. The sight of the Jag attached itself to his nerve endings, hanging there in a rough jangle. The two of them were in a tan Bronco jacked high on oversize tires, a four-wheel-drive all-terrain vehicle, the back end gutted to make room for equipment, tools, guns. Luther Lee didn't remember when the car had been stolen, only that he'd been driving it around the city for two years with tags that belonged to somebody else.

North on Hyde, up through Nob Hill neighborhoods, Zack wearing his black ensemble, turtleneck, chinos, sunglasses. Luther Lee drove, decked out in his camouflage army fatigues, like the hunter he believed himself to be. They stayed close in traffic for ten minutes, stopped at lights, trailing a cable car for three blocks as it halted for spring tourists. Zack tamped out the number and swallowed the roach.

"Did I tell you what this fuck said?" Zack remarked.

Luther Lee touched his green sock-cap.

"You told me," he said.

Luther Lee had a three-day growth, on the run and unable to shave. Zack knew Luther Lee fancied himself some kind of institutional rebel, the kind of man who would kill just to outrage the empty sky.

"Said to turn you, whack you, that shit," Zack said.

Zack enjoyed the ride, the city displayed for spring, green sycamores on the streets, women in short skirts up to their cracks almost, Zack glad they were coming back into style.

"Turn you," Zack repeated.

"Turn my ass," Luther Lee said.

"He's going in," Zack said.

The green Jag turned left down the ramp of an underground garage beneath an apartment building on Russian Hill. Luther Lee parked in a bus zone across the street.

"Dude lives in there," Zack said.

The building was gray and gilt, ten stories high, balconies with wrought-iron railings, a fancy, high-rent spot.

"He's got another crib too," Luther Lee told him. "Some kind of spare crib down on the Marina. I seen him go down there on the cable car. He got himself a green Buick too. Parks in the back."

"I tell you that motherfucker kicked me?" Zack said.

"You told me."

"Didn't say shit. Just kicked me."

"What'd you do?" Luther Lee said.

Zack rolled down the Bronco window and leaned outside.

"It ain't what I did, it's what I'm gonna do."

"I'm glad to hear it," Luther Lee said.

"Say, what'd you cap Jimmy Vine for anyway?"

"He turned me, didn't he?"

"Yeah, but he was a punk."

"He was a punk," Luther Lee growled. "You should have seen his nigger ass up there in Hunters Point. Drove that heap of his right up there and I walked him down to the Dumpster saying like this here is my stash, and Vine eating that shit right out of my hand. We get down to the Dumpster and he looks in and I ping him right behind the ear. You should have seen the shit fly, blood coming out of his mouth like a Pepsi you shook up. Fucker goes straight down on his face. You know what I mean?"

Zack laughed. "What's with the ice pick?" he asked.

"Everybody got a sign," Luther Lee said. "That's my sign, you dig?"

"Yeah, I dig," Zack said. "Like you wrote your name on him. Like graffiti shit and all."

"Only it ain't my name," Luther Lee said.

"It might as well be."

"Tell that to the cops," Luther Lee said.

"Fuck I'm high," Zack said, yawning.

"He's always alone down at that Marina place," Luther Lee said quietly.

"So cap him there."

"I could cap him there," Luther Lee agreed. "There's an alley that runs behind the place. I could get inside maybe and cap him when he goes down there. I think he takes chicks down there, so it might not be cool."

"Where else you gonna cap him?"

"There, I guess," Luther Lee said. "He might have a chick with him though. What else would he go down there for?"

"So cap the chick," Zack said. "Who fucking cares? You rather go down for doing Arthur Vine? Do life for that punk?" Zack spat on the sidewalk. "Besides, you capped that DEA fuck over in the East Bay too."

"You should have heard that guy," Luther Lee said. "I had him down by the racetrack and he was on his hands and knees begging me not to cap him. You should have heard him beg. It was beautiful."

"Don't play around with Avila. He's dangerous and he has moves."

"He kicked you? Is that what he did?"

"I said he did, didn't I?"

"I wish I coulda seen that," Luther Lee said. "I tell you man, I ain't gonna do five years. I'm too old for that shit."

"You can't stay in the city," Zack said.

"I ain't gonna stay in the fucking city. They say Phoenix is good. Yeah, they say Phoenix is really growth deluxe, industry and the trade and all that shit down in Phoenix. Shit like that. You go down to Phoenix and you can score steady work. It's a laid-back atmosphere, like that."

"Well, you can't stay here," Zack concluded.

They remained in the bus zone on and off for two hours, moving once, coming back, moving again, coming back. Zack smoked his third number and Luther Lee listened to tunes on the radio and they talked about the Lakers and the Suns, about Phoenix, the virtue of the West Coast trade. When the afternoon was gone, Luther Lee took Zack across town and dropped him at a bar called Two Fellas. Zack felt the feeling then, the one that made him whole.

What he called tight and on the loose.

Avila listened to the phone message five times, then erased it. He wanted the sound of her voice in his head, something to replace nothing. He wanted to hear the voice when he drove the green Jag, he wanted to hear it in his office, sitting in the dark afternoon. He wanted the memory to haunt him, he wanted it to bedevil him. In this way, he wished to admit to his mistakes. That night, he put a new tape in the machine and burned the old one, and headed to the Y to lift. He parked off McAllister, walked over two blocks, then changed to his workout clothes. He had been lifting for an hour when Zack came in and sat down on a weight bench, just across the way.

"How you doing?" Avila said nonchalantly.

Zack had the look, tightened up, red eyes, thin little smile, teeth drawn over his gums.

"Good, I'm doing good," Zack said.

Hopped up, definitely.

"How's Luther Lee?" Avila said.

Zack shook his head nervously. He was wearing surplus army fatigues, hooded gray sweatshirt, combat boots. It must have been the new look, paramilitary antigovernment, wild and dangerous. The Freeman look.

"You know two cops were at Luther Lee's house?" Zack asked. "You know that, did you?"

"I'm not surprised," Avila told him.

He watched Zack lick his lips, fried high and running warm. Avila did fourteen sixty-five-pound right-hand curls, reversed, did the left. Zack sat quietly, sucking his teeth, wired for more coke pretty soon.

"They gave his old lady a hard time," Zack said finally.

"Sarah? How is Sarah?"

"Oh, Sarah," Zack said, "she's just fine. She looks so good I'd do her myself. If I couldn't do better."

"Glad to hear it," Avila told him.

"They couldn't find Luther Lee and they said they'd be back."

"Should I be worried?" Avila asked.

"Like I said, they'll be back, whenever."

"One thing I hate," Avila said. "It's talking to fucks when they're high on coke. It makes everything fuzzy as shit. Fucker smiles, licks his gums, repeats what you say, looks like he thinks he could run a mile in two minutes. You should lay off that shit, Zack, it makes you stupid."

"I can handle it," Zack said.

"That's what they all say."

"Don't worry about it, all right?"

"All right," Avila said.

Avila did two sets of military presses, twenty, then forty total. Zack sat, blinked his eyes, licked his lips.

"Whatever," Zack said nonsensically. "I had a long talk with Miss Sarah. She said those two cops were all over her case about Arthur V. Some dude named Perry Lehigh. You dig? All over her fucking case."

"I'm not surprised."

"She thinks they'll come back with a warrant."

"She's a smart lady," Avila said. "A lot smarter than Luther Lee."

"They even asked some questions about you," Zack said.

Avila dropped the dumbbells at his feet.

"What kind of questions?" he asked.

"Had you ever been to his house? Did she know you, ever met

you? Did she know who worked with Luther Lee, that kind of shit. Like maybe she was going to give us up just for the hell of it. I hate to tell you this, bohunk, but they had a photograph of your pretty ass too."

"A photograph," Avila said dreamily.

"That's what she said."

"So, what's the bottom line, Zack?"

Zack flashed a childish grin.

"I guess the bottom line," Zack said, "is that Luther Lee is taking a long, long trip."

"What kind of trip?"

"A long one," Zack said.

"Is he coming back? Can I reach him?"

"I don't really think so," Zack said.

"So, he's out of touch?"

"Pretty much out of touch, I'd say. You couldn't fax the fucker if you wanted."

"And where did he go, Zack?"

"I think he's down in San Jose by now," Zack said. "In the landfill. Yeah, I'd say he's in the landfill down in San Jose. You ever see the landfill down there? Must be fifteen stories high of shit and garbage down there. Looks like hell with seagulls flying around it. Seagulls everywhere, pecking through shit, flying around, eating garbage, pecking through shit. Thousands and millions of seagulls pecking through shit. Fifteen stories of crap. It's much worse than I could ever tell you about, man."

"You know this for a fact?" Avila asked.

"I wouldn't be saying it if I didn't."

Zack stood up and made a gesture like hugging himself. The coke was spitting at him, tiny bursts of coke in his head.

"You won't be seeing me anymore," Zack said.

"This breaks my heart," Avila replied.

"You better watch those cops," Zack said. "I think they like you for something. I don't know what it might be. But I'd watch them if I were you."

"Hey, thanks for the advice, scumbag," Avila said.

"Good luck, lawyer," Zack said.

When Zack had gone, Avila showered and dressed. He cruised waterfront bars for two hours, then down along Clement, then finally at the edge of Chinatown, checking the scene, swimming the bottom as he called it. His needs defined the time he spent at each place, a map to the contour of his hate and desire. By the time he got back to Russian Hill it was past midnight. He took off his clothes and sat naked on his bed, playing back his answering machine. There was only one message for the day, something he was sure to remember: *This is Detective Vorhees. SFPD. Maybe you recall our meeting. I'm wondering if we could get together to talk about an incident at the Holiday Inn near the airport? Maybe you could help me out on that? Call me when you get a chance.*

Avila paced the low-ceilinged room.

Green walls, modern furniture, teak and Naugahyde.

Digital clock, humming.

What could he do to the memory of Karla's voice?

Erase it, that's what.


Lightfoot ferreted Sylvia Dorning, now Litchfield, in under thirty minutes. She came up clear and cold in green on a screen downstairs, E-mailed up to Lightfoot, who reported to Vorhees. Divorced, mother of two girls, living now in Oceanside. Lightfoot called the old law firm in Los Angeles first, then hooked up with the DMV, and that's all it took. Then, on Friday morning, Vorhees caught the early cheapie flight to LAX and rented a pink Lincoln Continental at a cut-rate price across the airport service road—tinted glass windows, electric power windows and seats, chrome bumpers, kit on the back, pimp style. He made it out of L.A. on the noon flow south on 101 and was in Oceanside an hour later. Sylvia worked as the drive-in teller of a small branch bank at a shopping mall, and they made a date to meet at a Wendy's nearby. It was a warm, overcast day as Vorhees drove above the beach, from where he could see the ocean curling away to the horizon, the smell of the water different from Northern California, warmer, seaweedy.

Vorhees took a seat near the front door of the fast-food restaurant and bought two coffees. When she came inside, she looked exhausted, as though her life had gotten completely away from her and she was both surprised and disappointed. From his notes, Vorhees had learned that she was owed sixteen thousand and change in back child support, and that one of the kids had chronic asthma. Sylvia Litchfield had once been pretty, but she was heavy now, with black circles under her eyes, chewed fingernails, a nervous hangdog look.

Sylvia sat down at the uncomfortable plastic table. "It was a woman who called me," she said meekly.

"That was my lieutenant," Vorhees said.

"I thought it would be her coming down."

Penney's blouse and skirt, cheap perfume.

"I'm sorry. Maybe she should have explained."

"I was hoping it would be a woman," she said.

She was wide-eyed, frightened. Vorhees put his badge on the Formica surface between them, just to ease her. Maybe it wasn't working.

"You want to talk to her on the telephone? That would be okay with me if it makes you feel better."

"No, it's just she said she'd be right down. Like that. I really thought she meant *she*. Not you."

Vorhees sipped his coffee.

"You want something to eat? This is your lunch hour, isn't it? I'm buying."

"I'm supposed to be on a diet," Sylvia said.

"Please feel free," Vorhees offered. "This won't take long."

"It's just that I've only got thirty minutes."

"We'll make it quick."

"I thought it would be a woman coming down."

"Let's give it a chance."

"I don't really know what this has to do with me. She didn't explain anything. Has my ex-husband done something?"

"I know you're unnerved," Vorhees explained. "This has to do with someone named David Avila."

Sylvia Litchfield paused in the act of reaching for her coffee. She looked out the brightly reflected windows at the mall parking lot, three acres of Audis and Mazdas, a border of ice plant, a set of beige condos in the near distance.

"I see," she said.

"You used to work up in L.A. for a firm of attorneys, didn't you?"

"Poole and Roberts," she said. "That was a long time ago. Or at least it seems like a long time ago."

Vorhees felt sorry for Sylvia Litchfield. Two kids in an expensive beachfront town, pulling down, what, ten bucks an hour tops?

"What did you do up there?" he asked.

"Legal secretary."

"Avila was a lawyer with the firm?"

"I really don't want to talk about this."

"It's important, Mrs. Litchfield," Vorhees said. "I could take the time to explain the problem to you in detail if you'd like, but we've only got thirty minutes. I hate cutting into your day like this, but I have to. I need background on David Avila. Maybe Lieutenant Lightfoot should have explained it in more detail."

"She didn't mention David Avila at all. She said something about a murder investigation. It scared me to death. I have to tell you, it scared me to death. I thought maybe Randy got hurt or something."

"Your ex?"

"Him, yes. Randy."

"You made a sexual harassment complaint to the bar association against Avila back in 1989, didn't you?"

Sylvia Litchfield said nothing. It was as though a bomb had exploded in her soul.

Vorhees said, "I just need to ask you two or three questions, and I'm out of here."

"I'm afraid," she said.

"I can tell you a man's life is at stake. I know that sounds pretty corny, but it happens to be true. Please believe me, I wouldn't ask you to dredge all of this up if it wasn't absolutely necessary."

"Has David done something?"

"You remember him?"

"Yes, I remember him," she said quietly.

"Why don't you tell me about him?"

"It was so long ago."

"I know," Vorhees said.

"What's he done?"

"I'm not sure," Vorhees said. "Maybe nothing. Why don't you just tell me about the sexual harassment complaint?"

"I don't think I can talk about it."

"Sure you can. You're safe. Nothing will happen to you. I promise."

"My kids. I have two kids."

"David Avila isn't going to hurt you."

Finally Sylvia sipped her coffee. She looked out the window and began to speak.

"I had worked for the law firm for about six months when they hired David Avila. It was the late eighties in Los Angeles and the law firm was doing great. They were into everything, real estate, criminal law, securities. There were five or six lawyers, I can't remember exactly, but he was one of the first new guys they hired when things were good. Right away he paid attention to me. You probably can't tell it, but I used to be pretty. I used to be really pretty. David was a smart aleck, but he seemed nice too, or at least I thought he was nice. The only thing, he was good-looking, and he acted like he knew it too. I guess he wasn't making much money then, and he lived in a little apartment in Venice. A few weeks after he came to work for the firm he asked me out. It didn't seem like such a good idea to me to date one of the lawyers, but it happens. I was going out with Randy then, but we weren't getting along too good, and so when David asked me for about the third time I finally said yes. I guess I went out with him partly to make Randy jealous. I hate to say it, but all I ever wanted to do was get married and raise a family. That's all I ever wanted to do, and maybe I thought going out with David would hurry things along that way. It was really stupid. Like really stupid. We only went out three times in all. Me and David. I still remember our first date too. He took me to a drive-in restaurant on Wilshire and we sat in his convertible and ate hamburgers and listened to music on the loudspeakers. David was really into his car, like really into it, you know? They say a person ought to know themselves, and sometimes I think I know myself pretty good, and when I was sitting in that convertible with David, I sort of knew I shouldn't have been there. It wasn't me. Anyway, we listened to oldies for a long time. I was thinking I was out of place there, what with him being a young lawyer and stuff, and me a secretary, but we rode around later and he took me to a movie and it wasn't so bad. It was kinda fun. I said yes when he asked me out again, but I didn't think I should go, but I did. We drove around again and then late we went to some clubs on the Sunset Strip. I wasn't used to that kind of date at all. It was scary with that heavy metal music and people dressed wild and strange too. I grew up in Glendale and we never went to L.A. that much in high school and all. We danced and had some drinks and then got something to eat and it was late and I was tired. It was kinda fun, but not as much fun as with Randy, even though David was handsome and all that stuff. I didn't get home until two in the morning. I wasn't used to that. All

I ever wanted was to have a nice family. That sort of life. You know what I mean?"

Vorhees nodded. "I know what you mean," he said. "And you do have a nice family, huh?"

"Me and the girls," Sylvia said. "I'm divorced now. I never thought it would happen to me and Randy like that. But it did, and I don't know why it happened. I can't figure it out. Sometimes I stay up late at night and think about it and I can't understand how things fell apart so quick. I thought we were in love and then the kids came along and then Randy left."

"Things will work out," Vorhees said helplessly.

"No they won't," Sylvia said flatly. "No, they won't work out. Not ever. Not for me."

"Don't give up hope," Vorhees said. "You were saying about David Avila?"

The woman glanced at her digital watch.

"We had another date," she said. "And then I quit going out with him. I didn't want to go out with him in the first place. I got back together with Randy and six months later we got married. You know how they say the rest is history?"

"What about the harassment complaint?"

"Oh, David started bringing in photographs to work. He'd leave them on my desk, maybe under a brief I was typing, and when I'd turn a page, there this photograph would be. I'd tear them up, but he'd leave another."

"What kind of photos?"

"He started with two of me," she said. "He took some photos of me on our third date. I guess I'd had too much to drink, because I don't remember it very well. They weren't nice photos either. After that, he'd bring photos of other women. He'd leave them on my desk. One of the photos was scary. After two weeks when it didn't stop, I told one of the partners about it and they made a big stink. They fired David. I didn't want to, but they made me file a formal complaint with the bar association. I think they were covering their behinds, but I did it anyway. All I wanted was to be left alone. That's all I wanted. I wanted him to leave me alone."

"Did he leave you alone?"

"Kind of, I guess."

"Kind of?" Vorhees asked. "We looked up Avila's record and there is a criminal complaint on file, but it was dismissed. Is that you?"

Tears came to Sylvia Litchfield's eyes now. Bright drops, poised.

"I really don't want to talk about it," she said.

"Did you go to the police about the photos?"

Vorhees knew better.

"No, not about the photos," Sylvia said.

"You mean there was something else?"

Sylvia Litchfield dabbed her eyes with a paper napkin. "Please," she said, "I've got to go back to work."

"Please, ma'am," Vorhees said.

"Did he do something to someone else?"

"It's very possible," Vorhees said.

"I don't want to go to court. I couldn't stand it."

"That isn't likely," Vorhees told her.

"I thought you'd be a woman," Sylvia said, almost giddily. "I thought you'd turn out to be a woman."

"I'm sure the lieutenant didn't mean to mislead you. She's a nice lady. She's my boss."

"Your boss?"

Vorhees smiled and nodded.

"It's hard to talk about," Sylvia said.

"I'm not writing anything down. It isn't like that."

"Has anybody been hurt?"

"Two people."

"Women?"

"Yes, I'm afraid. There might be a third."

"Oh dear God," she said.

"Why don't you have some coffee?" Vorhees asked.

"I've got to get back to work."

"Just let it out."

The restaurant was nearly empty now, lunch hour over. Muzak above yellow annoying light.

"Our last date," Sylvia said. "We went to some bars again. I wasn't used to drinking so much. Hardly at all. We went to his apartment in Venice. I don't remember why I agreed to do that, but probably because I was drinking, I don't know. Yes I do. I'd had another fight with Randy, that's it. He's my ex. We'd had a fight and I drank too much and agreed to go to David's apartment in Venice. He had his apartment fixed up like a surfer, Lava lamps, nets on the ceilings. He thought it looked pretty cool, but I thought it looked kind of silly. Like something out of a movie. That's where he took the photos of me, dancing and like that. I guess I was in my bra and panties. That was pretty stupid I guess. Dancing and carrying on like a crazy person. I thought we were having fun. That's what I thought was happening.

"I told him I had to go to the bathroom. When I was in the bathroom he came in, just barged in, and he said we should take a shower together. Maybe it seemed like a good idea, I don't know. But one thing led to another. He brought in a bottle of wine and I had a drink of wine right out of the bottle. I remember that much. The next thing I knew I was in the shower. Even then, it seemed like fun. It's not like I never had fun with a man, you know. Do you know what I mean? I'm not a prude. I've never been a prude and Randy wasn't the first man in my life, even then. But there weren't many, don't get me wrong. It wasn't something I did as a rule. I had been drinking, that was all.

"And then David got in the shower behind me and started doing things with his hands. I guess I got a little scared. At first I thought it was a big joke. He was having fun and things would be all right. But then he pushed me up against the tiles so that I could barely breathe and he put his arm around my neck. It scared me and I didn't cry, but I felt like it. I thought any minute he'd realize he was hurting me and stop. But he didn't. Then he took the wine bottle and he put it inside of me from behind."

"All right," Vorhees told her.

Sylvia let out a rush of breath.

"I'm sorry," she said.

"You dropped the case later?"

"Yes," she whispered. "I wasn't going to file it at all. But I had to explain to the lawyers what had happened between me and David, and they made me file the complaint. Later, I just dropped it. I was happy and I was going to get married and I didn't hear anything from David. I didn't want to get involved in courts and police and that kind of stuff. That sounds pretty stupid to you, but that was a long time ago and I thought everything was going to be all right."

"That's enough," Vorhees said. "You sure you don't want some hamburgers in a sack?"

"No, I just need to get back. I'm on a diet."

"We'll be in touch if we need you. I hope not."

"I hope not too," Sylvia said. "These women, will this help?"

"Oh, I think so. I know they'll appreciate it."

Vorhees stood and shook the woman's hand. He watched her rise and walk through the glass door. She turned back just before going out.

"I thought I was going to be happy," Sylvia Litchfield said. "I thought I was going to have a happy life."

"Take care of the kids," Vorhees said.

He watched her trudge across the parking lot, heading toward the small drive-in bank. If anything, the day was grayer than before, a hint of ocean rain in the air. Typical early spring in Southern California. Vorhees got in his pink Continental and headed north on 101.

Last call for Jack Darwin, sitting in the tiny shed, immersed in a chimera of dust motes. He had already begun to plan scenarios for his so-called escape. The newspapers were full of news about the manhunt. State police were haunting the bus and train stations, airports, highways. The CHP had established roadblocks and were checking cars, trucks, vehicles of all kinds. There were floating rumors of Darwin's flight, now to India, where he was a mendicant, atoning for his crimes, perhaps meditating on them, one hand to his forehead. When nothing presented itself, Darwin shaved his head with a set of horse clippers. He had already grown a tuft of blondish beard. At that point, he stumbled across something entirely unexpected, a Gold Card receipt from Sammy's Dockside restaurant near Belvedere, across the bay from Sausalito. He decided it was worth one more trip to the city in Angel's panel truck. If stopped, he would say he had stolen it, and nothing more.

Thank God for Friday rush hour, he thought, driving up 101 in dense junglelike traffic. He went through the city and waited forty-five minutes to get across the Golden Gate, moving slowly up the ramps, beside the defunct Presidio, the darkness of early evening sheltering him. If time was on his side he would arrive at the restaurant before dinner, perhaps be able to speak with the manager during a lull. Across the Golden Gate in a sparkling extravaganza of headlights and sunset, up to Mill Valley and across the cutoff toward San Quentin with the bay in the near background and acres of cool eucalyptus trees rustling in a soft breeze. Darwin would stop and say a small prayer for the soul of Dolores Hernandez, and then he would drive on, feeling the rush and tumble of the old panel truck as he accelerated through inclines, steep declivities, sharp curves that arced along the edge of the bay where the rich were already uncorking white wine. At the head of the bay he turned east and found Sammy's aglow with lamplight, its triangular entryway lighted by torches. Windows enclosed the restaurant on three sides, giving a perfect view of the bay, part of the parking lot, a slash of green hillside dotted with eucalypti.

Darwin parked and went to the main entrance, pausing to study himself in the mirrored glass of a door panel. Starkly bald, hollow-eyed, thin and tired-looking, a walking cadaver with a thin beard. Tan chinos covered with dust, flannel shirt, straw hat he'd found in the shed.

He found the manager sitting at a corner table doing napkins. Darwin explained that his Gold Card had been stolen six months before, and he'd tracked one of the bills to Sammy's.

"So what can I do for ya?" the manager asked him, looking skeptical.

"It's not your fault," Darwin said. "I just thought the waiter might remember something. You see, the police aren't excited about finding out who stole my Gold Card, so I'm relatively on my own. The card has been canceled and everything charged on it by these two has been voided on my bills, but I'm still kind of angry."

"You can ask, I guess," the manager said. "We've got two waiters. Todd and Jake."

"It looks like this was lunch," Darwin said. "Shrimp cocktail, Evian water, Caesar salad, that kind of food."

"Todd's your man," the manager said. "Hey Todd!" he shouted. An elflike young man emerged from the swinging doors to the kitchen. He wore black pants, a white shirt, black bow tie. "Guy wants to talk to you," the manager told him.

They walked to a corner table, opposite to where the manager was doing his napkins.

"This is a long shot," Darwin said. "But last November, somebody stole my Gold Card. They used it to have lunch here just after Thanksgiving. They had shrimp cocktail, Caesar salad, that kind of thing. You wouldn't happen to remember a couple like that, would you?"

"Are you kidding me?" Todd said. "We're crowded every day for lunch. I'm no genius."

"Look, it's important," Darwin said. "The lady is good-looking. Black hair, about middle of the back, might wear it straight or braided once down the back. She'd have a deep tan, almost mahogany colored, but you could tell it came out of a salon, not the beach. Green eyes. You saw her you'd probably remember her."

"You got some luck, pal," Todd said. He made a little click with his tongue. "That is a famous Sammy's Dockside couple."

"How's that?" Darwin asked in surprise.

"They're famous around here," Todd said. "Hey Marvin!" he shouted to the manager. "Guess who stole this guy's card! Liz and Dick!"

The manager smiled, gave a minuscule wink. Todd turned back to Darwin and said, "We call them Liz and Dick. Lady had green eyes all right. She looked a little freakish with that tan."

"And the man?" Darwin asked.

"Oh, good-looking guy. Dark bushy eyebrows, wavy black hair, some kind of weight lifter, muscles on his muscles kind of guy. Intense, expensive pin-striped black suit, red power tie, that kind of city type. They didn't say a lot and they came separately."

"How do you know that?"

"I saw the cars in the back of the lot. Hell, even the dishwashers saw the cars."

"How do you remember so well?" Darwin asked.

"Kind of hard to forget a gold Mercedes and a green Jag. And a vanity plate on the Jag that said LAWDOG."

"Thanks very much," Darwin said, remembering Avila's Jag, his vanity plate. Avila? Karla? "I'm glad you have such a good memory."

"Hey," Todd said. "It really isn't my memory. I'll tell you a secret. This lady, the tan one, she had her foot on this guy under the table and was, well, jacking him off. I'd come over with the shrimp cocktail and there she'd be, rubbing him with her foot under the table. Dishwashers came out from the back to watch for a while. She seemed to be enjoying herself. You don't see a thing like that in Sammy's Dockside and forget it very soon. They're legends around here."

Darwin thanked the waiter and the manager and went into the parking lot. Some puffy clouds had blown in from the ocean and the

air was damply chilled. Darwin got in the panel truck, thinking about
the target pistol Angel kept stored in the stables. Darwin hoped he
would be able to drive back to the Peninsula, then return to the city
without being stopped. David Avila could be only two places, and Darwin knew where both of them were.

Hello, David.

　　Hello, Karla.

　　I'm surprised you're calling here, David. And I didn't expect to
hear from you so soon. You told me you were busy with clients. I just
assumed, well. But I'm glad you called.

　　You sound strange, Karla. Are you all right?

　　It's just gotten dark outside, hasn't it? I've been sitting here all
day on the sofa thinking about you, David. Not just today. I've been
sitting here a lot, thinking about you. I'm sitting here in the dark now,
thinking about you, David, and I'm wearing a terry bathrobe with nothing on underneath it. I'm naked under the bathrobe, David, and I'm
wet. It's dark outside now, sweetheart. I'm looking outside the big picture window in the den and it's gotten dark. Hasn't it gotten dark?
Where are you, David?

　　Karla, you sound really strange. Have you been drinking?

　　No, David. I'm fine, I'm really just fine. It's Friday isn't it? It seems
like such a long, lonely day.

　　I'm coming over.

　　You're coming over? That's wonderful, dear.

　　Yes, I'm coming over right now. You'd like me to come over and
be with you, wouldn't you? The last time we talked on the telephone
you said the main thing was that we could be together. Me, coming
over to see you, that would be nice, wouldn't it? I've finished my work,
and I'd like to come over.

　　Wouldn't it be dangerous, David?

　　I've decided that it's a risk we should take.

　　Why, David, why? Aren't you afraid of the police?

　　What are you talking about, you bitch?

　　David, let's not quarrel. I'm all wet and I'm thinking about you,
so let's not quarrel. It's just that I've been thinking and thinking. I've
been thinking all day, sometimes all night too. I think the police are

after you, David. I don't know, but something is happening outside there. After all, you killed those women, didn't you?

Karla.

No, David. You killed them. It doesn't matter now because they're dead, aren't they? We can't change that, can we? But I just want it out in the open. That's all.

Karla, shut up, will you?

Let's not quarrel.

No, let's not quarrel. I'm going to come over. I've got to see you tonight.

You've got to see me tonight? David, you know I'm waiting for you. I'm wet and waiting for you. I've waited for you nearly two years, haven't I? Do you remember the little motel we used to meet at in San Rafael? Where the desk clerk even got to know us by sight? That was dangerous, wasn't it? But it was fun too, taking chances like that. I don't know what we thought we were doing, maybe having an innocent tryst, I don't know, but it was fun back then. I remember how the room smelled of Lysol and soap when we went inside, and then later, it would smell like us, you and me. People do that sort of thing, don't they, cheat on their husbands? My father never cheated on my mother, David, not once. Not once.

Karla.

No, wait, David. This is important. You've got to listen to me. My father never cheated on my mother, David. He wanted to make her miserable, and he wanted to hurt her badly, but he didn't have the energy to cheat on her. Neither of them had the energy for that sort of thing, David. Because what was going on in their heads wasn't sexual. I don't really know what was going on in their lives, David. What would make two people stay together when they're so miserable they could die? Maybe they lacked something vital. When I first met you in Marge's, and Jack was drunk, I looked at you and I thought you had something vital. Not like Jack. You had the look I thought I wanted. Like a panther, David. But there was this boy in high school my senior year. We went out to an orange grove together and he was my first. You remind me of him, David.

You're not making sense, Karla. What is it?

A detective named Cooley telephoned here late this afternoon.

He called you?

Yes, David. Of course.

What did he want, Karla?

He asked me if you'd ever been in this house. That's what he asked me. It was late this afternoon and I'd been sitting on the sofa thinking about you and Jack, and when the telephone rang I answered it and it was him. He was very polite. They're always very polite aren't they, policemen? Anyway, he wanted to know if you'd ever been in the house, if I knew you, if we'd ever gotten together, you know, socially.

All right, Karla. What did you say?

What could I say. I told him no.

Did he say anything else? Did he ask you any more questions, Karla? It's very important that you tell me exactly what he said.

David, it was late in the afternoon. I hadn't slept in weeks. I'm so tired. You have no idea how tired I am at this point, David. Do you remember when we started seeing each other at the Dockside, and then going up to the cemetery?

Will you shut the hell up?

Just answer me.

I remember. Yes.

I knew a back road from the bay, didn't I? You remember I worked selling packages at the cemetery? Well, do you remember going there for the first time?

Yes, of course. Will you shut up?

We made love on a grave. There were tombstones everywhere. I remember you wanted to do it on a grave. Why was that, David? Don't you think cemeteries are holy places? I don't really know why I ask, because I thought it was fun. I went with you, didn't I? I suppose for me it was a way of getting back at those men who ridiculed me at the cemetery offices. I don't know what it was for you. What was it for you? Going up to the cemetery and making love on a grave? All the tombstones hanging over us. Like boulders on a mountainside about to topple over.

I'm coming over, Karla.

Yes, come over. I'm wet now, just thinking about it. I forget. Do you remember the Dockside? When we drove up to the cemetery to make love. Well, I don't know if you'd call it making love, would you?

But it was something. I loved your body, David. What would you call what we've been doing?

For the last time, Karla. Please shut up. It's getting late and if we're going to be together we'd better get off the phone and be together. Will you wait for me, Karla?

What time is it? After four? Near five? It still gets dusk early, doesn't it? I hope it will be summer soon.

Will you wait for me, Karla?

I just want to hear you say it.

Say what?

That you killed those women.

What's going on inside your head, Karla? It's some game I don't understand. I think you know about that, Karla. Don't you really? Why shouldn't you know. It was never a secret between us, was it? What did you think was going to happen to your husband once I met him and helped him? Did you think we were going to ball games together? He's sad and he's weak, Karla. And I put him down. That's what happens to sad, weak people. It's a law. It's the only law there is, the oldest law. It's Darwin's law. Whatever it takes, Karla, whatever it takes. You like me for it, don't you, dear? Just as you hated Jack for following his own law?

You're saying yes? You killed them?

You heard me.

Oh, oh. The streetlights just came on.

Shit. What are you talking about?

They just came on, David. They're pretty. But sad. They've given them orange bulbs, David. I liked them better the other way, when they were white. They were pretty in the summer fog. When the streetlights had white bulbs you could sit in this room and look outside in the summer when the fog was in, and you could only see the halos of the bulbs, and mist, and the streetlights looked like hovering angels. It was beautiful.

I'm hanging up now.

Fine, David. Did I tell you that I'm naked in my bathrobe? Did I tell you that I'm all wet? I'd like you to come over as soon as you can. I'll tell you about my dad when you get here. What he used to do to me in bed when I was little. It isn't something I've ever told anyone before, but I'll tell you. I never talked to my mother about it, but she knew. My mother knew all those years, David. She knew. I know she knew and she knew I knew. Isn't that just pathetic, David? Isn't it sick? I've never told anyone in my life, and now I'm telling you. My lover. My beautiful lover who is coming to me in the night. I liked them better when they had white bulbs, David.

I'm coming over, Karla.

I'll be in the shower, David.

You'll what?

I'll be in the shower, waiting. I'm going to take off my bathrobe and jump in the shower and wait for you. That's how you like me, isn't it? Naked and facing away from you so we can't see one another? You'll be here in what, thirty minutes? I'm just going to pour myself a vodka rocks and wait for you in a hot shower. It will be wonderful, won't it? Just you and me in the shower. I'll tell you about my dad. Don't worry, David. You don't remind me of my father in the least. He was weak, like Jack, and you are strong. Like that song they taught me in Sunday school. Jesus loves me, this I know, for the Bible tells me so. Little ones to him belong, they are weak but he is strong. I'm weak, David. But you're strong, aren't you? Do you think Jesus was watching us on the graves when we went to the cemetery?

I have to change clothes. Then I'll be over. Did Cooley say he was going to telephone or come over tonight?

Cooley. Oh, him. No, that was all he said. I told you what he said.

He's not coming to the house tonight?

No, David. I told you what he said. If you're in trouble David, perhaps I can help you.

I'm fine, Karla.

It was never about money, was it?

What?

The money, Jack's money. It was never about the money, was it? You were never interested in the money, were you? You just enjoyed what you were doing. You just wanted to see if something like that could be done.

We're beyond that now, Karla.

Yes, I suppose we are.

I'm coming over.

I'll be in the shower waiting for you. The front door will be unlocked. I can't wait to see you. I'm wet and hot for you right now and it's making me crazy. I want you to hurt me like you hurt those other women.

(Dial tone)

Voice out, as they say in Hollywood, just a dial tone hit Avila's ear, like a nervous bee. He hurried into his bedroom and changed into a pair of black sweatpants, black athletic shoes, white T-shirt, and heavy leather bomber jacket. A certain cool music played inside his mind, as though a heavy curtain had lifted and there in the sea-drenched night a small orchestra had appeared, topside, moon shining in the background, gentle swells of ocean on matte. Before he took the service stairs to the parking garage and went out the side entry, he put on a pair of thin calfskin gloves. He seemed to glide along the pavement as he ran, nothing left of his incorporeal being, only bone and skin and muscle and the delicate attention to detail that was the hallmark of his personal style.

The run to Hyde took two minutes, tops, but it was time he took to be with himself, to luxuriate in the heedlessness of everything, his own life, its limited attainments, the pros and cons of dropping down from the thick-spined acacias and onto the hot floor of the savanna. Crouched and ready.

When a cable car passed, Avila hopped it in midblock, paying a jovial East Indian his fare. He walked to the back and stepped onto the rear platform, then grabbed a brass rail and leaned into the night air, away from the tourists omigoshing at Alcatraz and Angel Island, all the other bright night shit in San Francisco, their eyes brilliantly lit with wonder. The cable car plunged downhill precipitously and you'd think death was imminent. The conductor shouted, "Hang on, folks!" followed by mixed hurrahs and screams, pointed exclamations. Oh, the beauty of the city, Avila thought, its glamour and mystery, its steamy back streets and opium dens and treasure troves of desire, its Carol Dodas and Fatty Arbuckles grunting over starlets in seedy hotel rooms, and Sam Spades, its tinsel and lust and aromatic coffee smells and naked Chinese chickens hung redly upside down in butchers' windows. "Here we go again, folks!" the conductor cried, hilariously, bang-a-bang, Rice-A-Roni, the San Francisco treat, Avila swinging out, apelike and touching parked cars, snapping one radio antenna as he passed, watching it roll downhill harmlessly. Vandal! Scourge! Down past crooked Lombard they fell, the tourists gawking awkwardly out of the car, the rhododendrons of the street in purple and blue like war wounds or cancer lesions. "End of the line, baby!" shouted the conductor. Avila watched the bay approach, the strip of Aquatic Park where bocce players smoked cigarettes and squawked unknown dialects. "Hey, end of the line," the conductor said. Avila hung out the back of the cable car, nearly unconscious.

"End of the line, sir," the conductor said again.

Avila hopped down and walked into dark neighborhoods away from the park, rows of parked cars in the dark. He fancied himself invisible. Then, in the darkened garage of the Marina apartment, Avila got into the old Buick. It started on the first try.

He drove. How far was it? Let's see, from David's world to Jack's world, just a few blocks, two up, one over, and so on, a ride into upper worlds from nether ones, up to where Karla lived in the shake-shingle house with a monkey puzzle in front, up to where Jack had been a boy, a quiet world of stucco mansions and manicured fescue and curved streets that begged for professional photographers to snap them, a world of lawn parties and society luncheons where matrons wore wide-brimmed straw hats and the air smelled constantly of peonies. Avila parked down the street from Jack's house and walked up fifty feet. Jack's house was dignified, a redwood roof, the monkey puzzle tree, faint light in two windows like holes in a jack-o'-lantern. Mist hung in the trees. As Karla had promised, the front door was unlocked, slightly ajar.

Inside, Avila saw a lamp leaned against the den sofa, an odd trapezoidal patch of light on the carpet. Tony Bennett was singing that old song, and from where he stood in the entryway Avila thought he could hear the hiss of the shower. He walked up the stairs and stood, breathing heavily, outside her bedroom door. He took off the bomber jacket and let it fall, slipped out of his shoes. He went through the darkened bedroom and opened the bathroom door.

He was met with a flood of steam.

"Karla," Avila said. "Karla," again, louder.

He could see nothing.

Two steps farther in, he touched the shower glass and drew an imaginary circle on it with his index finger. With his other hand he touched the drawstring on his sweatpants, then touched a finger to his forehead, sweat forming there already.

"Karla baby, I'm coming in with you," he said.

"David," he heard behind him.

When he turned he saw her in the bathroom doorway, standing still in her white terry cloth bathrobe.

"Karla," he said.

The sound compressed their distances. There was no pain, only a flash of recognition. Avila looked at the red tea rose forming on his lower abdomen, just above the groin. Petals foiled on petals, a medallion of red with a tiny blue nucleus. He fell down on his rump and looked at Karla above him, standing in the steam. He relaxed and put his head on the tile floor. He felt no pain, only a frightening numbness.

"Oh, David," Karla said.

Avila placed his hands low and they came away wet and he looked at them. An awful roaring noise entered his head, replacing the orchestra.

"You shot me, you bitch," he said.

"I know, David, I'm sorry."

Avila managed to sit up.

"Oh, you goddamn bitch," he said.

His T-shirt was hot, his skin was burning him.

Karla held the .32 in her right hand, barrel down. The front of her bathrobe came open and Avila could see the hair between her legs. Across his vision furry microbes flitted, the dots and squiggles of confusion.

"Why, Karla?" Avila said.

"Why, David?" she answered. "Because I love you."

"Oh, you bitch," he said.

He got to one knee, unable to rise. Then he got on two knees, beads of blood on the floor. The flower on his groin was as bright as fresh paint.

"Why did you come?" Karla asked him.

"It doesn't matter," Avila said.

He counted the pulses of pain, timing their arrival. His heart pumped, then pain would rise, then subside. He inhaled deeply and rose to one knee again. Yoga pose: Wounded Man, knees and hands on tile, breathe, release, breathe, release. He struggled to remain conscious. Against the odds, his mind worked its way back through time, back to the cats he'd tortured as a kid in L.A., cats with their tails snipped off by a hedge trimmer, blinded cats, tiny needles in their eyes, cats burned by ignited aerosol spray, strangled cats, hung cats, cats bludgeoned with rakes and hoes and shovels, kittens placed inside coffee cans under hot sun. Back through the dust-ridden light of the Pico house he fell, its sour breath smells, its torn curtains. He heard clocks and organs and hailstorms in his head, all the sudden organization of his outrage.

"Do you want some help?" Karla said.

She took one arm and he rose. Against the bathroom door he slumped, unable to go farther.

"Let me help you," Karla said softly.

"Get me to the front door," Avila said.

Slowly they made their way to the stairs, where Avila balanced against its banister.

"I wish you hadn't shot me," Avila said.

"It was the only thing."

Down two steps they went, then three, Avila draped over the banister. Yoga pose: Wounded Man, arm crooked on banister, right leg on stair, brilliant drops of blood on white carpet.

"I feel sorry for you, bitch," Avila said.

"It's all right, David, it's all right."

"You just lost focus," Avila said.

"Yes I did. I lost focus."

Karla was holding the bomber jacket and athletic shoes in her free hand. They made it to the bottom step and Avila sat down heavily while Karla put on his shoes, right first, then left, laced them, touched his face, bathed in sweat. She helped him on with the jacket.

"I want you to tell me," Karla said. "About the cemetery. Did you like what we were doing there? Did you think it was fun, or did you think it was bad?"

"It doesn't matter, one way or the other, does it?"

Karla wiped his face with an edge of the bathrobe.

"I'll help you up," she said. "We won't be seeing each other again, you know."

"Yes, I know," Avila told her.

"Doesn't that make you sad?"

"It doesn't matter, one way or the other, does it?"

They stood up together, Avila mummified with pain.

"What do you want me to tell Detective Cooley if he calls again?" Karla asked.

"I don't care," Avila said. "Tell him nothing."

"Tell him nothing," Karla said.

"Not that it matters now."

"No, not that it matters now," Karla said.

The front door was open. Avila stumbled into the night air. It made him feel as though he'd been burned in a fire. As though his skin had been scorched and charred. There were false sounds in his head, dry rustle of palm fronds in hot breezes. He dragged his pain toward the green Buick.

Darwin had a theory. Maybe the state police and highway patrol believed he was in India. What else could explain luck like this, driving an old panel truck up and down the freeways of California and never being stopped?

On his way back north, Darwin stopped and used a pay phone to call Avila's Russian Hill apartment. The phone rang five times: Leave a message.

Darwin decided he would stop by the Marina apartment and see if David Avila was there, just an off chance. If not, then he would wait on Russian Hill. Darwin had the target pistol in his lap. For one last time, he thought of his father and mother, his brother Adam, the times he and his brother had spent on the front porch of their cabin in Tahoe, waiting for the first scouting hummingbirds of summer to approach. Beautiful green slashes, red throats, heaven-sent evenings of soft gold light falling on turquoise water.

Killing was not supposed to be a part of Darwin's life, but now it had to be.

Getting inside was suck-ass easy.

Luther Lee cruised the Russian Hill apartment, stopping every twenty minutes or so to park in a bus zone across the street for half an hour, then moving on, coming back. Just before evening rush he saw Avila go in the front door. Half an hour later he emerged from a side entrance off the garage. Luther Lee took off in his Bronco, just in time to see Avila hop a cable car on Hyde. Because there wasn't any doubt where Avila was going, Luther Lee cut downhill on a side street and spent twenty minutes circling the Aquatic Park public lot before finally parking in a handicapped zone. He ran the four blocks up to the Marina apartment where Avila kept a second crib, by then almost dark, and the green Buick in the garage, gone. Luther Lee decided to wait in the alley, crouched behind a Dumpster where nobody could see him. He had settled in for a long wait when the green Buick returned, only about thirty minutes later.

When the Buick went by, Luther Lee stood and watched it creep down the alley, going too slow, no lights, as if Avila wanted to get a ticket. The Buick nudged against a trash can, then turned into the garage, almost deliberately, the engine idling for a full minute. Luther Lee could see the outline of Avila's head on the driver's side. Staying in full shadow, Luther Lee closed the distance, Luther Lee at one with the dark in his blue stocking cap, black T-shirt, army fatigues, the ensemble of a night hunter. To his surprise, Avila sat in the car for a long time without moving before his hand emerged and balanced on the pavement. Then Avila poured himself out of the car, left hand on pavement, hunched at the waist, hands on concrete, then hands and knees. Avila struggled to his feet, collapsed against the hood of the Buick, moving slowly and tenaciously, foot by foot, toward the back door of the apartment.

Luther Lee posed at the back of the car, watching Avila just inside the door. Avila disappeared into darkness, the door still open.

Once he got inside, he saw Avila sitting in an armchair directly across from a sofa. It was nearly pitch-black in the room, but Luther could tell it was him, soft in outline against drapes. Luther Lee took out a silver-plated .45 automatic and went on in.

He turned the corner of the breakfast nook and confronted Avila. Holding the gun to his face, Luther Lee told Avila, "Move, motherfucker, and I'll kill you."

Avila was silent. With his left hand, Luther Lee turned on a table lamp. Avila's black hair was plastered with sweat, his face bright and fearful with some kind of nameless pain. He held himself with both hands, as if he might suddenly crumble like an ancient basket just uncovered. Something gray had stained his T-shirt, a huge maddening mudhole of muck.

Luther Lee backed away and sat down on the sofa.

"Man," he said. "Somebody done fucked you up."

Avila turned his head. His eyes were wide, as though he were intoxicated and couldn't see.

"And you smell like shit," Luther Lee said. They passed a few moments that way together, each in a world. Luther Lee put down the gun. "Did you shit your pants or what?" Luther Lee asked.

Avila breathed twice, deeply. The sound of a crosscut saw passing through soft pine.

Avila rested his head on the back of the chair.

"Get the fuck out of here," he said.

"Did you get stabbed, man?" Luther Lee said.

"Go on, get the fuck out."

"Oh, I will," Luther Lee said.

Avila sighed deeply, like a disappointed man who is very tired.

"I guess you surprised to see me," Luther Lee said, smiling.

"Not really," Avila told him.

"You done thought Zack offed me."

"You were next," Avila managed to say.

"So, that's probably true," Luther Lee said. He took a few moments to observe the small apartment. "You ought to get you a new decorator. Green walls, green carpet, green furniture. It looks like crap, man. I think somebody ought to let you know that."

Avila closed his eyes. His nose was running, his breath shallow, tiny rasps.

"You bring chicks here?" Luther Lee asked.

"That's right," Avila said.

"You could do better, man, all the cake you got."

"I suppose so," Avila said. He leaned forward and spit a glob of grayish blood onto the carpet.

"That was ugly," Luther Lee said. "What you been into?"

No sound from Avila, just a deep organic bending forward of his torso, head between knees. In time, he sat up, balanced himself.

"You ever been to Phoenix?" Luther Lee said. "I heard they got a good trade down there, trade could keep me in business for a long time. I hear they got lawyers down in Phoenix too. The kind who could help me when I get into trouble. That's what a man needs in this life, a good fucking lawyer. I get into the trade down there, I'm gonna get me a swimming pool and a good fucking lawyer. Then I be living the good life. I guess that's what you been doing, living the good life?"

"Get the fuck out," Avila said.

"Hey, hey now," Luther Lee said happily. "Let's take it easy here, okay? Say man, did you kick Zack in the stomach like he said you did? That dude was ticked off as hell. I guess you shouldn't have done that."

"Zack is shit," Avila whispered.

"What's that you say? Well, never mind."

Luther Lee put a toothpick in his mouth. He worked it around and around, studying Avila. The gore on Avila's hands and forearms was sticky.

"Go ahead," Avila said. "Do your thing."

"Don't rush me, man. I got to drive to Phoenix tonight. It's a long trip down there. What is it? Like, eight or nine hundred miles, something like that? Man, I got the Bronco gassed and ready to go. My shit is packed. I got a new life waiting down in sun city. Hey, you ever been down there? I heard trade was good down there. The downside is they got a lot of Mexicans and that shit down there too."

Avila balanced himself on one arm of the chair, tried to sit up. In another context, he might have been said to have a beatific glow.

"Whoa, partner," Luther Lee said. "Just you relax."

Avila grunted once.

"Hurts huh?" Luther Lee asked him. "You never did tell me if you been shot or stabbed. You're a fucking mess though, either way. I'd be curious how it happened to a dude like you. Zack, he told me you had moves. He told me you were dangerous. I guess your dangerous fucking days are over now, huh?"

"Go on," Avila said nonsensically.

"Hey man," Luther Lee said. "Where'd you go tonight you got fucked up so bad? Twenty minutes you get fucked up bad. You try to stick up a Quik-Trip or what?" Luther Lee unzipped one of his fatigue pockets and extracted an ice pick. "I guess you got one foot on the other side already." Luther Lee stood in front of Avila, towering over the wounded man. He held the ice pick at his right side, point out. "I'll just slip you over nice and easy," he said.

Avila's eyes were wide again. He looked to Luther Lee like a bad angel, ready to fly away.

"What's you sign, man?" Luther Lee said. "Mine is this ice pick right here." He raised the pick, eyed it once, put it down. "Everybody got to have a personal sign. Zack, he doesn't have no sign. A man got to have style, a sign." Luther Lee raised the pick again, cut an imaginary Z in the air. Whoosh, real fast. "Zorro, he had a sign, you know. And let's see, Batman he had a sign too. Oh, I get it, green, that must be your sign. That ain't much of a sign, man. I'd think you should get a cooler sign than that. Like, you know, Robin Hood and all that shit. Get yourself a new sign, man."

Avila raised his right hand to cover his eyes.

"You want I should stop the pain?" Luther Lee asked. He walked behind Avila, who tried to turn his head.

"Easy, brother," Luther Lee said. He walked close to Avila then, grabbing Avila under the neck with his left hand, choking up quick. Avila grabbed the wrist weakly, tried to lift his left arm and failed. Avila's right hand found air, waving like a disembodied tentacle. Luther Lee pushed away the hand, then flicked the ice pick quickly into Avila's left eye, half an inch or so, Luther Lee letting out a rodeo yelp. "Hooree!" Luther Lee shouted. A string of red squirted onto Avila's white T-shirt. Luther Lee stood back as Avila dropped his head into his chest. "Oh man, you do smell bad," Luther Lee said. "You'll have to clean yourself up." Forward again, Luther Lee choking Avila with a hand beneath the chin, raising the head high, flicking again with the ice pick, half an inch or so into Avila's right eye, another long string of red and yellow erupting from the wound. Through the closed lid, half an inch, another string of blood and mucus.

Luther Lee let Avila's head drop. He put the ice pick into his fatigue pocket and walked in front of Avila, peered into his face. The eyes were closed, filigreed with laced blood, turning blue as a carbuncle. Avila was breathing softly, like a child. Luther Lee went out the back door, without bothering to close it all the way.

Delayed at LAX, delayed by air traffic around SFO, and delayed by heavy rush-hour traffic on the Bayshore, Vorhees got back to Potrero Hill about nine that night. "Don't ever fly on Friday in California," he told Alisha. The baby was asleep, so Vorhees ate a bowl of chili and crackers in the kitchen with his wife, catching up on the day. He took a shower after dinner and telephoned Cooley at home.

"It's Friday night," Cooley said in mock whine.

"I know," Vorhees consoled him. "But I had a good talk with Sylvia Dorning."

"Yeah, I figured," Cooley said. "Hey, I'm trying to watch boxing here."

"You'll want to hear this, partner," Vorhees said.

"Sure, go ahead. I'm all ears. By the way, I called Karla Darwin when you were heading south. I asked her if David Avila had ever been over to her house for a visit. You should have heard the silence."

"Well, did she say anything?"

"Nah," Cooley said. "I mean for about five minutes she was stone dead. Then she said no, Avila hadn't been at the house. But it wasn't like you'd believe her or anything like that. It just wasn't that strong."

"Okay, listen to this. David Avila was a lawyer in Sylvia Dorning's firm. He asked her out and on their third date he got her in the shower and sodomized her with a wine bottle from behind."

On the line, Cooley himself went silent. Vorhees could hear TV noise in the background.

"Guy just got knocked down," Cooley said.

"Come on!" Vorhees shouted.

"I'm just screwing around with you," Cooley laughed. "We better get up to see Karla again."

"I'm calling Lightfoot tonight," Vorhees said. "I think it's time we brought Avila in for a talk."

"Search warrant type talk?"

"That too," Vorhees agreed. Vorhees could hear Alisha in the nursery, talking to the baby. "How about we go up and see Karla first thing in the morning?"

Vorhees managed to get about six hours of sleep that night. He got up early and dressed quietly, then drove over to Cooley's house in the Avenues and picked him up in the station wagon. They drove over the hills to Pacific Heights and parked in the driveway of the Darwin house, just behind the gold Mercedes. It was a cold morning with an ice blue sky and a few puffy clouds high over the coastal foothills. A gardener down the block was pruning tree roses, and two kids were shooting hoops next door.

"Well, she's home anyway," Cooley said, gesturing to the gold Mercedes.

"Front door is open a crack," Vorhees said.

They got out together and walked up the flagstones to the front door. Vorhees rapped on the door hard enough to push it a foot or two wider.

"Mrs. Darwin?" Vorhees called out.

Cooley shrugged and stuck his head inside the house.

"Holy shit," he said.

Vorhees went around him and from the entryway he could see Karla Darwin curled up on the sofa, about twenty feet away, up three stairs. The terry bathrobe she wore was matted with blood and a small automatic was in her right hand, down at her side on the sofa. Cooley and Vorhees went upstairs slowly. The woman had her hair pinned up as if she were going to take a shower, but her robe was half open, and you could see the lower part of her naked body. Vorhees kneeled in front of her and pulled the robe closed. Cooley slipped around him and eased the gun out of her hand.

"I'm bagging it," Cooley said, going away.

"Mrs. Darwin?" Vorhees asked tentatively.

She opened her eyes.

"Mrs. Darwin?" he said again.

"Hello, Detective," she said.

Rosy morning light dusted the picture window of the den. Through its gauze curtains you could see a slab of green lawn, a monkey puzzle tree, lines of eucalyptus going downhill.

"Are you hurt in any way, ma'am?" Vorhees asked.

"No, I'm not hurt."

"What happened in here?"

"David came over," Karla told him.

"David Avila?"

"David came over."

"Did he try to hurt you?"

"He wanted to take a shower. It was going to be just like San Rafael. You know, in the motel when we used to meet and take showers and spend the whole afternoon together."

"Sure, San Rafael," Vorhees said.

"I told him I'd wait for him," she said.

"Are you sure you're okay, ma'am? You're all covered with blood. Are you sure you're not injured? Maybe I should call an ambulance."

"I'm not injured, thank you," Karla said. Her face was tan-lined, but not tanned.

"You stay right here," Vorhees said. "I'm going to check the house." Vorhees unholstered his Glock and did a walk through every room. When he came back he said, "Nobody inside, Mrs. Darwin."

"That's nice," Karla said.

"Can't you tell me what happened here?"

"I told you. David came over. We were going to take a shower together. Have you seen Jack?"

"Your husband?" Vorhees asked.

"Have you seen poor Jack? Is he all right?"

"He's gone," Vorhees said. "He's on the run. It probably isn't very good for him, being on the run."

"No, I don't think it is."

"Please tell me what happened here, Mrs. Darwin."

"Did Jack ask about me?"

"Well, he wondered why you told lies about him."

"I shouldn't have," Karla said.

"Maybe you can make it up," Vorhees suggested.

"They used to say things behind my back," Karla said.

"What?"

"They used to say things. In high school, behind my back."

"I'm not following, Mrs. Darwin," Vorhees admitted. His knees ached from crouching on the floor. "What happened here, Mrs. Darwin?"

"I never told anyone about those things," Karla said quietly. She bit her lip. "After all these years, you'd think I'd forget all about it. You know, when I worked at the cemetery, they said things behind my back there too. The men. It was cruel. They used to say things."

"There's a lot of blood in your bathroom, Mrs. Darwin. There's blood in the bedroom and on the stairs. Did you shoot David Avila with that gun we took? Is that what this is all about? You need to tell me, ma'am. If that's what happened, we have to do something about it."

Vorhees sighed, then got up and met Cooley at the front door.

"It's bagged up," Cooley said. "What's she say? What the hell happened to her?"

"We'd better call Lightfoot now," Vorhees said. "I think she shot Avila. Let's get Lightfoot on the phone and alert all the hospitals. We need to bring him in. Mrs. Darwin and our lawyer Avila were having a thing together."

"No shit," Cooley said. "I'll use the phone upstairs. I'll get a couple of uniformed females out here along with the Mattingly crew. Maybe we should get her to the hospital too before we take her in." Cooley hugged the wall going upstairs, staying out of the blood. Vorhees went back up to the den.

"Did David Avila kill those women?" he asked. Finally, he decided to sit on the carpet in front of Karla Darwin. "Can you tell me everything you know about this?"

"Do you think Jack would have me back?" Karla said.

"I don't know, ma'am," Vorhees told her.

Cooley came back downstairs. Vorhees heard him on the landing. Karla Darwin sat quietly, hands folded, eyes unfocused.

Vorhees walked down the landing.

"Lightfoot is on it," Cooley said. "Two females are on their way over along with Mattingly's forensic unit and an ambulance if we need it. They'll take her downtown and to a hospital if that's what she needs. Lightfoot is headed to the magistrate about a search warrant for Avila's Russian Hill place and office. They'll be here in just a few minutes."

Cooley dragged Vorhees by the shirt cuff into the morning air. It was brisk and bright, a beautiful day.

"What happened in there?" Cooley whispered.

"She shot Avila," Vorhees said.

"That's really cool," Cooley said. "Where is he?"

"I think she's in orbit," Vorhees said. "And I don't know where Avila is. But he isn't going far trailing all that blood."

The gardener had put down his shears and was watching the two detectives like a hawk. A few minutes passed, then a patrol car rolled up with two female cops inside. Vorhees and Cooley spent five minutes getting them up to speed on procedures. Mattingly arrived then, and they roped off the house and sent in a crew.

"The Marina crib is only five minutes away," Cooley told Vorhees.

"And it's your day off," Vorhees said.

"Okay, I'm really interested now," Cooley said.

"If Avila isn't down at the Marina, we'll circle up to Russian Hill, then go over to his office. Maybe by then we'll have a report on the hospitals from Lightfoot."

Vorhees and Cooley got in the station wagon.

"Oh, I forgot to tell you," Cooley said.

"Yeah."

"Something even cooler than cool."

"I'm dying to hear."

Cooley leaned over the seat conspiratorially.

"Lightfoot told me they got Luther Lee Dokes in custody," he said.

"No shit?" Vorhees said. "What, how?"

"Get this," Cooley said happily. "Last night early, Dokes parks in a handicapped zone at Aquatic Park. Some old fart bocce players spot him and call it in. Meter maid shows up, then a tow truck. Luther Lee comes back and raises holy hell, pulls a gun on the tow truck guy, who splits up the hill. Two patrol cars roll and they chase him down to the ocean, where he finally gave it up. They took him in on the gun charge. Guess what? They search him and they find an ice pick in his pants pocket. It has fresh blood on it."

"That's so great," Vorhees said. "I wonder who he did?"

"Gets me," Cooley said.

Vorhees pointed the station wagon downhill, toward Avila's Marina apartment.

In the dark, Darwin waited, sitting on a sofa across from David Avila. He had driven through an alley behind the Marina apartment, and he had seen the Buick parked slightly off-center in the garage, a garbage can nudged over, some of its contents spilled near the back door, which was ajar, unlocked and open. Darwin didn't know how long he sat that way, watching Avila. He only knew that sometime later a swatch of gray light filtered over him. Darwin felt as though he'd just awakened after a lengthy and difficult surgical procedure.

"Take it easy, Mr. Darwin," he heard someone say. The black detective named Vorhees. Darwin glanced at the man, who was standing in the entryway, followed by Cooley. "You have a weapon there, Mr. Darwin?" Vorhees asked.

Darwin placed the target pistol on the floor at his feet.

Vorhees came forward. He kneeled down and pushed the gun away lightly, then stayed on one knee.

"You all right, Mr. Darwin?" Vorhees asked.

"I will be," Darwin said. "Avila is dead."

"It looks that way," Vorhees said.

Cooley flipped on a floor lamp, and David Avila came into view, a white corpse with dark-lidded eyes.

"I'm not telling you anything," Darwin said.

"Hey, I don't blame you," Vorhees told him. "I don't think you need to say a thing. We've pretty much figured it out."

"It takes a special kind of person, doesn't it?" Darwin said, almost to himself.

"What's that?" Vorhees asked.

"A special kind of person," Darwin repeated. "To do something like this to Dolores and that other girl."

"I guess so," Vorhees said. Cooley had gone outside to make a call on the radio. "You didn't do anything to Avila with that gun, did you, Mr. Darwin?"

"Nothing," Darwin said. "I just talked with him, that's all."

"You talked with him?"

"I told him how much Dolores meant to me."

"He say anything, Mr. Darwin?"

"He was dead I think. But I talked to him anyway."

"It's over now, Mr. Darwin. You come downtown with us and I'll make sure it gets straightened out." Vorhees got up and put his hands on his hips. "There's been enough trouble now," he said. "It's time this ended so you can get back to the job of living."

"You want to hear a story?" Darwin said.

"Sure, go ahead," Vorhees answered. "We've got time."

"There was a tong war in Chinatown once," Darwin said. "A fellow had been shot and was dying in the street. Another rival gang member cut his head off. Lawyer told the judge his client had just accelerated the inevitable." Darwin looked at Vorhees. "Isn't that funny?"

"Funny?" Vorhees said. "I don't get it."

"Accelerating the inevitable," Darwin said. "That's the definition of murder."

"I guess it is," Vorhees said. He touched Darwin on the shoulder. "You need some help, Mr. Darwin? Can you make it all right? Can I help you? We all need help, don't we?"

# epilogue

On Sunday afternoon in late April, Vorhees drove down to Burlingame with Alisha and the baby. He took the Junipero Serra in order to see the whole bay, what was left of open country between San Francisco and the Peninsula, Alisha and the baby in the backseat, Vorhees driving with the windows open, a great windblown scene below.

It took him about thirty minutes of easy cruising to find Highway 92 and the county road that cut off it to the south and west. When Vorhees arrived at the stable, there were about fifteen cars parked in a gravel lot under the main office of the stable and riding academy. He saw Cooley's car, an old gray Chevy, and he recognized Lightfoot's car too, a red Audi. The office stood on a grassy knoll above the lot, surrounded by a white fence. Up the hill were corrals, open grassland; down a narrow grassy path, the barn and more corrals, a stable, some outbuildings. The day was high and dusty blue with a warm spring breeze kicking through the eucalyptus leaves. Alisha had made two gallons of potato salad, and Vorhees had brought down three cases of his special home-brew root beer. On the porch of the office, card tables had been set up, arrayed with punch bowls, jars of pickles, cheese boards, crackers, cans of nuts. The air was rich with the smell of eucalyptus gum and horse.

Vorhees saw to it that Alisha and the baby were settled in at one end of the card tables, he said hello to Cooley and his wife Rose, and then he walked up the grassy path and found Tom Fullerton leaning against a fence rail, smoking a big cigar. Vorhees said hello, and refused a cigar.

"How's Jack Darwin holding up?" he asked Fullerton.

"As well as can be expected," Fullerton told him.

Vorhees could see Darwin across the corral, sitting alone on what remained of a watering trough. He was wearing gray slacks and a powder blue Izod shirt. Darwin didn't seem to be looking at anything in particular, his gaze somehow grazing on the brown hillside and the oak trees on top.

"You guys were really great," Fullerton said.

"Just doing our job," Vorhees said. "I'm sorry it had to happen. It's a terrible thing." Vorhees put two arms on top of the fence rail. "I guess Karla Darwin is going to get better. I heard she was in pretty bad shape."

More cars entered the parking lot, people unloading lawn chairs, heading toward the main office.

"You think this party is a good idea?" Vorhees asked.

"Sure, why not? Angel is the man responsible. He has a surprise for Jack. Why not do it? It's a nice day and Jack has nothing to be ashamed of, does he?"

"No, it's not that."

"I heard the law school is giving Jack back his old section of legal research and writing to teach. They're even adding a section on professional responsibility this summer. Jack's on his way to a teaching career I'd think. I don't believe he ever wanted to practice law, but teaching might be his place. He's living in his house, he's going to AA. He's going to be fine."

"I'm glad," Vorhees said. "What's happened to him, I don't see how anybody could stand it."

Fullerton puffed his cigar and let smoke feather into the breeze.

"God, it's a beautiful day," he said. "How's your new baby?"

"She's great," Vorhees said. "Sleeping through the night now. That's a big change for us."

A mariachi band arrived in a used black hearse and began setting up under the eucalyptus. You could hear them tuning their instruments, guitars, bass, a single trumpet doing trills. Vorhees smelled barbecue, a subtle smoky aroma in the air. Fullerton excused himself to talk with his partner Max, share a cigar and open a can of beer. Vorhees walked down to the office again and intercepted Mad Dog Paiewonsky, who was about to get a soda from an icy tub.

"Hello, Detective," Paiewonsky said. He popped a can of soda and sipped it reflectively.

"Got a second?" Vorhees said.

"Sure," Paiewonsky said.

They walked to the corner of the porch and sat on its floorboards, legs dangling over the bare ground. The mariachi band began to play their first number. Half a dozen kids played tag on the grass.

"I see the DA came down. That's nice," Vorhees said.

"Oh yeah, she came down."

"I was just curious."

"Why? What's on your mind?"

"We received some faxes over at the Hall," Vorhees began. "You wouldn't know anything about them, would you?"

Mad Dog looked away and drank some soda. He looked back and shrugged.

"Whoever sent those faxes," Vorhees said, "had Avila's trial work nailed. They even managed to get into the bar association's confidential files. Imagine that."

"Yeah, imagine that," Mad Dog said. "Does it matter?"

"Not really. I'm just curious."

"Well, let's just let it go."

"You got into the bar files, didn't you?"

Mad Dog smiled and set the soda down between his legs. "You know," he began. "Nola Gettes told me one time that beneath her bullshit exterior there was a *her* inside. You know what I mean?"

"I think I do," Vorhees said.

"I'm glad it turned out like this," Mad Dog said. "I was thinking about giving up prosecuting before now."

"You changed your mind?"

"For now," he said. "I feel like we did some good work here. For a change."

Mad Dog shook Vorhees' hand and left to join the DA staff. A crowd had assembled at one of the corrals, so Vorhees gathered up Alisha and the baby and walked up to the grassy path. At least twenty-five people were around the corral where Jack Darwin and Angel were standing. The mariachi band was playing loud now, and Darwin stood inside the ring of people looking helpless. Angel walked back to the barn and returned leading a beautiful young colt. He neared Darwin and stopped.

"This colt is yours," Angel said. "He's been gentled but not broke.

I think you and I will have to break him together. He's yours, Mr. Darwin. Everybody here bought him for you. He doesn't have a name, so you'll have to name him soon."

Darwin took the rope, looking stunned. He was crying, holding the colt around its neck.

"Thank you all," Darwin choked.

"He's a beauty, isn't he?" Angel said.

"He's a beauty, Angel," Darwin said.

There was applause. The baby woke and Vorhees tossed her on his shoulder and began to rock gently back and forth.

"Let's get some barbecue," he told Alisha.

"Sounds good, honey," she said.

Vorhees and Alisha walked the baby down to the serving line. Just before he got to the barbecue table, Vorhees turned to look for Darwin. He saw the man leading his new colt uphill through brown grass toward the last live oaks in that part of the country.